PENGUIN BOOKS

RUN WITH THE HORSEMEN

Ferrol Sams is the author of seven works of fiction, including the novels *Run with the Horsemen*, *The Whisper of the River*, and *When All the World Was Young*, all available from Penguin. Also published by Penguin are *The Widow's Mite & Other Stories* and *Epiphany*. Ferrol Sams lives in Fayetteville, Georgia, where he practices medicine.

run
with
the
horsemen

Ferrol Sams

PENGUIN BOOKS

PENGUIN BOOKS
Published by the Penguin Group
Penguin Books USA Inc.,
375 Hudson Street, New York, New York 10014, U.S.A.
Penguin Books Ltd, 27 Wrights Lane,
London W8 5TZ, England
Penguin Books Australia Ltd, Ringwood,
Victoria, Australia
Penguin Books Canada Ltd, 10 Alcorn Avenue,
Toronto, Ontario, Canada M4V 3B2
Penguin Books (N.Z.) Ltd, 182–190 Wairau Road,
Auckland 10, New Zealand

Penguin Books Ltd, Registered Offices:
Harmondsworth, Middlesex, England

First published in the United States of America by
Peachtree Publishers Limited 1982
Published in Penguin Books 1984

30   29   28   27   26   25   24

LIBRARY OF CONGRESS CATALOGING IN PUBLICATION DATA
Sams, Ferrol, 1922—
   Run with the horsemen.
   I. Title.   II. Series.
PS3569.A46656R8   1984   813'.54   83-25111
ISBN 0 14 00.7274 8

Printed in the United States of America
Set in Caledonia

To
Helen

run with the horsemen

I

In the beginning was the land. Shortly thereafter was the father. The boy knew this with certainty. It was knowledge that was in his marrow. It predated memory and conscious thought as surely as hunger and thirst. He could not have explained it, but he knew it.

The father owned the land. He plowed it, harvested it, timbered it, and hunted over it. It was his. Before that it had been the land of his father and his father's father. Before that it had belonged to the Indians, who since Creation had held it by God's will in trust for the family, just waiting until it could be claimed by its rightful owners.

The boy knew all this. No one told him. He also knew that in turn the land owned his father. Everything the father did eventually revolved around nurture of the land. Without the land there would be no family. The ungodly were not so and lived in town. They were like chaff which the wind bloweth away. Their feet were not rooted in the soil, and they were therefore of little consequence in the scheme of things.

There were also humans who tilled the soil and owned no land. Their plight in the here and hereafter was too dreadful to consider, and consequently they merited a special compassion from the father and the family. Not owning land was an affliction too embarrassing for comment, like being cross-eyed or feeble-minded, and surely was visited on one by God.

All these things the boy knew before he could talk, and nothing to which he was exposed later, either theosophical or

1

scientific, ever completely erased these atavistic convictions. This was the way it was in the Piedmont of Georgia between World Wars.

The father was a giant. He was slim almost to the point of elegance, but he was still a giant. Born into the rural poverty of Reconstruction, the sixth of nine children, he had from early childhood shone like a gem among his peers. There were no public schools, but illiteracy was so unthinkable a condition that most families in the county sacrificed other necessities to send their children to cooperatively employed schoolmasters. The father was an enthusiastic student and was one of four of his parents' children who were sent on to prep school at Locust Grove Institute. Maintaining academic excellence, he was one of three who were sent to college.

All of this activity was financed largely by his mother, who sold butter and eggs and took in boarders to raise cash to educate her children. Her ambitions were fulfilled in the boy's father. He lettered in three sports at a Baptist university and after graduation taught English and Latin and coached football and baseball in a small college.

Immediately after the *Lusitania* was sunk, he enlisted in the Army, married, and went to France. There he fought Germans mostly, but occasionally on leave he got drunk and fought British officers. He was twice wounded and came back to the county as a retired Captain of Infantry, a condition no one in the family was allowed to forget. After one frustrating year of farming the land, he entered Emory Law School, came home as a lawyer, and began his political career by being elected County School Superintendent. He held this position forever and never plowed a mule again. By the time the boy knew him, he was a giant.

Only a little less important than the land was the house. It had been built from timbers hewn and hand-planed on the spot and sat approximately in the middle of eight hundred acres, give or take a recession or two. After the War the yankees and carpetbaggers almost got it at auction, but the intrepid young grandfather walked twenty miles and bought it in for taxes at the last dramatic minute. Where he got the money was never plainly set forth, but it was a very heroic act. On a romantic impulse he had the house deeded to his young wife. This was a very wise move, for the grandfather later developed a taste for whiskey and gambling that kept the family coffers careening between full and empty. The grandmother developed a streak of Irish stubbornness and never allowed a mortgage on the house, never mind the degree of penury.

After the father grew up and married, he remodeled the house and moved into it. This so increased his already considerable stature in the eyes of the grandmother that she deeded it to him. It was a safe haven for any relative. The family consisted of the father, the mother, their four children, the father's parents, the grandmother's brother, the father's sister, and the sister's husband. The extended family consisted of whoever needed a place to live for awhile, whoever was visiting from outside the county, and occasionally whoever needed to hide from the law.

The father was the center of all this feudal menage. So bound was he to blood, so gracious and generous to any kin, that none of his womenfolk ever knew what the dinnertime census was likely to be. His control over the family, albeit benevolent, was so absolute that the boy never heard one voice raised in criticism. He was the most courtly and gallant person to women that the boy ever knew. In return he received more female adulation than the boy ever observed anywhere else. At home he came in late, slept late, was served separate meals except for Sunday dinner, and was waited on hand and foot by all the women in the house. The boy at an early age confused him with Jehovah, Moses, Cosimo Medici, and Black Jack Pershing.

In addition to the family, the father was intimately bound to another group. The number of Negroes living on the land varied according to the number of children in individual families and the amount of cotton being planted in any given year. Usually there were from fifty to eighty of them, and they lived in the ten tenant houses which were dotted in weathered punctuation around the fields. They and the father revolved around each other in the mutually supporting and mutually demanding system called sharecropping. Listening at an early age to stories of the grandparents and also to reminiscences of the more ancient blacks, the boy had puzzled over the vanished condition of slavery. For the life of him he could see only superficial differences in the former and present systems. Once he mustered the temerity to ask Aunt Lou, who had yellow eyes and white braids. She was also reputed to have Indian blood, a condition which licensed her frank speech and short temper.

"Co'se we better off, boy. Whatcher talkin bout? We free now. Whatcher talkin bout what free mean? Hit mean we do what we wanta. Hit mean we go where we wanta. Hit mean we kin leave anytime we git ready, do we pay out and kin we find another place to stay. I ax my maw the same querstion when I was a little gal. Co'se we better off. Git outta here!"

Since Aunt Lou and her husband had lived on the place for over twenty years and her father-in-law had belonged to the grandmother's father, the boy was still puzzled. He finally decided that freedom meant you could move off the land to Cincinnati or Detroit and that it might be desirable for blacks but was unthinkable for whites.

The father superintended the hands from the vantage point of the upstairs front porch on Sundays or from his automobile window on weekdays. They raised some corn, a few pimentos, pigs, chickens, and cows. The main crop, however, was cotton. Cotton was king, they said, and this was because cotton was cash. Cotton was the opportunity to pay out each fall, the chance to buy Christmas and new clothes. Cotton was the only avenue to the ultimate in opulence, the ownership of a car.

The family was poor. It was "poor but proud" they said. The confused boy grew up thinking one should be proud of being poor. One of the in-laws slipped around occasionally and made liquor. He had plenty of cash, did not read books, and was tolerated but not admired. A cousin had surrendered to the boll weevil, moved out of the county, and bought Coca-Cola stock. He was rich, but there was unspoken disdain for him because he had left the land.

The grandparents told horror stories of having to boil dirt from under the smokehouse to retrieve salt after the yankees had been on the land. They had learned to eat a weed called poke salad as a means of survival in those days, a custom that they passed on as a springtime ritual of communion to their descendants. Things apparently got a little better for awhile, but then the Great Depression hit the South like aftershock from the earthquake of Reconstruction, and the children knew poverty firsthand. They also, however, knew pride. No one in the county had any money to spend, and there was a security of blood that transcended the possession of material things. When one is convinced that one is to the manor born, the actual physical condition of the manor itself is of negligible importance.

In unspoken collusion with his wife, his mother, and his sister, the father set such an example that his four children were convinced that being a Southerner in that particular spot and in that particular family was so enviable a condition that comparison was an idle exercise. They believed, almost as devoutly, in Jesus Christ, Santa Claus, and the Democratic Party. Very early they knew the distinction between "genteel," "common," and "tacky," which they learned from the ladies, but the difference between "big" and "little" they learned from the father.

Despite the father's royal prerogative of lying late in bed and having a separate and special breakfast prepared for him, the establishment was truly a working farm. During planting and cultivating seasons the hands were expected to be at the barn by daylight and in the cotton fields by sunup. There were no tractors, and each able-bodied male who could see over the handles of a plowstock was assigned a mule and sent to work the cotton.

Early in the spring the one- and two-horse turning plows were used to break the soil, which had "lain out" all winter and been compacted by the winter rains. Next a flat cultivator with iron teeth was dragged over the freshly tilled soil. The rows were laid off and fertilizer, pungent gray grit imported from South America and called "jew-anah," was strewn in the rows with a clacking guano distributor. Then the fuzzy little pussywillow-like seeds were tucked into the rows with a cotton planter.

When the greasy-looking green plants appeared, they were shortly attacked by a host of enemies living in the row with them and crowding them out—cockleburs, jimson weed, and the ubiquitous crab grass. This invasion precipitated frenetic activity called "chopping cotton." Men, women, girls, and boys assembled in the fields with flat hoes fitted with homemade handles. They thinned the cotton plants and uprooted the weeds and grass. There were dozens of people in the same field, absorbed in the rhythmic to-and-fro motion of the hoes, the baking sun on the shoulders and back, the rhythmic clanking when the hoes struck a rock and the swish when the blade hit rich loam.

After this the crop had to be plowed. The cotton was "run around," with each row having the dirt listed to it from both sides by a mule drawing the plow twice down each row of cotton. This was followed by a process called "busting the middles," in which the central pone of earth left between the rows by the running around was plowed up and the crab grass therein uprooted to the hot sun to shrivel and die. This involved an overwhelming amount of activity when one considers the number of rows in an acre of cotton.

The vocabulary was rich, and the boy enjoyed hearing the black men instruct their sons about preparing the tools and the mules for different tasks. The language was studded with terms like hames, collars, singletrees, doubletrees, Johnson wings, scooters, scrapes, trace chains, and plowlines. A camaraderie developed between each man and his mule, and it was a prestigious event when a boy became a good enough plowhand to be assigned a specific animal which was known as his mule and which no one else could plow when he was present. Each mule had a name and as distinct and individual a personality as the man who plowed her. Everyone on the farm knew Maude, Kate, Red, Clyde, Worry, Pet, Emma, and Joe by sight and knew what to expect in the way of reaction and behavior from each of them.

There was a dependence in those days between man and mule, the one upon the other, that was more than complement; it was symbiosis—the one was necessary for the survival of the other. It was important to have a mule that was obedient but spirited, and it was essential to have a mule with a good gait. There was a rhythm to plowing that was almost musical. The stride of the man matched that of the mule in a one-plane dance down a cotton row with the ears of the mule plunging forward then backward in unison with the pull of the forelegs, now the hindlegs, as the heavy plow was dragged smoothly through the whispering earth. The hands of the man provided lateral counterpoint to guide the plow between the rows to the accompaniment of creaking harness, deep sonorous animal breathing, the padding of heavy, rapid feet in the loose dirt, and the occasional, directional monosyllables from the human. "Gee," "Haw," "Whoa," "Back," "Come up in there" could be heard in low, satisfied gutterals or fractious impatient high notes according to the performance of the animals.

Over and above and beyond and around could be heard bird song—the trills of thrush and mockingbird, the chirrs of the catbird, the sad, seductive two-note of the mourning dove, and the fulfilled cackle of a laying hen back at the barn. Until the middle of the Depression, when times got so bad they took up the tracks, one could hear the ten o'clock train blow for Harp's Crossing two and a half miles up the dirt road, and then one knew it was only two hours before time to quit for dinner. The older men could look at the sun and tell time within fifteen minutes, but the boy liked to hear the train.

After the cotton was chopped and plowed the first time, brigades of children and women swarmed over the fields with pails of poison. This was a concoction of molasses laced with arsenic. It was applied directly to the crown of the cotton plant and the squares of unborn blooms with a mop made of rags wrapped

7

around the end of a stick. The pails were old syrup buckets or old lard buckets and could be red, blue, orange, silver, or varying shades thereof, according to their age or origin. The children were of varying shades of black or brown, according to their origin, and of staggered height and weight. They lined up at the ends of the rows and began stepping off to individual rhythms, dipping in the bucket, then mopping the top of each cotton plant lightly, and because of different degrees of speed and efficiency, they would soon be scattered all over the field.

The blue green cotton plants snuggled the contours of the rich red land, the color and pattern interrupted and accented by the spindly black legs of the children invading the rows like giant wading birds. When the cotton was knee high, powdered arsenic, which was bright pink, was dusted directly onto the plants while they were wet with dew. This was done by jolting a flour sack full of the powder immediately over the plants while walking briskly down the rows. Later, when the cotton was higher, a man or adolescent male would walk between two rows with a tank of powdered arsenic on his back and a forked blower protruding in front of him which he operated by turning a hand crank, thus dusting two rows of cotton at the time. This latter job had to be done while the air was still and the plants were wet with dew, and so it was not uncommon to hear the soft whirr, whirr, whirr of the arsenic blower at night when the moon was bright and no breath of air stirred.

Running-round, busting middles, and poisoning were re-peated over and over until the sunny days and hot nights had produced a foliage so rank it cut the sun off the weeds and grass at the roots of the flourishing cotton. Then the work was at a standstill until time for the bolls to burst open and the mature cotton to be picked by quick black fingers. This catching up with the work usually occurred in July and was called "laying-by." The sunup to sundown toil was over for another year, and the hands could take time for a little recreation. This was the time of revival meetings in the churches of the whites and protracted meetings or "big meeting" in the churches of the blacks. Each year when laying-by came, the father was host at a fish fry in the pecan orchard in front of his home—the traditional "big house"—where a barrel of mullet imported from Florida was fried in washpots of sizzling lard and served up with coleslaw and cornbread. Lemonade was on hand for the women and children and a modicum of "shine" or white liquor for the men. It was a time of conviviality and release and predictions of crop outcomes and remembrances of things past.

One summer the fish fry was dominated by tales of "what that boy done to that mule right out there in front'n the house" and "what that boy gwine do nex" and "at boy a sight an at'se truf."

In early June the boy had been told to join the hired hands next day in tending the father's personal cotton patch, which occupied twelve acres directly across the road from the big house. This was cotton that was not sharecropped but that the landlord paid cash to have worked and harvested. The plants, which were a good eight inches high, had been run around but had grassy middles. These had to be busted, and every available hand was pressed into service, even such an inferior plowman as his spindly son, whose heart swelled with pride to be so casually included in an adult assignment. He had plowed before, but not all day, and he felt very important.

The next morning he pulled on his overalls in the half light of dawn, raced downstairs through the kitchen, grabbed the milking buckets with water to wash the cows' bags, and half-ran to the feedhouse. Here he mixed a whiteoak basket full of cottonseed hulls and sprinkled it liberally with cottonseed meal. He put this in the cows' troughs in their stalls in the rickety shed where they had been confined all night since milking time the evening before. While the animals sighed and munched and made chewing sounds or rasped their tongues across the wood of the trough, wood worn smooth by tongues still rough, he leaned over and bathed their tits, cleaning from them the manure encrusted thereon during a night of lying in their own waste. He smelled the acrid odor of fresh dung mixed with urine, the musty scent of old dried manure, the sweet breath of the cows, the spicy odor of the cottonseed meal, the smooth, almost velvety odor of the fresh warm milk, and felt very much a part of the universe. He rinsed the second cow's bag again, settled on his haunches with the milk bucket between his knees, and began milking with both hands directly into the big heavy tin bucket—first the left hand, then the right—in a steady, strong, and rapid rhythm. His grandfather had taught him to milk, and he did it with his thumbs tucked into his palms, a position which gave greater leverage.

He was always fascinated by the sounds of milking. The notes of the alternating twin streams changed from the tinny ping, ping, ping on the bottom of the empty bucket to ching, ching, ching as the bottom became covered to shig, shig, shig as the milk became deeper, obscuring the metallic resonance, to a steady purring as the bucket filled and the foam rose. Milking was a satisfying activity for him because he performed it well, and everyone else acknowledged as much. He gathered up his full buckets of milk and the empty feed basket, propped open the rickety door to the cows' stalls so they could go out to pasture all day, and hurried back toward the house.

When he went by the bigger barn where the mules were kept, the yard was swarming with men and mules getting harnessed up for the day's plowing. He spotted Darnell, prolific father of two-thirds of the baseball team, and shouted to him, "Darnell, please fix my plow with a big scrape. I'm going to bust middles today, and I'm running late."

His mother had breakfast for him when he got to the house, fresh hot biscuits made of homegrown graham, rolled by hand to the size of a loving woman's palm. There were no eggs this morning; the hens were moulting and the few eggs obtained were saved for the father's breakfast and for Sunday cakes—in that order. There was thickened gravy made from middling meat, however, and there were hot buttered biscuits with ribbon cane syrup, all topped with a glass of the fresh warm milk which his mother had strained through cloth and served him as soon as he sat down. He ate rapidly and hurried to the lot to catch his mule.

10

The sun was just rising, an embarrassment involving minor loss of caste with his black friends, since a dedicated plowman was already in the field by now.

He grabbed a bridle from the harness room, which always smelled of sweat-soaked leather, neatsfoot oil, and the musty mouse nests in the corners. He squeezed through the slatted entrance gates into the vaulted main hall of the barn and gasped with dismay. The only animal in the vast empty space before him stood munching corn from the long communal trough, occasionally raising her head to jerk a frond of fodder from the rack above, swishing a fly from her back with her tail, or indolently raising a hind leg to get a fly off her belly with the hoof.

This was a mule named Pet, and everyone dreaded her. She was a farm legend. Pet had been bought as a young mule along with her sister, Clyde. During her first season on the farm she had stepped on a nail, a cruel, treacherous tenpenny spike, which had punctured deep into the frog of her right front foot. A terrible infection ensued, and the boy's grandfather, amateur veterinarian by necessity through a long postwar generation of tending crops, children, and animals, had undertaken the treatment of Pet. An affinity developed between them which soon became love. The crippled animal would hobble to the plank fence of the barnlot and whinny when she saw the whiteheaded old man with the walking cane coming down the lane between the privy and the barn, bearing a bucket of hot water and numerous boxes of medicated powders and ointments. As she improved, a slow and tedious process, she began following him around the pasture when he was checking cows and calves or locating the nests of guinea hens cleverly hidden deep within blackberry thickets by many branching trails.

The old man had worked animals all his life, but he developed a special affection for this one and began treating her as a favorite child. She got special rations and extra delicacies at feeding time. He demanded special attention and rubdowns for her from the Negroes when they brought their own tired mules in from the fields. For one solid year she was not allowed to work, and as surely as that coat won Joseph a trip to Egypt, she became a spoiled brat. She rapidly learned how to manipulate not only the other animals but the humans on the farm as well. Fortunately, she was not vicious, a trait that would not have been tolerated, but she became a mistress of passive resistance.

She learned to walk so slowly that a plowhand would be tripping over his own feet within five minutes. Curses and lashes with the plowlines along her flanks would produce a momentarily quickened gait accompanied by persecuted sighing and sneezing. Soon her progress degenerated again into a head-drooping, slothful gait that was infuriating. Tabitha, mistress of objective wisdom, the wife of Freeman and mother of Buddy, who was the boy's best friend, had remarked that Pet had a certain number of steps she would take each day and she counted to be sure she didn't take an extra one. The only reason the mule was not sold was that the grandfather would have been to bury. Also Pet could be worked in a team. Hitched to the two-horse wagon with Clyde, she could be forced to step out and pull her share of a load of firewood or guano or cotton, but plowing her as a single or trying to deal with her on a one-to-one basis had been known to make grown men weep with frustration.

Central Johnson was the biggest, fastest, strongest man on the farm and could lift a bale of cotton by himself. On the one occasion when he had plowed Pet all day, Latisha, his wife, reported that he jerked and quivered for an hour after supper and his right shoulder was sore for a week from lashing Pet with the plowlines. Furthermore, Freeman and Darnell swore that at feeding time that night Pet grinned while she ate her twelve ears of corn and two bundles of fodder. Whenever there was any choice whatsoever, Pet was bypassed as a plowing partner, and she had become so proficient at modifying human behavior that she spent most of her life eating and standing and getting sleek and fat.

The boy had counted on having the young red mule this morning. She had not been assigned permanently to anyone, and she had a short, quick gait to match his own stride and was eager to work. He surmised that Darnell's fourth son, Menfolks, must have taken the red mule, leaving him with Pet. This was the penalty for being the last one to the lot, and he shrugged philosophically. If positions had been reversed, he would have done the same.

He stood on tiptoe, slipped the bridle over Pet's head, and forced the bit between her teeth, ignoring the impression that she seemed to slobber on his hand deliberately. He fastened the throat latch and pulled her, groaning and resisting, through the barn door into the yard where Darnell had left the plow for him. He threw the harness on her back, fastened the collar and tied it with the hame string, adjusted the back band, managed to back the reluctant animal into position, and hooked the trace chains to the singletree. Lifting the plowhandles so that the scooter would not plow up the lane and the driveway, he clucked to Pet and said, "Come up in there." She blew air through her nose with a wet, flubbering sound and leaned over to snatch a bite of morning glory vine off the back garden fence. He hit her with the plowlines and she eventually condescended to move, but at her own pace, and the boy felt that he was being tolerated but not obeyed.

When they finally reached the cotton field, he noted that Central and his second son, Snooks, were already plowing in the lower part of the field, their mules moving briskly and purposefully along, heads wagging, ears flopping, knees coming up in perfect cadence. He set the plow in the middle of a row directly across the road from the big house and said to Pet with confidence and assurance, "Git up." Thirty minutes later he was already sweating, and Pet was moving on her queenly way up and down the cotton rows, now fast so that he had to run to keep up, now suddenly slow so that he rammed full tilt into the plowstock, never consistent, always frustrating, often infuriating.

About this time she abandoned passive resistance and became openly aggressive. She began passing flatus. In plowing there are certain unwritten and even unspoken rules based on mutual consideration between man and beast. One of them is the acknowledged prerogative of stopping to urinate. The signs are obvious: the mule stops, puts her front feet together, spreads her hind legs apart, raises her tail straight up in the air, hunkers her hips down, and ejects a torrent of yellow urine behind her. This done, she cleans herself with a vaginal activity which can only be described by a close observer as winking, lowers the tail halfway, winks some more, moves her hind legs closer together, lowers her tail to normal carrying position, and then resumes walking without any command from the man behind the plow.

This is a deliberate activity, not to be rushed, not to be interrupted by human impatience or orders, and as stylized a ritual as her human counterpart's straightening a skirt and applying comb and lipstick. Urinating requires a full stop, but any decent mule can defecate in full stride, the tail raised only halfway, the huge brownish green fibrous balls tossed almost contemptuously out with a plop-plop-plop, the complete activity accomplished in an offhand manner with never a break in stride. Passing gas is an inconsequential activity which ordinarily attracts no notice whatever.

On this lovely June morning with wine-sweet air, warm not yet hot sun on the back, the muted crow of a rooster and the darting hum of an occasional bumblebee in the ear, Pet chose to demonstrate her power by deliberately pausing to pass flatus.

She would lumber along, ignoring the blandishments, imprecations, and threats of the boy, and suddenly come to a full stop. Slowly and importantly she would assume the urinating position, tail heisted straight up, and the boy would patiently and courteously respect the ladylike pause. Then, blasphemous and bitchy, she would expel flatus, not short staccato bursts, but long, drawn-out, sighing whooshes which sounded like a dirigible settling. Each one took minutes. The more the boy fumed over these unnecessary pauses, the longer and more frequent her pauses became. She recognized the new advantage she had acquired over the puny human who was trying to direct her activity this morning, and she was happily exercising it. Long inactivity, green grass, and an inexhaustible gas supply all combined to serve her well in bringing this upstart to his knees.

In the midst of his frustration, leaning on a plowhandle, the boy chanced to think of something. He felt in his pockets. He had a match. He palmed it in readiness while Pet plodded down the row. She stopped, braced her front legs, spraddled her back legs, flaunted her tail on high and began. Swiftly the boy leaned over, scratched the red and white head on the plowstock beam, and raised the match.

A flame leaped out as long as a man's arm. There was a clear zone between the source and the beginning of the flame. The blaze was blue, and it hissed and crackled and had long, feathery projections on the upper side of it, and it kept on and on and on and was altogether awe-inspiring to witness. Pet's reactions were the swiftest in a decade of laziness. First she tried to clap her tail down to cover the flame, but apparently this was painful, for she raised it again with alacrity. Still with her haunches hunkered, she jerked her head around, eyes rolling so that the whites gleamed in alarming exophthalmus, and beheld the great blue torch over which she had no control. With a loud snort that expressed wonder, disbelief, terror, and rage, she lowered her head, kicked both hind feet straight back into the plowstock, crouched, and then launched herself into a furious gallop.

The boy was never sure when the fire went out. Of a sudden he had more activity than he could handle. Hollering, "Whoa! Whoa, please whoa!" he clung desperately to the plowstock, which was bouncing along behind the mule, now in a dead gallop. He pulled back on the reins. Nothing happened. He dug his heels into the dirt and pulled back. All this accomplished was his heels plowing up two extra rows of cotton. Central, hearing the commotion and seeing a runaway mule in a perfect stand of beautiful cotton, yelled to the boy to drop one line. By doing this and clinging to the other, he managed to pull Pet's head to one side so that she ran in a circle. But run she did. She circled and circled. She had completely demolished a half acre of cotton by the time Central could grab her head and rein her in. She stood trembling and blowing, lathered of groin, eyes flashing and rolling as helplessly and uncontrollably as if she were in the midst of an epileptic seizure, for once totally intimidated and conquered.

While the boy stood in shock and wonder, trembling almost as much as the mule, viewing the horror he had wrought, thankful for the still and quiet, Central said, "What got into dis ole mule? A whole nest o' yellow jackets wouldn't a got dis much action out'n her."

Then from the upstairs front porch, where he had witnessed the incident, the father roared, "Boy, if that's the best you can do, put that damn mule back in the barn! Get your mattock, and spend the rest of the day getting sassafras sprouts off the terraces."

That was his only punishment. Freeman later told the boy that his father had confided to him: "He's not a bad boy. He minds well. I just can't think of enough things to tell him not to do."

the father provided a permanent home for his parents in the house. He also provided a home for his old maid sister, who accepted her spinsterhood cheerfully until the father imported a war buddy from Tennessee who married her and moved into the upstairs southwest bedroom. The new uncle was not fond of little children in general and this little boy in particular, and their bedroom door was kept locked at all times, a situation which lent it some of the fascination of Bluebeard's Chamber. In later years the boy was disappointed to find that it contained neither headless maidens nor trunks of treasure. This uncle was nicknamed Comp, and he was an impressive figure indeed. He must have felt lost and bewildered in the polyglot of the family into which he married, and he established his individuality early on by an obsessive-compulsive display of personal dignity. In the Depression, when everyone else wore homemade clothes and had the collars and cuffs of their shirts turned when they frayed, Comp wore Hickey-Freeman suits on Sunday and washed his automobile at least once a week. This was a Whippet and lasted for years and years because of the tender care he gave it.

Comp adopted as his personal contribution to the family welfare the responsibility of the vegetable garden. The rows were laid out with geometric precision and plowed free of crab grass before it could become more than a green fuzz on the surface of the earth. The yearly yield was a deluge of agrarian wealth, and the family rarely bought food at the grocery store. There were

17

beans, butterbeans, peas, tomatoes, okra, corn, squash, onions, potatoes, turnip greens, mustard, peppers, beets, radishes, carrots, and eggplant. They grew prolifically and they poured into the large back porch and kitchen in an overwhelming volume in season. They were eaten and they were canned and they were dried for the winter. The boy's mother had a tendency toward excessive generosity with the produce and would lade city kin with enough vegetables for a week when they came visiting. This infuriated Comp, who thought two tomatoes comprised a handsome enough gift for a thank-you note.

The boy had always accepted as a fact of life that one automatically liked his kin, respected his elders, and was generally loyal to the family charisma. Comp demonstrated the fallacy of this. With the universal attitude that small children are either deaf or noncomprehending to the point of stupidity, he used to vent his ire in the boy's presence when his in-laws came visiting and hauling. He would fling himself out of the house, his nose and lip curled in a sneer of contempt, and mutter such character analyses of various aunts, cousins, and uncles that would have left Sigmund Freud nodding in sage agreement. It rendered the boy round-eyed at this not unsatisfying contemplation of clay feet on people he had been taught to revere. He learned early on to accept imperfection in idols and to cherish hidden virtues in varlets.

Comp had a flaw in his projection of dignity that always left the boy titillated and the sisters subdued. Before the father prospered enough to buy a Delco system and install electricity and running water in the house and before he had yielded to his wife's pleadings for a chicken yard, Comp had a feud with a rooster. This was a huge fowl with a large amount of Rhode Island Red in his pedigree. His eye was yellow, shrewd, and malevolent. He announced impending sunrise each morning with a deep-throated crow that was such an emphatic declaration it could not be ignored for a mile. He was fearless in protecting his domain and the occupants thereof. With his head down, neck outstretched, wings spread, and tail feathers lowered to cut wind resistance, he would charge any interloper that was a fancied threat to his hens

18

or baby chickens. Cats, dogs, other roosters, and even small children traversed his domain with a wary eye and a hurried step, prepared to run when he appeared. He was a worthy model of the word "cockiness." Comp hated him.

Comp would throw rocks at him, would chase him with sticks upon sight, would turn red with rage and bolt out of the house after him if he heard his crow. He did not kill the rooster because it was under the benign protection of the boy's grandmother, but he did everything short of carnage. His attacks would cause the magnificent Chanticleer to flee through the yard, over the garden fences, through and over shrubs, tail feathers rippling in the wind of his own speedy passage, staccato shrieks erupting from his parted beak, hens flying and running in cackling hysteria, the yard erupting into total noise and confusion.

These encounters would leave the man heaving and hissing and red-faced with fury, the rooster high stepping, wary, and stuttering with indignation and disturbed aplomb, and the children awed and silenced by such a maniacal outburst. The girls privately thought the feud was triggered by the noisy crowing. The boy knew better. He had witnessed the inception of the hostilities and had been present when war was declared.

The privy stood at the end of the garden lane, some two hundred feet downhill from the well, and off to one side of the big barn. It was made of unpainted, weather-silvered pine boards and looked like a vertical box with a slanted shingle roof and a flimsy door. Another name for the edifice was "closet," and it resembled one. When in use the door was fastened from the inside with a big wooden button impaled on the doorframe with an eightpenny nail. Inside was a bench about three feet high with an oval hole cut in each side of the seat. The very shape of the holes informed one instantly of their function. On the floor was a stack of newspapers, a box of corncobs, and an old catalog, any of which could be used for cleansing. Under the seats was open space, the ground beneath each hole punctuated with an odorous, conical minaret, smelly monuments to hearty diet and healthy alimentation.

These piles so enriched the surrounding soil that it was teeming with earthworms and grubs, making it a rich hunting ground for chickens and mandating the confinement of fowls in a coop on a diet of pure corn for at least a week before slaughter.

Coming through the pasture one afternoon behind the privy, the boy was crawling on his belly beneath the lowest strand of barbed wire when his quick eye noted that the privy was occupied by a male member of the family. No person can appreciate like a man over fifty who has wintered innumerable sessions in a privy the hippy expression "Let it all hang out." Beneath the back of the privy was the old red rooster, king of the barnyard, provider for his flock.

As the boy watched, the rooster's attention was attracted upward. His neck craned forward, his head tilted first to one side and then slowly rotated to the other side while first one yellow eye and then the other peered intently above, striving for recognition of the cluster of pendulous objects on high. Then, dauntless, curious, aggressive, his decision for action was obviously made. He bent his yellow legs, half spread his mighty wings for balance, stretched forth his great red neck, and with a jubilant spring leaped high in the air and caught the middle one in his strong stubby beak.

Cause and effect were never more immediately demonstrated. There was a great bellow of pain and surprise followed by several high-pitched yip! yip! yips! as though an Indian were on the warpath, succeeded by a long, drawn-out, howling crescendo. This was accompanied by much thumping and banging within the wooden structure until it actually rocked and tottered as though to fall. At this moment the imperturbable rooster chose to flap his wings, stand on tiptoe, arch his neck and let forth a bugling and triumphant Cock-a-doodle-doo. With this the flimsy door banged all the way back against the wall and Comp exploded forth, flinging corncobs like a Gatling gun. The reserved, dignified Tennessee veteran turned into a red-eyed, furious demon bent ever thereafter on revenge. Associating the rooster's crow with Comp's activity facilitated later grasp of Pavlov's experiment with the dog, not to mention the principle of inertia and its division into potential and kinetic energy.

Another member of the family circle was a great-uncle, only surviving brother of the almost deified grandmother. At age eighty, he permanently abandoned his wife of sixty-two years, declaring that he could no longer endure her nagging, and returned to the ancestral acres to live out his last years. He had married above him. At least his wife thought this. He was either too obtuse or disinterested ever to recognize or admit it himself. His wife was the granddaughter of General Israel Putnam, who had distinguished himself during the American Revolution, as far as the boy was ever able to learn, by escaping on a black horse from the British after being lax enough to be captured by them in the first place. Impoverished gentility was stylish, and Aunt Carnela was in the height of fashion on both counts. She bore Uncle Bung four children, all of whom bore in turn, both badge and burden, the middle name of Putnam and all of whom he regarded askance as strange and foreign beings.

About all that could be said for Uncle Bung was that he felt friendly. Like the rooster he was under the divine protection of the grandmother, a condition which would have been negated in a moment by his brother-in-law, the grandfather, who never adjusted to sharing the serenity of his dotage with this never particularly admired interloper. Uncle Bung was small, chubby, bowed of back, and bandy-legged. He had round, apple cheeks, a silver moustache, and wavy silver hair. He looked like Santa Claus with the beard shaved, and his soul belonged to the great god Bacchus. Like an aged leprechaun he would roam the woods for miles around and ferret out the illegal liquor stills of neighboring blacks and poor whites. These forays would result in homecomings both irreverent and ribald, with much dancing of Irish jigs and lusty singing of lewd songs. He had a delivery that could make the most staid Baptist hymn sound obscene. His contribution to the family welfare was to keep the seat of the back porch swing warm. From this self-imposed enthronement, toes barely touching the floor, supporting chains rattling and whiteoak rattan creaking and squeaking, he spent the long summer afternoons fanning himself with pasteboard advertisements from morticians. Apparently dozing or muttering incoherently, he was actually making acid and penetrating comments about the various members of the family. The boy listened, absorbed, discarded, and learned.

One of the facts the boy learned from Comp and Uncle Bung was that most of the adult members of the tribe shared the children's opinion of Hollis Bolton. Hollis was the husband of the grandmother's oldest daughter, and he enjoyed the offhand, disinterested attention afforded an American vice-president or Victoria's Albert—nominally necessary, materially present, but in reality unimportant. He swept into the family circle when the Depression hit, starved out of Atlanta and forced back to the farm, which he had fled in laziness and an exaggerated sense of self-importance a generation earlier. Clad in seersucker or black serge, reeking of cheap cigars, pompous and braggadocian, he seemed to the children as flat and false as his teeth. Given to bombastic ultimata toward the boy and nonavuncular fondling of the girls, he earned their enthusiastic loathing.

The mother and father were courteous to him and demanded the same of the children. Superficially this was granted. The grandmother's benevolent mantle could protect the red rooster and Uncle Bung, but even her divine sanctuary was not a haven for this repugnant intruder from the city. He was fair game, and he welded the four children into a tight federation of revenge.

He lived three miles away in the hamlet of Peabody, but he made at least four trips to the big house weekly. Ostensibly he came to visit the grandmother, but he always managed to convert the filial pilgrimage into a self-serving foray that would have made William Tecumseh Sherman blush. He and his wife hauled away apples, peaches, watermelons, sausage, shoulders, hams, flour, meal, and vegetables by the ton. They even brought their dirty laundry once a week for Tabitha to wash and iron, paying her with old clothes or discarded hats and trinkets, which she promptly threw away.

Once the baby sister, who knew how to operate the family sewing machine, turned down the hems of Uncle Hollis's pants, which were folded atop the basket of clean clothes, and sewed the bottoms of the legs together. The boy had the satisfaction three days later of overhearing his aunt complain to the grandmother of the one-legged, off-balance, room-wrecking havoc that had followed. He and the sisters hugged each other in surreptitious glee.

One day Uncle Hollis came by the big house to leave his wife while he attended the Old Soldiers' Reunion in Tyrone. He hung his coat on the back of a porch rocker, and the boy spied two Tampa Nuggets in the inside pocket. A city cousin had brought him from a trick novelty shop in Atlanta some little wooden pegs impregnated with an explosive material which caused them to blow up when heat reached them. It took only a few minutes to tease open the cellophane on one of the cigars and implant the load deep within. All day the children had excited spasms of snickering over the vision of the pompous Hollis, thumbs hooked in suspenders, digesting a free lunch, puffing the cigar while assuming his member-of-the-cabinet stance, and having the thing explode to smithereens in his face.

This was not what happened. He met a man in Tyrone from whom he had borrowed money and, seeking to placate him, grandly bestowed upon him a conciliatory Tampa Nugget. Only the forceful intervention of mutual acquaintances prevented a severe altercation a little later, and Uncle Hollis returned to the big house with his necktie still twisted under his ear and his shirt collar wrinkled and wilted. The children looked innocent and concerned.

The boy delighted in deviling him by tampering with his truck. This homemade vehicle, Uncle Hollis's pride and joy, had been improvised by sawing off the back-end of a Chevrolet car and substituting a big wooden box. About once a week the boy would cram a raw sweet potato well into the end of the exhaust pipe. When Hollis tried to crank the truck, his wife sitting beside him waving farewell to the grandmother on the front porch, the motor would catch once, hiccup, and die. Then the children would all come forth to help push the truck off. Hollis would sit under the wheel, foot on the clutch, car in second gear, while the children strained and heaved to get the truck going down the sandy driveway fast enough for the motor to start. His wife continued to wave to the grandmother the entire time.

Jumping the clutch always worked, but whoever was directly behind the exhaust pipe had to be careful lest he get hit in the shin with the forcefully expelled sweet potato when the motor did catch. All this activity was worthwhile, since Hollis invariably drove straight to Mr. Tom Druid's garage (located in Mr. Tom Druid's back yard, side yard, and sometimes in his front yard) with the complaint, "It won't start again, Tom—I want it fixed this time." Investigation by an honest mechanic cost Hollis only piddling sums, but he developed a reputation for being mechanically stupid and very neurotic about his truck.

Once the boy risked their lives in this very truck. One Sunday afternoon, watching in indignation while Hollis ate four dishes of homemade ice cream, he longed for some form of revenge. Fanned by Uncle Bung's sotto voce scathing comments from the swing and reinforced by Comp's contemptuous mutterings, this longing produced an inspiration. South of the big house about a half mile down the hill at the crossroads, a big postoak tree towered some forty feet in the air and leaned over the red clay road. The boy hurried toward it. The clay of the road, not completely dry from rain two days before, was cracked into deep, irregular octagons by the baking sun and felt deliciously smooth to his bare feet. Skimming along the road, he detoured to a nearby watermelon patch. Selection was a speedily resolved problem. The forty pound giants were more than he could carry, and the five pound runts were unworthy of his project. He picked one that was between fifteen and twenty pounds, thumped it carefully, and checked the curling tendril at the base of the stem to determine that it was dead ripe. After lugging it tenderly to the roots of the tree, he cast about for a way to climb to the first branches, which were a good eight feet off the ground. He found an old oaken plank discarded by the chain gang after a bridge repair and managed to tug it to the tree. Inch by labored inch, the boy slanted it upward against the tree trunk at an incline he could mount.

Hastily he unfastened his overalls, let the galluses out as far as they would go, lay on the ground by the melon, rolled it over the apron of his overalls against his naked belly and chest, and clicked the fasteners securely closed. Staggering to his feet, he lurched around, assuring himself that this improvised sling was dependable. It was. They might fall together, but nothing could separate him and that watermelon unless he unfastened the overalls. Waddling to the plank, he managed to mount it by imitating a two-toed sloth and finally reached the haven of the lowest branch in the postoak.

Pausing to rest, he kicked the plank back down into the weeds so that no passerby on the road would have any reason to look up into the heavy foliage of the tree. Then, pushing with his feet and pulling with his arms, he managed, slowly and laboriously, to climb to the very top of the tree, fearful all the time that he would either burst the melon in his overalls or that he would be too late to hit the target. On the top branch, well out over the road and some forty feet above it, he locked his legs to insure balance, undid the overall bib, and balanced the melon gingerly on the limb before him. Then he waited.

He began calculating how far ahead of the truck he would have to drop the melon in order to hit the hood. Then he waited some more. He leaned over carefully and sighted down through the leaves to be sure he would have a straight drop to the road below. He would. He waited. He waited so long that he became fearful his prey might have gone home by Harp's Crossing and more than half hopeful that they had. Then he heard the chugging motor and saw the bright blue truck cresting the hill. As it coasted down toward the ambush, he grasped the melon and leaned over empty space with feet tightly entwined beneath the supporting branch. Mouth dry, heart thumping wildly, he desperately gauged speed of truck, height of tree, speed of melon, and launched his missile. Instantly he saw that he had misjudged. He thought with horror that the plummeting melon might hit the windshield, then with fleeting disappointment that it might land on the roof. Instead, it struck with a cataclysmic crash in the empty wooden body of the truck.

What he had not anticipated was the deadly combination of gravity, velocity, and weight. The entire truck leaped sideways in the road, the hind wheels skewing dangerously near the deep ditch. The melon had completely disintegrated on contact. The biggest particles remaining were the seeds, which were concealed by the high wooden side bodies of the truck. The vehicle ground to a halt. Hollis got out. "What in the hell was that?" he asked.

He circled the truck and kicked each wheel. "It wadn't a blowout."

He got on his knees and looked underneath. "Maybe the transmission dropped out," he ventured.

The boy hugged the tree as tightly as a koala bear, beseeching divine providence that the man would not look upward.

"Maybe it was an earthquake," his wife volunteered. "It felt sort of like that in 1910—it made me dizzy."

"Hell, Haynie, that wadn't no earthquake. There's something bad wrong with this truck. Let's take it by Tom Druid's before we go home."

Still shaken by the danger of his feat, the boy clung to his perch for long minutes after they were safely gone, too weak and too trembling to trust an immediate descent. Walking home later, the moist clay patterns cool beneath his feet, the sun still hot on his head and back, he noticed a grasshopper suspended in chirring vibration head-high over the road and smelled the warm fresh odor of opening cotton bolls. He realized that summer was almost over. In sudden maturity he decided that he would wait awhile before he told his sisters about the watermelon.

* * *

One week in midsummer the aunt went visiting and Hollis came to the big house every day for dinner. This was long before lunch was invented, and the meal consisted of two breads, buttermilk, multiple vegetable dishes cooked with hog fat, whatever meat was available, and pie made of the seasonal fruit. The farm bell tolled promptly at twelve from an oak post erected by the smokehouse. Dinner was served at twelve-fifteen, and the farm bell tolled again at one to send the hands and mules back to the fields.

It did not toll for Hollis. After his almost reptilian engorgement he ensconced himself daily on the wicker sofa which stood on the back porch just under the window of the kitchen where the two younger girls assumed the Herculean task of washing the dirty dishes and pots after each meal. While everyone else labored, Hollis slumbered and snored for at least an hour every day in totally limp and abandoned relaxation. His very presence was an annoyance to the children; this performance constituted insult.

There is an unspoken Southern axiom that if a lady complains about something, a gentleman immediately assumes the responsibility of rectification. It is based on the principle that if Mama ain't happy, ain't nobody happy, and it is an early molder of family attitudes and activities. When the sisters complained, therefore, about this gross snoring outside their working zone, this blatant flaunting of privileged indolence, the boy felt challenged to do something about it. He found the uncle sprawled on his back, left arm wedged beneath him, right hand trailing on the floor, legs slightly bent in the eversion of deep relaxation. His head was tilted back, with the mouth agape and the upper plate vibrating with each deep, chest-racking snore.

While the boy watched this phenomenon, an idea was born. He eased outside, located a good-sized wooden chip, and then searched for a fresh deposit of dark green chicken manure, thinking that cat would really be meaner but was not so readily available. This provided, he picked up a chicken feather from the corner of the yard and stole back into the porch. While the sisters watched through the window in happy horror, he liberally smeared Hollis's right forefinger with the fresh, rank, still-warm chicken dropping.

Icing on a cake was never applied more thickly, deftly, or lovingly. The snoring continued as regularly as waves on the seashore. Next the boy crept behind Hollis's head, held the screen door open with one hand, stretched his skinny frame as far as possible, and tickled vigorously under the nose with the feather. Then he bolted through the open door, legs pumping like pistons, heading for the deep woods and a secret hole where he could hide. Even as he ran, disappearing from sight of the porch in an all-time record sprint, he could hear the roars from the bewildered and sickened enemy behind him. Fear made his feet fleet, but it was exultation that made his heart race. "That'll fix him good," he whispered as he scampered through the creek into the white mud cave, where he crouched in safety for at least an hour while the storm he had generated subsided. Getting a report later from the second sister, who was gifted in both observation and expressiveness, he was assured of the success of the project.

"Both nostrils were stuffed," she said. "There were little peaks and curls sticking out."

She paused to consider and then added, "It looked just like black meringue."

The children hugged each other ebulliently. Hatred can, on occasion, be a lovely bond.

The grandparents had a great influence in the family circle, especially on the children during their formative years. No real Southerner has ever been able to consider very seriously the highly touted ancestor worship of the Chinese. It is watery by comparison. Teethed on "what we had before the war," weaned on the accomplishments of successful kin, nurtured on the pronouncement of dominant family traits, and lullabied by the recitation of genealogical alliances of several generations, no Southerner could ever mature without a profound sense of family. This spilled over into awareness about other families in the county, and one learned what to expect from different tribes in both looks and actions.

This knowledge came largely from the grandparents and usually in the long, conversational family evenings before television, radio, or accessible automobiles. In the winters the gathering was around the crackling fire in the grandmother's room, in the summers on the wide verandah outside her bedroom door. The grandfather was the raconteur, the grandmother the critic, prompter, and censor. Before they were five, the children knew that "Blood will tell," and "Pretty is as pretty does," which they learned from the grandmother. From the grandfather the boy learned "You can't make pound cake out of cow manure," a comforting maxim indeed when one is forced to assume responsibility for the actions of others, which happens frequently to a farmer.

Diminutive, serene, and regal, the grandmother was rigidly loyal to her generation. Never having read Ruskin, she was assured that she had been placed on this earth at the opportune time and place to have all matters social, moral, and religious disclosed to her in absolute truth. Her codes of conduct and conversation were inflexible and inviolable—she once automatically slapped the boy full in his mouth for saying *bull* in her presence instead of *male cow*. At family gatherings all males rose when she entered the room, even if she had departed it only five minutes earlier. This was in deference to the grandfather, who would have your head and ears if you did not comply with this courtesy.

She and her friends wore shawls, and nobody but their husbands had ever seen their legs without stockings. Her clothes were either gray, black, or lavender, and she always smelled of rosewater and glycerin. She hated the devil, yankees, and Roman Catholics, although she had seen none of them, equating Abraham Lincoln, the Pope, and Satan in haughty dismissal. She also hated alcohol but had seen a great deal of that.

Her temperance sermons far surpassed any efforts in the local Baptist pulpit and had the added cut of personal reference.

Her darkly prophetic pronouncement that "Osborne men can't drink," brought shudders to the boy's spine. His own observation was that indeed they could, more than anyone else he had seen, and he was in his late teens before he finally comprehended her meaning. It was even later before he was sophisticated enough to understand fully her other oft-repeated advice of "Marry out of the county, boy."

Her love for flowers enriched the boy's life. She had borders on each side of the sand-covered walk leading to the verandah, and she also had a flower yard. Whenever the boy was on the verge of excessive punishment for fussing with his sisters, the grandmother would lure him away on the pretext of needing his help in her flower beds. There she taught him the difference between weed and choice plant, the effect of chicken or cow manure on growing things, and the joy of pulling weeds and grass out by the roots so the flowers would flourish. She also managed gently to counsel him about temper, the virtues of manhood, and family pride.

She made him feel special, and she imbued him with a reverence for womanhood that he never forsook. She became a part of the boy's life, of the warp and woof of his structure, and he loved flowers in homage to her. Years later, the characteristic tints and fragrances of petunias, snapdragons, sweet William, or phlox would conjure up instantly the sight of her tiny, shawled figure in high-buttoned shoes, the sound of her gentle, patient voice, the faint tremor of her thin-skinned, heavy-veined, fragile-boned hands; and he would feel again accepted, loved, and encouraged in an otherwise harsh and hostile world. Every child needs a grandmother, preferably in residence.

Her snuff was like sex—one was supposed to ignore it. She used it as daintily as she did everything else. Special brushes, or dipsticks, made from fresh blackgum twigs were de riguer. The brush was moistened in the mouth, rolled lightly in the little tin box of snuff until a small ball adhered to it, and then placed back in the mouth, precisely between the lower bicuspid and the gum. Here it rested in contentment and serenity while the rocking chair creaked, the fire crackled, and the Seth Thomas clock ticked on the mantel. If some visitor, called "company," was announced, there was a genteel flurry while she hid the box and brush, rinsed her mouth with water, and wiped her lips with lace or a wisp of embroidery. The boy thought there were a lot of adult idiots around if no one comprehended the reason for that bucket of sand beside her chair.

The only time the boy ever saw her dignity violated or her equanimity destroyed it had been his fault, and he felt conscience-stricken about it for years. In the summertime the long mornings began before day and were filled with breakfast, housecleaning, churning, washing of clothes, feeding of chickens, and canning, plus the preparation and serving of dinner. After the definitive twice-tolling farm bell had brought the men to dinner and sent them back to the fields, after the dishes were washed and the kitchen floor was scrubbed with hot water and lye soap, after the victuals remaining from dinner were stored in the pierced-tin safe awaiting supper, after every woman on the place had energetically performed every labor known to God or man, there came an interval known as nap time. The ladies retired to their high-ceilinged, shady, lace-curtained, breeze-kissed, feather-bedded corner bedrooms, removed their shoes, and "stretched out" for an hour. Peace descended. Total quiet prevailed. The hum of a bee was a musical intrusion, and one almost felt that if it got a little quieter, the rays of the hot sun or the growing of the cotton would be audible.

The children were not permitted even a whisper of communication, and any journey in the house had to be accomplished on stealthy, barefooted tiptoe with exquisite care not to slide or slur a foot across the floor. For the boy these were daily periods of tedium which he aborted by slipping silently from the house and exploring the yard, the garden, the barn, and its environs.

One day he was visited with an inspiration so fascinating and challenging that he abandoned all logic in pursuing it. His Atlanta cousin had a cow pony quartered on the farm. She was an intelligent, individualistic, fiery beast only slightly smaller than a horse and had been evicted from the Georgia Baptist Orphans'

Home for maiming more orphans than the Baptists could repair. The boy had mastered the animal and could ride it when others could not. Having learned the secret that Brownie could not abide a saddle, he simply rode her bareback, and a mutual respect and tolerance existed between them. On this hot summer nap time, the boy, fantasizing about Ivanhoe, d'Artagnan, Lassiter, and Francis Marion, decided to ride the pony up the steps of the big house, across the front porch, down the long narrow hallway to the steep, dark stairwell at the rear of the hall, mount these stairs, and emerge eventually onto the unrailed upstairs front porch which circled two sides of the house. From this vantage point he would then survey, in grand and splendid isolation, the terrain beneath him, searching for enemy Knights Templar, French Royalists, Mormons, or British Redcoats.

In almost dreamlike sequence the performance was as easy as the inception. Brownie was unusually amenable to accepting the bridle, and she mounted the seven concrete steps to the front porch as though she did it daily. Entering the hallway, however, evoked a sense of unease in the little horse. With the boy astride her, she lowered her head, eyeing and snuffling each article in this strange darkened tunnel in which she found herself. Her feet made an echoing, clumping sound on the polished hardwood floor as she slowly proceeded down the hall, obedient to the encouraging nudges of the boy's knees.

The grandmother's bedroom door opened onto the hallway across from the foot of the stairs. Just as the horse, diffident, cautious, and suspicious, arrived at this point and stretched her head toward the stairs, the grandmother, curious, disbelieving, and investigative, opened the door and thrust out her head.

For one frozen moment in time, eyeball to eyeball, not twelve inches apart, they stared at each other, the Southern matriarch serenely entrenched in the home built by the slaves of her forebears and the tousled western maverick, unwilling interloper in a foreign element. Simultaneously the grandmother gave an outraged squawk of surprise and indignation, the pony reared on its hind legs, and the door slammed. The horse wheeled, and a scrambling ride ensued back down the hall and across the porch. Brownie leaped down the steps, and the wildest gallop the boy ever experienced carried both culprits safely back to the haven of the barn.

The boy anticipated with dread but resignation the severe punishment to follow. To his amazement, the incident was never mentioned. His misdemeanor fell into the category of snuff and sex—it was so improbable that it was ignored. For months when he recalled that afternoon, his buttocks would tighten at thought of the undelivered thrashing he justly deserved. For years he felt guilty thinking how similar were the rolling eyes of the grandmother and the horse at the moment of their confrontation.

lthough the grandmother was a patrician representative of her area and generation, the boy's mother was unique. Born and raised in a north Georgia city, she had adjusted to this Piedmont farm with unbelievable poise. She was as romantic as the father but in addition possessed a pragmatic and realistic streak that served as spring steel when the breaking point of a family crisis occurred. Surrounded by her husband's people, living in his mother's house, constantly overseen and advised by his spinster sister, beset by hordes of kin arriving unexpectedly at mealtime, she maintained her own distinct personality and moved within the family group as a glory. She was the happy pivot that kept the entire highly improbable group from flying apart. Everyone was heavily dependent on Vera.

Though she never opened her mouth during the genealogical recitations to question the blueness of her in-laws' blood or the impoverished nobility of their lineage, she also never opened her mouth to confirm it. On occasion, with a silence that almost shouted, her unspoken message was that somebody better pick the cotton.

She was completely submissive to the dominating manhood of the father. She adored his person, obeyed his orders, indulged his whims, admired his intellect, applauded his accomplishments, waited on him hand and foot, and defended his mistakes. She thus created such an ideal of masculine behaviour and exhibited such an unswerving belief in the reality of this superior image that the father was challenged to the limits of his really rather remarkable powers to fill the role so subliminally but steadfastly outlined for him. Chafed by the armor of the Southern gentleman, rigidly confined by the concept of Christian chivalry, mired in intellectual Romanticism, he was trapped by his own codes of heroic conduct. Bound by the demands of his patriarchy to the innumerable problems of multiple relatives, weighed down by responsibility for the material welfare of his family and hands, the man sometimes would weary of his empire. Then he would say to hell with it all and release his humanity.

Since the grandmother allowed no liquor in her home, never mind who was financing the home, the father's relaxing episodes invariably occurred in town. They began with whiskey consumed secretly in the back of the drugstore as token acknowledgment of the prohibition laws. Rapidly the Southern gentleman, medieval knight, and benevolent father and husband disappeared. A berserker emerged. A rampage followed which was sure to include fist fighting or pistol whipping, maybe both. There would be wild and heedless driving, recklessness on muddy roads, occasional womanizing, and frequent bodily injury, both to self and others.

These explosions, occurring in the still frontier-flavored county seat and ignored by law enforcement officers, were devastatingly embarrassing to the family. The children were deaf as loftily as possible to the snickering comments of classmates on Monday.

The mother's reaction was consistent. She consoled the children by blaming these violent manifestations of released passions on the War and the mysterious tortures their father had endured while "overseas"—a distinctly different condition from being "abroad." She conquered the father by never evincing the slightest show of anger but by being "hurt." This is a Southern synonym, usually used by women, for genteel and refined, slightly Christian, and very martyred suffering. In the hands of an intelligent and artistic expert it is a formidable weapon indeed.

It guarantees forgiveness, a condition which the offender may not desire but can hardly refuse, and promises a fairly immediate return to the emotional status quo, a state the offender most devoutly covets. It involves grief, but the grief has to be silent, manifested by brimming eyes, the wordless splash of a reproachful tear, the very slight reddening of a beautiful and aristocratic nose. It is a condition which can never be utilized by a coarse-featured, simple peasant of a female susceptible to abandoned sobbing or other uninhibited behavior. A Southern man with any sophistication of breeding who hears, "I want you to know that I'm not mad, I'm just hurt," in soft controlled tones knows immediately that the ballgame is over, the race has been run, and that his shoulders are pinned firmly to the mat.

Usually by Monday, never later than Tuesday, with the mother bracing it, the father managed, burdened but brave, to remount his pedestal. The ship of their marriage, another patch in its sails, once again safe after a squall, would right itself and sail on, managing an occasional skip across the waves and shining in the sun. It was a state secret whose hand was at the wheel. The boy observed, absorbed, discarded, and learned.

His mother had huge blue eyes, even white teeth, a warm, generous smile, and long brown hair which she wore in one thick braid around the top of her head like a tiara. She was considered a very beautiful woman. The boy knew her as a very happy one. The huge old house was a perfect sounding chamber for her voice, which was melodious in speech and lilting when raised in song. She sang when she churned, canned, cooked, or swept and hummed when she sewed. One of the most beautiful scenes of the boy's early memory revealed her in a low utilitarian rocking chair that had belonged to her Grandma Bradley. She sat in the upstairs southeast bedroom, next to the small wood-burning stove, which held an aluminum kettle of water steaming busily and audibly.

Holding the baby sister cuddled to her breast, mother and child blending in a single projection of bliss and security, one dimpled hand of the baby exploring in idle wonder the hollow at the base of the mother's throat, she rocked the little chair and sang her lullaby. It was a simple evening before prosperity had overwhelmed the Southern whites and precipitated the blacks into a prickle of social consciousness. In that bare-floored, cavernous box of a room, lit by the flicker of fire from the jack-o-lantern face of the little stove and one small kerosene wall lamp with a tin reflector, she sang in innocence and joy to the contented child a lulling tune. The words a generation later would have produced street harangues and a shrilling cacophony of reverse intolerance on nationwide television:

> You my little black baby wid a turned-up nose,
> And a little patch o wool upon yo head.
> You got wrinkles in yo elbows and dimples in yo toes,
> And a mouf lak a watermelon red.
> You my ripe ripe tomato; you my sweet sweet potato;
> You my pretty little brown sugar-bowl.
> You des a little bit o honey what de bees ain't found —
> You my own pickaninny—dat's all.

She also sang hymns in church. This was a white one-room building planted squarely on exposed brick pillars with two doors at each end, and a graveyard behind it which smelled of magnolias and moss The interior looked sparse and bare. The tall, narrow windows were uncurtained, clear-paned hosts to cylindrical, corner-hugging rows of dirtdauber nests, the tenants of which attended summer services regularly. There were three rows of highbacked square benches made from hand-planed boards of heartpine. Designed for disciplined, masochistic adults, the backs were so straight that they almost tilted a resting spine forward. The seats were so wide and so high off the floor that the legs of a child either stuck stiffly straight out or dangled limply in thin air.

The pulpit was a simple square column of pine topped by a Bible and a limp lace doily. It stood squarely behind the huge potbellied iron stove that burned coal and was heated until it glowed red in a feeble attempt to warm the House of the Lord in the wintertime. If one sat in the center of the church, the pulpit was invisible. Much craning of the neck was necessary to see the preacher, an act which was usually balanced out by craning of the ministerial neck to determine who was sleeping safely behind the shield of the old stove.

The floor was bare and announced with piercing creaks any foray to the outdoors and Cousin Tom McEachern's privy. Most of the children wore shoes to church, and these heavy, hobbling encumbrances made clumsy, clumping sounds any time they touched the echoing wooden floor.

Wires were strung across the room at a height of approximately six feet. These supported green curtains which were pushed back against the wall for church services but drawn out during Sunday School to form individual cubicles for the various classes. Biblical descriptions of Solomon's grand new temple with its curtains always produced in the boy's mind an image of hangings that were green, cotton, musty smelling, and cut on the bias.

Overhead light was provided by large nickel-plated Aladdin lamps, hung from the ceiling by chains. They had white china shades and gasoline mantles nested inside clear glass chimneys. When lit, they emitted a distinctive noise, half purr and half hiss, and shed an eerie white light which attracted hundreds of moths and an occasional praying mantis, beetle, or devil's walking stick. Periodically an obsessed bug, irresistibly attracted to the death-dealing lights, would find his way down the chimney and fall into the whitehot maw of one of these miniature Molochs. Those quick cremations were always announced by a fiery flicker of intensified light and a hiccuping gulp in the steady hiss of the burning gasoline fumes, awe-inspiring background to awe-inspiring sermons.

The church had a steeple, a white and shingleroofed projection with a bell which could actually be tolled, a solemn act reserved for the portly deacons. The bell had no melodious tone at all but clanged loudly and uncompromisingly to announce preaching once a month on first Sunday and revival services every morning during the second week in August. The rope to the bell hung through a hole in a trapdoor just inside the church between the two doors. It ended in a large loop stained and greased by pulling hands, suspended well above the reach of children and adolescents. It was clearly visible from the boy's Sunday School cubicle and added an extra neck-prickling thrill to the power struggle of Esther, Mordecai, and Haman.

The summer of his tenth year was a religious landmark. Revival in the church occurred during laying-by time for the dirt farmers and supposedly between the fruiting of the Georgia Belles and Elbertas for the peach-picking hands. It consisted of six consecutive days of church in the morning and church in the evening. The preacher came with his entire family and lived in the community for the week, sleeping at one house most of the time but eating dinner and supper in different homes. This was a gastronomic feat which would have challenged the digestive powers of a Roman emperor, since each housewife tried to outdo her sisters in quality and quantity of food prepared. Also with arch and coquettish but iron-willed insistence they urged seconds on the poor man. How preachers bore the onslaught is a mystery, but they seemed to enjoy it.

No one ever joined the church during regular services. Revival was the time for that. It involved a march down the aisle to shake the preacher's hand, a vote of admission by the church membership, and a Sunday afternoon immersion in Mr. Walt Toler's cold fresh-water swimming hole while the congregation lined the bank and sang, "Shall We Gather at the River?" The voices of the singers and the preacher sounded muted and flattened by the outdoors and the absence of sound-rebounding walls and ceiling.

The girls had to be careful about their skirts when they waded out into the creek. If they got air trapped beneath them, it would be released during the holy, upending process of baptism and flip the garment up in embarrassing exposure of hidden flesh. There were two schools of thought on this problem. One advocated the stiff, thigh-clamping extension of hands to confine the skirt while the preacher held the nose; the other advised sewing rocks into the hem of one's skirt and holding one's own nose. One had to weigh the trust one had in the preacher against the suspicions one had about the creekside voyeurs.

Anyhow, it was great fun to see the fully clothed girls

carried under the water by the arms of the preacher and more fun to watch them part the water in Ondine-like emergence, hair and eyes streaming, wet clothes clinging revealingly to nubile bodies. Young spectators learned quickly from observing their elders that in this paradox of solemnity and joy it was forbidden to laugh.

The older sister, four years his senior, unquestioned and adored superior in all matters intellectual, had joined the church the previous year. The other children had occupied only the periphery of family attention while her decision was discussed, her convictions confirmed, and her attitudes applauded. Basking in the center stage of family approval for several weeks, she managed to excite no small degree of envy in her little brother. He privately resolved that, if it was all that important, he himself might some day join the church, an act which he had never considered previously as anything other than a spectator sport.

Certainly he had not planned it. Salvation had never challenged him. Believing with childish arrogance the family myths of superiority, living in a two story house that still had paint on it, eating hot graham biscuits with plenty of butter and ribbon cane syrup, being the only son of a Southern mother, it never occurred to him that he did not already dwell in some superior state of salvation.

The mother was deeply religious. She not only attended Sunday School and church regularly, she scrubbed and shined four children and had them there every time the doors opened. This was no small feat, since the baths were administered in a large gray enamel tub with water drawn by hand from the deep, raw-smelling well and heated on the kitchen stove in an iron kettle. In addition, the second sister had hair that tended to curl, a natural resource that necessitated exploitation and display. A strand of hair was isolated and trained around the mother's finger with a moistened brush until it formed a bouncing coil. This was repeated until the hair ran out and resulted in a head full of shoulder length curls that shimmered and quivered in the light like a peck basket full of fresh pine shavings. This caused all the women on the church ground, addressed according to kinship or

40

marital status as "Cuddin," "Miz," or "Miss," to sigh and say she looked like a little angel, fully rewarding the beaming mother for the extra thirty minutes of preparation. No one ever referred to the youngest sister, who had a head full of wheat straw and a breathtaking proclivity for frank speech, as an angel.

The mother, in addition to taking them to church, gave the children a Bible education which they accepted as part of family routine. Every night for an hour she read to them from the Story Book Bible, a highly entertaining, simplified version that skipped the begats, abstractions, and sex of the original, and modernized the language while sacrificing none of the details. The boy became immersed in the Old Testament.

He reveled in and shivered with delighted horror at the accounts of Abel's murder, the destruction of the Flood and Noah's drunkenness, the unbelievable denial by Abraham of his wife, the justified punishment of Lot's wilful wife, the incessant involvement of Jacob in some type of family fracas, the mighty words of Moses, the vamping and duping of Samson, the reluctant leadership of a God-bedeviled Saul, the venality of King David, and the vanity of Solomon. He secretly admired Jezebel as an imperious, disdainful, highborn lady thumbing her nose at fate and able to endow with dignity a debasing death. He had more canniness, however, than to proclaim such heresy. The Old Testament heroes were real to the boy, as was Jehovah, their just and terrible director and judge.

Jesus seemed to the undersized boy an ineffectual, unrealistic, effeminate aspirant to the overpoweringly masculine and mighty attitudes of His Father, Lord God of Hosts. The boy could not help being bored by stories of a man who had never done anything worse as a child than run away from home and then talk mildly like a smart-aleck when finally apprehended. He not only had more sense than to voice this attitude, he felt horribly guilty in the depths of his soul for having it. He always shrilled forth his lusty and off-key contribution to the favorite song of the Sun Beams with a hidden quiver of shame for secretly loving the Father the best: "If I love Him when I die, He will take me home on high, Yes, Jesus loves me." He, like Naaman, learned to give lip service in one direction while the allegiance of the heart went elsewhere.

Although he delighted in descriptions of a heaven in some permanently temperate zone and shuddered at the horrors of a malodorous and flaming hell, personal salvation had not been important to him heretofore because its virtues all seemed to pivot on the eventuality of death and life beyond. He vaguely and blissfully assumed that in the unlikely event of death ever overtaking a member of the family, the mother would see them through and get them in, clinging safely to the skirts of special privilege. He had no real concept of sin. If pressed for a definition, he would have been dishonest, for he identified it nebulously with sex, and no power could have forced such an admission from him. This probably stemmed from being caught with a whole gaggle of cousins one sunny afternoon perched buck naked on the top rail of the cowlot, tickling each other with oat straws and giggling gleefully.

After the expected peppery punishment with a keen peach-tree switch, he received a puzzling discourse from his mother, the mysterious slant of which was that the body is the temple of the soul. Ever thereafter he tended to regard the center of his being as an erect penis, and he seemed to get in more trouble with the temple than with the soul. He got caught so many times with a hard on—in the pecan tree, in the holly tree, under the front porch, under the back porch, behind the engine house, behind the smokehouse, in the hay loft—that as surely as a compass needle points north when released it was a marvel that he did not become aroused at the mere sight of a switch. Although they must have been reported to him, his father never mentioned these peccadilloes; it was always the mother who meted out punishment, followed by the exhortation to preserve the purity of his temple.

Sin, and being saved from it, were the furthest things from his mind that hot night during revival when he seated himself midway down the church next to JoJo Peabody, the only other boy

42

his age in the congregation. The preacher that year was named Mr. Lawson. He was tall and bony-thin with grizzled gray hair, steel-rimmed glasses, and a steel brace that held him ramrod straight. His dentures were too big for his face, causing sunken cheeks and spraying sibilants, but he was filled with the fervor of evangelism. He could yell and shout and whisper and weep and stamp his feet and wave his arms with the best of them.

He was a Baptist to the bone, a consummate actor, and a shrewd judge of human nature. The text this night was from the New Testament, and the boy noted that here was another one getting excited over Dives and Lazarus. Mr. Lawson portrayed the rich man in the depths of Hell as being filled with social indignation upon seeing the beggar from his old domain lolling in the bosom of Abraham. As the preacher enlarged and elaborated on this theme and enriched it with endless illustrations of people dying just before they were saved, the boy went to sleep.

He and JoJo were sitting directly behind Cuddin Alice and Cuddin Exor, old maid daughters of Cuddin Deuteronomy Fernandey Malcolm (called Cuddin Dew for short). Both ladies looked like drying skeletons with their skin stretched tight over bony prominences and then hanging in loose folds and wrinkles to the next bony anchor. Their eyes were bright and darting, Cuddin Alice's blue above tiny gold-rimmed spectacles and Cuddin Exor's brown behind large horn-rimmed spectacles. They quavered and hissed when they sang the hymns, and they sighed when they prayed. They had no malice in them but did not miss one breath of gossip, and man had known them not.

When he read Greek mythology, the boy always thought of them when the Harpies were mentioned. Tonight they were fanning themselves in unison with advertisements from Haisten's Funeral Home. This slow regular motion, coupled with the hissing of the Aladdin lamps and the resonant metronome of the preacher's phrases, completely hypnotized the boy.

He dreamed that he was dying, that Cuddin Alice and Cuddin Exor were bending over him murmuring that it was time to call Haisten's, wisps of hair straying from the tight, uncompromising buns on the backs of their necks. The boy actually felt that he was dying. Then it dawned on him that he was not rising. He was falling. He jerked awake on the hard bench, heard the louder hissing of the Aladdin lamps as an insect hit the flames, saw the planes of earnest Christian faces shine whiter in the eerie light, and the eye sockets loom darker. The preacher thumped the pulpit, stamped the wooden floor, and bellowed that this young man had wanted to make a commitment to the Lord but was killed in an automobile (the voice now sank to a whisper) on his way home. His soul was lost (crescendo again), his life wasted because he had not professed Jesus Christ as his Lord and Saviour.

"If there are any in the house who have heard the call but are trembling on the brink, while we sing this closing hymn won't you come, won't you come, won't you come before it's too late?"

The piano whined and thumped. Cuddin Tom stood to lead the singing, watch fob hanging from the precipice of his pendulous belly, chin tucked into fat neck, mouth opened wide in solemn slowness.

> Tomorrow's sun may never rise
> To greet thy long deluded sight.
> Poor sinner, harden not your heart,
> Be saved, oh tonight!
> Oh, why not tonight?
> Oh, why not tonight?
> Wilt thou be saved?
> Then why not tonight?

Heart pumping audibly, quivering with terror, soaking wet with sweat, the boy faced his own mortality for the first time. Fear propelled him from his bench and down the aisle to grasp the outstretched hand of the surprised preacher. He was saved from hell, saved from falling when he dreamed, saved from burning in eternal flames, saved, saved, saved! Jesus never crossed his mind. What a preacher!

Having impulsively got himself into this center of church consciousness, this quagmire of embarrassment, this fresh nightmare state, he heard the murmurs of his elders: "How sweet," "Just precious," "So young." He heard the tremulous query of his mother, "Son, do you know what you're doing?" There was no way to renege.

At the age of ten he embraced religious hypocrisy. Guiltily he never let his mother know that he had joined the church under the simple stimulus of "God's gonna getcha!", that he revered Jehovah but didn't feel Jesus was real, and hadn't the foggiest notion what they were talking about when they discoursed on the Holy Ghost. JoJo, loyal to the end, joined the church the following night, and they were baptized on Sunday afternoon in Toler's Pond. The heavens opened not, and no dove descended. Nor did lightning strike. Selah.

The mother had a job. There was a two room schoolhouse in the little community of Winship some four miles west of home for which only one teacher had been procurable. The mother had taught school prior to her marriage and at the last minute was pressed into service to fill this vacancy. Like most other things, it was a family affair. The grandmother and aunt would keep the three younger children. The oldest daughter would ride to school with the mother and indeed be one of her pupils. Because of the job the mother was given a car of her own, a square four-door vehicle, the top of which gave the impression of being wider than the bottom.

For rain or cold weather it had flexible sides which could be snapped onto metal supports around the car. The windows in these sides were made of a wonderful substance called isinglass, which was semiflexible and in the beginning allowed penetration of vision and light, although one always had the sensation of peering sideways under water. With a little age, a little exposure to the sun, a little wear and tear while folded on the floor of the car during the hot days of summer, these panes became yellowed or opalescent with an opaqueness that challenged the keenest eye.

Fortunately the windshield, which could be cranked straight out for ventilation, was made of glass, and after all there was little motorized traffic on the narrow dirt roads. A lot of people still used buggies or wagons for transport.

This automobile gave the mother a new independence and mobilized her to an unbelievable degree in happy vagabondage. It was so important to her that the father, in characteristic generosity, saw to it that for the rest of her life she had a car.

She enjoyed her first year of teaching so much that a family conference was convened about continuing the arrangement. The aunt assured her that she did not mind one bit keeping the little girls; they were precious children, quick to mind, easy to entertain, and sweet of disposition. The boy, however, was another story. He picked on the little girls, kept them in a constant uproar, sent them screaming and crying to tell on him for one hundred offenses per day, and was apt to give her a "complete nervous breakdown." This was a mysterious but important condition of the aunt—incipient throughout the boy's preteen years—and apparently such a státus extremis that it must be avoided at any cost. It was the supreme threat, a gauntlet-flinging, die-casting, last-ditch ultimatum that required very sophisticated thespian expertise to be credible. For a Southern woman to say, "I declare I'm going to have a nervous breakdown," was much heavier theater than "I want you to know I'm not mad, I'm just hurt," and was a declaration of untenable frustration. The only stronger statement was, "I'm going to kill myself," a plebian attempt at gaining one's own way to which no genteel mistress of manipulation would consider stooping.

Auntie had brought it on herself. Upon the departure of the mother to the sanctuary of Academe, the boy blithely assumed that this surrogate would automatically afford the same adulation and comfort it was his custom to enjoy by virtue of being the only male child in the family. This was a condition of exalted eminence. It involved at some far-off point in time a mysterious activity, firmly declared but not specifically outlined to him, called "carry on the name."

He hadn't the faintest idea what this entailed, but he was ready. Saul or David or Elisha could not have felt more anointed. After all, this came straight from the mouth of the grandmother herself in direct communication during a flowerbed session. In addition the slim and magnificent grandfather, who had a gold tooth and a great gold biscuit of a watch with a gold chain the size of a small boy's finger and might be a king in disguise, had told him while sitting on the wooden plank laid across the top of the two-horse wagon as it jolted, rattling and empty, down the clay road, "Someday, boy, you'll have to carry on the name." He hugged this nebulous assignment to his breast as a sign of unassailable superiority and assumed that all people would know that he was set apart.

Auntie, favored sister of five brothers, practiced in the ancient wiles of domesticating males to harness, productive labor, and compliance, was not impressed. She actually favored little girls over little boys. She thought they were cuter; she thought they were sweeter and prettier; she thought they were superior. She even had the audacity to say so. The boy was bewildered and disbelieving. He suffered rejection and disapproval. It seemed to him that the harder he strove to please her, the more unobtainable her approval became. He came to feel like a dog jumping vainly for a tantalizing morsel that was being held farther and farther out of reach. He learned firsthand the destroying quality of indifference.

"Well, is the little baby crying again? The sweet girls aren't crying. Does he want us to fix him a sugar tit?"

This was such an infuriating affront that he soon abandoned honest exhibition of grief as a weapon. He cried no more himself. He made others cry.

The aunt would chide him with "You know what little girls are made of? Sugar and spice and everything nice."

It was her warm and approving tone that made this formula seem so admirable and desirable.

"You know what little boys are made of? Snakes and snails and puppy-dog tails," with a sneering tone accompanied by the contemptuous curl of her upper lip. He felt totally unworthy.

Never mind the snakes and snails—he knew nothing of them. But what was wrong with puppy-dog tails? He had to confess that he had one, of which he was a little in awe and very proud. It would even wag from side to side under proper conditions. Having assumed heretofore that it was an addition and an asset, he was now forced by these repetitively chanted insults to consider the opposite.

He soon learned to hide honest anger in the same closet with grief. He became angry no more. He made others angry. He became adept at annoying the little girls. Physical assaults such as hitting, biting, pushing, or pinching were out. Psychological assaults such as snatching of dolls, breaking colors, making fun of games, or laughing derisively were tools just as effective. When the girls cried, the aunt got angry. When the aunt was angry, she whipped the boy.

She was a whipping wonder. She could beat a tattoo with a wooden hairbrush on a boy's tight-stretched bottom that would have made Gene Krupa pause in admiration. In the selection of switches she was mean and cruel. She used privet hedge, a weapon of power and sting that was far worse than the mother's customary crepe myrtle branches, which tended to be a little dry, creating a lot of rattle and noise but not an unbearable amount of pain. Both women reserved the acrid-smelling new growth of the peach tree as the ultimate punishment, used only for infractions approaching capital offenses.

When the aunt whipped the boy, she held him by one hand. Eyes squinched shut, bare legs jerking and fast feet stamping, he would wheel round and round his privet-wielding tormentor, screaming in rapid, rhythmic penance, "I won't do it no more, I won't do it no more." His aunt had stopped him in mid-punishment once to correct his delivery: "I won't do it any more, boy." It was important to stop the dancing and the shrieking when she stopped the switching. If she suspected overreaction, she might resume the punishment.

When the aunt, dizzy and exhausted, rested her baton, and the boy, stinging and snubbing, stopped his lyrics, the two little girls standing against the wall round-eyed with attention, mouths slightly agape with concentration, would complete the act. Silent and solemn, they would raise their shoulders in a final-curtain shrug, lower them with a long sigh of applauding satisfaction, and resume playing with their dolls in a sweet, cunning, cherubic fashion. Watching another child get a switching is great fun.

The more the aunt punished, the more stubborn the boy became and the more dedicated he was to precipitating the uproar. Becoming caught up in the stimulus-response chain, the more switchings the little girls watched the quicker they ran crying to the aunt. By the end of the school term the boy could produce sibling hysterics by simply appearing in the same room, and the aunt had begun routinely gathering a bundle of privet shoots every morning on her return trip from the privy.

Unseen participant beneath the heavy tablecloth, he overheard the aunt: "I declare, Vera, I think I'll have a nervous breakdown." The grandfather: "I don't know what he does to those girls, but it raises more fuss than a weasel in a henhouse." And the coup de grace from the grandmother: "He's not a bad boy, hon', he's just mischievous." And from the aunt the whispered finale, "I declare, yall, I really do think I'll have a complete nervous breakdown." Under the table the boy hugged his bony knees and silently breathed, I'll say, snakes and snails.

The father was consulted that evening and the decision was made. About three weeks before his fifth birthday the boy was enrolled in school, sharing with five other students for seven months the benches reserved for the first grade. These were in a room that accommodated under one teacher all children in the first three grades. He was soon absorbed in the milksop activities of Baby Ray, central figure in the first book he ever owned. His academic career had begun. His life was forever changed. He could read. "Baby Ray loves the dog. The dog loves Baby Ray."

Getting to and from school was as much of an adventure as learning to read and write. The dirt road was so narrow that there were many places where meeting cars had to take turns. The hills were steep, the ditches precipitous and deep, and the roads ungraded. In the valley between two of these steep hills flowed a creek with a wooden bridge just at water-level. In rainy spells the creek rose over the bridge, overflowed its banks, and formed a shallow muddy torrent which covered the entire roadbed for approximately two hundred feet. It took a skilled driver indeed to sight between the tops of inundated bushes and roadside weeds accurately enough to maintain an automobile precisely in the center of the rocky road so that the valley could be safely crossed.

It took shrewd guesswork, dexterous hands, and cold courage to navigate the invisible bridge. With water swirling above the hubcaps it was a sobering certainty that a slip off the edge would mean submersion in the channel of the creek. The father solved the problem handily. In rainy weather, No-legged Joe went to school with Miss Vera and the children.

He was a strong, muscular, well-built black man who had little to say but was kind to children. In his mid-twenties he got drunk one Saturday night and went to sleep on the railroad track between Stonewall and Peabody. A fast freight cut off both his legs midway up the thighs. In those prewelfare days the father had paid the doctor and hospital bills and then later had bought him two artificial limbs made of polished wood with shoes and socks lifelessly in place.

Joe managed well. For picking cotton, he left his legs in the wagon and padded his shortened thighs with wads of rags and old automobile casings which he wired around his stumps like rubber rockers. With the cottonpicking sack slung around his neck and dragging behind him in the dirt, long brown fingers would nimbly empty crisp brown bolls of their fleecy load. He could waddle down the cotton rows with plants now sometimes taller than he and pick two hundred pounds a day. The grandfather always bragged on him in the autumn-spiced, sun-slanted afternoons when he came to the field with his steelyards to weigh the individual spreads and baskets of cotton.

Joe could plow fairly well. With both legs strapped in place, he could grip the plowhandles for support and walk behind a slow, even-paced mule for better than half a day, leather reins looped around his neck so that he could give a directing pull with strong tobacco-yellowed teeth. He could hoe and chop cotton by using the hoe as a support but was much slower at this activity than the other hands and always showed as a lone figure in the field, trailing the chattering group. He could not pull fodder, use an axe, catch a mule, or milk a cow.

Watching him walk would tear one's heart out. Balanced on his long wooden legs like an adolescent awkward on stilts, propped unsteadily upright by a walking stick in each hand, bowing and bobbing from the waist, swaying sideways and thrusting forward with his hips, he lurched grotesquely down the paths and trails of the farm and even along the side of the big road. The boy, old enough to feel embarrassment at the fortune of having his own two good legs and ashamed of being whole in the presence of this half man, delighted in scampering around to perform little errands for Joe. He handed him his reins during the mule-harnessing ritual, toted him a fruit jar of water in the field, and even on occasion lugged the heavy wooden legs to him one by one. He always, however, averted his gaze, and he never talked of the handicap. Neither did Joe. The boy never heard him complain, but he never saw him smile.

Another tenant, trying to avoid confusion when another Joe moved onto the farm, labeled him No-legged Joe, a non-teasing, clarifying, almost compassionate nickname which the other blacks did not use in his presence. In the winter when the creek rose, Joe would wear his legs and go to school with the boy. It was his job to get out of the car, grope with his canes through the muddy water, and outline the bridge for the mother to cross. Comprehending that Joe's legs did not get wet nor did his feet get cold, the boy still felt uncomfortable when he saw Joe's overalls wet to the knees when he reentered the car. When the boy was six years old, Uncle John and Aunt Lou, parents of Joe, had a good cotton year, clearing over three thousand dollars after all expenses were paid. They bought a white Buick touring car and moved to some place called New Jersey, taking Joe with them. They never saw each other again. Baby Ray loves the dog. The dog loves Baby Ray.

The mother quit teaching after his first year, and the two older children transferred to Peabody school. Peabody was a much more cosmopolitan and sophisticated community than Winship, containing some twenty houses, two general stores, a post office, the train depot, and a cotton gin. The school was much more luxurious also, having a privy with a real wooden door that would button securely closed, in contrast to the one at Winship which had only a hanging burlap bag which blocked vision but not wind.

They attended school in the old wooden, unpainted, two story Masonic Lodge, a vacant, silent structure which the boy entered uneasily. Some of the older children said it had maybe some skeletons in it and that grown men used it at night for mysterious meetings protected by a guard at the door. Upstairs there was a locked closet extending the length of the room, and the walls were hung with various incomprehensible charts. Student speculation was intense about the contents of the closet, even after a sixth grader came to school one day sagely reporting that his father had told him there was a goat in there.

A new school was being built that year, practically in the drip of the old one, and it was made of bricks, the only such building in all of Peabody except the bank which had gone broke years before. It even had an auditorium in it, with a stage. They moved into the new school midway through the year, elevated and important.

The lessons were a snap for the boy, just repetition of classwork he had overheard during his rest periods the previous year. His real learning experiences in the second grade occurred at recess, where he became skilled in interpersonal relationships and reactions to outside events. He learned to practice deceitful restraint by watching his peers. When the school bully, who happened to be a sixth grade girl, hit an unyielding line playing

52

"Red Rover, Red Rover, let Leslie Thomas come over," tumbled head over heels into the wood pile, and broke her arm, he did not cheer. He learned that an affected look of big-eyed innocence was an invaluable aid when lying to adults. He told the upper grades teacher that he didn't mean to pull the big red ball off the end of Mary Plunkett's wool stocking-cap after he had snatched it deliberately and maliciously. When Linnie and Minnie Plunkett joined Mary in a fifth grade female triumvirate to tell him they knew better, he was able to feign nonchalance in the face of terror. He learned that solemn silence can cover guilt and imply agreement with adult projections. He used this ploy when he accepted condolences for the springtime death of the only other boy in his grade. He had despised Luther Richardson. He discovered the comfort of having someone in a more miserable condition than himself the afternoon little Willis Marshall bore the finger-pointing humiliation of stinking up the whole bus with his union suit full of fresh feces. His own drawers were wet.

In short, at age six he had become, at the very least, a good apprentice in the arts of deceit, dissembling, evasion, artifice, fraud, and outright lying. Thereafter he was frequently ignorant but only rarely innocent. The skills he developed to disguise his real feelings and motives were useful in staving off the pain of total attention and derisive comments that followed childhood blunders and faux pas. Because he knew how much he himself was lying whenever he said, "I don't care," he learned to look beyond that statement and see the distress it covered when uttered by others. He learned awareness of other people's feelings.

transferring to Brewtonton for the third grade was a cultural shock. There were eleven grades in one big two story building which had concrete steps, steam heat, and wooden floors greased by years of antiseptic-smelling sweeping compound. It had indoor plumbing. It also had an electric bell to announce changing classes for the high school students. The bell rang for recess and lunch for the grammar school grades. There was a total student body of two hundred fifty. The first six grades were housed on the bottom floor, and the seventh through eleventh grades upstairs. When the bell rang to let the high school students out, a drove of mules clattering through the loading chute from a freight car could not have made more noise than the upperclassmen coming down the wooden stairs. The new third grader on the end of the hall below was prevented from bolting outdoors only by the presence of his blasé peers who disregarded the periodic floor-shaking migrations of the barbaric giants.

It was difficult to adjust to having only his grade in an entire great room. All day the teacher focused on her class of twenty children. There were no long periods of listening to older children recite. There were no periods of delicious daydreaming while other grades absorbed the attention of the teacher. His concentration was demanded daylong and his every move was directed. There was even an hour every day devoted to an activity called art. Each child was required to bring a packet of thick drawing paper, a box of wax crayons which everyone called "colors," a pair of blunt-ended, dull scissors which would cut nothing but paper, and a jar of glue.

In those Depression days before a distant entity called government had concerned itself with providing basic necessities and with preventing the psychological effects of cultural deprivations, it was interesting to observe how the children responded to the demand for furnishing art supplies. Some parents did not have the money to provide the luxury of art paper, scissors, colors, and glue; and some, contemptuous of such frippery, refused to acknowledge it seriously. The resultant variety of materials presented was an ingenious hodgepodge of what was on hand back at the farm.

Instead of art paper, which came to two sheets for a penny, there were the paper writing tablets, always Blue Horse brand because if one saved enough covers one could win a prize, maybe even a bicycle. One boy brought a length of brown wrapping paper from his regional general store. For scissors, several girls were allowed to substitute their mothers' sewing scissors, and a tall, lanky farm lad even brought his father's mule shears, a long, sharp-pointed, dangerous weapon which the teacher kept in her desk drawer until the following spring when the mules needed shearing again.

For glue, the majority of the students substituted jars of homemade paste, concocted from plain flour and water, that had to be renewed frequently because it would either turn sour or dry out. Only the more affluent had the bottles of storebought mucilage, rubber-capped with a red cone which could be flattened with pressure to extrude glue through a small mouth, or the little jars with a brush suspended from the center of a screw cap.

Some of the bigger boys brought nothing in the way of art supplies and would announce this either with false bravado or with open embarrassment, hanging their heads and shuffling their feet. The understanding and compassionate teacher would pat the tousled heads or hug the bony shoulders and assure these nonconformists that she had some supplies of her own which they could share. Only the more obtusely imperceptive children felt compelled to reveal the Emperor's nudity by proclaiming: "His paw ain't got no money this year." Then they in turn were made to squirm before the withering glances or open rebukes and admonitions of their more intelligent and sensitive classmates. The uncouth offenders would be forced to slink away from the group, still muttering in defiant, unenlightened, stubborn factuality, "Well, he ain't."

Colors, however, were something that nearly everyone had. Most of the children were able to produce at least the nickel box, containing eight of the brilliant-hued cylinders, the waxy odor of which was as reminiscent of the first day of school as the spicy leather of new, squeaking shoes or the dry, flat smell of a fresh piece of unbroken chalk. Some of the bigger boys had, as a legacy from older siblings, uneven bits and pieces of secondhand colors that they carried in Prince Albert cans in the bib pockets of their overalls. Marston Gallaway had a multihued disc which he had procured by melting unmanageable small bits of crayon in a jar lid on top of the stove. He had trouble staying in the lines, but he was good on blended backgrounds, and everyone admired his penurious ingenuity. Thrift has been defined as what your pappy left you.

Art class was an hour of happy confusion each day. The rigid rules against talking were relaxed, and everyone was busy—drawing, coloring, cutting out, and pasting. The sand table was kept decorated to illustrate current stories in reading class, and the windows were pasted over with seasonal efforts at colorful, if not expert, art. There were pumpkins, cats, and witches for October; Pilgrims and turkeys for November; Santa Claus, red bells, and stylized Christmas trees for December; hatchets, cherries, and log cabins for January and February; white lilies and leaning crosses for March and April; and clean windows for May. The bulletin board was adorned with the best efforts of individual students, and it was a moment of open jubilation when the teacher selected an exhibit. Striving unsuccessfully month in month out for bulletin board recognition, the boy resigned himself to academic achievement. He was no artist, but he had an edge. These city children had never heard of Baby Ray.

Recess was a midmorning recreation period when everyone screamed and yelled. The girls were given to walking sedately around the yard in bevies with their arms around each other's waists while the small boys darted around them chasing one another. Each group professed to be unaware of the other, but frequently the promenade was interrupted. and there were delighted feminine shrieks when the running boys came too close. In the grassless, red-clay yard, the older girls involved themselves in red light, hopscotch, jump rope, or granny, according to the season, and the older boys spun tops or played marbles, stick ball, or pop-the-whip; but the third graders were content to run and scream.

Lunch recess in the middle of the day lasted an entire hour. The teacher sat at her desk and ate her meal and the children did likewise. There again variety was in evidence. Lunch consisted of what was available on the farm. It was packed in a brown paper sack with translucent grease spots and usually started with two biscuits as a base. These contained either sausage, shoulder, ham, or middling meat, according to the point the family had reached in consuming its yearly supply of hog meat, or else preserves of some sort, or sometimes just plain butter. Side dishes were an occasional luxury and consisted of a baked sweet potato, an apple, or even a hard-boiled egg if the hens weren't moulting and the grandmother was not hoarding eggs for Christmas cakes or Easter settings. The sack was supposed to be saved and returned to the family kitchen, folded neatly in an *Elson Reader,* which became in time faintly greasy itself.

One girl had a tin lunch box and a thermos bottle and daintily sipped milk or hot soup. Her mother rode the big yellow bus and spent the first day of school each year sitting in the desk with her. Despite these advantages, she was not as robust as the rest of the class. Indeed, she was "delicate." This is a rural Southern term, always feminine, which tells one automatically that this person is so involved in a relationship with her mother that she will never, never play pop-the-whip or perform any chores. If threatened or frustrated, she is given to closing her eyes and trembling uncontrollably, lips moving silently as though praying. She never plays at recess, speaks only to other little girls, and always makes A-plus. She never cries because she has spent enough mirror time to know how horribly unattractive this makes her appear. If her mother doesn't die or she doesn't discover abandoned fornication by the time she is in the tenth grade, she grows up to be "peculiar" and will never sweep a floor or make a bed. "Delicate" is not to be confused with "frail," which implies that a child will grow out of it.

There was another little girl with dimples, a pouting smile, and saucy brown eyes who was "cute." When a boy uses this term, it means that the girl may not be the prettiest one in the class but who cares? She lived so far out in the country that she had to walk two miles even to get to the school bus route. One frosty morning she brought a pint jar of blackeyed peas for her lunch. The boy was so envious and so acquisitive that at recess he talked her into trading half her peas to him for lunch in return for one of his sausage biscuits and half his sweet potato. It was the first luncheon date for each.

He also persuaded her to sneak into the classroom before recess was over and put her jar of peas, cold and tightly lidded, on the radiator in the back of the room, anticipating with relish a hot meal. The radiator, huge, silver, snoring dinosaur, dutifully sighed and hissed, responding to distant metallic clankings with watery rumbles in its cast-iron bowel. Precisely at the moment the lunch bell rang, the radiator emitted a blast of steam from its escape valve, the little girl screamed, and the pint jar exploded, slinging peas and bits of glass all over that end of the room.

After the teacher quieted the sobbing child and announced to the class that nothing should ever be placed on the radiator, the boy dutifully shared his cold, dry lunch with the tear-streaked, puffy-eyed, hiccuping girl, acquiring thereby a reputation for being thoughtful, unselfish, and generous. A practiced manipulator from years of maneuvering between the aunt and the younger sisters, he managed to guarantee her silence about his participation by convincing her that it was all her fault.

The students who lived within walking distance of the school went home for lunch each day. They were called "the town children." This automatically grouped them in a clique so far as the rest of the class was concerned, since they were referred to as "the country children." The town children were very sophisticated, being perfectly at ease in the unpaved county seat of Brewtonton and entering with insouciance such imposing and intimidating emporia as Rosenbloom's Dry Goods and Notions, Carmichael's Drug Store, Bennett's Pharmacy, or Pike's Mercantile. Pike's was presided over by Miss Beauty Graves, over-powdered, jet-dyed bellwether of the UDC, whose radiating mouth wrinkles were as deeply stained by carmine lipstick as those of country crones by snuff. The town children were not even afraid of Miss Beauty. They went home earlier in the afternoon while the other children waited for the bus and were generally pushed by time and events into a special category. The class became divided into town and country, and the division, despite warm and bridging friendships, lasted throughout the school career.

Other relationships lasted also. The older sister, now in the seventh grade, had long ago established herself as the doyenne of the family children, including all the cousins who visited every weekend. Her authority and royal prerogatives were not to be questioned, and to the third grade boy she was the epitome of dignity, grace, and beauty. He worshipped her, and he worshipped her from afar, for her aloofness, virtue, and intellectual superiority forbade any close or warm relationship. He coveted her approval and dreaded her disdain. She could lift her chin, tilt her nose, and arch an eyebrow while sniffing ever so daintily in disapproval and make him feel as uncouth as if he had dirty socks, had not brushed his teeth, or had been caught picking his nose. Most of the time she ignored him. Occasionally, in gracious condescension, she would read to him, not Bible selections and not Uncle Remus, but marvelous stories of knights and ladies, goblins and princesses, *Black Beauty, At the Back of the North Wind, Hiawatha,* and *Evangeline.* He would have died for her. One day he thought the time had come for him to do just that.

The sister had been born without a hip socket on the right side, causing a distinctive gait which unobservant people called a limp. In reality it was a dipping, gliding, flowing, rhythmic, graceful locomotion that made the conventional walk of her peers seem awkward and ordinary, like the lurching of milkmaids or the shuffle of ribbon clerks. So charismatic was her nobility, so strong the gentility of her presence, that none of her friends even noticed that she walked differently. Staring was gauche, covert glances were tolerantly overlooked, but comment was unthinkable.

One afternoon the two of them were walking around the northeast corner of the school building to rendezvous with their ride home. She was on the narrow concrete walk, her arms loaded with her customary bale of books, and he was walking his usual unnoticed three steps to the rear and left of her. Around the corner, loudmouthed, sweating, and terrible, came the terror of the third grade, Harold Butts. He rode the last bus and was the bully of the grammar school. With flaming red hair, shining blue eyes, and rubbery red mouth, he towered over his classmates and had spent six months of play period strutting and bragging. He had completely cowed and intimidated the boy, who was convinced that any confrontation with Harold Butts would result in immediate annihilation or at least maiming for life.

Now this puffing, fire-spitting dragon of a human came charging around the corner of the school building on the narrow ribbon of concrete and caught the sister a glancing blow, tumbling her books and pencil box into the red clay of the schoolyard. For a moment, not able to believe that he had violated the aura of personal dignity surrounding this superior creature, even the oafish Harold stood in temporary slack-jawed silence. Then, gathering his bluster and bravado again to him, he hurled the ultimate blasphemy, "Git outta my way, ole hippity-hop."

This insult struck the boy's ears like a galvanic current. Death-dreading fear exploded into overpowering rage. Screaming, "You can't say that to her!" he flung himself with abandon into his Armageddon. Lowering his head, he charged squarely into the hated, redhaired hulk before him. Equilibrium is difficult to maintain while being butted in the belly, and Harold tumbled backwards off the walkway to sprawl supine beside the scattered books. Surprised but still supremely confident he yelled, "So you're finally willing to fight—now I'm going to kill you!"

The words were hardly out of his mouth before the maniacal boy, frenzied as a shrew, was astride his chest, both fists pummeling at the fleshy face. One blow landed squarely on the nose, and a satisfying geyser of blood erupted, spurting copiously over the face, hair, and even into the eyes of Harold. Everything about the bully collapsed at the sight of his own blood. He began crying and bellowing. Loving the advantage, the boy struck the nose again and again until he felt a strong grip on his shoulder. He looked up into the eyes of his sister. "That's enough," she said. "Get up and let's go."

The released Harold, blubbering and blowing bloody bubbles, howled, "I'm gonna tell the teacher."

"I just wish you would," was the icy rejoinder from his sister. "I would like for her to know about it."

The boy, removed from the maelstrom of his fury, looked in wonder and disbelief as the brassy bully, now a craven coward, trotted around the corner of the building, still sobbing and moaning. Reaction set in, and he began trembling as violently as the dog he had heard his elders describe having problems with peach seeds. Fighting was every bit as bad as he had dreamed it would be.

They waited in silence for their grandfather to appear in the open black Chevrolet which had a thermometer in the radiator cap. The grandfather did not drive, but relegated the chore to Coot, a rotund, shiny black man who had the whitest smile and friendliest disposition in Georgia. He unfailingly responded with genial "Yassuhs" to the minute instructions the grandfather gave about how fast to go, when to turn the wheel, when to shift gears, and which ruts to try to miss. The sister sat behind Coot and the boy had to sit behind the grandfather, leeward of the tobacco juice which the grandfather spat out the front window while the car sped along at twenty miles per hour. As the car chugged into sight on this afternoon, the sister lifted her chin, arched an eyebrow, sniffed daintily, and looked down her royally tilted nose at the boy. "You did the right thing," she said, calmly and without inflection.

He felt six feet tall. For five miles his heart sang while he periodically wiped tobacco spray off his right cheek. The unexpected approbation he received from other boys the following day at school did not allay his shyness, but it did keep him from feeling so painfully alone in this huge city school. He no longer regarded Baby Ray as his best friend.

The king of the school was a marvel. Instead of knee pants and robes he wore a suit and tie, with his portly stomach smoothed roundly into a vest. He was so straight that he leaned backwards, and the vested stomach was always the presenting part of his anatomy. He had the first rimless spectacles the boy had ever seen, and they sparkled and glittered even more than his polished bald head. The teachers referred deferentially to him as "the principal," but the boy recognized monarchy when he saw it. He periodically passed out typed sheets of paper to his teachers, stood immovable in the hall during the stampede of recess, presided over something called "faculty meetings," and efficiently managed his domain.

He had an unqueenly wife whom the boy regarded as the royal toy. She had very white skin, a Betty Boop mouth, marcelled hair, two chins, and extremely high heels. She wore a coat with a black fox collar and belonged to the American Legion Auxiliary, a much more frivolous organization than the United Daughters of the Confederacy, memorializing as it did the smug joy of victory rather than the sad grandeur of defeat. She had bright red fingernails which matched her bright red lipstick, and she twinkled and sparkled when she laughed. She looked like a Campbell Soup ad with titties, and the boy secretly wished that some day she would hug him.

Her job was to bring lunch to the king on a Coca-Cola tray which had a picture of her when she was thinner painted on it—she had a straw in her mouth. She could also drive their A-model coupe with the rumble seat and all in all was very grand.

Her husband's main job was to whip the big boys. For the most part his attention was required only for the high school students, since the ladies who taught the first seven grades were capable of enthusiastically managing their own discipline problems. Occasionally, however, some of the younger, more timorous, or city-bred teachers would send their bigger boys to the office. These were usually students who were fast on their feet but slow in their books and who possessed at least two social promotions. The principal would have them bend over his desk. Then he would remove his belt and strap them furiously until they hollered. Nobody messed with Mr. Benton.

The sixth grade teacher never sent anybody to the office. Gaunt and cadaverous symbol of inviolate spinsterhood, she stalked the halls like a female Ichabod Crane and looked for all the world like a nest-bound Dominecker hen. She had been teaching since she was fifteen years old and most of her students were children of former students. Two were even grandchildren. Known for dedication to arithmetic, grammar, and Christian principles, she commanded over the county a deferential respect usually afforded only to blood relatives. Every year she shrewdly evaluated her new class from a disciplinary standpoint and seated all the bigger boys and the loudmouths who thought they were going to be bigger boys in a single file next to the window.

Any time that whispering or other outlawed activity became strident enough to breach her deafness, her reaction was simple. Having long ago wearied of futile efforts to establish blame when bad boys were involved, she snatched up her stick, marched up and down that outside aisle, and frailed the daylights out of every occupant thereof. The number of trips she made depended on the seriousness of the offense. The degree of pain inflicted depended on how adroitly one was able to duck and twist as she approached, flailing her arm and crying out, "Shhp, shhhp, shpp, quiet, quiet, quiet, naughty, naughty, naughty."

If she struck hunched shoulders or bowed back, the pain

was negligible, but a solid lick on the head could bring instant tears and make one's ears ring for an hour. Once she apprehended a fourteen-year-old second-year holdover involved in a vigorous game of pocket pool and aimed for his head with repeated blows. He finally wept and fell sideways from his seat, thrusting his battered head beneath the desk and exposing his buttocks, like a Moslem on a prayer rug. She wielded the stinging stick with righteous fury until she was exhausted. Nobody messed with Miss Dorcas.

Nobody messed with Miz Culpepper either. She had taught school almost as long as Miss Dorcas and spoke in the same carefully selected, grammatically correct, and precisely perfect sentences. In addition she was an arbiter of etiquette, conduct, and morality. She had a chin, prominent even in repose, which jutted forward in moments of confrontation as a most alarming implement of accusation. Endowed with square shoulders and a formidable bosom, she could shake her finger, thrust forth that chin, ice down her voice, and become transformed immediately into a juggernaut, dreadful, terrible, and irresistible to student, fellow teacher, and even principal.

She believed in divine intervention and intercessory prayers, but her supplications to the Almighty every morning sounded to the children like carefully chosen directives to an obedient and slightly junior assistant. She never whipped even the bad boys. There was absolutely no point in striking anything which had been reduced during the first week of school into a quivering, subservient end-organ trained to respond to her raised voice with a meek and docile "Yes, ma'am." She ruled the fourth grade long before Adolph Hitler, Francisco Franco, or Indira Gandhi rose to prominence, but she could have served as a role model for any of them.

At some time during the third grade the boy had calculatedly developed the silly and annoying habit of sucking the little finger on his left hand. He did this in response to an intense effort among the adult members of his family to break his younger sister of her habit of sucking her thumb. They had decided she was "ruining her mouth" and "bucking her teeth." They pleaded, begged, cajoled, flattered, and even bribed. She accepted nickels, dimes, and quarters, smiled demurely, blinked her eyes promisingly, and sucked her thumb more than ever. She modified their behavior.

On the day that the boy heard the father offer a five dollar bill and the aunt promise a birthstone ring, he decided that he had better encroach on this fertile field that was becoming quite attractive financially as well as offering a surfeit of adult attention. Discarding as too obvious the ploy of sucking the right thumb in direct imitation, he slyly began sucking his left fifth finger. It was awkward and tasted horrible. He persisted. No one noticed. He persevered. Everyone ignored him. Finally he became truly habituated, at which point the father growled at him on the same day he upped the sister's ante to ten dollars, "Why don't you get that silly damn finger out of your mouth?" Frustrated and hurt, he experienced the consolation and comfort to be gleaned from finger sucking and thereafter became a true addict, enduring switchings, admonitions, sessions of reasoned persuasion, and even the humiliating indignity of having his father smear the offensive member, shriveled clean and white, with fresh chicken mess.

By the time the bribes were proffered, it was too late. He was hooked. At any moment he was not actually busy he would pop that little finger in his mouth. One afternoon during reading period in the fourth grade, Miz Culpepper suddenly whirled, snatched a piece of chalk, and while the entire class watched in solemn attention wrote dramatically across the blackboard in horribly clear and shockingly large Spencerian script, "Porter Osborne, Jr., sucks his little finger." Belshazzer could not have seen "Mene, mene, tekel, upharsin" appear in divine accusation across his palace walls with greater consternation and horror. For years, in unexpected flashbacks, he could hear the resultant explosion of delighted derision from his classmates, but he never sucked his finger again.

The only time he ever saw Miz Culpepper retreat from a position was on a hot April afternoon. The hated union suits had been abandoned, the boys all came to school barefoot, the girls wore short-sleeved dresses, and there was a general sense of accomplishment in the realization that school would be over in less than a month. Some of the bigger boys were already missing days to help with spring plowing. The town children had come back from lunch, and everyone had lined up and filed back into the classroom. They were a good fifteen minutes into the geography lesson when one little town girl timidly raised her hand. Stopping in midsentence, the teacher inquired frostily, "What is it, Betty Lou?"

"May I be excused?" came the barely audible petition.

A quick look at the white gold octagonal watch, a judicious pause, then the forward tilt of the positive chin, and the divine decision came. "Certainly not. It is only fifteen minutes since recess. You should have attended your personal needs then."

The businesslike recitation of the chief agricultural products of Brazil resumed. Of a sudden, Betty Lou's head went down on the desk, cushioned by protective forearms, and her shoulders began shaking with silent sobs. For about as long as it took the geography lesson to halt and teacher and students alike to turn their attention to the stricken child, there was universal wonderment at what could be the matter with Betty Lou.

Then enlightenment came. First a trickle, then a veritable hot torrent poured through the crack in the rear of her desk seat, splashing off the dusty bare feet of her boyfriend, whose declaration of love involved sitting behind her in class. Bewildered and then shocked into action, the swain finally managed to uncross his legs, whereupon he leaped into the seat of his own desk and yelled, "Good Gawdamighty!"

Miz Culpepper, still not in total comprehension of the problem, automatically gave him two swats on the seat for using the Lord's name in vain and bent over the stricken girl, inquiring what was the matter with Betty Lou. This only intensified the sobs. The urine by now had formed a sizable puddle on the floor and had begun running in rivulet overflow down the row of desks in silent testimony to the uneven condition of the aged floor. It took the pointing finger of Annie Ruth Barton to attract Miz Culpepper's attention to the freshet. She helped the sobbing child to her feet and escorted her to the door. Betty Lou's head was still encased in shielding forearms when Miz Culpepper directed her homeward in the company of the solicitous Annie Ruth and announced magnanimously that neither girl had to return to school for the rest of the afternoon. Her aplomb once more intact, she turned to the still solemn and shocked class. "Let us pray," she intoned.

Ever thereafter Miz Culpepper was known as an easy touch for piss call, and nobody messed with little Betty Lou.

Ulysses was the janitor. He ran the school and made the boys pick up trash and paper on the grounds at recess. He scattered the sweeping compound, emptied the trash cans, and was never in a hurry. He had a lair in the basement of the building. Here he kept his coat and lunch and fed the great red-mouthed, cast-iron dragon of a furnace by shoveling huge scoops of fine coal into its roaring maw. This produced, by some strange alchemy, a grand condition called "steam heat," even in the corner rooms. The boy did not understand this magic, but he learned that the nerve center was located in that darkened, crowded hole in the basement where the man's arms, in their rhythmic to-and-fro sweeps, were lighted and accentuated by the flickering red tongues of flame leaping in the throat of a dreadful demon. It would have taken four grown men to drag him into the furnace room.

This man who controlled the monster, who served as high priest for the squat iron god of the school, had a nickname. The town children called him "Bill." The boy discovered that his son, "Punk," who had died when he was six, was really named Telemachus; so he never called the janitor anything but Ulysses. Such was his awe and respect for the man that he would gladly have called him "Mr. Ulysses, Sir, your Honor," but doing so was unthinkable.

To have addressed him as "Mister" or "Sir" would have violated too many rural Southern taboos of that era. The boy felt it would have been like finding a loose piece of yarn and pulling it until the entire fabric of his regional civilization lay in a tangled snarl at his feet. Such a prospect was dizzying to consider and hastily discarded before any responsibility could be assumed or guilt assigned. Ulysses was a Nigra. He was not a Negro or an Afro-American or a Black. The two former terms were not in the vocabulary, and the third was used in a callous, impersonal manner by landowners in much the same way they referred to "cattle" or "stock," emphasizing thereby physical prowess or brute capacity for labor. "Colored" was an acceptable adjective usually coupled with a collective noun. "Nigger" was an unthinkable crudity, permissible when used ribaldly by colored people, but intolerable on the lips of gentry. A white person who used this word was also likely to say "have went," "I seen," or "I taken," and produced exactly the same attitude of pained and awkward sufferance in his listeners.

The sainted older sister, usually exempt from corporal punishment, got popped squarely in her mouth at the supper table one night when she experimentally said the word. The grandparents indulgently and affectionately referred to black children under age five or six as "pickaninnies," but this was regarded as old-fashioned. The accepted term, polite, respectful, genteel, and refined, was "Nigra."

White children did not say, "Yes, sir," or "Yes, ma'am" to a colored person. They did not say, "Mister," "Miss," or "Miz." All colored people were expected to use these words in addressing whites, and they dutifully complied, even with their social or intellectual inferiors. Adults used "Aunt" or "Uncle" to avoid being flippant or impolite when they addressed older Nigras. This made the white people feel very virtuous and respectful and comforted them in upholding their rigid social rules. It made the Nigras so favored seem too venerable to have sexual intercourse.

One never referred to a "colored lady." It was "colored woman," and infractions were corrected as patiently and carefully as grammatical errors. In conversing with Nigras about whites who were not present, one always went to great pains to apply the appropriate courtesy titles, with the unspoken fear that a lapse would condone familiarity. One used the same technique in training one's children. This rule applied even when speaking of family or intimate friends and imparted a certain formality which was woefully needed in areas of Southern speech other than titles. It became ludicrous when nicknames were involved. To hear local characters referred to in absentia as Mr. Mouse Sams, Mr. Tit Turnipseed, Mr. Custard Brown, Mr. Babe Burks, Mr. Boss Stinchcomb, or Mr. Hoss Harp put one quickly down the rabbit hole with Alice. Nobody laughed.

All males were expected to remove their hats when entering a house or when in the presence of ladies. Whites who overlooked this nicety were ignored and dismissed as louts. Blacks were reprimanded for the oversight. White boys could mingle freely in play with black children; white girls could play only with colored girls and then only at the home of the white. Eating at the same table was unthinkable. Drinking from the same glass would produce a lingering but certain death.

It was very important to whites for a Nigra not to get the reputation of being "uppity." To hear grown people say that "Uncle Edmond has always known how to stay in his place" added an impressive aura of sagacity and diplomacy to Uncle Edmond's ability to walk the knife edge of survival, both physical and social. By being so conscious of the Nigra's place, the whites locked themselves securely in their own place. The possessors became the possessed; the dancemaster also had to dance. The tune, however, was compelling. The notes were clear and simple, and the dance was ritualistic and traditional.

All these rules were learned at such an early age that most children were not even aware of having been taught them. Their absolute verity was reinforced by the cooperation of the blacks. By the time he was four or five years old, the Southern white was so subliminally convinced of his superiority that later Supreme Court decisions, demonstrations, and riots served only to confirm his belief. Nowhere could there have been a keener consciousness and awareness of race and racial differences than in the close associations of daily life on a Georgia farm.

There it was all laid out. One didn't talk about being superior; one lived it. No matter how bad things were for the rural white Southerner, they had to be worse for the colored. It was simplistically tempting to attribute this condition either to divine will or natural law, and if one ever dared to consider how the Nigras felt about the situation, it was comforting to conjure up memories of laughter and joy in assurance that they were happy with their lot.

A feeling of superiority often breeds also a feeling of responsibility, and most whites instinctively practiced some degree of noblesse oblige. It was a rare individual, however, who learned how to separate compassion from condescension. It was also rare to experience any honest and open exchange of feelings about race between whites and Nigras.

When he was nine or ten, the boy was visiting Tabitha one afternoon while she ironed clothes. He watched her substitute a cooled flatiron for a hot one sitting on the freshly whitewashed hearth before glowing hickory embers, flicking it with a spittle-moistened finger to see if it sizzled satisfactorily. Hearing the hiss of hot, heavy metal as it touched moistened linen and smelling the steam rising from iron and starched fabric, relaxed and filled with contentment, he was moved to tell her earnestly and sincerely how much he loved her. She stopped midway between fireplace and ironing board, swung around, and looked him squarely in the eye. "You love me so much, boy, that when I die you goan say, 'She sho was faithful'?" Their glances locked for an interminable, naked moment. The boy's ears rang with the dizzying silence of unseen spinning planets, and he walked home without another word being spoken. He never forgot the question, and he never forgot the look.

In the basement of the school, between the foot of the stairs and the furnace room, was the boys' toilet. It had three commodes, of which at least one was usually overflowing. Flat against one wall there was a slate urinal, five feet tall, the back of it covered with running water. In those pregraffiti days, it was scratched with initials and with valentines encircling the coupled names of the latest schoolyard romance. Jeff Barlow and Gerald Hansard in the fifth grade would stand three feet away and hit the pipe that carried the cleansing water across the top. Lee Hugh Moore could stand in the middle of the floor and pee completely above the urinal, splashing the rough plaster wall behind it. Lee Hugh had grown off early and already had hairs.

The toilets were frequently stopped up because country boys did not know that newspapers and lunch sacks were not to be passed through piping. The floor was constantly wet, and sometimes the water would be over one's shoetops. The stench was unbelievable and was only accentuated by the nose-stinging addition of Lysol, which Ulysses poured generously over everything. The porcelain was never cleaned. Even the heartiest boys stood on the seats of the toilets, squatting briefly on their feet when number two was so imperative it had to be indulged.

The girls' toilet was across the hall, and the girls were fearful of going to the rest room because of the wharf rats which were likely to go running across their paths at the foot of the stairs. These were huge, evil-looking beasts, as big as a feist terrier, which would run humping and squealing across the room, their tails lifted high to keep them out of the fetid water. Because of the odors, the water, and the rats, some of the girls who rode the bus did not go to the toilet all day long. By the time they were in the fifth grade they must have had the biggest bladders in the state.

Once the boy heard a member of the Board of Education telling the King that there had been multiple complaints from parents about the condition of the rest rooms. In fleeting disbelief he heard the glittering, plump, fastidious ruler of the school explain that Ulysses was frequently instructed in the care of the sanitary facilities but that it was impossible to stand over him all the time. He ended his explanation with, "You know how niggers are." As the boy watched the two men walk away, sagely nodding their heads, his illusions of royalty vanished.

The next day on the playground he swaggered over to Joe Junior Wallis and Clyde Bilson and joined them in referring to the principal as "Old Man Benton." The following week he was walking on tiptoe through the basement, leaping from one relatively dry spot to another, his nose clogged with the smell of Lysol, urine, and feces, when he met Ulysses coming out of the furnace room.

"Good morning, Bill," he said.

V

at periodic but infrequent intervals the boy was given a dime and sent to get his hair cut after school. This involved a two block walk to the courthouse square. He had to go past Babcock's barn, a long, low, cavernous structure emptied for years of any livestock. Then came the two story wooden Lodge Hall, always empty and always reputed to be filled with skeletons and coffins, its upper windows blankly staring like dark, dead eyes. He went all the way to the corner where he encountered the paved sidewalk and turned right through the entrance to Babcock's bank. This was a yellow brick building with its door in the corner. It was vacant, busted, so they said, in final defeat by the rival Marsengill clan. Comp was wont to mutter darkly that the Babcocks had taken mortgages on dead mules and in addition had ruint Dr. Landers. The father and grandfather, Babcock loyalists through years of political warfare, were never heard to comment. The grandmother was never heard to comment either. She just rocked, dipped snuff, smiled, and put all her money in a fruit jar in the bottom of her closet.

From here he walked the rest of the block beneath the tin sheds to the two story brick building on the other corner. Here was Mr. Isaac Harte's barbershop. On the wall outside was fixed a red and white striped cylinder which revolved endlessly, looking like a huge candy cane being augered constantly from nowhere to nowhere. This was a great fascination to the boy and never ceased to puzzle him.

He hated to get his hair cut, but he loved to go to the barbershop. Mr. Isaac Harte had a long cigarette holder, a taciturn attitude toward life in general, and a stern intolerance of small boys. Everything he used in his shop made one either itch or sneeze. Wiggling was forbidden. Since he always had clippers or wickedly slim scissors in his hand and would mutter threats of cutting one's ears off, it was most important to sit motionless on the board stretched across the arms of the barber chair. It was interesting to consider that he was the father of Tater Harte, who kept blowing his fingers off playing with dynamite caps. He also had five other children. He raised them all and fed them well by cutting hair for ten and fifteen cents and shaving men for a dime. He took frequent fishing and drinking breaks, usually on Mondays, and had the best vegetable garden in town. The only words he ever addressed to the boy were, "Sit still or I'll cut your ears off," and "Hey, Lord," the latter uttered on the expiratory phase of a deep sigh. With grownups, however, he was quite sociable, although always serious. The information exchanged between him and the adults in his shop was varied and fascinating and made the ordeal of the haircut worthwhile.

Particularly interesting was Mr. Lum Thornton. In warm weather Mr. Lum Thornton always sat in a wooden chair leaned against the light pole on the sidewalk outside Mr. Isaac Harte's barbershop. In cold weather he sat inside the shop, but he didn't come to town as much in the winter. He lived at the Poor Farm. The Poor Farm was located two miles from town near the convict camp and consisted of a row of five houses. They had no foundation planting or flower beds but just sat there on rock pillars by the side of the dirt road, each in the middle of a bare dirt yard.

Whenever the county commissioners were petitioned to help a pauper, they investigated the case, and, if the person qualified, he or she was moved into one of the stark little cottages to measure out a drab and pitiful life. The inmates were fed the same fare provided for the chain gang, cheap, ribsticking victuals consisting mostly of dried peas, fat meat, and lots of syrup.

This was a very convenient arrangement. The church

people had no difficulty knowing where to take boxes at Christmas, Easter, and revival time. The non-church-goers who had clothes to discard in those prewelfare days could do so virtuously and charitably without being afraid they were donating them to someone who secretly had a radio or a daughter with a Cadillac. So abject was the poverty involved, so patently miserable the people, so profoundly horrible the conditions that it was a perfect example of the life to avoid. Even the most indifferent children were round-eyed with awe when they drove by and saw the row of houses with dulled, motionless people sitting on the porches. They had the fires of capitalistic ambition ignited forever within them. Thus were recruited the slaves to the Protestant work ethic.

It was humiliating, degrading, and shameful to have to go to the Poor Farm, and any child in the county would rather die than have a relative of his wind up there. This contributed to making Mr. Lum Thornton as fascinating and puzzling as the revolving barber pole. The boy never tired of watching him. He gave no sign of feeling either humiliated, degraded, or ashamed about being an inmate of the Poor Farm. In fact he gave the impression that he felt he was just as good as anybody else and a sight better than most. He had definite opinions about everybody in town and a total lack of inhibition about voicing his opinions. In addition to this, he laughed a lot. He was the only one who could get a smile out of Mr. Isaac Harte.

One afternoon the boy hunched immobile beneath the cloth apron, fearful for the integrity of his ears, looking at the piles of varicolored hair on the floor. The owner of the building pushed down the brass latch of the front door with his thumb and stuck his head in. "Just want to remind you that the rent is due tomorrow," he said. With this he closed the door and retired to his law office in the other half of the building.

Mr. Isaac Harte put another Camel into his cigarette holder and said, "Hey, Lord, hold still or I'll cut your ears off. I ain't never failed to pay the rent yet."

With this, Mr. Lum Thornton raised the lid to the small stove, spit tobacco juice audibly on the hot coals, and said, "Hell,

Isaac, don't pay no attention to that pissant. He'd still be the letter carrier if his wife wadn't rich as six inches up a bull's ass."

Mr. Isaac Harte smiled, took a long draw through his cigarette holder, and said, "I expect you're right, Lum."

Once Mr. Lum Thornton took note directly of the boy. "What grade you in, boy? The sixth? Well, I know you're scared you goan be a runt all your life, but you ain't. All yo family grows up to have big dicks and be mean as hell." He paused and added judiciously, "They bad to git drunk, though, and shoot theyselves." While the boy's cheeks flamed hot, Mr. Isaac Harte said, "Hey, Lord, hold still or I'll cut your ears off." The boy saw in the mirror that he was smiling.

One spring day Mr. Lum Thornton was rared back in his chair on the sidewalk, leaning against the light pole. His shirt sleeves were rolled halfway up his forearms and his collar unbuttoned at the neck. He had such thick, vibrant body hair that the boy was reminded in amazement of an animal pelt. Mr. Isaac Harte, temporarily out of customers since he had finished shearing the boy's neck and scalp to its summertime scantiness, leaned laconically against the doorjamb with his cigarette holder clamped between his teeth. Up the sidewalk, regally erect and self-assured, on her way to call on Mrs. Babcock, swept the venerable and proud Miss Hess Meriwether. Pausing to acknowledge the nodding heads and respectfully murmured greetings of the group, her eyes fixed on the contented figure seated at the edge of the sidewalk. "My word, Lum," she said, "are you that hairy all over?"

The chair never budged. The eyes of the pauper met the eyes of the aristocrat. "Miss Hess," he drawled, "hit's a damn sight wuss'n that in spots."

As the rebuked lady bustled hurriedly across the street, Mr. Isaac Harte smiled.

Once Mr. Sam Percy was waiting his turn on a Saturday morning for a haircut and shave. He was making detailed anatomical comments about each and every female who walked down the street or across the courthouse square. Finally one young girl hove into view, and Mr. Sam was silent. Mr. Lum

Thornton loudly remarked, "Now there's a fine one. That's as big a pair of tits as you'll find in the county, and her ass looks like two coons fighting in a croker sack."

"Dammit, Lum," complained Mr. Sam Percy, "watch your mouth. That's my daughter."

Mr. Isaac Harte flipped his brush around the neck of the current customer, creating a cloud of talcum powder. "Sam," he said softly, "ever one of them girls was somebody's daughter."

Then he smiled.

One Sunday Mr. Lum Thornton was sitting on the porch of his house at the Poor Farm with Old Man Tom Pearce, who shared the house with him. These men were equally poor, there being no degree of poverty below the absolute; they were equally ancient; and they were identically garbed. Yet one was called "old man," a Southern title used behind a person's back which denoted condescension, familiarity, and just a soupçon of mild contempt, while the other was accorded the courtesy title of "mister." The boy never figured out the difference in this situation, but he conformed.

The men waited on this Sunday afternoon for the chance call of a relative or a carload of Royal Ambassadors, gangling adolescent Baptist boys bent on Christian charity under the tutelage of their knowing elders. Old Man Tom Pearce fell to bemoaning his fate. "Oh, the pity of it all!" he wailed. "To think that I've worked as hard as I have all my life, made as good a living as I have, and now here I am in my old age reduced to living on the Poor Farm with nothing to comfort me but the prospect of a pauper's grave. Oh, it's terrible! Oh, it's tragic! To have prospered like I have and to wind up a pauper!"

As he warmed to his subject, repetition inflaming him, Old Man Tom Pearce began keening like a Jew at the Wailing Wall. Finally, just as the Royal Ambassadors rolled up, Mr. Lum Thornton growled at him, "Aw shut up, Tom. I've knowed you for seventy years, and you ain't never been nothing but a pauper."

"That's a damn lie!" shrieked Old Man Tom Pearce.

He launched himself in arm-swinging fury upon the other

old man, knocking him in surprise out of his chair. Locked in combat, they rolled across the porch and finally tumbled four feet to the ground. Still fighting, they wallowed in the yard before the startled boys until finally Old Man Tom Pearce got Mr. Lum Thornton's thumb in his mouth. He clamped down with a bite that would have shamed a possum and delighted an alligator. Mr. Lum began yelling, "Get him off, get him off, get him off!" precipitating the onlookers into the delighted activity of forceful peacemakers. They finally managed to prize Old Man Tom Pearce's jaws open and extract Mr. Lum Thornton's mangled thumb, but it was a job.

Old Man Tom Pearce never forgave his former housemate and had to be moved for peace and safety to another cottage at the Poor Farm. Mr. Lum Thornton had to have a lot of attention from Dr. Witherspoon. When he finally made it back to the barbershop, some of the shock the event had created in town had worn off, but he was still an object of curiosity. It takes some kind of courage to appear in public for the first time after being whipped by an octogenarian. His hand was still swollen to twice its size, swathed in bandages, and carried tenderly in a sling. Mr. Lum rolled his eyes sheepishly at Mr. Isaac Harte and gruffly spoke his first word, "Hell, Isaac, I wouldn'ta thought the old buzzard had a tooth in his head."

Mr. Isaac Harte took a deep breath, sighed deeply, and smiled. "Hey, Lord. Hell, Lum, I woulda thought you woulda been right," he said. "Come on in."

When Mr. Lum Thornton died, Mr. Isaac Harte stayed fishing for ten days. When he came back, his eyes were red and puffed, and his hand trembled when he held his cigarette holder. The boy went for a haircut, and the whole time he was in the shop he never saw a smile. He felt empty. Later he persuaded his parents to let him walk all the way across town, three blocks farther, to the other barbershop. This one was run by Mr. Arthur Masters, an immaculate, softspoken bachelor. The boy opened the door to the new place timidly and slid inconspicuously into a seat which held a fattened, two-year-old copy of *Collier's Magazine*. He pretended to read while he diffidently studied the strange surroundings. The door opened, and Mr. Boss Chapman walked in. Fascinated, the boy looked at the short, pudgy, erect figure with a head too big for the body, hat cocked on one side, two inches of battered cigar stuck in the folds of his face approximately where a mouth should be. A gold ring with a huge yellow set blazed on one finger.

" 'Y golly, Arthur, you remember that old blind Nigra I was telling you about? The one that's made me so much cotton and that I think so much of? Old Uncle Will? Well, I sent him to a specialist, and, 'y golly, he's got a cadillac in both eyes and it's gonna cost me near a thousand dollars, 'y golly, to have em took out."

Mr. Arthur Masters inserted a Lucky Strike cigarette into a long holder. He grinned broadly. "Tell us about it, Boss," he said.

The boy gazed at his magazine and contentedly waited his turn.

VI

Occasionally the boy would pretend he was sick in order to stay home from school. It was preordained on these occasions that he would be doctored, either by the mother or the grandfather. Both generations had the philosophy that any illness known to God or man could be improved by a laxative. The mother always administered a teaspoon of baking soda dissolved in a glass of water, which tasted horrible but moved on through an empty alimentary canal with speed and relative gentleness. The grandfather, made of sterner stuff, purged one with either Black Draught or Dr. Hitchcock's Powders. He calculated dosage by putting as much of the foul-smelling powders as he could balance on the end of his knife blade into a cup of boiling water. This evil brew was then decanted into a saucer for quick cooling but had to be drunk therefrom before it cooled completely. There was no reneging, since the grandfather personally supervised each step of the procedure.

His treatment produced such violent stomach cramps and such subsequent explosive and watery bowel activity that it took at least half a day to recover from the remedy. When one did play off sick, it was with a prayer for the ministrations of the mother rather than of the grandfather. In those days there was no freedom of choice for home medical care. There was, however, incorporated into the language a phrase advising courage in the face of inescapable painful punishment: "Stand up and take your medicine like a man."

One of the farm events that made school attendance almost unthinkable to the boy was hog-killing. This involved so much planning, organization, expertise, and total group participation that the boy likened it to feudal preparations for siege. The frantic activity and excitement were exhilarating, and the boy was attracted to it primarily because so much of the ritual horrified and repelled him.

It all depended, first of all, on the weather. There was no refrigeration or cold storage. The hog had to be butchered when the temperature was below freezing, preferably in the lower twenties and preferably when there were going to be several continuous days of such weather. This assured adequate time to process the fresh meat and preserve it. Nothing could be more tragic than losing meat because of unexpected warmth or maggots.

All this made weather prophets of every adult on the farm. They paid great heed to *Grier's Almanac* in predicting weather. This was a compact little magazine, printed on cheap rough paper and distributed free of charge each year to "Rural Boxholder." Packed between the advertisements for trusses and remedies for piles was a profusion of information which the initiated regarded as a little less totally accurate than the Holy Bible and a little more so than *The Atlanta Constitution*. It all began on page two with a mysterious drawing of a naked man, his arms outstretched, his belly wall cut away to reveal all his viscera, and a blank spot where his genitals belonged. From every conceivable part of the man's body, including the blank spot, there radiated little arrows to the different and appropriate signs of the Zodiac.

On succeeding pages there were calendars with more mysterious symbols. Jessie Johnson, Central, and Freeman referred to all this information simply as "the sign." They would pore over the almanac to find out when they should plant cotton, castrate a hog, or have a tooth pulled. The sign could be going up, coming down, or stationary, but its position was very important. Woe betide if "the sign ain't right." The boy learned to read Caesar, Virgil, Chaucer, and even Robert Browning, but he never learned to read *Grier's Almanac*. Some of the more devout even wanted to kill hogs by the sign, but the grandfather went strictly by the weather for that.

The early hour of hog-killing had a feeling of sacrificial preparation to it. The grandfather, like a whitehaired Druid, heavily cloaked against the brittle clear air of the frigid dawn, was busily supervising every detail and sharpening knives. At least a half dozen black men were on hand, hunched and bundled into so many layers of clothes that they bent their arms and legs with difficulty. It was so cold that each had a rime of frozen breath on his moustache. The boy had noted that all grown Negro men had little moustaches like Charlie Chaplin, except Leemon, who had a huge bristling one the entire length of his upper lip. No whites had moustaches, but his Negro friends would have looked strange without them. They moved now with subdued voices through the icy, preday dimness in easy performance of long-familiar tasks.

The well windlass rattled constantly while bucket after bucket of water was drawn from the depths of the family well and carried in tubs to the washplace. Here they filled the large iron pots around which a fire was built and fed until it roared heavenward, snapping glowing sparks even past the bare winter branches of the tall chinaberry tree. When the water began its preboil singing, the grandfather, still sharpening knives, gave the signal, and everyone trooped down the garden path toward the privy, veering left to the hogpen.

The pen was a tightly constricting enclosure built in one corner of the mule lot and made of puncheons with a raised wooden floor. Herein the hog had been confined ever since September, drinking slop and eating corn from a wooden trough nailed securely across one end of his prison. In the beginning, tall and thin, he had been voracious, gobbling everything given to him and squealing loudly for more. The owners kept feeding him in a profligate manner that made the dames of Strasbourg look like Old Mother Hubbard, until finally he began fattening. His squeals had subsided to throaty and contented grunts. Still they fed, and further he fattened. Finally he reached a point where he lay on one side, mired in obesity and his own waste, eating only a fraction of his previous ration, too somnolent and fat to do more than grunt lazily and twitch an ear when a chicken hopped into his pen to peck up the undigested grains of corn. At this stage in his career the humans began praying for a freeze and consulting the almanac.

Now he lay trusting and lazy, while the men knocked the boards off the back of his pen with an axe, and four of them reached in to grab a leg apiece and haul him, now squealing in protest, into the lot behind the pen. Then, his squeals reaching an unbelievable pitch, they turned him on his back and another man hyperextended the head. The squeals were now muted into the throat of the animal by the man's rigid grip on the snout. The boy clung like a barnacle to the top plank of the lot fence, and the sun showed a half disc bright on the far edge of the pasture.

The grandfather stepped forward and slashed the presented neck with one quick, sharp stroke through a good ten inches of pure white fat that did not bleed at all. While the men held legs and head determinedly and the animal subsided into bewildered deep grunts, the new white wound gaped wide and bloodless. The grandfather raised a longer, sturdier knife. The boy noted that the breath of the men, the breath of the hog, and the vapor from the fresh slash in the throat all produced visible steam that rose in the cold air and mingled in a vague mist above their heads. He thought of Elijah at Carmel, Aaron at Sinai, the prodigal son's return, and, for a horrifying, quickly repressed moment, of Abraham on Mount Moriah.

The grandfather's arm flashed like a striking snake. The long knife searched downward through the bottom of the preliminary wound until it struck a great vessel, and a gurgling, gushing fountain of blood erupted to send its steam also into the stinging air. The men released the hog and sprang back, blowing their neglected wintry noses with a thumb and wiping them on the arms of their coats. The animal staggered to its feet, spreading them wide apart, and reeled around the lot. His blood poured in an ever-diminishing stream from his throat until terminal weakness toppled him over and he unprotestingly pumped the last of his blood out and died.

Then, for the first time, shouting voices were heard in the morning, and bedlam erupted.

"Bring the drag over here."

"Roll him on it."

"Now, all together, pull. Pull! You need to git a mule? Pull!"

"Leemon, you ain't pullin on yo side."

"I is, too. Nis sapsucker heavy. Pull yoself 'n nemmine bout dis side. I got de world licked. Pull!"

The carcass was hauled to the washplace and upended into boiling water in a hundred gallon drum tilted in the earth. A singletree was then secured by its hooks to the tendons of the hind legs, a plowline thrown over a thick chinaberry limb, and the body hoisted up until the nose cleared the ground by a good two feet. More scalding water was flung over the carcass to soften the outer skin, and the men quickly swarmed around, scraping the hair off with long knives. Within minutes the animal was completely cleaned. It hung glistening in the early sun, slowly revolving on its suspending rope, its belly bulging obesely. It was the whitest thing the boy had ever seen. It was the most naked. It was as white and as naked as a corpulent aunt without her corset. It seemed profane for it to hang there in the sun before the gaze of everyone.

Pans, tubs, and buckets suddenly appeared from everywhere. The hog was opened with careful strokes of the knife and the entrails came tumbling down into a waiting tub. Each end of the intestinal tract was carefully tied off with a string, and the full tub carried to the waiting women who had set up a bench in the garden. Their job was to empty these intestines, wash them, wash them, wash them, and finally bear a pan full of pale, slick, sliding tissue into the house. They were now called chitlins, but spelled chitterlings.

Grown people parboiled them for hours, dipped them in batter, fried them, and ate them. The boy could close his eyes and see Tabitha's hand holding a length of the fresh intestine, two fingers deftly stripping its contents with plop, plop, plops onto the ground and passing it on to Delia. He could see Delia pour water in one end, hold it high between outstretched hands, slosh the water back and forth several times, and then sluice the nasty liquid out before passing it to Mitt. Mitt would turn the gut wrongside out, wash any clinging particulate off, and then scrape it with a knife. The smell was unique. No matter how white the table linen, how bright the silver, how soft the lampshine, how brownly beautiful the platter of crisp meat, the boy never had hunger pangs strong enough to make him eat a chitlin.

Everything moved fast now. The liver and lights went in one pan, the heart, spleen, and pancreas in another, leaving a cavity in the carcass with ribs showing through like rafters in an empty hayloft. The kidneys were stripped from the backbone and discarded. No one liked them. Leemon would peel and split one, cook it on a hot brick around the washpot, and eat it on the spot. Freeman told the boy that Leemon thought it would help his nature but would answer no further questions nor make any definitions. The boy privately thought that Leemon must have a really bad disposition if he needed to eat something that smelled like pee while it was cooking.

The hog was now lowered, placed on the wash bench, and its head cut off. The skull was opened with an axe and the brains carefully extracted from their secret nest of glistening bone. Boiled, scrambled with eggs, and served with grits and fresh sausage, they were considered a delicacy, but they had to be eaten soon. The carcass was halved down the backbone and butchered into standard cuts, the hams and shoulders reserved for curing along with the middlings. Fat was stripped off in great wads and sheets and diced into squares. This would be placed in the washpots the following day and boiled down until pure white lard was rendered, leaving as a residue brown cracklings which were used to season cornbread. Lean meat was diced and set aside to be ground that afternoon with salt, red pepper, and sage into sausage. The mother saved out as much as could be eaten fresh, and the remainder was stuffed into long, thin cloth sacks and hung in the smokehouse to dry.

One clear, cold morning the boy was excitedly prancing around a freshly hoist hog, which had just been scraped and which Central was preparing to open and gut. The grandfather had gone to the hogpen with the remainder of the men to slaughter another animal. Central began his pattern of incision, swerving to each side of the penis, removing it separately, and flinging it aside. With nonchalant stealth the boy recovered the taboo organ and sauntered off to examine it surreptitiously. Enthralled, he slipped the slender, firm white gristle in and out of its protective sheath. The older boys at school were right. It certainly was shaped like a corkscrew or a brace and bit on the end, only it was flat. No wonder the old sow squealed so loud and the boars grunted and huffed when they were breeding. Curiosity overwhelming him, he wondered if it also went round and round as well as in and out. He was so intent on this prize that he walked around the engine house squarely into the arms of Tabitha, who was headed for the chitlin bench.

"Boy, what you got in yo hand? Nemmine puttin it behind yo back—I done seen it. I am gwine tell Miss Vera, Miss Sis, and Miss Sally on you! Ain't you shame o' yoself, boy! You thow at nasty thing down dis minute. I mean it! You heah me, boy? Lawd have mussy, you better mind me! Put it down!"

Startled into nerve-tingling jitters, the boy tried to stammer a reply: "But, Tabitha, I was just looking. I was just seeing what a hog's looked like. I didn't mean any harm."

"Hit doan make no difference what dey look like. Dey all de same. Dey all nasty. And hit doan make no difference whether you *mean* no harm—you goan *do* plenty of harm. Das all menfolks study bout. I tell you it was two weeks atter I got married fo Nig knew whether I wuz a man or a woman. My maw hadn't told me nothin, and he come tryin to put his nasty self in ne bed wid me. I wish I hadn't let him wear me down. I wish I'd a jus made him get him another woman den. He had plenty of em since. He doan bother me no more, but hit still make me mad. I mean for you to thow dat thing away right now! You gonna be jes lak all de rest of em. You gwine think dats de mos important thing in de world, and you gwine think you got de answer to everthing swingin tween yo legs. Thow it down! Now!"

His jaw agape, stunned by this passionate tirade, the boy dispiritedly slung the limp hog penis over the garden fence.

Years later, there were moments when he agreed with her.

dvancement to the seventh grade meant moving upstairs. Plans were underway for a new high school, and it was already being built next to the cemetery across the road from Dr. Winston's house. For this last year, however, the high school was still upstairs in the old building, and it added to one's sense of importance to be quartered on the same floor with grown boys, some of whom even had to shave.

The high school girls had "developed." This caused some of them to begin walking in a perpetual ungainly slouch, trying to get their shoulders to meet under their chins in an effort to conceal the existence of the embarrassing protuberances. They carried their books in a stack clutched protectively in both arms over the chest.

Other girls threw their shoulders back, raised their chins, and thrust their new additions proudly forward. They rarely carried their own books, but when they did it was in a stack on one hip. The former group was likely to have reputations for being sweet, refined, and dedicated churchworkers. The latter was likely to begin dating early and have all their proms filled at the Junior-Senior Reception. Among the eighth grade girls, the former outnumbered the latter about ten to one; in the eleventh grade the ratio had become reversed.

One girl in the ninth grade stood out from all the others in the boy's seventh grade eyes. She didn't stretch, and she certainly didn't slump. She was totally natural and unaffected, he thought.

She seemed no more conscious of her mammary development than she was of her rolling brown eyes and flashing white teeth. She had a lot of wool sweaters. The boy used to scuffle with a friend to see who would stand across from her in the seventh grade line when the ninth grade was lining up to reenter the school building after recess and lunch. She never walked but always ran up the flight of steps, and the resultant activity was beautiful for a prepubescent country boy to behold. Her breasts seemed to have a life and an exultation of their own, joyfully and capriciously leaping like gamboling kids when their owner, shoulders back and head erect, trotted up the steps.

The boy, slack-jawed and adenoidally gawking, appreciated for the first time the puzzling imagery in the Song of Songs, which is Solomon's. He knew that he stared and feared that the adult and unapproachable goddess would notice his preoccupation and be offended. She might even report him to the principal. She never became aware, however, of the boy and the direction of his gaze. She never even noticed him. For an entire year he was privileged to observe in secrecy such happy bouncing, rolling, and quivering that ever thereafter he would grin in boyish glee when he heard the particular word "titty."

The seventh grade teacher was a gifted educator, and he admired her. In her first year out of college, she was already an accomplished disciplinarian. She took absolutely no sass off the older, bigger boys, and most of them would rather get a whipping from Mr. Benton than a tonguelashing from her. When a boy did sin extensively enough to have to be taken to the office, she usually led him there by his ear, a stance at once so painful and ludicrous that the embarrassment thereof was to be avoided if at all possible. Once Gerald Carstairs jerked his ear loose from her grasp, whereupon she snatched him along the hall and down the stairs by his hair, for all the world like a recalcitrant mule being led to work.

She introduced the boy to diagraming, and he was consequently enthralled by her. She was frequently absent on Mondays, suffering from a mysterious malady called "toe-mane poison." On these days the boy loyally ignored the snickered suggestions of Jeff Barlow and Lee Hugh Moore that there was more than coincidence to Buster Pike's simultaneous absence from his job at Bennett's Pharmacy.

One sunny day, immediately after lunch, the teacher announced that the entire class was going to march downtown and get a typhoid shot. There were no exceptions. Everybody had to go. Such were the legend of her stern discipline and the strength of her personality that she arrived at the doctor's office with all her students. Of course she had to make a side trip through Babcock's barn to recover Lee Hugh Moore, Gerald Carstairs, and Jeff Barlow, but the good little boys and girls were such obedient robots that the line of march never wavered.

The boy was afraid of Dr. Witherspoon. He was the county physician, however, and he was going to administer the free typhoid shots. He had an office on the second floor of Carruthers's store, across the steep, dark stairwell from the room where the Carrutherses stored their coffins. He was hardly ever in his office, though. If someone wanted the doctor, he could be found on the street and would treat the patient on the spot for everything except surgical procedures. He had one vest pocket full of powdered calomel, and a good-sized pinch between his thumb and forefinger was a dose for an adult. He could stand on the sidewalk, peer at a protruded tongue, look at an eyelid pulled down, measure a pinch of powder into a twist of paper for the patient, and still maintain a reputation for being a good doctor. He never forgot to caution that the calomel should be followed with a dose of castor oil or a broken dose of salts so one wouldn't get salivated. This was a mysterious and dreaded condition reputed to begin with blackened teeth and to end with an agonizing death. He made house calls in a Model-T after it supplanted the horse and buggy and was said to be very good on pneumonia.

He was fat, whitehaired, and as old as God. His fingernails were dirty, and his hands were always chapped and scaly. They trembled and shook. His head trembled and shook. Before speaking he had the habit of grasping his nose firmly between a thumb and forefinger and beginning an inhalation. Then he snapped his nose loose, producing a noisy, moist sniff of a breath while his head lurched to the side. He then extended the thumb and forefinger on down to his neck, where he pinched his Adam's apple while flinging his head backward. These motions were habitual and were repeated incessantly as punctuations to his speech. The boy, in fascination, always half expected the great, trembling head to jerk out of the hunched black coat and roll on the floor.

Mr. Lum Thornton said that Dr. Witherspoon had more twitches than a wagonload of old maids on a hayride. The boy wondered what would happen to the nose, Adam's apple, and calomel if he lost his thumb and forefinger. Mr. Lum Thornton wondered out loud if he used the same grip while urinating and whether he could piss a steady stream.

The boy loved to hear the grandfather tell about Dr. Witherspoon attending Miss Maggie Lewis when she was fifteen and in labor with her first baby. Uninformed and uninitiated, she kept jumping out of bed and yelling every time she had a labor pain. Dr. Witherspoon, in ponderous and unassailable dignity, sitting in a canebottomed chair by the feather bed, kept admonishing her to save her energy and bear down. The pains got closer and harder, and finally Miss Maggie ran plumb out the front door into the yard, yelling and hollering. When Dr. Witherspoon finally got her back into bed, he sternly chided her.

"Maggie, if you don't settle down and behave yourself, I'm going to leave you."

The bewildered and frightened girl indignantly replied, "Well, Dr. Witherspoon, I don't much care if you do. I've been gettin wusser ever since you got here."

As the seventh grade thumped up the dark wooden stairs and the echoes of their feet reverberated down the empty hall past the coffin room, the boy steeled himself for the ordeal ahead. He resolved not to cry. It was for sure and certain that Marie Vondenbacker would cry. That was the way she greeted any event. Once she had even cried because she did not get called on in spelling. All the teachers had learned to pat her automatically without interrupting their class recitations, and they no longer even bothered to ask why she was crying. She cried so easily that it was considered poor form to tease her. The important thing was not to cry yourself. If you did, the big boys called you Vondenbacker, and then you had to fight. The time that Gerald Carstairs cut Mr. Benton's finger with a knife while getting a whipping, Mr. Benton hit him so hard that Gerald cried like a baby. Lee Hugh Moore laughed and called him Vondenbacker, and Gerald chased him all the way past Miss Rosie Massey's house down to Mr. Bobby Lee Babcock's driveway, throwing rocks and begging him to fight. It was much better not to cry.

As all twenty-one students crowded into Dr. Witherspoon's office, the boy looked around in horror. Never had he seen so much dust. It covered the cluttered desk and everything on it with a fine, brownish gray powder. It was so thick on the windowsill that Jeff Barlow had written, "Lee Hugh loves Cleo" in startlingly clear letters before they had been in the room two minutes. Even the windowpanes were dirty, transforming the clear sunny day into a dismal shadow of indeterminate time within that office. Hanging on a nail was a partial skeleton that had been missing bones and parts of bones for at least the forty years it had hung there. It was so covered with dust that the eye sockets were fuzzy. It was an object of pity rather than terror. Beside it, on another nail, hung the doctor's hat and coat. Under the desk and in the corners were long, thick rolls of dust that moved easily with every current of air. These were disdainfully referred to as "cat fur" by housewives and were regarded as a sign of sloth and indolence.

In the midst of this depository of professional memorabilia moved the gargantuan, lurching bulk of Dr. Witherspoon, preparing the vaccine for administration. A towel was laid on the dusty desk. He picked up a round-bottomed glass saucer, blew the dust out of it, uncapped the rubber-stoppered bottle of opalescent fluid, and poured the vaccine into the saucer. Raising the creaking metal lid to a dingy sterilizer, which one assumed had once been boiling hot, he extracted with his thumb and forefinger the barrel and plunger of a syringe which he jerkily assembled. He attached a needle next, tightening the hub with the same thumb and forefinger. He then sucked up a syringe full of vaccine from the saucer.

Shaking a bottle of alcohol against a pledget of cotton torn from a blue-papered roll, head bobbing from side to side, thumb and forefinger going from nose to neck, the venerable and respected dean of the medical community rumbled in a shaking profundo, "Which one of these fine young ladies and gentlemen is first?"

Since Marie Vondenbacker had already been crying ever since they passed the horse trough at Rosenbloom's corner, it was a foregone conclusion she would be first, and the docile, sobbing girl was pushed unresistingly to the head of the line. The boy, by virtue of being the smallest student in the class, was placed second by peer pressure. Even the girls pushed him. He was thus in ideal position to watch Marie get the first shot. Sleeve rolled up, snubbing and sobbing, eyes tightly shut, head hanging on her chest, the girl stood still as a subdued animal. Dr. Witherspoon grasped her limp arm, made a halting swipe across it with his alcohol sponge, and picked the loaded syringe from the towel on the desk.

The boy watched in eye-protruding fascination, his face no more than eighteen inches from the target, as the scabrous white hand with the gray-rimmed fingers shook and trembled and finally managed to rest the needle on the flesh. It pricked jerkily in and out three times before it was finally embedded deeply enough, and the vaccine was injected—ever so slowly and carefully. In triumph at completing such a dexterous physical feat, Dr. Witherspoon raised his shaking head and said, "Next!"

The boy, with disbelieving horror, realized that his arm was going to be swabbed with the same sponge and that the same needle was going to be used on him and everyone else. He looked in panic at the open door, blocked by the stern and frowning teacher, and realized that the only route of escape lay in diving between her legs and down the open stairwell. Even if he were successful, he knew that she would have one of the older boys catch him and haul him back. In that event he was sure to cry, and everyone would call him Vondenbacker. Caught between Scylla and Charybdis on the second floor of Carruthers's store, he resolutely raised his bared arm. Trying to pretend that this was really happening to someone else, he also tried to move his arm in phase with the doctor's shaking hand and get the job done more quickly.

On the way back to school there was much chattering and giggling in the high-spirited release of a group of children leaving a dreaded ordeal behind them. He heard Gerald Carstairs: "Boy, did you see old Vondenbacker? She cried more than the day Miss Dorcas made her leave her books in the seat for the fire drill."

And Jeff Barlow: "Yeah, and did you see Doc trying to git the needle into that little bitty arm behind her? It was like a peckerwood on a broom stick. I mean ole Osborne was tight."

The boy was silent and reflective. Regardless of Dr. Witherspoon's having saved the grandmother's life one time with calomel, Epsom salts, and mustard plasters, there must be more to medicine than this.

He was midway through his next class before he had the teeth-chattering chill and began running fever.

Eugenia Densmore was still in the seventh grade when the boy passed through it. She was twenty years old. Her mother had four boys before Eugenia was born, and none of them had graduated from high school, dropping out to work at odd jobs as soon, to quote John Seelbend, "as they wuz big enough to smell they own piss." Fascinated on overhearing this, the boy calculated that for the Densmore boys this phenomenon almost always occurred in the eighth grade, and he privately thought that it might have something to do with exposure to algebra and Julius Caesar.

He kept these conjectures to himself, however, since it was unthinkable temerity to challenge the opinions of John Seelbend, who didn't amount to much but knew everything about everybody. Whenever he heard the Communion phrase "to whom all hearts are open and from whom no secrets are hid," he envisioned John Seelbend spitting tobacco on a sizzling stove in Rosenbloom's store and proclaiming authoritative character analyses.

By the time she had spent thirteen years getting from the first grade to her second year in the seventh grade, Eugenia Densmore was taller than anyone else in the class. Her legs were longer than those of the teacher and were covered with little red bumps in the back and purple marbling in the front. She was a definite slumper, carrying her shoulders folded forward and bowing her back to a degree that made her neck protrude forward and upward so that it carried her very small head like a full blossom on a crooked stem. Everything about her was thin. She had long tapering fingers, a little upturned on the ends; a long twisting neck; small bright eyes barely separated by an unusually long, down-curving, sharp nose; and a bony head, the white scalp of which protruded ever so faintly through the thin hair straggling limply from the apex.

She was always very neatly dressed, usually in gray. She wore long gray jumpers, the tops a little higher and the skirts a little longer than those of the other girls. With this she wore a white shirtwaist, the little round collar of which folded down precisely over a gray button-down-the-front wool sweater. She kept her lips slightly ajar at all times but breathed noisily through her nose. Covertly studying her face, with its bumps and small cratered scars, the boy thought that her skin looked like the pinfeather areas on a chicken wing that had been plucked for cooking. He thought, in fact, that nearly everything about her reminded him of a bird of some sort. Walking around she looked like a great blue heron with carefully placed long strides, sharp eyes flashing as it peered from side to side in search of minnows. Hunched motionless in her desk, she resembled a shitepoke, patient and expectant by the side of Mrs. Murphy's goldfish pool.

Released at recess, she played joyfully with the first and second graders, towering above them in their shrieking games of chase. She ran dartingly among them in coquettish spurts and starts, now stopping abruptly to cock her head to one side and then rushing forward on tall thin legs. At these moments, in the boy's mind she became a killdee, and the packed, rocky schoolyard became fleetingly a loamy, sweet-smelling, fresh-turned field. Her speech consisted of high birdlike chirps, and the boy could imagine her at night perched on the footboard of her bed with the tiny head and neck tucked sleepily into an armpit.

In the days before free schoolbooks were provided, Eugenia had more of them than anyone else. Despite her family's scarcity of cash, her books were not secondhand. They were brand-new and shiny. The pages were still slick. She also had a pencil box with a ruler, a big rubber eraser, pen staffs, colored pencils, and a small pencil trimmer. She had a box containing fifty pointed wax colors. She had a brand-new Blue Horse tablet. She spent a great deal of her time stacking and rearranging her things so that they made an even rectangle which she could carry comfortably. She must have had at least twelve new seventh grade books, which she religiously carried to and from school each day. She couldn't read a line in a one of them.

She was a town girl. Her folks lived two and a half blocks from the school, next door to Burness and Fanny Mae Carson. Usually she walked to school, neatly stacked collection of books clutched tidily and possessively to her with both arms. On rainy days her brother Stoney, who had dropped out of school in the eighth grade and had a job driving Dr. Witherspoon's Model-T for him, would bring her to school. One rainy morning as she slammed the car door shut, making its isinglass windows shake, she dropped her entire load of books on the sidewalk right at the feet of the arriving boy. As she began scurrying around to pick them up, clucking and fussing like a nervous hen, he automatically stooped to help her. He picked up *Elson Reader, Seventh Grade* and *World Geography for Seventh Graders,* both pristine and unviolated. He reached for a thin, dingy volume that had slid from the center of the stack, its cover so worn that the title was no longer legible. It fell open in his hand, revealing a familiar blond boy, with a head too big for his body, gazing forever at a dog in the background.

"Eugenia," he gasped, "where did you get this?"

Flustered, she peered over his shoulder. "Oh," she said, "that's my very first book. I like to read it for pleasure." She looked around and then said in a confidential twitter, "Besides, Little Porter, Baby Ray is my very best friend. Now don't you laugh, you hear?"

He didn't.

No one was ever mean to Eugenia. No one ever teased or taunted her. Some of the girls automatically used a mothering tone when they addressed her, and all of them unknowingly patronized her. The teacher called on her once, and this produced such snickers in the back of the room and such a red-faced, muted "I don't know" from Eugenia that she was never called on again. The girl had a perfect attendance record, but except for saying "Present" at roll call and an occasional "May I be excused?" she never uttered a sound in class.

Despite a resolute, semimature attitude of tolerance, her classmates were uncomfortable in her presence. Her very existence embarrassed them, pointing up as it did a difference between Eugenia and themselves which they were equipped neither to understand nor tolerate. Among the boys there was a fear of guilt by association, and not one of them would have been caught dead talking to her. The supreme taunt that year was "Ain't Eugenia Densmore your girl friend?" and this produced more group ridicule and laughter than to be called Vondenbacker. The boys were careful, obstreperously shoving, to avoid being caught next to her in line. Early in the year she became as isolated and obvious as an abandoned lighthouse.

On School Day at the County Fair that fall, the students had been lined up and marched to the open field where the carnival folk had erected their rides and exotic tents. Usually there was sparse attendance in the daytime, the fair coming alive only at night when the farmers came in from their fields and thronged the midway, charmed by the thumping roar of the carnival generator, the recorded calliope music, and the chanted supplications of barkers. On School Day, however, there was a mob in the daylight hours. All the school children were admitted free, and rides were half price. Everything was open as usual except the bingo tent and the dancing girls.

As the seventh grade lined up to pass through the gate into the fascinating foreign land beyond, the boy heard Roy Dougherty and Dan Henson pushing and whispering, "I'm not going to stand by her. She's your girl friend. Go on up there."

Something happened. For a moment cowardice died, and shyness vanished. Extracting two dimes from the tobacco sack in his knickers pocket, the boy stepped forward, ludicrous Ivanhoe to unlikely Rebecca. "Eugenia," he said, "how bout riding the Ferris wheel with me?"

Later, trying to eat elusive cotton candy without pulling it off its paper cone by hand, holding tightly to the swaying seat balanced momentarily and dizzyingly against the sky while new riders entered the gondola on the bottom, Eugenia looked over at the boy.

"You know something, Little Porter? Next to Baby Ray, I like you best of all."

Comfortably, he laughed.

"I know what you mean," he said. "If you got a nickel, I'll get us some popcorn."

Right after Thanksgiving, preparations for Christmas began. The windows were decorated with paper wreaths and stars which were pasted to the glass panes. A tree was provided by one of the boys a week before the holidays, and art class was given over to making chains out of colored paper strips to hang in decorative festoons. The girls brought strings of popcorn they had prepared at home, and excitement spiced all the school routines. Names were drawn among the students so that every one would have a present. On the last Friday before Christmas the students brought their gifts to school and stacked them under the tree. Scripture was read, carols were sung, names were called off, and the gifts were distributed. This was called "having the tree." There was a welter of handkerchiefs, Evening in Paris talcum powder, chocolate-covered cherries, music boxes, toy automobiles, and celluloid dolls, all wrapped in red or green tissue paper, and none costing more than a quarter. That year at name-drawing, the boy got Summerfield Hammond's name. He was quickly approached by Mattie Mae Simpson, who had a real crush on Summerfield, and he let her talk him into swapping for Cleo Barfield. In the process he overheard the boys begin their banter about Eugenia. One of them had drawn her name and was making frantic efforts to barter.

"Naw, I ain't goin to swap with you. Everybody knows she's your girl friend."

"Hell she is! I'll just lay out of school that day."

"You better not. And you better quit that cussin. Some of the girls will hear you and tell the teacher."

The boy began thinking more frequently than he wanted that Eugenia might not even get a present on the tree. The prospect was terrible to consider. He was troubled and uncomfortable.

On the Saturday before the last week of school, the mother drove the children to Atlanta to let them do their Christmas shopping. The boy had spent his spare time that fall picking up black walnuts, knocking the soft, staining outer hulls off them, and storing them in sacks. He was allowed to carry these to Cottongim's Feed Store on Broad Street, where he sold them for one and a half cents a pound. The proceeds constituted his Christmas money. This year he had the princely sum of ten dollars and twenty cents when the man weighed the walnuts and paid him. From this he had to buy only fifteen Christmas gifts. He felt wealthy. The children accompanied their mother through Rich's grand and glittering palace, where they kept repeating politely to inquiring sales clerks, "No, ma'am, we're just looking."

After splurging on a twenty-five cent lunch in the Peachtree Arcade Cafeteria, they were finally carried to Kress's, McCrory's, and Woolworth's, where they were turned loose to shop on their own. The boy quickly bought a velvet pincushion for Cleo for a dime. He spent more time shopping for the teacher and finally selected, for twenty cents, a handkerchief with red roses in one corner and a gummed gold sticker in the other that said "Handmade in Ireland." He bought gifts for aunts, uncles, sisters, grandparents, parents, and some cousins. He still had some money left.

He stood a long time in thought and finally flung caution aside and spent the grand sum of thirty-five cents for a pair of fancy pictures of George and Martha Washington, painted on a blue background and framed most elegantly in gold. He wrapped them in a gift box and put Eugenia Densmore's name on it.

The afternoon they had the tree she received two gifts, which attracted a lot of attention to her. The boy who drew her name had given her a ten-cent jar of storebought mayonnaise. The other girls were all clustered around her when she unwrapped the pictures. It was quite the grandest gift to come off the seventh grade tree that year, and her chirrups, twitters, and clucks were appropriate. Summerfield Hammond sidled up to the boy and said, "How much did you pay for those things, anyway?"

The boy drew himself up disdainfully and replied, "That's the rudest question I ever heard. I was taught not to ask how much things cost."

After Summerfield reddened and shrank away, Jeff Barlow leaned over conspiritorially and said, "You're right. My mama taught me that, too, but I saw some just like em and I know you gave fifty cents for them. That's a heap of money."

The teacher came by and said to him, "That's the sweetest thing I ever saw. And thank you for my handkerchief, too."

All in all, he felt pretty good on the way home. The semblance of virtue, he decided, was better than no virtue at all.

Eugenia Densmore came to him at the seventh grade Easter egg hunt, her gaily colored straw basket brimming with candy eggs and hard-boiled painted chicken eggs.

"Little Porter," she wheezed, "I'm going to be twenty-one

this year. You tell your pa that if he'll pay my poll tax I'll vote for him."

"I'll tell him, Eugenia," the boy promised.

"Little Porter, I don't ever want to be in the eighth grade." She paused a long moment. "I'm going to quit school, no matter what my ma says, even if it hurts her. What do you think of that?"

"I think that's all right, Eugenia," he said. He immediately wondered what John Seelbend would think.

That summer her folks sold their house to Clarence Martin and moved off to East Point or College Park or some place like that. The boy apprehensively prepared for eighth grade matriculation. He wasn't sure he was ready, either.

VIII

The eighth grade was a significant milestone. In the first place the new one story school building was so modern that it was challenging to attend classes there. There were brand-new rest rooms at either end that were well-lighted and ventilated and had smooth, clean concrete floors and no rats. There were eight classrooms, the windows of which went all the way to the ceiling and had metal frames. Straight across from the front door there was an auditorium that would seat three hundred people. The stage at the end of this reverberating canyon was bare until some ladies organized the first PTA in the county and raised money with cake sales and shows to hang a velvet curtain across the front. It opened and closed just like the one at the Fox Theater in Atlanta.

There was a new janitor for the new school. In those days before anyone had coined the descriptive word "redneck," he was known as a white man. He had a high voice, a mouth full of snuff, and a back which was humped across the shoulders but erect at the waist. This resulted in a loose-legged, arm-hanging gait that shrieked "country" from a half mile away. He had a five pound bunch of keys, a massively puffy wife, and a houseful of crusty-nosed, snarl-headed children. He did not wear overalls but dressed in khaki pants and a white shirt with the top button always fastened. His best friends were the ninth grade boys, and at lunch he could be found under the cedar tree at the rear of the building, where this worldly and highly sophisticated group of males gathered. Here they conducted their own version of the Kinsey investigation and provided, without tuition, raucous and graphic sex education classes long before such a service was even imagined by the Board of Education. The janitor, when interrogated by this group, had slurpingly asserted through his snuff that at age forty-four he still beat his meat every month when his old lady had on the rag. This was greeted by such delighted laughter and repeated so gleefully to absentees that the boy was ashamed to proclaim the disquieting embarrassment and almost panicky nausea he experienced when told about it. It was simpler to avoid the cedar tree. Everybody else called the janitor "Edgar," but the boy invariably addressed him as "Mr. Bannister." He had learned at an early age that polite formality can be a very effective social barrier.

Heretofore the boy had been the smallest child in his class; now he had the dubious distinction of being the smallest in the entire school. There were four grades in the new building and eight classrooms. The students changed rooms for each class, creating five minutes of always exciting hustle and bustle at the end of each hour. The banging of the lids of the screened wall lockers lining the corridor, the exchange of information about classes, and the hollow boom of many feet marching along the wooden floor from one class to another all contributed to the busy confusion. The boy was so small that he had to stand on tiptoe to reach into his locker.

If he walked in the middle of the throng of students in the hall, he was so short that it was twilight down there where he was, and he had to be very agile to avoid being accidentally trampled. His shyness hurt. He would do anything to avoid being noticed. He dreaded doing anything foolish that might result in the attention and derision of his classmates. He had noticed that some of the earthier ones not only laughed but even pointed their fingers at the object of their ridicule. He thought he would die if he ever became the focus of such attention. He had frequent dreams of appearing in public naked and less frequent ones of flying. He was so timid that he blushed if anyone spoke to him. Events transpired in the eighth grade that changed all this and transformed him, at least on the surface, into a garrulous smart-aleck who would stop at nothing to make other people laugh.

Miss Harriet Duncan was his homeroom teacher. This meant that she called the roll and gave the spelling lesson every morning before the bell rang to signal the changing of classes for first period. In addition, he had her for civics and English classes. She was young, beautifully groomed, and blonde. He thought she had the most voluptuous figure he had ever seen, with wide flat hips that looked lovely and enticing when clothed in a pink skirt that matched the deep pink lipstick on her wide, generous mouth. She was scrupulously clean and had hard convex fingernails enameled with the same pink as her lips.

In the first year of her career she was poised, gracious, and completely in control of all situations. In a day when all schoolteachers were automatically assumed to be perfect ladies, she had an additional advantage. The boy had heard his father, the County School Superintendent, say that this new teacher was bound to be superior because her mother was the former Miss Henrietta Carter from Franklin, who was one of the finest ladies and best schoolteachers he had ever known.

He consequently entered the forbidding and unknown high school with a preconceived confidence hiding his timidity. He knew he would have at least one teacher he liked. Within a week he was infatuated with her. By the end of the second week he was head over heels in love.

The lady had a blemish, one flaw in her physical perfection—if one overlooked the huge, flat, brown suede shoes she wore to school. On the left side of her face, just out from the angle of her lips, was a large, dark mole. Within this mole, bristling noticeably therefrom, were three stiff hairs, two black and one white. When she spoke or laughed the mole moved up and down, and the hairs glistened and shimmered, catching the light. The students wondered why she did not pluck these offending hairs, but Mattie Mae Simpson said if you did, it made the mole turn into cancer.

One afternoon he had study hall in the back of a ninth grade class she was teaching. It was the last period of the day. He had finished all his homework and sat quietly watching the teacher and other students. Taking his notebook, he turned to a clean page and started trying to draw her. He soon became frustrated. How in the world do they draw noses so that they stick out? He was satisfied with the wide, flat planes of her face. The hair was pretty good—at least you could tell it was hair. The eyes and mouth, he fancied, really looked like her.

Absorbed and oblivious to everything else, he held the paper away from him, cocked his head on one side in appraisal of his creative effort, and then bent over for the finishing touch. Ever so carefully, at just the right spot, he drew the black mole. In the throes of artistic inspiration, he gripped his pencil and flicked three hairs into the mole. This was the best he could do. It wasn't good, but he had seen worse. At least you could tell who it was. At precisely the moment he realized with hair-prickling consternation that he was not alone, he heard her well-modulated voice over his left shoulder.

"That's very graphic. Let me have it."

Startled worse than he had ever been in his life, he bolted upright and forward in his desk, hiccupped loudly, broke wind, and urinated an uncontrollable squirt into his pants. He turned brick red and unbearably hot and yelped, "What picture?"

Biting her lips and almost laughing, the teacher calmly said, "Give it here, Porter. And you had better see me after school."

The agony he endured for the next fifteen minutes was excruciating. How can I lie out of it? There is no way. How can I erase the mole? That might hurt her feelings. There is no way. How can I possibly be smart enough or act cute enough to give it some nonchalant and lighthearted explanation? No way! She's going to think I am crude, cruel, and coarse.

Oh, God, how I love her. How could I possibly have done this? If she didn't have those rubbersoled suede shoes, she never could have slipped up on me. Why won't everyone quit staring at me and giggling? Dennis Rockmore has his head on the desk behind that book and is outright laughing at me. He even keeps crooking his finger goody-goody-goody at me.

What if she shows it to the principal, and I get a whipping? If I do, there is no way I can keep from crying. What if Dennis Rockmore sees the wet spot on the front of my pants? I'd rather get a whipping. What if she keeps me late after school? Comp will leave me, and I'll have to walk to the drugstore and catch a ride home with my father. Who will milk the cow for me? What will my mother and father say about all this? What would happen if I just ran away and disappeared? If it weren't for that mole, there might be some salvation in sight. As the bell rang and the students all filed out of the classroom, he silently wailed, Oh, what am I going to do?

He soon found out.

The teacher sat at her desk, quietly stacking books and papers. The boy sat in his desk, head hanging, face so crimson he feared a permanent stain, his body jerking with every thudding heart beat. This was the absolute bottom in humiliation, the ultimate in mortification. He thought of a line from that poem his older sister had recited the time she won the district meet in Reading:

> . . . there is no weight
> Can follow here, however great.

The halls of the building grew quiet. Miss Duncan raised her head and looked at him. "Come here, Porter."

Rooted in his seat, eyes downcast, he mutely shook his bowed head. Why can't I die? he wondered.

She rose and came to him. A smooth white hand with pink-tipped nails laid the hated picture on the desk in front of him.

"As soon as you have drawn me one hundred of these, we'll both go home." She calmly resumed her seat at the front of the room and began grading papers.

Never looking up, amazed at her intuitive grasp of the cruelest way to punish him, the boy pulled his notebook toward him. He had twenty-six sheets of paper by count. If he put four pictures to the page he could complete the assignment without having to ask for more paper. He would have died before trying to speak to her, since at this point he trusted his voice no more than he did his treacherous sphincters. Carefully he began drawing. With practice he became more expert, and at the end of an hour he had picked up some speed.

When he eventually finished, pants finally dry, face now only bright pink, he raised his hand, but still averted his gaze. When she came and stood over him, he handed up the sheaf of drawings, and that remarkable woman leafed deliberately through them. Finally she placed them once again on his desk and, with dulcet silkiness, said, "Aren't you forgetting something? These have to have everything the original does."

Horrified, he raised his eyes, met her level and serene gaze, blushed deep red again, and found his voice. "Yes, ma'am," he quavered.

It took thirty minutes to draw one hundred moles at the corners of one hundred mouths. This time he was able to rise and carry the finished product to her. She raised her head from the book she was reading, glanced casually at the first two pages, and said, "They're still incomplete, aren't they? Go back and finish them. I'm in no hurry."

Completely mastered, feeling that this woman was looking at his very soul, unmasked before benign divinity, he stumbled back to his desk and, deliberate as a robot, placed three hairs in one hundred moles at the corners of one hundred mouths. This time she accepted the papers, looked at each one, and said, "This is fine. You may go now."

Just as he reached the door, drooping with emotional exhaustion, she said, "Wait a minute, Porter."

She rose from her desk, walked over to him, placed one finger under his chin, and raised his head. She pushed his hair back with her other hand, leaned over, kissed him softly on the mouth, and pushed him out the door.

He was halfway to town before he realized what had

happened to him. Confidence hit him like a bullet. As if propelled by taut rubber bands, his legs began pumping, and he sprinted all the way to the drugstore. Just as the sun went down, he sauntered past the soda fountain with its humming ice cream box, under the whispering ceiling fans, past the pool table with its clicking balls, and entered the dim, unfurnished, raftered room behind the latticed rear wall. Here he found his father, tilted back in a captain's chair, his white-trousered legs crossed and white-shod feet resting on the cold iron stove, a glass of whiskey in one hand and a glass of water in the other.

"Hello, Daddy," he said. "I got kept late at school to do an assignment for Miss Duncan, and Comp left me. I'll have to ride home with you."

He never again dreamed that he was naked in public.

One day in civics class, the lesson was on county government and the fact that county offices are located within the courthouse. In reading the chapter he had thought it all very obvious and simple, but then it was rare to run across anything in civics that he had not learned as a toddler from either his father or his grandfather. Miss Duncan called on Rooster Holcomb. It was apparent immediately that Rooster had not read his assignment. It was also apparent that he did not care.

"Where are the county offices, Royston?"

"I don't know."

"Oh, come now, Royston. Where is the Ordinary's office?"

"I don't know," with a degree of superficial defiance.

"Well, Royston, everybody knows Mr. Russell Carpenter. He's Clerk of the Court. Where is his office?"

"I don't know," Rooster repeated, this time with some degree of bravura, as a couple of his cronies began tittering. It was becoming a contest between Rooster and the teacher, and Rooster was winning, just by maintaining his aplomb and refusing to be drawn into this educational process. Determined to stimulate class interest and at the same time assure Rooster that he knew some civics, the teacher patiently pursued the subject.

"All of you students know our County School Superintendent and where he has his office. Where is it, Royston?"

With a raffish grin, Rooster sat up in his desk and stole a glance at the boy. "In the back of Carmichael's drugstore," he triumphantly announced.

There was total silence for a moment. It seemed to the disbelieving boy that the entire world went into slow motion. It was deathly still. This was his father Rooster was talking about. He was making fun of the boy's father. He not only recognized imperfections in the giant, he was announcing in public a peccadillo that was not even discussed at home. This can't be true, he thought; I'll wake up and it'll all be a dream. Several heads turned to look at him. The teacher's mouth was agape for a moment. Then the room exploded with laughter. Everyone, he felt, turned and stared at him. They laughed until the walls bounced sound waves tumultuously and rapidly into his ringing ears. He looked from the corner of an eye at Rooster. He was laughing, too. He was laughing as though he had excelled at something, was being congratulated, and was trying to act modest about it. I'll get you, the boy vowed. Never mind that you're twice as big as I am and have to shave every day and can plow and split wood like a man. I'll get you if it's the last thing I do. I'll get you if I get killed for it.

Under the insistence of the teacher, a semblance of order was being restored. The cacophony subsided to a roar and then dwindled rapidly to sporadic giggles and then to a studious hum as the teacher, poised and elegantly unruffled, resumed the lesson. The boy sat at his desk, chin on his chest, face and ears flaming. He heard nothing for the rest of the period except the swish of his own blood through his ears. No one at home ever commented about his father's hanging out at Carmichael's drugstore. They ignored it. I'll get him; I'll get him; I'll get him.

The bell rang and he gathered his books and filed out of the room with his classmates. No one mentioned the incident to him.

He heard Miss Duncan, in low, cultured tones, say, "Royston, I want to see you after school." He was almost jealous of Rooster. I'll get him, he thought again; I'll get him.

He slept poorly that night. There was a lot of laughter in his dreams, but none of it was fun. None of it was happy.

"Do you feel all right, son?" his mother asked the next morning when he brought the milk in from the cowlot.

"Yes, ma'am, I feel fine." No use to confide in anybody about this.

When he arrived at school, Rooster was waiting for him and walked up to him in the presence of two or three other boys.

"I'm sorry if I embarrassed you yesterday," Rooster said, and stuck out his hand.

The boy shifted his books to his left hip, took the proffered hand in a firm grasp, and gazed upward into the older, bigger boy's eyes with an open, steady look.

"Don't worry about it for a minute. I didn't pay any attention to it. It's all right and I don't care." When Rooster turned away, he looked at the broad shoulders and muscular legs.

I don't know how in the world I'm going to do it, but I'm going to get you, he silently reaffirmed.

Once the boy, silent, unobtrusive, and consequently unnoticed, had overheard Mr. Dean Burdette recount a fascinating tale, reported to be true—as in fact most of his tales actually were. Around the turn of the century a young man was about to get married and had sought out his family physician, a crusty old character known for his earthy wit.

"Dr. Redwine," the youth earnestly began, "I'm fixin to get married and I want your advice."

"Well, Joe, that's fine. What can I do to help you?" the grayhaired physician genially inquired.

"Well, Doc, it's like this," Joe stammered. "I've heered all my life about women gittin ruint on they weddin night and never bein wuth nothin later. I don't know nothin about stuff like that, but I love this girl I'm marryin and I sure don't want nothin I do to

110

ruin her. So I thought I'd get a doctor to tell me what to do. I'd just die if I ruint my wife."

Incredulous at being presented this opportunity, the doctor lowered his voice to a confidential level and in professional-sounding cadence responded, "Joe, I'm glad you asked. If more young people thought about this, there'd be much less trouble later on. You're right, of course. It all depends on what you do that first night. After that, you can relax, but that first night is crucial. Now listen, son. Go ahead with the sex act. That's all right. Go right ahead with it. The important thing is how you do it on that first night. Now listen, son. Here's the secret. It's very simple, but it's very important. On that first night, don't put in anything but the first inch. Just the first inch, right on the tip of it. After the first night, it doesn't matter, but on that night, if you don't want your wife ruint, don't put in anything but just that first inch. You listening, son? You got it now, son? Just one inch. No, boy, you don't owe me a dime. I'm glad to accommodate you."

The night of the wedding, at a decent interval after the ceremony, the bridal pair retired to their nuptial chamber upstairs while family and a few guests continued the revelry below. Of a sudden there was a loud commotion above. The guests all quieted themselves and looked toward the stairs. Just behind the sound of banging door, thudding footsteps and loud pleas for help, Joe appeared halfway down the steps. Clad in a white nightshirt that came midway between his knees and ankles, he yelled, "Call Dr. Redwine! Call Dr. Redwine!"

As everyone stood stunned and silent, all attention riveted on him, he implored again, "Call Dr. Redwine! For God's sake, call Dr. Redwine! Effen she dies, she done it herself!"

The boy loved this tale. He thought it taught many lessons and fancied that it contained deep philosophical undertones. He thought about it often.

One Friday afternoon in early spring, sitting in Miss Duncan's study hall, he idly noted that Rooster had requested and been granted permission to be excused. I bet he's sneaking around to smoke, the boy thought. What if I could catch him? I could scare him good.

He let five minutes elapse and raised his hand to catch the teacher's attention.

"What is it, Porter?"

"May I be excused?"

"Not now. Royston is out of the room, and you know the rule about two excuses at once."

He knew from long experience how to handle this situation. He squirmed vigorously in his seat. "I just can't wait. I really can't."

She looked at her watch. "Well, all right. Go ahead. Royston should have been back before now anyway. If you see him, tell him I said to get himself back to the room immediately."

He hastened down the hall and slammed open the door to the boys' rest room as hard as he could. With a start, Rooster dropped something into the commode, but smoke still floated in blue tendrils above the urinal.

"Oh, it ain't nobody but you. You scared me. I thought it might be the principal, the way you busted in like that."

"Naw, it's just me," the boy replied and went immediately to a commode and forced himself to urinate. While he was washing his hands, Ballard Giles from the ninth grade sauntered in. "Hey, Holcombe, gimme a cigarette, huh? I'm about to have a nicotine fit."

The boy opened the door to leave the rest room. Turning, he said to Rooster, "By the way, Miss Duncan said for you to get yourself back to the room immediately."

Rooster was busy giving the upperclassman a match. Nettled at the peremptory interruption, he directed, "You tell Old Lady Duncan I said to kiss my goddam ass."

Giddy with a mixture of horror and delight, the boy sped back down the hall. Did he dare? Of course he did. What would happen? Who knows? What would happen to Rooster? Slowing to a nonchalant stroll as he reached for the doorknob, the boy muttered under his breath, "Effen he dies, he done it hisself." He opened the door and slid ever so modestly and quietly into the classroom. Easing the door carefully closed behind him, he was the perfect picture of diffident courtesy.

Miss Duncan looked up. "You're back already, Porter?"

"Yes'm," he said, lowering his eyes.

"Did you see Royston?"

"Yes'm."

"Well, did you tell him what I said?"

"Yes'm, I told him."

"Well, what did he say?" she pressed.

Raising his head and widening his eyes innocently, in clear and distinct tones, he told her.

The resulting pandemonium was deeply thrilling. Miss Duncan nearly knocked him off his feet in her plunge through the door and down the hallway to the boys' rest room. A few of the girls screamed, but most of them and all of the boys laughed so loudly that Miss Garrett came out of her room next door to see what was the matter. They laughed so loudly and Miss Garrett shouted so vainly for them to stop that the noise brought Mr. Gill out of his office down the hall. Just then the red-faced and furious Miss Duncan approached the group with a stunned and crestfallen Royston in tow. They rang the bell ten minutes early to dismiss school that afternoon, and the boy was halfway home before he could breathe evenly or trust himself to speak without his voice trembling.

"How did your day go, son?" his mother asked that evening as he filled the woodbox behind the kitchen stove.

"It was fine, Mother, just fine." No need to confide in anybody about this.

The weekend sped by. When he arrived at school Monday morning, he saw Rooster talking to Oliver Turnipseed and Mortimer Harris. He walked straight up to the group, looked squarely up at Rooster, and said, "I'm sorry if I embarrassed you Friday." He stuck out his hand.

Slowly, Rooster reached out and limply shook it once. "It's okay," he mumbled.

At noon, reaching on tiptoe into the locker to get his greasy lunch sack, he turned to Summerfield Hammond. "Let's go eat our lunch outdoors today. Under the cedar tree. Okay?"

As he pushed through the ninth graders to find a sunny spot to sit, he decided that although he was the only one who knew it, his balls were going to be as big as anybody's. Some day.

about midway through the eighth grade, the boy decided that he would try to be first honor graduate when he finished school. All students were required to take four subjects each year. He was already taking five and making excellent grades in them. Each A gave one five honor points, each B three, and each C two. As he assessed his competition, it was readily apparent that his only rivals were three of the girls in his class. There were a couple of the boys who would accept valedictorian if it were conferred on them like the crowning of King Saul, but not one of them was likely to work for it.

There were three girls who really studied hard and liked to make good grades from the philosophy of virtue being its own reward. They were the ones to watch. Even if he took the upper limit of five subjects per year, they would certainly do the same. Assuming he made straight A's, there was one of the girls who was sure to do likewise. She had made one B-plus in the fifth grade and had cried for a week. She was consequently not likely to subject herself again to such ego-destroying trauma.

An additional option included extracurricular activities. Each spring the school was involved in competition with other schools in multiple areas of academic achievement. The best student was selected in Debate, Music, Home Economics, Ready Writer's Essay, Declamation, and Girls' Reading. Local contestants were chosen by judges in open competition before the student body, and later in the District Meet, and even later in the State

Meet. It was an honor to represent one's school as a contestant in the District Meet. It was a rare and anointing achievement to win an event on the district level, and no local person had ever placed first in a State Meet except the fabled John Mark Cowan, who had won a place on the winning debate team. This had excited the whole town and welded everyone together into an amalgam of admiration.

While eavesdropping at UDC and American Legion Auxiliary meetings, the boy had been impressed at how long this youth had remained the center of conversation, a position usually reserved for less virtuous and less intellectual accomplishments. John Mark had even been spontaneously granted what the boy privately called "The United Daughters of the Confederacy and American Legion Auxiliary and Women's Missionary Union Combined and Holy Go Far Award." To win this supreme award required congenial and unanimous vote of the ladies of the organizations.

Hiding behind a curtain or beneath an open window, the boy was the secret and self-appointed recording secretary. A nomination was made by a powdered lady, teacup in midair, little finger rolled daintily into a tight curl, who would proclaim solemnly and sincerely, "I tell you, that boy will Go Far." The vote followed immediately. In order to vote Yes each lady had to stop chewing, sipping, swallowing, or visiting with her neighbor and nod her head in sage and enthusiastic agreement.

By the boy's reckoning John Mark Cowan, after he won the State Meet in Debate, had received the Go Far award more quickly and overwhelmingly than any other nominee in history. The boy had never met the fabled youth nor spoken to him, but his sister knew him as the older brother of one of her friends and had pointed him out on the street one day. For several years thereafter, the boy had regarded severe acne as an indication of intelligence.

After graduation, John Mark had gone to the University of Georgia to study law and died of a ruptured appendix during his senior year. When meetings convened after his funeral, the boy had noted how quickly and enthusiastically John Mark had received "The United Daughters of the Confederacy and the American Legion Auxiliary and the Women's Missionary Union Combined and Holy Cut Short Award."

Several years later the older sister had won District Meet in Girls' Reading and gone to State. Listening to the open adulation this evoked in the family and watching the beautifully simulated modesty of the mother and aunt when the resulting Go Far nomination occurred, the boy was permanently impressed. He consequently entered the eighth grade with preconditioned awareness of the importance and desirability of District Meet competition. When he discovered that one was given five points for representing the local school and an additional ten points in the unlikely event one got first place in the district, he was filled with resolve. This just might be the edge he needed to win his goal of becoming valedictorian three years hence.

He went out for the debate team. The subject that year was "Resolved: that a unicameral legislature is more beneficial than a bicameral legislature." This alone was enough to limit the field of contestants. He won a place on the team, learned a lot of new words, and pocketed an easy five points. So far, so good. The only trouble was that Betty Lou Braxton and Annie Ruth Barton were both going out for basketball. If they made the team, that was also five points for each of them. If he and they all made straight A's, they were still even. Without ever voicing his goal to anyone, he cast around for an advantage.

There was no way he could go out for basketball. He was waist high to most of the team. He decided to try out for Declamation. True enough, his voice had not changed yet, and Summerfield Hammond had a booming baritone and ministerial ambitions. Emmerson Ware, a senior, had a deep voice and lots of presence and had won last year's contest, but Emmerson pronounced every syllable and used the long *e* even when it preceded a consonant. Summerfield worried him, but the boy smugly thought he could beat Emmerson.

He had a secret weapon. For over a year he had been "taking" from Mrs. Parker. This meant that he was being given private elocution and expression lessons. Most parents who went to this expense did so in an effort to wind up with a child who habitually said "get" instead of "git." Occasionally it was a successful venture.

Mrs. Parker was his teacher, and she was an unusual person indeed. Like so many other people in his life, he had heard about her from his father before he saw her. She had taught the father when he was at Locust Grove Institute, and this had apparently conferred sainthood upon her. Following the two maximum opportunities for a real lady in the Reconstruction South, she had become first a schoolteacher and then a minister's wife. Material considerations were beneath her notice. She was interested only in the cultural and the spiritual and gave the firm impression that the two were inseparable anyway. When she first began teaching expression, she was driven to the students' homes by her retired husband in their Model-A Ford.

The boy would never forget the first time he saw her. The Ford chugged to a stop, her husband turned off the ignition, and she remained motionless until he walked around and opened the door for her. As she placed one foot on the running board and extended a hand to her waiting husband, the Ford became a royal carriage and Queen Mary was being assisted therefrom by her loyal footman. She swept regally up the steps to the verandah and acknowledged introductions with such dignity that she seemed to bestow royal favor when she inclined her head and repeated a name.

She was tall for a woman, full-busted, and thick-waisted. Obviously corseted, she held herself so erect and moved with such dignified grace that one had the impression her flesh would have remained molded like marble in the unlikely event her foundation garments were ever removed. When she sat, her feet were crossed at the ankles, and her hands were folded in her lap. Her straight, proud spine had never been known to touch the back of a chair. She wore her long hair in an iron gray bun on the back of her neck, and she had never been seen in a short-sleeved or low-necked dress. Her only concession to cosmetics was face-powder, and the only way one could be sure she wore this was to see an occasional fleck on her gold-rimmed bifocal spectacles or a faint frosting on the fine black hairs of her dainty moustache. She spoke in a melodious, carefully inflected, unaccented English that was precise and almost painfully correct, and she had the mannerism of frequently closing her eyes while speaking. This imparted both emphasis and sincerity to certain phrases.

He thought her the grandest creature he had ever met. Once he had tried to imagine her naked and discovered to his amazement that she had no navel, no nipples, no hair and that the only orifice she possessed was her careful and proper mouth. This did not disturb him at all, since her husband was exactly like her except for a bald pate with white tonsure and white bushy eyebrows. They even spoke alike and called each other "Mr. Parker" and "Mrs. Parker." The boy wondered if they did this to discourage any possible familiarity from other people but finally decided that they addressed each other this way, even in private, to discourage possible familiarity from each other.

He had never met a more asexual person, but he loved her devotedly. She would have recoiled from a double negative with the same instinctive aversion he would have felt for a highland moccasin. He had approached his first session with her in some dread. He assumed that she would give him some "piece" to memorize that was in Negro dialect and supposedly humorous. Instead she sandbagged him with Robert Browning's "Prospice," followed in rapid succession by Markham's "Man of the People" and Emerson's "Each and All." She taught him what a comma meant in the spoken sentence, and she taught him to interpret what he read. He would have done anything in the world to please her, and pleasing her involved much memorizing and oratory.

She finally accumulated so many students that she took an apartment in Brewtonton. This consisted of a bedroom, bathroom, and kitchen in a private house. She had a blue and white linoleum rug on the floor and a red and white oilcloth cover on the kitchen table. The boy now walked from school to take his expression lesson and was even excused from study hall for this purpose twice a week. He was surprised and entranced by the place she had found lodging. She was staying in what the boy regarded as one of the strangest and most interesting menages in the county. She had taken rooms with Miss Ina Rhodes.

Miss Ina was unmarried and somewhere in that indeterminate age between thirty-five and seventy that the boy regarded as "old." She was the head of the household and made her living by running a boarding house. She was aggressive, positive, and forthright. She was also endowed with the Rhodes sensuality. She had horrified the boy once by loudly proclaiming that one of the male teachers who boarded with her ought to be dating the girls more, citing as evidence for this assertion the spotting of his bed linen, which she changed every Monday. The boy had heard of wet dreams from the older boys, but it had never crossed his mind that a lady knew of such phenomena.

She had a black hat that sat squarely atop her head every Sunday morning as she sat squarely in her church pew. Mr. Lum Thornton had said that Ina Rhodes was a wonder, jumping in that Baptist Church every Sunday and frigging like a mink any night of the week. The boy had never seen a mink, but the remark captured his fancy and made Miss Ina more interesting.

Miss Ina was responsible for her younger sister, May Belle. May Belle was also "old" and was one of the few people anywhere that the boy could look straight in the eye. He didn't understand dwarfs, and anytime he asked at home, his aunt and mother circumvented his questions by murmuring vaguely about "afflictions." His father and grandfather were willing to be explicit about May Belle but got vague about Miss Ina.

He thought to himself that the Lord had fashioned May Belle's body and head full size from two potatoes and then stuck little sausages on for arms and legs. He did not call her "Miss." She swept the front porch with a broom that was twice as tall as she was, but she had an easy time with the dustpan. She was not endowed with the Rhodes sensuality.

The third member of Miss Ina's family was her father. He was short, stooped, and whiteheaded and tottered around on a cane. He was so old that he was disoriented to time, place, and person. He was not, however, disoriented to purpose. He was a real Rhodes. Occasionally, waking from a doze in the sun, he would forget who May Belle was and start making sexual overtures toward her. This would cause May Belle to run stumpingly around the side of the house, beating her short arms like rudimentary wings and screaming for Miss Ina, who would come out and break off the confrontation with her usual vigorous and positive approach.

One time at the barbershop the boy had heard a terrible commotion, and Mr. Lum Thornton, after investigating, announced, "That is some sight to see. That midget running and hollering and that old man chasing her on a walking stick and Ina behind him with that hat on, frailing hell out of him with a broom. If I didn't know I was in Brewtonton, I'd think I was dreaming."

Once the boy, striving for the right inflection in his recitation, had overheard Miss Ina using her broom. "Papa, you leave May Belle alone, you hear me? Hold still and I'll knock that piss-hard plumb offa you."

Mrs. Parker, apparently, was deaf. "Go ahead, Porter.

> Yon heifer, lowing on the upland farm
> Far heard, lows not thine ear to charm. . . .

You like Emerson, do you not?"

"Oh, yes, ma'am, Mrs. Parker. I really do. I mean, really I like Ralph Waldo Emerson."

He could not imagine her and Mr. Parker sleeping together in that double bed, but neither could he imagine them being so congenial with the family from whom they rented.

When he approached her about entering the Declamation contest, she showed not the slightest surprise. She gave him a book of famous speeches to read, and they finally selected Patrick Henry's fervent plea to the Virginia House of Delegates. He memorized it quickly and easily in sing-song cadence, and then that marvelous muse of poetry, that female version of Professor

Higgins began producing the remarkable metamorphosis that made him sound real and believable. She taught him to roar; she taught him to whisper. She taught him the art of the dramatic pause, and she taught him how to plan gestures and then use them so that they seemed natural and unplanned. She taught him to be such a consummate actor that it did not seem incongruous for a prepubescent boy to deliver the war cry of a redhaired Virginia firebrand.

"Our brethren are already in arms! Why stand we here idle?"

Emmerson Ware declaimed Henry Grady's "The New South" for the third year in a row. Summerfield Hammond delivered a Christian exhortation by Bruce Barton in a beautiful bass monotone.

The boy exulted: "What is it that gentlemen wish? What would they have? Is life so dear or peace so sweet as to be purchased at the price of chains and slavery? Forbid it, Almighty God!" Arms stretched downward with palms up and head thrown back: "I know not what course others may take, but as for me,"—right arm raised above the head, with forearm and fist moving backward and then forward in rhythmic and final emphasis—"give me liberty, or give me death!"

The decision of the judges was unanimous. He won first place. As he walked modestly with downcast eyes out of the auditorium, he thought, Those big peckerwoods might as well have been reading "Baby Ray loves the dog."

He had five more points to his credit. How he loved Mrs. Parker.

For three weeks she forbade him to think about Patrick Henry. She made him memorize a "piece" in Negro dialect, the humorous point of which revolved around a ripe watermelon going "plunk" instead of "plink." She made him memorize an inane thing, just mastered by his fifth grade sister, called "The

One-legged Goose," which featured a dialogue between a black slave and his master. May Belle used the broom on the porch whether it needed it or not. Miss Ina used the broom on her father when he needed it. The days grew longer and warmer.

Two weeks before the night of the District Meet, Mrs. Parker began again on Patrick Henry. She made him leave off all gestures for one session; then she resumed them. She lectured him about onstage conduct. She cautioned him about appearance.

"There will be ten contestants. They will most likely be seated in a semicircle on the stage. You will draw straws for the order of the speaking. Sit erect. Do not cross your legs. Keep your feet together and do not shuffle them back and forth. Do nothing to call attention to yourself. Do not lean back in your chair. Keep your hands folded loosely in your lap. Remember that the judges are watching everyone. Be completely inconspicuous except when you are speaking. When another boy is speaking, look at him and really listen to what he is saying. Do not try to go over your speech in your head. You know it well. I have done all I can for you, and you have performed beautifully. Keep it up."

As if this weren't enough to make him nervous, the father sent him to Atlanta with his mother. At Kibler-Long, for fifteen dollars they bought a brand new suit which had a vest and two pairs of pants. They were the first long pants he had ever owned, and he was conscious of the milestone as well as the financial extravagance. One week before the contest, they sent him to Mr. Isaac Harte's barbershop for a haircut he didn't think he particularly needed. On top of that, when the day arrived, his father, who left Brewton County only for emergencies and never attended out-of-town school functions at all, drove to Griffin that night to appear, unannounced and unexpected, fifteen minutes before the Declamation contest was called.

By now the boy was scared half to death. As he left the sanctuary of his family and walked alone down the aisle toward the stage, he could hear his blood swishing through his ears again, and he wanted to bolt and run. Dutifully he mounted the steps to the stage and approached the moderator's table with the other boys, where he drew a slip of paper. It had the number four on it. He would be the fourth speaker. He found the fourth chair in the semicircle in front of the table where the moderator, the timekeeper, and the Griffin principal were seated. We're from the fourth district, he thought, and I'm speaking fourth. Maybe that will be good luck for me.

He tried to remember everything Mrs. Parker had told him about stage appearance. For one insane moment he had an urge to suck his finger, but he folded his hands quietly in his lap. Thank God for the footlights, he thought. There must be ten thousand people in that auditorium, but they're just shadows beyond those bright lights. He was glad his mother had made him urinate a half hour earlier. He resisted the urge to cross his legs. Are the judges already looking? he wondered. Don't do anything to call attention to yourself, he cautioned. The first speaker had risen. Keep your eyes on him and listen to him; don't cross your legs; sit erect, he warned himself.

"Fourscore and seven years ago," the first speaker intoned, "our forefathers brought forth on *this* continent. . . ."

For Pete's sake! the boy thought, who picked that speech for him? Nobody in Georgia likes Lincoln, and, besides, why did he emphasize the word *this*? Mrs. Parker would have his hide.

The second boy stuttered twice in his delivery. The third boy used two periods where obvious commas were intended, and a very faint question mark instead of a period. As number four was called, followed by his name and hometown, a sudden surge of confidence unexpectedly carried him calmly to the front of the stage.

"Mr. President," he began in measured, reasoned tones.

Minutes later, with impassioned patriotism, he thundered, "Give me liberty, or give me death!"

As he walked back to his seat, it seemed to him that the applause was the longest and loudest of the evening so far.

He remembered to sit up straight as he looked at the faces of the following contestants, although he was too absorbed in the backwash of relief to hear a word they said. He noted, however, that the applause they received was scattered and brief. As number seven rose to speak, the boy's eyes drifted beyond him to number eight. This was a boy he had met that afternoon, a member of the debate team from Carrollton.

He was a senior named Tom Henderson, a self-assured, confident, polite, and cordial young man with a handsome face and beautiful voice and manners. As he introduced himself to everyone, he had seemed so suave that the boy felt ten years old again and wondered if his ears were clean. The boy assumed that he must be a real genius if he was representing Carrollton in two district events, and after he watched his easy assurance and listened to his well-modulated conversation, he realized that this guy was a preconfirmed winner in declamation. Tom was so likeable that the boy was not even jealous, only resigned.

As he looked at him now, he saw that Tom sat with his legs crossed and was tilted ever so slightly backward in his chair. His thumbs were hooked in the armholes of his vest, his head was bowed, and his eyes were closed. His lips were noticeably moving. As the boy jerked his eyes away to gaze raptly at the face of speaker number seven, he thought with consternation, Oh, Lord, he's going over his speech, and he's not remembering where he is. It never occurred to him that this splendid sophisticate might not have had the blessing of advice from some Carroll County Mrs. Parker.

The moderator announced, "Number eight, Tom Henderson, Carrollton, Georgia, representing Carroll County High School." Tom rose from his chair, walked to the front center of the stage, looked in confidence across the footlights, and stood silent as the grave. The entire audience grew still. After an unbearable interval of startled silence, a feminine voice from the audience, obviously reading, delivered the first line of his speech. Tom folded his hands behind his back, rose briefly on tiptoe, cleared his throat, swallowed hard, settled back to a flatfooted stance, and repeated the sentence woodenly. He stopped. The silence came again. Silence from that many people became more than a lack of noise.

It was a listening, attentive force that throbbed and waited and impelled and pushed.

Just as it had lasted to the point the boy felt that he must scream to destroy it, Tom raised his shoulders in a resigned shrug, mumbled, "I'm sorry. It's no use," and shuffled back to his seat.

It took the stunned moderator a painful moment to recover his composure and announce, "Number nine, William Westmoreland, Route One, Griffin, Georgia, representing Spalding County High School."

The boy fastened his gaze on number nine's face while his brain whirled. I can't believe Tom forgot that speech. How in the world did he manage to do that?

He succumbed to the comfort of comparison. Boy, I'm glad I didn't do that. I didn't forget a word in my speech. I didn't stumble the first time. Of course the credit for that goes to Mrs. Parker, but still I didn't forget my speech. Poor Tom. Underneath he must be just as scared as anybody. This really isn't fair. If he hadn't forgotten, he would have been sure to win. He can't help it because he forgot. It really isn't fair.

As speaker number nine walked to his seat, the boy rose from his chair. Propelled by a force he did not understand, he found himself unbelievably tipping across the stage, only dimly aware that the eyes of everyone must be on him, oblivious of everything except the compulsion of what he had to do. He gripped the edge of the moderator's table, leaned over, looked that startled man in the eyes, and with quivering chin and quavering voice, launched his plea: "Please, sir, can you give the boy from Carrollton another chance? Anybody can forget."

As he made his way back to his seat, he heard as if in a trance the moderator intone, "Number ten, final speaker in this contest. Charles Willingham, LaGrange, Georgia, representing Troup County High School."

He forgot about stage presence and appearance. He sat with hanging head and hot cheeks while number ten manfully spoke. He had doubled his embarrassment about Tom by becoming personally embarrassed himself. What could I have been thinking?

The rules plainly state the disqualifying conditions. A speaker is allowed only one cue. Now I've killed any chance I might have had. That moderator thinks I'm a fool. Now I'll be disqualified. I couldn't help it because Henderson forgot his speech. Why did I feel called on to make a spectacle of myself? None of the other boys let it bother them. Oh, call Dr. Redwine for the whole bunch, he thought.

As speaker number ten bowed to polite applause and resumed his seat, the moderator rose and announced in formal tones, "There has been a request that contestant number eight be granted another opportunity. Although the rules are clear on this point, I have consulted the other officials and we have decided to grant this request, which, I might add, is the most unusual I have ever received in my twenty years of teaching. Ladies and gentlemen, I again give you contestant number eight, from Carrollton, Georgia."

As Tom Henderson got up, the applause leaped across the footlights like something alive.

Well, thought the boy, regardless of what the judges are thinking, at least the crowd approves. Everybody likes that Henderson boy.

That Henderson boy was standing, easy and relaxed, at the edge of the stage, holding up his hand for quiet. He spoke in an assured and confident tone. "Ladies and gentlemen, I appreciate this more than you can know. The officials are most kind, and my young friend from Brewton thoughtful and unselfish, but I must decline this second chance. I do not think it would be fair, and to be perfectly honest, I'm not at all sure I would remember my speech this time. I apologize to you and I apologize to my school for letting them down. Thank you, but no, thank you."

He smiled warmly, bowed, and sat down.

Ashamed of the relief that filled him, the boy applauded with the rest.

The moderator announced, "We will now dismiss the Declamation contestants. Remember, all awards will be announced from this stage at ten o'clock tonight. The next event is in music. Will all the piano contestants please come forward?"

The boy found his way back to his family group in the rear of the auditorium, where he self-consciously submitted, in embarrassed acceptance, to a kiss from his mother.

"That was wonderful, son," she beamed. "You never spoke better. Mrs. Parker would be very proud of you. I just know you won. You were better than anybody else."

"Thank you, ma'am," he replied, silently expostulating, I wish she wouldn't say that. Everyone sees her kissing me in this crowd and then hears her talking like that and I'll be a mama's boy for sure.

"Where's Daddy?" he inquired.

"Oh, son, you know how your daddy is. When you got up out of your chair and went across that stage, he got so nervous he couldn't stand it. He's gone outside to smoke a cigarette. Go see if you can find him."

As the first music contestant got well into her piece and the strains of Mozart's "Turkish Rondo" stormed across the darkened auditorium, the boy tiptoed out to find his father. He was well aware of the high honor he had received by this greatest of all men interrupting his Friday night routine at the drugstore to come all the way to Spalding County to hear his speech. Spying the tall, familiar, white-clad figure standing alone at the end of the hall, he rushed toward him. His father stretched out his hand and grasped the boy's in a grip so strong that the boy felt anchored.

"Let me tell you one thing," the man said with emotional huskiness. "That was real sportsmanship and it took guts. I don't give a damn whether you won or lost that contest. If you never do another thing in your life, tonight you are a man. You are bigger than anybody here." He clasped the astonished and wondering boy to him with an arm around his shoulders. As a freshet of tears rolled down his face in blessed release, the boy happily thought, I don't give a damn, either.

At ten o'clock when the principal of the host school finally got around to the Declamation awards, the boy sat alone with his mother. The father was nervous and smoking again. Third place went to Butts County, second place to Troup, and finally the man said, "I am sure the decision of the judges will be approved by everyone here. First place goes to the gallant young Patrick Henry from Brewton County. Will you come up for your medal, Porter?"

The resultant explosion of sound almost blew him down the aisle. He had never heard such a roar of clapping or seen so many smiling faces. When he was halfway to the front there was a great rumble, and the people in the audience rose to their feet, the applause increasing like a sudden gust of summer rain on a tin roof. He was walking through a tunnel. It's pretty nice down here, he thought.

He was sliding back into the seat by his beaming mother before he surreptitiously opened the blue box with "Balfour" printed on it. The shiny gold medal threw reflected lights into his shining eyes. For the first time he thought of the ten points it represented. Hello, beautiful, he greeted it silently.

Three weeks later the UDC meeting was held at the big house. He yielded to his childish urge and crept on all fours beneath one of the living room windows opening onto the verandah. He slowly raised his head and peered through a breeze-floated lace curtain. Miss Beauty Graves sat on the edge of her seat, teacup gripped in rigidly curved talons, glittering chain to her pince-nez fastened daintily in her jet black hair, her mouth a scarlet slash in the stark whiteness of her powdered face. "I tell you, Mrs. Osborne," she announced—all the hum of ladies stilled—"that boy of yours is sure to Go Far."

The boy ducked his head, crawled softly past the line of windows, then rose and raced on bare feet down the length of the high front porch. As he leaped exultantly off the end of the porch, flailing his arms in the air in simulated flight, he startled the dogs from their cool, moist bed in the drip of the house. Soaring over them, he exclaimed, "Better look out, ole Spot and Big Boy! Here comes ole Combined and Holy!"

As he hit the ground and ran around the corner of the house, he added, "Now then, if I just don't get the appendicitis."

that summer he overheard his mother tell the aunt they were getting low on cornmeal. She said that until someone could go to mill, they had better put more bran in the pans of rough cornbread they cooked for the pack of dogs that lay around the yard.

There were three grist mills operating on Whitewater Creek in the county. Each one had a lake impounded above it to assure an adequate source of power for turning the huge stones that pulverized the corn or wheat between them. The boy loved to go to mill. The machinery there was always so rusty and old looking that he thought it improbable it would work. There were huge iron gears with cogs like giant brown teeth and big rusty iron bars disappearing through the floor and ceiling.

It was always a thrill to hear the rhythmic flapping and slapping of the great moving belts. He liked the rattling, rumbling, yet even beat of the rusty conglomerate as it meshed into action, crushing the grain with ponderous and indifferent grinding that made the whole mill tremble. The vibrations came from the floor through one's feet so strongly that they caused a vague shimmer in one's vision. It was similar to but stronger than the sensation received while sitting on the church bench by Mr. Charlie Sorrells when he was singing bass. The great nets of cobwebs in the rafters and corners, outlined by the fine white dust of flour, looked like ragged curtains. The miller was the cleanest looking man in the county, with flour on his clothes and hat, a dusting of it on his eyebrows and lashes, and a definite powdering on the air-straining hair within his nostrils. The mill was a place of unbelievable excitement, even enchantment, and the boy never tired of observing the activity there. Some parts of it, however, remained a mystery to him.

He figured out the process of shelling the corn, which produced a pile of discarded red and white cobs and a bin full of hard, pearl-like kernels. He understood that these kernels were then dribbled between a series of water-driven revolving stones which ground the meal progressively fine. He saw it finally come sliding out the wooden chute, which had been polished by years of use to an unbelievable smoothness. The meal fell into its bin, not in a steady stream, but in shifting starts and spurts which were in perfect rhythm with the flapping of the belt, the rumble of the wheels, and the shaking of the floor.

He never fully understood how the miller determined how much of the finished product was to be delivered, warm and fragrant, to the customer in sacks and how much was reserved as toll for the service of grinding. He was too polite to ask. He had noted that the grandfather, purchasing supplies in a store, would meticulously count every penny of change before snapping it shut in his leather coin purse. This same grandfather would deliver a load of corn or wheat to the mill, leave the premises for a couple of hours to yarn with friends, and return to load the finished product with never a word about shares or weights. The boy thought to himself that this was an unparalleled opportunity for graft. He decided that millers must be the most trustworthy of men and that they were not to be questioned. He had never seen a rich one.

Overhearing his mother on this occasion, he decided to carry a load of corn to mill all by himself. He had not seen any of his friends since the end of school, and he thought it would be fun to pick some of them up as he drove the wagon through Brewtonton and carry them to mill with him. He asked the father about the plan. He tried not to cringe as the father gave one quick, involuntary glance at his frame before averting his eyes in embarrassed kindness.

"I don't expect you're quite filled out enough yet to handle a wagonload of corn and a team of mules all by yourself. That's a good seven miles, and by the time you wait for your meal, it'll be an all-day trip."

He paused, sensing the unspoken disappointment of his son. "I tell you what," he decided. "Go tell Freeman and Tabitha I said to let Buddy off this afternoon to help you shuck corn, and tomorrow to go to mill with you. Tell them I'll pay him. He's about through with his plowing anyway. Tell them if they're out of meal they can send some corn along with yall. You can be in charge, but I'll feel better if Buddy is along with you. You never can tell what a team of mules is going to do when they're out on the big road that far from home."

"Yessir," the boy replied as he turned to leave the room.

"Come back here a minute," his father commanded. He chucked a knuckle under the boy's chin and looked into his eyes. "I'm expecting you to act like a man."

As the boy ran barefooted down the barn lane and up the path across the cotton patch to Tabitha's house, he didn't feel at all like a man. There's not very much to taking a load of corn to mill, he told himself.

He and Buddy shucked corn that afternoon with the enjoyment that an anticipated event can give to routine tasks. They worked rapidly and congenially with comfortable and compatible small talk. They were used to one another. In fact, the boy regarded Buddy as an accepted part of his universe. In some ways he really looked up to him and tried to emulate him. Some three years older than the boy, Buddy was already physically a man. Quick-witted and dexterous, he was also very kind and gentle. He did not have a mean bone in his body and exhibited a genuine love for people. Fun-loving and quick to break into contagious laughter, he was also very thoughtful and accommodating. Blacker than either of his parents, his sleek, clean skin actually shone, and his gums seemed redder and his teeth whiter than those of anyone else the boy had ever known. He had been raised strict. He was not allowed to go "catting," an activity that involved wild behaviour with females, or "skinning," an illegal card game which the boy could not master. He had never been known to "lay out," which implied drinking liquor and not coming home until daylight. He dated only one girl, and he was homerun king of the cowpasture baseball team. He was, in reality, a black Galahad, and the boy had sense enough to know it.

The previous year, during an afternoon baseball game in the pasture behind Wes's house, a sprinkle of rain had driven everyone to shelter. Some of the players dashed home, some took shelter in the cowshed, and some were invited into Wes's two-room home. Wes, one of Uncle John and Aunt Lou's sons, was a tall, muscular high-yellow man, married to a thin, wiry, quick-tongued black woman named May. In the hierarchy of farm life, they were said to belong to the boy's grandmother.

If anyone, black or white, was ever teasing about this, the boy was unable to discern it. It never occurred to him to question it. His grandmother had been born before the War to slave-owning parents, and he noted that although Wes sharecropped under the supervision of the father, he always plowed the grandmother's land with the grandmother's mule, and she pocketed the owner's half of the profits each year. He also noted that during work time the grandmother was the only one who could have a maid come once a week. This was invariably May, and she cleaned only the grandmother's room, washed only the grandmother's linen, scoured only the grandmother's slop jar, leaving the rest of the big house to the aunt and mother, who had no household help until laying-by time.

Wes and May were in the highest circle of the local caste system and were subject to no disciplinary action or admonition from anyone except the grandmother herself. The dwellings of the rest of the families on the farm were consequently not exempt from jealousy. It was not the devouring or revenge-taking type of jealousy, but just everyday annoying and irritating envy. Wes and May belonged to Miss Sis.

On this rain-interrupted afternoon in Wes and May's front room, the conversation turned to boxing and the world of prizefighting. Darnell and Wes fell to arguing about techniques and styles of various boxers. The boy piped up with the information that he had some boxing gloves and volunteered to go to the big house and fetch them. Santa Claus had brought them to him the previous Christmas, in an effort on the father's part to get him interested in manly competition and to discourage his proclivity for gouging, choking, and biting in his inevitable occasional fights with bigger cousins.

They were four big puffy pillows of soft red leather, and he had never had them on. In fact, they were unused except for one occasion when he had persuaded his two younger sisters to don them when they were fussing. This had resulted in such roundhousing blows and nose-flattening humiliation that the girls had finally snatched off the gloves in favor of the more familiar and effective technique of hairpulling.

He hastened down the half mile of clay road through the light rain, procured the boxing gloves quietly enough to avoid waking the napping ladies, hung the gloves around his neck, and returned to Wes's house on his bicycle. This was another gift from an earlier Santa, which he never used for pleasure because it was no fun to ride a bicycle on rutted roads that rattled one's teeth. It was faster than walking, however, and by now he was in a hurry.

He pedaled furiously back, ignoring the fact that the combination of wet clay road and a fenderless bike was laying a red stripe down his back. Dashing into the room full of dry ballplayers, he found Wes and Darnell still discussing their differences of opinion about boxing. The boys crowded around him to feel and squeeze and exclaim over the boxing gloves. Everyone encouraged Wes and Darnell to put on these gloves and demonstrate their respective points. Overwhelmed by this youthful clamor, Wes was soon persuaded to remove his shirt and have a pair laced onto his hands. Tall and powerful, the paler glint of his usually unexposed shoulders shining beneath his overall galluses, he danced sideways around the room, exhorting Darnell to confront him. Darnell, older and shorter, with prudence and courtesy, kept declining. The crowd of boys was not to be denied.

Even Menfolks, beloved third son of Darnell, implored, "Come on, Paw, do it! We know you kin whup Mister Wes."

As Darnell persisted in his refusal, the disappointed groans of unfulfilled enthusiasm filled the little house. Wes kept dancing around, hitting his gloves against each other, a condescending smirk growing wider and wider on his face.

"Come on, man," he admonished, "these old gloves like feather pillows. Ain't no way I could hurt you with em."

Darnell regarded his twisted Bull Durham cigarette carefully, blew on its smoldering tip, and flicked an incipient ash with his little fingernail. "I ain't studyin you, man," he announced.

As Wes threw back his head and tauntingly laughed, Buddy unexpectedly stepped out in front of him. "What about me, Mister Wes? You jes soon try me as Uncle Darnell?" he queried politely.

The room stilled immediately in surprise, and the boy, recalling briefly an earlier, younger volunteer, felt like a frail and diffident Jonathan. What guts, he thought. Wes looked down at the challenging youth and spoke happily and confidently, "Don't make no difference to me. Come on, do you be man enough."

The center of the room was soon cleared, the sides and corners filled with some fifteen noisy, chattering black children and adolescents, their staccato shrieks to each other as unintelligible as a foreign tongue. Most of them were either nephews of Wes or cousins of Buddy. May was moving swiftly around the room, as barefooted and excited as the boys. Darnell was puffing on his now-glowing cigarette as he tied the gloves on Buddy. He's the only one in the room with shoes on, the boy thought inconsequentially.

He watched the two contestants tap gloves and begin circling each other, both of them shirtless in overalls rolled halfway to the knees. Wes was a good six inches taller than Buddy, with wide, flat shoulders and long tapering muscles. He was thirty-five years old and as erect as an aristocrat. As he pranced sideways around the room, he held his shoulders back, his head up, and had both arms extended in front of him and curled upward at the elbows and wrists.

He looks like pictures of boxers before they wore gloves. He looks dangerous, the boy thought. He darted up behind the man and impulsively pled, "Don't hurt him, Wes, please."

Looking at Buddy, he was aware for the first time that this teen-aged boy was as big as he would ever be. Nothing tapered about Buddy. He was built in blocks and chunks. He looked like a rectangle of black marble, thick and squat, and there was no fat on him. He moved slowly and smoothly sideways, crouched behind the protective gloves, in a stance that exaggerated his comparative-ly short stature. Wes danced on the outside of the circle, flinging blows at Buddy's head, hitting the soft gloves, recoiling in bounces and jumps, darting in for another flurry of blows, always moving, always quick.

Buddy, on the inside of the circle, looked to be moving slowly as oil by comparison, always facing the antagonist, ducking behind the gloves as the blows rained, raising his sleek shaved head in cautious assessment, always gliding, always shifting, never in a hurry, never striking a blow. The boy thought he looked for all the world like a black snake in a coil, all motion fluid, no effort wasted, all attention concentrated. In the corners, the Bandar-log screamed.

May was hopping around the periphery, encouraging her champion. "Go on, Wes, put him away. Hit's done quit raining. Git dis over and git dem chirren outer my house."

All the young people were solidly behind the younger contestant. "Come on, Buddy," they implored. "Hit him, Buddy. Hit him just wunst anyway, Buddy."

Still the improbable waltz continued. Wes began to slow. As he began dancing back after delivering a series of licks against the protecting gloves, Buddy suddenly launched himself out of his crouch and lashed at Wes with the one blow he struck all afternoon. His fist collided solidly with the left side of Wes's jaw. Wes's head snapped back, his feet left the floor, and for a split second he was arched rigidly in mid-air. Then, like a sheet of floating newspaper which hits an unseen downdraft, he buckled in the middle and crashed to the floor in limber unconsciousness.

Before the house stopped trembling from the force of the falling body, it was empty. The children crowded through the door in panic, the usually mature Darnell leading them. May was right behind them screaming, "I'm goan git Miss Sis. Buddy done kilt her nigger!"

Only Buddy, Wes, and the boy were left in the room. The boy yelled at May, "Come back here, May! He ain't dead; he's just out. Besides, Miss Sis is taking her nap."

Buddy stood without moving, dripping and blowing, arms dangling limply. "I didn't go to do it at bad, Sambo. You sure you right?"

The boy knelt by the prostrate giant. He had never seen an unconscious person before, and he was frightened and uncertain. The great chest was moving up and down, however, and as he raised an eyelid, it flickered under his touch.

May was still insisting that Wes was dead and that the boy ought not to have brought those gloves up there in the first place.

With a confidence he did not feel, he directed her, "Don't just stand there! Get me some water and a rag. Quick!" He thought fleetingly of his grandfather and added, "You're hanging around like the dead lice were falling off you. Get a move on!"

Turning to Buddy, he said, "He's all right. Take off those boxing gloves and help me."

"I can't. I been trying," Buddy wailed.

"Untie em with your teeth. And tell those chillun to get out of the door. We need all the air we can get."

He and Buddy straightened the limp and sleeping Wes on the floor. He put a pillow under his head. He crossed his arms on his chest. At least he looks better, he thought.

"Here's de water, Sambo," proffered May deferentially. He began bathing Wes's face and slapping it gently. Wes turned his head and ground his teeth. Finally he opened his eyes in a long blank stare and looked around the room in bewilderment. "What's goin on here?" he asked.

"Buddy knocked the stuffing out of you, and you've been out for five minutes, but you're all right. Just be still," the boy replied.

After a long moment of silence and more gaping around the room, Wes raised himself on one elbow. He drew a long, shuddering breath and pointed a finger at the floor. "I stumbled on dat loose plank," he announced. "I been aimin to fix it."

The boy didn't hang around the yard to enjoy watching the adulating children congratulate the victorious Buddy. The hero of the hour was handling himself modestly and well. The boy was filled with such admiration that he longed to stay, but he knew that he had better get on his bicycle and try to beat this news to the big house. He had found long since that whoever broke a story first had a precious opportunity to slant the news to his advantage. As he went by Darnell's house, he heard one little girl in the local telegraph chain announcing loudly to another, "Buddy kilt Mister Wes, but Sambo brung him back to life." Quelling a sudden irrational surge of vanity, he murmured to himself, "Well, whatta you know? Move over, Lord Greystoke."

He leaned over the handlebars and pedaled faster, uncaringly flinging mud up his back from the naked rear tire.

A year later, shucking corn in preparation for what they both regarded as a holiday on the morrow, the boy realized that he was uncomfortable about Buddy going with him. That's crazy, he thought; if it were just me and Buddy, we'd really have a frolic. What's wrong with you? He realized that it centered around his plans for collecting some of his school friends as they went through Brewtonton. He pondered this. Buddy was his best friend on the farm, and he was going to meet his best friends in town tomorrow. He was mixing worlds that had never met before. If Buddy goofs up, I'm the one they'll laugh at, he thought. For Pete's sake, you're acting like your mother was going to the class picnic with you. Relax. How can anyone keep from liking Buddy?

He looked across the freshly shucked corn at the shaven head. They better be nice to him, he thought fiercely.

"Buddy," he spoke out loud. "You'll like these fellows we're going to meet tomorrow. They're good boys."

"I know I will," Buddy responded. "They bliged to be nice boys if dey yo friends. Les put dese shucks in de lot for de cows. We got enough corn."

The next morning he ate a hurried breakfast and ran to the barn to help catch the mules and hitch up. Buddy already had the team harnessed and was loading the sacks of corn from the slatted crib. Pet threw up her head, rolled her eyes, and backed to one side as the boy went by to help finish the task. He ran back to the house to get his paper bag with two ham biscuits in it for his lunch and to kiss his mother goodbye.

"Have a good day, son," his mother said, "and I'd rather you didn't go in that lake. It's so deep I'd worry about you."

"I won't go in the lake, Mother," he promised. "We may wade a little in the creek for mussels, but don't you worry."

Minutes later he and Buddy were on their way, sitting side by side on a plank laid across the front of the wagon body. The boy was driving. He glanced around his world. The sun was about an hour high in a cloudless sky. No breath of breeze stirred. The dew, in heavy drops on the flat cotton leaves, sparkled in the glow of early morning. In a crepe myrtle bush a mockingbird was trilling a rich and complicated melody in repetitious insistence. Far off he heard Lucinda's rooster crow. A foraging bumblebee zoomed indolently across the wagon toward a patch of purple vetch. He took a deep breath of honeysuckle-fragrant air and looked over at Buddy. No use to try telling him about "Pippa Passes," he thought. Buddy caught his eye and grinned at him. "Ain't it a pretty day, Sambo? We goan have a good time."

In Brewtonton they stopped at successive houses and collected Tom Dowman, Warren Mitchell, and James Kelly, all of whom seemed pleased and excited over the prospect of taking a real load of corn to mill. They were all familiar with picnic and swimming activities surrounding the old mill and the adjacent lake, but none had any experience of the actual working side of it; they bought their meal and flour at the store. They laughed and chattered all the way out to Lake Marston, catching the boy up on all the news in town since school had closed. Buddy was easily and smoothly accepted into the group. The boy felt pretty good.

Arrived at the mill, all five of them unloaded the corn in record time and were told by the miller that it would be about three hours before the meal was ready. Buddy drove the empty wagon in bumping, bone-jarring clamor across the rocky yard and tied the mules to a tree. The boy untied two bundles of fodder before them and left them munching contentedly, swishing their tails and stomping a foot to dislodge an occasional fly. Then the boys set out in high spirits to explore the area. They waded in the creek below the dam and dug the secret-looking, heavy black mussels out of the mud and skipped them like stones across the water. They marvelled at the smooth, mother-of-pearl interior of the rough, hairy shells. With prodigious leaps from boulder to boulder they crossed the creek just below the dam, feeling the mist from the cascading water excitingly cool on their faces. The tremendous rocks on either side of the creek were defaced with scripture references in white paint—giant letters slanted in primitive script across the barren rock surfaces.

They were all the same reference: Deuteronomy 27:17. The paint, while wet, had trickled and spattered enough to add unexpected flourishes to the crude lettering. A strange feeling of anger emanated from these lurid messages that flaunted themselves amid the grays and browns and soft greens of the weathered mill and creek and woods. They were reputedly painted there by Mr. Bennett Marston, whitehaired eccentric bachelor who lived in a very small house across the road with his old maid sister.

"His family used to own all this land, and he doesn't like it cause it's not his any more," James Kelly explained. "You can run up on him out in the woods and he won't even talk to you. He's crazy as a betsy bug."

"Naw, he ain't crazy," Tom Dowman authoritatively corrected. "He's just strange. He couldn't learn in school, and he's half-witted. He wouldn't hurt nobody."

Since the boy and Buddy lived out of this area and Warren Mitchell, the Methodist minister's son, was a newcomer, the three of them knew nothing of the local legend. They were interested, however.

"Tom, you're wrong," said James. "That ole man's crazy as a loon. I come up on him one day with a shovel and a bait bucket, and it scared hell outta me. He just stood there and looked at me."

They were walking up the far side of the lake and were temporarily and delightedly distracted by a pair of blue jays that dive-bombed them when they approached their nest. Tom, whose father was a lawyer and whose grandfather was a lawyer and a Witherspoon to boot, was not to be corrected by the grandson of a tenant farmer who had been named Prince Albert Kelly in honor of a pipe tobacco and signed his name with an X. He returned to the subject of Bennett Marston. "That old man is harmless. He comes from good folks. My mother knows the family, and she says Mr. Marston's just an idiot."

Well away from the painted rocks and the eerie feeling they inspired, the boy could stay out of the conversation no longer. "Tom," he invited, "let me see you close your eyes and spell 'Deuteronomy.'"

As Warren and Buddy laughed, the subject was dropped. A little later they had the good fortune to stumble up on a battle between a king snake and a cottonmouth moccasin. The shiny black and white constrictor had already mastered the dull brown, venomous pit viper, and they were grappled together in an interlocking coil like a huge ball of knitting yarn. As the boys watched, the king snake slowly and sinuously squeezed his victim, slithering another loop of his body in gliding grace over the moccasin for a progressively surer grip. He looked at the boys and flickered his split black tongue in quivering investigation at them but kept his head low and flat, never abandoning his hug of death. The boy had not witnessed nor even imagined such a scene. He raised the question that perhaps they were mating.

"Mating, hell!" Tom snorted. "You know better'n that. That king snake's goan eat that ole water moccasin. That's why folks like king snakes. They'll keep poisonous snakes away. As soon as that moccasin's good and dead, that king's gonna swallow him. If you'll be right quiet, we can watch em. He'll lick him all over good and get him good and slick and then he'll swallow him whole."

Warren Mitchell, tallest of the boys and stronger than any of them except Buddy, picked up a stick. "A snake is a snake," he announced, "and I'm going to kill em both."

"Dat's right, Warren," assented Buddy. "I know what you mean. Truf is de light. Hit em hard!"

"Don't kill em, Warren," begged the boy. "Let's watch."

"Naw," said Warren, "I've watched enough. Those things give me the creeps. Get back."

The ball of snakes still moved in slow, constricted sliding as Warren advanced with his stick held high. From the woods immediately behind them came a deep, slow, sepulchral admonition, the last syllable accented and prolonged: "Leave them alone!"

Everyone looked up in startled immobility to see the old man standing tall beside a pine tree, his white hair erect on his head in a shining aureole. The only sound was the crashing of underbrush as James Kelly raced downstream, convinced forevermore of his original opinion.

Warren slowly lowered his stick and slung it blindly behind him as he stepped backward, his eyes never leaving the old man's face. "Yes, sir!" he said.

'That's what I was telling him, Mr. Bennett," Tom volunteered. "I was trying to get them to leave those snakes alone and let that king snake finish what he started. That's exactly what I was telling em."

In the presence of an unwavering blue gaze and stolid lack of response, Tom's voice tapered uncertainly to silence. The old man never moved, never blinked, and never spoke. As the boys retreated slowly in the footsteps of the distant James, the boy ducked under an alder branch. He looked back over his shoulder. Mr. Bennett Marston was still standing by the pine tree, his hands empty by his sides, still not moving. Before him on the ground, the boy thought he detected a slow, writhing ball of snakes.

Later, below the mill, having exhaustively rehashed their recent adventure, James suggested, "It's hot. Let's go swimming."

"I can't," said the boy quickly. "I promised my mother I wouldn't go in the lake." He was glad of the excuse, for he was an inexpert swimmer and was not at all proud of his high-headed dog paddle.

"Who said anything about the lake?" asked James. "There's the best wash hole you ever saw about a hundred yards around the second bend down yonder."

"Don't worry about the water," offered Tom. "I took a Red Cross course in lifesaving, and if anybody gets in trouble, I'll fish him out. Come on. Let's go."

Buddy entered the conversation as they started downstream. "Sambo, last thing my maw told me was not to git in no water. I can't swim a lick."

"Don't worry, Buddy," said the boy. "I can't swim much myself. You can go wading and we can at least sit down in the shallow part and cool off. I won't tell your maw. Come on."

They followed the others on a faint path along the creek, dodging briers, bushes, and leafy limbs and jumping over fallen logs, the firm moist sand and patches of sleek mud cool beneath their bare feet. The dank smell of the wet earth was everywhere, and every few feet they crossed a fresh pocket of honeysuckle fragrance. They soon emerged from the dimness of the leafy path onto a large sandbar which slanted down to the muddy creek as a fairly respectable beach. The creek was some forty feet wide here, flattened out after its constant attack against the restraining earth banks, and its current seemed slow and deliberate. It curled beneath the steep, undermined red clay concavity of the opposite bank as though snuggling its back into the comforting arms of a sleeping partner. It, in turn, curved around the sandbar in protective embrace.

This was the wash-hole spot. It looked placid and inviting. A hickory tree, its roots washed out by previous high water, slanted across the upstream boundary of the swimming hole. Below, a huge willow extended almost horizontally across the stream where it channeled again into narrow flow. Between the two trees the long and wide expanse of water was glittering in the searing sun. It was a perfect place to swim.

Within minutes they were all stripping off their clothes, taking care to fold them on rocks so that redbugs would not get in them. As the boy hopped on one leg divesting himself of his underpants, he became acutely conscious of his lack of physical development. He had never before been in a group of naked adults. Prepubescent nudity was commonplace on the farm among the blacks, it being much easier to let a child run around in just a shirt than it was to change diapers and pants when they were wet. Among adolescents and adults, body consciousness appeared suddenly and demandingly.

The genitalia were called privates and were just exactly that. Modesty was more than a self-conscious fetish; it was an ingrained tenet of conduct. When a male was forced to urinate in the presence of another, he always stepped to one side, turned his back, and even then shielded his privates with a protecting hand. The boy, despite devious and ingenious curiosity, had never had a good look at an adult penis, catching only covert and fleeting glimpses of these sacred objects as they were shaken dexterously after voiding and flipped quickly back through the overall fly by a quick withdrawing movement of the hips.

Now, prancing unashamedly in the sunlight, his friends from town, older than he and fully matured, were exhibiting themselves completely. He was startled by the sight of flat, stark white bellies accented by the vibrant growths of rich curly black hair and decorated by swinging genitalia. They acted proud of themselves. James Kelly was even popping his between thumb and forefinger with a slapping sound against his belly to make it bigger. Try as he would to avert his gaze and pretend indifference, the boy felt surrounded by big penises.

He looked around for Buddy. His black friend, great muscles bunched and gleaming in the hot sun, was sitting in the

144

edge of the water, its muddy surface covering his lap like a loin cloth, his eyes studiously and intently fixed on some distant horizon. Their glances did not meet. He looked down at himself. Well, he thought, it looks for all the world like a grub worm.

Fearful of attention and comment from his peers, he slid unobtrusively into the shallow water by Buddy. No one said a word to him, but the conversation on the sandbar was penetratingly audible.

"Look at ole James. He done worked himself up a semi," yelled Tom.

"Yeah," observed Warren. "Ain't he got a whopper?"

"You think that's something—you ought to see ole Dave Dillapree," responded James. "He's got the biggest one in town."

"How do you know?" asked Warren, laughing.

"Yeah, that's right," confirmed Tom. "He showed it to a bunch of us in the cemetery one day. When it's hard it's ten and a half inches long and four inches around at the bottom. He measured it right in front of us."

"My God," said the minister's son. "How come it got so big?"

"We asked him," answered James, "and he said he puts nitrate of soda poultices on it."

"He puts what on it? What's nitrate of soda?" asked Warren.

"Aw, it's fertilizer—you know. The farmers use it a lot, and his daddy puts it on beans and things in the garden. I don't know whether he's lying or not," James replied.

"I believe he's lying," opined Tom, "but then he might not be. It sho is big. You oughta see Benton Bishop's, though. It's crooked. And have you ever seen a coon's? It's got a bone in it with a hook on the end. Mr. Buck Ritter down at Brooks totes one in his shirt pocket to pick his teeth with."

"Where can you get nitrate of soda?" asked Warren.

Fascinated but repelled, embarrassed to his marrow, envious beyond description, the boy sought the same spot on the horizon that still claimed Buddy's attention. He would have died before he looked again. Buddy leaned toward him, looking at the white toes protruding from the current. "Don't dis water feel good on such a hot day, Sambo?" he said gently.

The town boys were soon climbing out on the tilted hickory tree and diving into the muddy wash hole. They emerged in bursts that brought them out of the water almost to their waists, simultaneously jerking their heads sideways to sling the heavy, sodden hair out of their eyes. They didn't belly-flop when they dove; they went in headfirst. Their feet weren't always together and most of the time their knees bent, but it was the grandest diving the boy had ever seen. In addition they swam overhand with their heads low in the water and their feet going like flutter wheels.

"Come on in," Warren yelled at him.

"I can't swim like yall. I'd better just play in the shallow water."

"Come on," commanded Tom. "I'll watch out for you. Don't forget, I'm a certified Red Cross lifesaver. I can tow you around like a rowboat."

"Come on in," added James. "You ain't goan have any fun in that shallow water."

The boy rose and waded away from the sandbar toward his frolicking friends. He thought how much better they looked with their bodies covered by the tawny water. "They look like people again," he muttered.

About twenty feet from the bank, waist deep, he suddenly hit a drop-off where the eroding current had made a precipitous shelf of the gently sloping creek bed. He disappeared from sight, finding himself suddenly submerged, weightless, in the amber swirling water. He clawed his way to the surface, blinking, coughing, and belching and began dog paddling furiously, keeping his chin as high as he could above the water. His friends were delighted.

"Fooled you that time, didn't we?" laughed Warren. "Nobody knows that ole drop-off is there."

The boy swam busily around like a woundup toy, pretending to be amused, determined to appear a good sport, eager for the approval of his impressive friends.

"Let's see if you can trick ole Buddy out here," suggested Warren. "He'll have a fit when he hits that hole."

"No, you don't," directed the boy. "He can't swim. Besides, his maw told him not to go in the water, and he always minds. Besides," he added deprecatingly, "I think he's scared of the water." He paddled frenetically in another tight little circle.

"His maw?" scoffed James. "He's full grown. He ain't as tall as Warren, but he's bigger than any of us. He's muscled up good as any white man in Brewtonton."

"Hey, Buddy!" yelled Tom. "Come on in—it's fun!"

"Naw, I ain't comin," Buddy yelled back. "I can't swim, and I'm scared a dat water anyhow. It's over my head. Yall have fun and doan worry bout me. I be fine jes lak I is."

"Look, Buddy, it's not deep right here," enticed Warren, treading water with his hands held up by the side of his head. "I'm standing on the bottom. See my hands?"

"Yeah, Buddy," added James. "I am, too, and I ain't any taller than you are. See my hands? I'm on the bottom."

"Tread water," Tom advised the boy. "Short as you are, he'll come on out if he thinks it ain't over your head. He'll be all right. He's gonna find that drop-off and jump back. We just want to scare him and have a little fun. Can't nothing bad happen to him. I'll look after him."

"I don't know how to tread water," said the boy.

"Ain't nothing to it," said Tom. "Just stand up straight in the water and pump your legs hard as you can like you're riding a bicycle. Then you can hold your hands outa the water. Get out in front of us, though, cause we're taller than you."

Following directions, the boy was pleased to discover that he actually could tread water. Holding his hands aloft, he called to the shore, "Look here, Buddy."

Buddy stood up, brown water running in rivulets down his massive black thighs, gleaming and shiny in the bright sun. "You on the bottom where you at, Sambo?" he asked.

"Of course I am," the boy lied. "See my hands? Wade on out."

"Hurry, Buddy," encouraged Tom. "We ain't got much longer. We got to go home. Come on."

Obviously studying the situation, the massive and phlegmatic figure suddenly sprang into unbelievable activity.

"Here I come!" he yelled and came charging through the shallow water like a dinosaur, whooping and waving his arms. He ran straight for the startled boy, who was treading water just at the edge of the drop-off, but such was the power of his pumping legs and his speed that his momentum carried him directly into the center of the creek. With a great splash and terrified bellow he plummeted beneath the concealing muddy surface of the deepest part of the creek. The boys, overwhelmed by the surprising violence of this charge, scattered like chickens to the shallow water. Buddy erupted from the creek like a leaping whale and with a scream of panic fell thrashing back therein, flailing arms churning the water around him into a froth. He emerged again and again. His eyes were rolling in his head, and his great red mouth was gaping wide. His wordless cries were bone-chilling and piteous.

"Get him, Tom!" screamed the boy. "He's drowning! Get him out of there!"

Tom made a racing dive and swam swiftly to the maelstrom in the center of the creek. Instantly Buddy grabbed him in his powerful arms and they both went under the water, rolling over and over like primordial beasts grappled together in rage. For moments nothing could be seen except the turbulence of the surface. Buddy was the first to reappear, bursting up again to scream, gulp, and go gasping under once more. Finally Tom bobbed to the surface. The boy watched unbelievingly as he dog paddled to shore, eyes red, nose streaming, and lips blue.

"I can't do it. He nearly killed me. Sposed to knock em out first. I can't do it," he gasped. He fell prone on the bank, chest heaving in the agony of air hunger.

The boy turned in desperation. "Warren," he began, but the tall lanky boy was already running through the shallows to launch his rescue effort. Approaching the fury in the center of the creek, he yelled, "Buddy, don't grab me. I'm coming in behind you and put my arm under your chin. I'll pull you in, but you've got to let me do it. Don't try to help me. Got it?"

Buddy was still going up and down like a weight on a spring, but he was obviously tiring. His prodigious leaps from the water were shorter and weaker. He nodded in agreement with Warren, went under the water again, bobbed up, spun around, and in the unthinking reflex of survival grabbed his would-be rescuer by the shoulders and pushed him under. He rode Warren like a submerged log, holding his own head out of water at last, huge rib cage pumping like a bellows, sucking in great draughts of air through the gurgling water in his throat.

The boy, in horror, sought further help. Tom was sitting up, but his head was between his knees like a chicken with the limberneck. He turned to James Kelly. "Get him, James," he pleaded. "You could get him now."

"I ain't about to go out there," replied James. "He ain't got no business in that creek, anyway."

The boy turned back in panic. Buddy was being ducked repeatedly by the violent efforts of the submerged Warren to escape, but there had been no sign of Warren.

"Buddy!" he screamed. "You've got to turn Warren loose. You're killing him. Do you hear me?" He looked around in desperation and grabbed up Buddy's overalls.

"Look here, Buddy." He waved them over his head. "I'm going to climb out on the willow tree and throw you one end of these overalls. You grab them and I'll pull you in. You hear me, Buddy? You got to turn Warren loose! You're drowning him! Turn him loose, Buddy!"

He never knew whether Buddy heard him or not. As he ran for the willow tree, Warren bobbed up like a cork a good ten feet from the center of conflict. He was blue all over and could hardly speak. He crawled through the shallow water, whimpering like a baby.

"It's no use. He'll just have to go," he sobbed and collapsed on the sandbar.

The boy was slithering along the willow trunk, some four feet above the creek. Buddy had disappeared. He expectantly waited for him to emerge violently again, frantically pleading and snatching at the air. He didn't. As the boy searched in terror, the back of the slick head drifted to the surface of the water some ten feet upstream from his despairing reach. The current played against the relaxed shoulders, and the unresisting body turned slowly over, and he saw Buddy's face. The eyes were closed. The mouth was relaxed and partly open. A few bubbles emerged from the flat nostrils. As he watched, the face sank placidly from sight. All he could hear was the peaceful swirl of the current.

Oh, God! he cried within himself, be with us now. Help us, God. Lord, have mercy!

Trying to remember the formula for prayer, he added in earnest propitiation, I'm a sinner, Lord. Through Your sweet Son, Jesus, help me and Buddy. It's all my fault.

As he clung with one arm to a limb, his friend's body drifted to the surface directly beneath him, carried passively along at the pace of the stream. His still face was turned upward. With desperate care the boy leaned out and cast the loop of the overalls gallus. Miraculously it caught under the chin and held. He felt the tug of the great body being pulled downstream and realized that this was serving to help secure the hold he had. The head was now completely out of water. He began inching back on the rough willow trunk, oblivious to the tearing, snagging bark, towing his quiet and precious load.

Roused by the excitement of renewed hope, Tom and Warren rushed out to help him. James stood on the bank and helped lift the inert form from the water, its great weight restored by loss of the creek's bouyancy. Limber and shifting, Buddy was turned on his belly, head down on the slanting bank. James folded one arm under the head, Warren turned the head sideways, and Tom straddled the waist. He began pressing the massive thorax with all his weight thrown through extended elbows into propelling wrists and hands. Beautiful rhythm. Forward, then spring back. Forward, then spring back.

The boy trembled so violently he thought he would shake to pieces. He watched in disbelief as the water poured from Buddy. It flowed in a steady gush from the mouth and both nostrils, increasing with spurts at the pressure of Tom's hands on the chest. Finally it slowed to a trickle and stopped. Buddy still lay flaccid and limp. The boy knelt and called to him. The eyes flickered and opened.

They have that wondering look, just like Wes's did when he came to, the boy thought.

Buddy belched loudly. The boy turned to find his under-pants while sudden tears blinded his eyes.

"Say something, Buddy," Warren implored. "Say something to us."

Buddy slowly turned his head and looked over his shoulder. "Git off my back, white boy," he obliged.

As the other three rolled in the helpless relief of laughter, the boy fastened his pants with shaking fingers. "Thank you, God," he breathed. "Oh, God, I thank you."

Later, as the mules pulled the load of meal eagerly up Gingercake Hill, well aware they were headed for the barn, Tom and James chattered with forced animation. The others were silent. Buddy and the boy dropped the town guests off at their houses with the most perfunctory of farewells. They rode together toward the farm, each wrapped in the isolating mantle of his own thoughts.

When they were a half mile from the big house, Buddy gave a long, shuddering sigh. He spoke almost as though addressing himself. "I always liked to bathe. I git up ever mornin and fill de ole washpan plumb full of water and stick my face down in it plumb up to my years and shot my eyes and blow bubbles like a hawg drinkin slop. My maw say I the craziest boy she ever seen bout water. Fum now on, I just goan barely dampen a rag and rub my face. An I gwine keep one eye open whilest I do that." He glanced sideways at the boy, who did not laugh.

"Sambo, do me one favor, please. Doan tell my maw bout dis. I promised her I wouldn't go in dat water, and she'll half kill me if she find it out." In total agreement with this proposal and relieved that he didn't have to suggest it himself, the boy nodded his assent.

The wagon drew near the field road going to Tabitha's house.

"I'll unload the meal and unhitch the team, Buddy. I know you're tired. Go on home."

"Aw right, Sambo. Thanks. Dat's mighty nice of you. Be sure you put de gear up right and hang de bridles up." Buddy clambered over the side of the wagon.

He stood on the side of the road, looking over the wheel at the boy.

"Well, goodbye, Sambo."

The boy met his gaze. For one crazy instant he wanted to hurl himself over the wheel into the great black arms and cry his heart out.

"Buddy," he said simply, "I'm sorry."

Buddy looked away and then back into the eyes of his friend. "I am too, Sambo," he said softly. "And dat's de God's truth."

When he returned to school that fall, he was in
the ninth grade. While registering for classes on the first day, he
encountered a problem. He discovered that he could fit only four
ninth grade subjects into his schedule. His female competitors had
no difficulty because home economics was available to them. His
homeroom teacher this year was Miss Hightower, a lovely
mountain lass who had close-cropped curls and wore no make-up
at all. She was very earnest about her teaching duties and tolerated
no foolishness. He sought her help, and together they examined
the master schedule. The only course available when he had a
vacant period was economics. Miss Hightower was the teacher.
Excitedly he placed a finger on the square.

"Here's one you teach, Miss Hightower. Why can't I take this?"

"That's a course that's supposed to be only for seniors,
Porter," she responded. "There's no way you could take that
without special permission. Besides, you already have me for
homeroom, spelling, history, and second year Latin. I'm afraid too
much exposure to one teacher would bore you. It might make
school stale for you. I don't think it would be a good idea."

"Oh, Miss Hightower, I couldn't get too much exposure to
you. You're a great teacher. I'll be taking English and math from
other teachers and, besides, I'd just be sitting in study hall if I
don't get another course I can take. Who do I have to see to get
special permission?"

"Well," the beleaguered lady answered, "no one this side of
the principal could possibly change this schedule. That means you

would have to see Mr. Gill, and he's awfully busy. Besides, Porter, look at this: second year history, second year Latin, and senior economics all follow one another. That would give you three consecutive hours in one of my classes. That's just too much. I don't believe you could stand it."

"Miss Hightower, don't you worry about me. I know I can handle it," the boy reassured her. "I'll run see Mr. Gill and be right back."

As he left the room on his way to the principal's office, the teacher ran one hand through her short hair, let her shoulders sag, and leaned forward on her desk with bowed head.

The principal was an elderly man of at least fifty-five who was very reserved and stern. He looked like a gray flannel stork whose yolk sac had not absorbed. Whenever someone presented him with a problem, he stood with his right hand in his pocket and jingled his keys while he rocked from one foot to the other. He cocked his head to the side and seemed to be listening, but his eyes always walked on off somewhere else. When particularly thoughtful, he would rhythmically loosen his bottom plate, thrust it forward with his tongue until it made his lower lip bulge, and then return it with a little click to its original position. The effect of the clicking teeth, the jingling keys, the rocking shoes, and the shifting eyes was one of such Olympian detachment that most petitioners were hypnotized into mistaking aloofness for intelligence. He shaved so closely that the skin where his beard grew stood up higher than the rest of his face, but his head was so bald it looked polished. His detachable shirt collars were stiffly starched and bunched his loose jowls into a choked ruddiness. Enthusiasm had never quickened either his voice or his step, and his occasional smile was thin as whey.

When he had replaced Mr. Benton as principal of the school, it was as severe a cultural shock as Cromwell's supplanting King Charles. He controlled the students and teachers alike by stifling them. He did not even bother to administer the whippings to the boys but relegated this vigorous act of authority to whatever hapless male subordinate happened to be designated assistant

154

principal. The boy was in awe of him but not truly afraid of him, and he approached the man with some degree of confidence in the success of his mission.

"Mr. Gill," he began deferentially, "I need to talk to you about the schedule. I need to take another subject besides the four regular ones, and senior economics is the only one I can fit in. Miss Hightower says that it's against school policy to let a sophomore take a senior subject, but that it's all right with her if you give me special permission. Do you mind, please, sir?"

The rocking began; the keys danced methodically under the manipulation of the pocketed right hand. Slowly the lower jaw protruded, and the semicircle of white teeth rimmed by unnatural bright pink slid forward and then backward with an audible snap. The principal's glance swung almost accidentally into fleeting contact with the boy's direct gaze and then slid smoothly out the window. The lower lip caressed and cleansed breakfast remnants with a little sucking sound. "Why do you want to take the course?"

The boy, having not the faintest notion what the course involved, was momentarily thwarted. He had long since learned, however, that an artful dissembler never shows indecision. Refusing to let his eyes flicker even momentarily, he quickly replied, "Because I want to be a doctor."

The keys were suddenly stilled; the gray, humped figure was motionless. Then he rocked upon one black shoe, and the lower plate plopped softly. "I had never thought economics was a requirement for the study of medicine," the principal intoned, "but from the attitude of a couple of the doctors in this town, it might be useful." He smiled fleetingly at some vision approximately two feet above the head of the boy. "That is a senior course, and you have two more years to work it in. There's no way I will give you special permission to take it this year."

"But, Mr. Gill," the boy implored, "I really do want to take it this year. It's terribly important to me. I'll work hard."

"No," the principal answered with finality. "The only way you could take that course would be for the County Board of Education to overrule me. You're too immature for senior economics, anyway." He turned to the desk and began shuffling papers, flexing his head backward so he could peer at them through his bifocals. The boy understood that he was dismissed.

As he walked disconsolately back toward the ninth grade homeroom, he realized suddenly that the Brewton County Board of Education was having its monthly meeting at this very moment in his father's office at the courthouse. Hope fired his imagination.

No, he thought, he'd never give me permission to go see them. Besides, I wouldn't have the guts to do it anyway. I never heard of any student appearing before the Board. I'd be scared to death. Besides, Mr. Gill would be as mad as an old wet hen. That old goat! I'll bet he knows the real reason I want to take five subjects, and he just won't let me. He's partial to the town kids anyway, and those girls are his pets and make over him so much because he's in their church.

He cast around in his mind for a suitable epithet. He was still too much under the influence of his mother to use real cuss words and too deeply in awe of the Decalog to take the Lord's name in vain.

"That old fart-buster," he murmured under his breath and felt immediately taller.

He stopped at the white porcelain water fountain mounted in permanent glory on the wall, as marvelous to the boy as the rock at Ramah must have been to Moses. Standing on tiptoe to reach the jet of water with his lips, he longed for the day when he would have to stoop to drink like everyone else in high school.

Suddenly he resolved, They can't do this to me. I'll die before I just sit back and take it.

Wiping his mouth on the back of his hand, he walked briskly into the classroom and approached Miss Hightower, who was still busily filling out index cards and arranging schedules. Widening his eyes in an effective imitation of innocence, he spoke in confiding and deferential tones. "Miss Hightower, Mr. Gill said I would have to go see the Board of Education to get permission to take your economics class. They're meeting at the courthouse now; so I'll have to hurry and get back before time for Mr. Gill to go to lunch."

Never before having been sandbagged by a Machiavelli, that uncomplicated mountain lass with a double major in Latin and history from the University of Georgia did not know she should fall to the floor, screaming and rending her clothes. She merely sighed and shook her head as the boy sped out of the building toward the courthouse square.

He went up the dusty street under the great oak trees, past the two-storied white frame houses with their wide verandahs. He marvelled again at these town folks who planted grass in their front yards and then bought special lawn mowers to trim them. Such opulence impressed him and made the bare, swept yards to which he was accustomed look austere.

He suddenly became aware of the audacity of the project upon which he was embarked. As individuals, the members of the Board of Education were not intimidating. They were local farmers and businessmen appointed by the Grand Jury in staggered terms to set policy for the administration of the county schools. His father, the elected County School Superintendent, then had the responsibility of enforcing their policies. The Board as a group, however, was formidable indeed. As a result of conversations overheard at home, the boy had formed an image of the Board of Education as a living, separate entity which became now an enemy to be defeated and now a compliant tool to be manipulated in the daily struggle of his domineering father to run the schools in his own fashion.

He faltered now and started to turn back to the schoolhouse. He didn't really have to take five subjects. He could probably win first honors even if he didn't. He thought of Mr. Gill and heard again his accusation of immaturity. He gritted his teeth and thought, I've got to try. I'll show that old pissant. Bowing his head as he scuffed his bare feet in the deliciously granular sand of the roadside ditch, he fervently entreated, "Oh, Lord, Thou knowest that I'm small and weak. Stand by me now in Thy majesty and might. Gird up my loins with Thy divine strength that I may smite them hip and thigh. Help me, Lord, I pray."

He paused and judiciously added a phrase to which the evangelist of last summer's revival had introduced him and which sounded impressively mollifying: "And I'll be very careful to give Thee all of the honor and glory and praise." He paused again and added the finishing touch to the magic incantation, "For I ask all these things in the name of Thy sweet and blessed Son, Jesus Christ. Amen."

Feeling immeasurably better, he scampered across the intersection between Rosenbloom's Store and Miss Roxie Huddleston's house and mounted the steep granite steps at the back of the courthouse. Holding his breath to diminish the stench from the men's rest room, he tiptoed down the cavernous hall with its eighteen-foot ceiling to the office door of the County School Superintendent. Pressing his ear against the solid heartpine door, he could hear the rumble of muffled male voices. They were in there all right. Courageously he knocked and heard his father shout, "Come in!" It was not an invitation but a command.

That gentleman, primed for his monthly session with the Board and arrayed impeccably in fresh white linen, was startled to see his small son swing the big door open but afforded him the same cordiality he would have extended to a real voter.

"Good morning, son. Just wait outside a few minutes. I'm busy with a very important meeting right now."

"Yessir, I know that. That's why I'm here. You see, I have to talk to the Board of Education," the boy managed to stammer in reply.

Concealing his surprise, consummate politician to the bone, his father immediately became very formal. "Well, we're always glad to have one of our students at a Board meeting. These gentlemen are certainly interested in the welfare of every school-boy and girl in the county. I believe you know all of them: Mr. Stancil from Winship, our chairman; Mr. Lawson from Dempsey; Mr. Melton from Helman Station; Mr. Gooch from Montclair; and Mr. Burkes from Black Rock. Gentlemen, this is my son, a member of the ninth grade class just starting this morning. I have no idea why he wants to address you, but with your indulgence, we'll interrupt our agenda to hear him and let him get on back to school. Go ahead, young man; the floor is yours."

Thrust into the relative comfort of ritual, the boy began to feel better. Solemnly he went around the room and shook hands with each of the five Board members. They were all dressed in their Sunday suits for this meeting, thereby underscoring the importance of it in the scheme of things. All the suits were black except that of Mr. Gooch, who was the youngest member of the Board and was dressed nattily in gray plaid with a dark maroon tie. He was also the only member of the Board who did not farm. He quietly failed in all economic endeavors and was currently floundering very affably in an unsuccessful general merchandise emporium in his section of the county. He sat on the Board by virtue of his family connections and was known to be an ardent champion of Mr. Gill. The boy pulled this bit of information quickly to the surface of his mind as he went around the room.

He decided that Mr. Stancil, the chairman, looked the most dressed up of any of the members, although he was the only one there without a necktie. He had on a shiny black suit and a white shirt buttoned at the collar, and he gave the impression that he really felt dressed up. He had many children who worked on the family farm and who were personally aware of the social stigmata in high school of being from the country. When the boy shook his hand, Mr. Stancil smiled in such a patronizing and indulgent manner that for an instant the boy feared he would be patted on the head and offered a nickel for an ice cream cone.

"Gentlemen," he earnestly began, "thank you for this audience on such short notice." He thought of Mrs. Parker and forced his hands to hang relaxed at his sides. "This is a personal problem that I bring before you, but one that may in the future affect other students. I have a vacancy in my schedule that can be filled only by taking economics. This would give me five subjects instead of four, but I know I can handle the load. I did it last year.

"The problem is that economics is a senior subject and I'm just a sophomore. The principal says that it's against policy to let a sophomore take a senior subject, but that if it's all right with the Board of Education, he'll give me special permission." He paused, widened his eyes, and glanced at Mr. Gooch. "He doesn't want to do anything contrary to the Board of Education, but he says that if I'm going to be a doctor I'll surely need economics."

He shifted his eyes to Mr. Stancil. "He thinks that as a country boy I may not be mature enough for the subject, but if you gentlemen will give me the permission I need, I promise to work hard and not let you down."

Before he could go any further, Mr. Stancil let his chair down with a thump. "I've done heered all I want to hear," he affirmed. "Any of you men see how come this boy shouldn't take whatever that subject is?" Responding to the unanimous shaking of heads, he turned to the County School Superintendent. "Tell ole Gill to let him take it."

"Please, sir," ventured the boy, "could I have a note to take back to Mr. Gill? I'm sure he wants it for his records."

"Ain't no problem," allowed Mr. Stancil. "Fix him one on the typewriter and I'll sign it," he directed the superintendent.

Inserting a sheet of official stationery with the Board's letterhead into the huge, square Underwood typewriter, the boy's father, with two sure and rapid fingers, soon produced a document which he read aloud.

> Mr. Joseph Gill,
> Principal Brewton County High School,
> Brewtonton, Georgia.
>
> Dear Sir:
>
> It is the unanimous wish of this body that Porter Osborne, Jr., be enrolled for this academic year in the economics class. We understand that this is normally a subject for eleventh grade students, but it is our desire that he be allowed to take it in his ninth grade year.
>
> > Sincerely yours,
> >
> > T. N. Stancil, Chairman,
> > Brewton County Board of Education

Beneath Mr. Stancil's name were listed the names of the other four Board members. Fascinated by the various approaches to signing it, the boy watched as the document was passed from one to the other until all the men had either laboriously drawn or flourishingly scrawled their names. Mr. Stancil signed it last, twisting his mouth in earnest concentration while he painstakingly constructed his signature. Finally, he handed it to the boy. "There you are. Now show 'em what a country boy can do," he admonished benignly.

"Yessir, I will. Thank you, gentlemen, very much," the boy replied.

As the door closed behind him, he searched the hall carefully. It was empty. Quickly he dropped to one knee. "Thank You, God," he breathed exultantly. "To Thee be all honor and glory and praise."

When he entered Mr. Gill's office and proffered his authority for special privilege, that gentleman clamped his lower plate in rigid security, and even the top of his bald head flushed bright pink. He read the note a second time and looked up from his desk. "Who gave you permission to go to town?" he demanded.

"Why, Miss Hightower did," the boy answered. "At least, she didn't tell me not to go when I told her that I had to see the Board of Education. The Board doesn't meet but once a month, Mr. Gill, and if I was going to take that course, I had to go today. Don't you see?"

"Yes," the principal snapped, "I see. At least I think I'm beginning to see. I may not believe all I'm seeing, but I am beginning to get glimpses here and there, young man."

His closely shaven jowls turned a dusky purple. "Let me tell you something. You haven't done anything yet I can whip you for, but I'm seeing to it that you get an F in deportment for this month."

He paused and then abandoned all pretense at judicial detachment. He glared straight at the boy, right into his eyes. The boy thought that Mr. Gill's eyes were as red as a terrapin's when you finally got a good look at them.

"Let me tell you another thing," the principal snarled. "There's no way you're going to pass that course. Smart as you are, it's way over your head, and you'll flunk it for sure."

He drew a deep breath and abandoned his reserve completely. "I'm going to instruct your teacher that you are to sit in that class and not participate. You'll receive a grade on your written tests but you are to ask no questions in that class. She's too busy with seniors to wet-nurse a ninth grader. And you'll get no help from her. Is that perfectly clear?"

Of a sudden the boy thought of another of the old-timers' tales that he thought fraught with significance. He had overheard his father and a crony guffawing about old man John Cox's being carried to Atlanta on the train by one of the boy's uncles, who was described by the mother as "incorrigible." Old man Cox had spent all of his fifty years in the backwoods of Brewton County and was fiercely self-assured and independent.

The uncle had enjoyed showing him the sights of the big city, and as a special treat had carried him to a whorehouse on Whitehall Street. The uncle swore that he heard through the thin partitions of the cubicles everything that went on. Old man Cox had procured a woman with pride in her work who began a series of cooperative pelvic thrusts and twists. His primitive manhood outraged by such a demonstration of modern day female decadence, he growled at her, "Jes let it lay there, 'y God! I'll git it."

Now, standing before the indignant and quivering principal, the boy dropped his eyes and did his best to look cowed. He forced a tremor into his voice as he respectfully replied, "Yessir." Then he raised his eyes and looked squarely into the principal's face. When the man could stand the confrontation no longer and swung his eyes toward the ceiling, the boy thought silently but emphatically, Jes let it lay there, 'y God! I'll git it.

That afternoon, in the kitchen, his mother inquired, "How did the first day of school go for you, son?"

"Just fine, Mother, just fine." He reached up to get his milking stewer from the wall. "Mr. Gill is going to let me take economics with the seniors. Miss Hightower is the teacher."

"Why, that's wonderful, son," the mother exclaimed. "That's quite an honor, isn't it?"

"Yes'm, I suspect it is," the boy responded as he headed toward the barn. "I wouldn't be at all surprised to find out it is."

After supper that night the children gathered with the mother in the living room for the evening worship service. This was a daily ritual begun some two years earlier by the mother after a revival in the Peabody Church. The fervent, unmarried young evangelist who led the meetings advocated daily Bible readings and prayer as a guaranteed formula for raising children in the way of the Lord. The middle sister played the customary hymn, and everyone sang the familiar words:

> Day is dying in the west,
> Heav'n is touching earth with rest.
> Wait and worship while the night
> Sets her evening lamps alight
> Through all the sky.

As the chorus began,

> Holy, holy, holy, Lord God of Hosts,
> Heaven and earth are full of Thee,

the boy felt a sweet sense of peace and gratitude fill him. The mother then read from the Scriptures.

The boy paid closer attention than usual tonight as she read the admonition of Jesus to pray for one's enemies and those who despitefully use us. When silent prayer began and the boy was on his knees with his face buried in the musty-smelling mohair of the davenport, he added another small equation to his formula for success. Oh, Lord, he prayed silently in his heart, bless Mr. Gill, I beseech Thee. And forgive Thy humble servant for calling him a fart-buster.

That night he was awakened by his father talking in the adjoining bedroom. This happened frequently, and he had long since learned to lie quietly and feign continued sleep. In this manner he was wont to gather fascinating information to which he would not otherwise be privy. In addition, it was part of his educational process.

Tonight he heard the father say, with great good humor, "Vera, I wish you could have seen him. He acted like he was accustomed to petitioning groups every day. He'll make one helluva lawyer if he keeps on. It didn't make that prissy old Joe Gill look very good, either. Even Gooch wasn't taking up for him today. Maybe I can get rid of Gill next year. I tell you, that boy's all right. He may be built like a frail little ten-year-old, but he's got the heart of a lion."

The boy snuggled into his pillow, fulfilled and complete. He thought of something his grandfather had told him one time: "It ain't the dog in the fight, boy. It's the fight in the dog." Smiling, he thought, It's going to be a good year. He went back to sleep.

The academic hurdles in the ninth grade were more easily conquered than the personal ones. In one year's time the boy had been transformed from being painfully shy into being the crassest of extroverts, at least on the surface. He had such a quivering capacity for emotional pain that he would have been reduced to a moaning, pulsating raw blob if he had not developed a protective scab. He did this with laughter.

Fearing ridicule, he burlesqued and exaggerated the ridiculous. He expended so much effort hiding his real feelings that he became a master of the automatic quick quip and the double entendre. Dreading the snickers from his blind side, he protectively manipulated laughter with an expertly crafted phrase or twist of speech. He deliberately built an image of himself among his peers as a swaggering, irrepressible smart-aleck who was cynical and flippant and would hesitate at nothing to produce a laugh.

He had his fellow ninth graders well trained, and he coasted on his reputation with them. Taking economics with the seniors, however, filled him with misgivings and made him uncomfortable.

In addition to fearing the derision or disapproval of these older students, he entered the class under the warning from Mr. Gill. He sat dutifully in class for a week and neither spoke to anyone himself nor was paid the slightest attention by the teacher.

Miss Hightower gave written tests at the end of each week's work. On the first test the boy made 100. He made a point of showing his paper to Mr. Gill, who did not seem either impressed or particularly happy. The boy studied even harder. The second test was more difficult. The boy made 100, which was the only one made in the class. Six of the seniors flunked.

When he showed this paper to Mr. Gill, that worthy ran his entire tongue under his bottom denture so that it sat sideways in his mouth for a moment and the principal looked as though his jaw were broken. An eighth grade girl, waiting to get a bus permit signed, gave a little involuntary shriek of dismay at the dry rattling noise when Mr. Gill settled it back into place.

"You don't have to bring your paper in here every week and show me, boy," the principal snapped. "I've got better things to do than check exam papers. There are right at two hundred students in this high school and if I had to see each one of them every time they took an examination, I'd never get anything else done."

"Oh, Mr. Gill," breathed the boy, "I hadn't thought of that. You're exactly right, and I won't bring any more to show you. It was just that I knew you had been worried that I might flunk the course, and it's beginning to look like I won't." He resisted the impulse to add, "Don't you see?"

He had carefully analyzed the indicators for corporal punishment and always tried to stay well short of the extreme debasement of getting a whipping. He felt that Mr. Gill's nerves were getting a little frayed, however, and that he might do something erratic. It might be a good idea to avoid him for a while.

Miss Hightower, however, had to be seen every day. Good and conscientious teacher that she was, she was not able very long to comply with Mr. Gill's order to ostracize the boy from class participation. The break occurred the third week in class when she asked for a definition of "entrepreneur." None of the seniors had read the lesson, and the boy timidly raised his hand. She scowled in obvious inner conflict and then granted him permission to recite. From that day he led the class.

There was not one of his senior classmates taking the course for any personal reason, and not one was fired with any particular ambition to excel. The boy soon learned that he could make them laugh as quickly as his own classmates.

By the end of six weeks he had them so conditioned that a sigh, a shrug of the shoulders, or a rolling of his eyes at appropriate times in class would send them into spasms of tittering. This began when the teacher was standing by his desk trying in vain to reach a high window to push it open.

She turned and said, "Porter, do you have a long pole?"

His instantaneous answer flashed back, "Not yet, ma'am. Ask me next year."

As he sat wide eyed and innocent in his desk, Miss Hightower's furious efforts to restore order in the classroom afforded him a sweet sense of mastery. She may have given him F in conduct on his first report card at the direction of Mr. Gill, but he richly earned the rest of them. At the end of the year he had F for every month in deportment and A in every subject except economics. He expended extra effort on that course and had A-plus every month.

By Christmas Miss Hightower had developed a twitch at the edge of her right eyebrow. In addition, she was observed to scowl and snap her fingers even while eating her lunch all alone. By Valentine's Day she had started using nail polish, and by Easter she had taken up lipstick and begun having dates with the driver of the oil truck. The next year she moved to Atlanta and got a job working in a bank. This was a pity, for she was a good teacher.

XII

in February Sally Fitzgerald's mother died. She died in childbirth while having her eighth baby for Lewis Fitzgerald. Sally was in the boy's grade, having transferred to the high school in Brewtonton after finishing the seventh grade at Black Rock. She was probably the shyest girl in the class and, even in those days of universal poverty, most likely the poorest. She was certainly the saddest. Even when she smiled, it was a manifestation of melancholy. In the ninth grade she walked in a slump with her shoulders folded forward to deny the presence of her burgeoning breasts.

Lewis Fitzgerald was the worn-out, watered-down tail end of a once proud and prosperous clan. He still clung to fifty acres of family land that had been handed down in ever-diminishing portions for four generations. He made a halfhearted effort to farm it, but one could tell by looking at him that Lewis Fitzgerald knew he would never make it. He was so tall and thin that he looked as if he were walking on stilts.

The boy's grandfather said he couldn't plow worth a damn because he was forever stopping to light his pipe. He never swore, never raised his voice, and when he smiled it was with a sad and patronizing air as though he knew something that his fellows had not yet discovered. He puffed his pipe and looked wise when confronted with problems. Then he waited for them to go away. On a Saturday afternoon, settling onto a nail keg on the porch of a country store, he bent and crossed the long sticks of his arms and legs for all the world like a carpenter folding his rule. The boy thought that if a praying mantis wore black pants, it would look exactly like Mr. Lewis Fitzgerald.

His wife was a rosy-faced, smiling, pretty woman who carried her head and acted like somebody. She herded her brood into church every Sunday, all of them scrubbed and dressed in clean clothes. Everyone tried not to identify the previous wearers of the clothes. It was all right to wear hand-me-downs from sisters, brothers, or cousins, but beyond that charity became involved. When people one knew acknowledged the need for charity, it was an embarrassment.

Everyone wished that Lewis Fitzgerald would do better, but he was such an agreeable, affable fellow, was so kind to his children, and evoked such warm memories of his respected father and grandfather that no one had the heart to berate him. They just sighed whenever they thought about him. Everyone sighed with the same sense of realistic despair when they thought about the sad-looking children.

The boy had privately labeled them "the Clan of Gloom." He fancied Mrs. Fitzgerald as a captive princess who had fallen in love with a frog. She spent all her time walking through a foggy land trying to make the sunshine of her smile bring light to the resigned faces of the great Clan of Gloom and stifle their sighs.

When the boy heard at school that she was dead, he was not startled. Death was commonplace in the county and evoked more curiosity in him than grief. No one in his own family had died yet, and he rather enjoyed the community excitement of someone passing on. This always signaled a halt in normal routine for a couple of days while the necessary formalities were observed. Caste and wealth and community standing were nowhere so sharply delineated as they were in the presence of death. The first question to be settled in that Baptist land was whether or not the victim was "ready to go." The boy had learned that this involved not willingness on the part of the participant but the ubiquitous, all-important question: "Is he saved?"

He had long since learned that the answer could be found

by merely watching his aunt. Warm tears and a frequently applied handkerchief foretold that the departed was on the other side, better off, or with Jesus. A ramrod spine, rolling eyes, and tightly clamped lips assured the unspeakable tortures of Hell and also intimated that they were justly deserved.

Of only slightly less community interest than the spiritual condition of a deceased member was how much money the funeral cost. It was rare to find a family so poverty stricken that they could not manage somehow to pay an undertaker for embalming, which was required by state law. These unfortunates were assisted by public funds, and it was much more degrading to have the county bury you than to have lived out your last days at the Poor Farm. Families usually were able to borrow enough money for at least a simple funeral and a tawdry coffin with a sleazy lining. The community accepted an expensive coffin and the decision to use a vault as a manifestation of family devotion rather than as a tribute to the practiced salesmanship of the undertaker.

The boy was too unsophisticated to tell the difference between solid copper and plain wood covered with cheap velour. He thought all corpses looked impressively grand, lying waxen and still beneath plate glass, hands folded on chest, cheeks rouged, and a frosting of powder in their eyelashes. He had never seen a dead human until the embalmers had finished, and these professionals could make death in Georgia seem as remote as the tomb of the Plantagenets and just as dignified.

The supreme compliment for an undertaker was for the community ladies to murmur behind their handkerchiefs, "Doesn't he look natural," or "She's just beautiful," or "It looks like he's sleeping. It wouldn't surprise me if he opened his eyes and spoke to me." The boy, a veteran of many funerals, had discovered long ago that grown folks did a heap of lying when someone died. He assumed that this was part of the ritual.

The choice of pallbearers was another indication of a person's community standing. Only close friends were asked to officiate in this capacity, and it was an honor not to be refused or taken lightly. The boy had noticed, however, that frequently a man's closest friends in life were overlooked at his death, and men were selected by the family because of prominence or wealth. He had never seen a man's Saturday-night drinking or whore-hopping buddy chosen as a pallbearer. These cronies might show up at the house for the sitting-up the night before the funeral, but they were always uncharacteristically subdued and obviously uncomfortable. In the uncompromising presence of death in this community, there was absolutely no doubt, even among the Methodists, that Jesus was Baptist to the bone.

When Mrs. Fitzgerald died, Sally's classmates were told of the tragedy when her school bus arrived without her, and it was announced that the funeral would be the following afternoon. Mattie Mae Simpson and Elsie Stinchcomb asked all the class members who had any flowers blooming in their yards to bring them the next morning. There was no need to ask for money. No one had any, at least not for anything as transient as flowers for a funeral.

There was something universally compelling about the thought of Sally Fitzgerald's sad face. It was almost as though she had been foreseeing the funeral of her mother for years. It was uncomfortable to begin pondering that someone who had so little now had so much less. Even the rough boys remembered to bring flowers. There were large bunches and small bunches of yellow jonquils, paper narcissus, and heavy-headed butter-and-eggs. There were sprangling lacy handfuls of little Roman hyacinths, both white and purple. The long wooden sewing table in the home economics room was almost covered with flowers that bloom in February. There were even a few branches of flowering quince.

Mattie Mae and Elsie solicited help and fashioned a wreath by sewing the bunches of flowers to a stiff pasteboard circle. When they were finished and had attached a salvaged silver bow at the top, the boy thought it the most beautiful floral offering he had ever seen. It must have weighed twenty-five pounds.

Summerfield Hammond had borrowed his father's car for the day, and he and the boy carefully carried the ninth grade wreath from the schoolhouse and laid it across the laps of Mattie

Mae and Elsie in the back seat. The boy rode in front with Summerfield for the five-mile trek over rutted muddy roads to Mrs. Fitzgerald's church.

The conversation was all about Sally. The girls assumed that they knew her better than anyone else because they took home economics together. They were careful to mention how smart she was in her books, how sweet she was to everyone, and how clean and neat she was. The boy finally relaxed when he realized they knew her only at school. For some reason he very fiercely desired that they not know about the hand-me-down clothes and Mr. Lewis Fitzgerald's farming.

He noted that they were careful to avoid any mention of the cause of Mrs. Fitzgerald's death. Discussion of any part of human reproduction was forbidden when both sexes were present—this was a very strict taboo. The boy had learned about menstruation only the year before from overhearing the boys under the cedar tree at lunch time. He had learned that every time the moon came full girls behaved strangely and that accumulated poisons came pouring from them in an uncontrollable bloody ooze that necessitated a condition called "wearing the rag." A boy could always tell when this was happening to a girl because she had dark circles under her eyes and smelled like fish.

He was too timid to ask questions about this horrifying condition and remained in a state of confused skepticism. He was also confused about how a woman bled to death having a baby. Childbirth was too sacred a subject for even the cedar tree experts to discuss, and no one ever dared broach the subject at home. He thought for a moment of asking Mattie Mae and Elsie for particulars about Mrs. Fitzgerald but could not bring himself to such boldness.

The church was almost full when they arrived. Groups of men, uncomfortable in their Sunday clothes, cluttered the yard in muted solemnity, smoking cigarettes and conversing sporadically in controlled rumbles. Inside, the women sat in silence, the creaking of a bench or hollow bump of a shoe on the uncarpeted floor accenting their movement to survey new arrivals. The first four benches in the center were gapingly empty, waiting for the arrival of the family. Around the pulpit were arranged the floral offerings, space obviously reserved in their midst for the arrival of the casket.

This waiting space, coupled with the silent patience of the waiting women, created a feeling of anticipation that had a little of the carnival in it. The undertaker's wife was at the front of the church, busily arranging and rearranging the flowers and standing back from time to time, head bent from one side to the other, to appraise her handiwork.

Summerfield and the boy carried the heavy, homemade wreath down the aisle to her, and she had them prop it on the dais in an easily visible spot, giving each boy a sad, sweet smile and a little squeeze on the shoulder.

She was a woman in her middle forties, heavily corseted and painted in denial of her age. She was an outsider, born and raised in Atlanta, and she could charm everybody in town, but she would never really belong. She had not been born in the county and consequently was always a little suspect, even though she transferred her membership in the UDC when she came to Brewtonton.

She had married Mr. Billy Boy Carruthers just at the end of the World War and had been busy trying to make something out of him ever since. He was the only child of Mr. and Mrs. William Boyd Carruthers, Jr., and it had never entered his head that this exalted position was not the ultimate goal of existence. His folks had a lot of money, but nobody in the family had ever been further than high school. They sent Billy Boy to college after college, until finally he met his wife at a fraternity party and they came home from a midnight sortie to Alabama with an empty gas tank and a marriage certificate—but without a diploma.

Her in-laws set her husband up in the undertaking business. Since there were four other undertakers in the county and he had no other occupation, Mr. Billy Boy spent a large part of his time idly visiting from one business to another, waiting for someone to summon him. His wife insisted that he wear a suit and tie every time he left home, which should have made him look impressive. In rebellion against this sartorial subservience, however, he refused to shave but twice a week, an incongruity which made him look ridiculous.

Whenever he swallowed, Billy Boy crossed his eyes, and he swallowed a lot during his blustering conversations around town. He consequently belched a lot, too, but the boy had noted that he did not cross his eyes for that function. It was said that the only reason anybody ever used him for a funeral was that they owed his father either money or a political favor.

Once in Mr. Arthur Masters' barber shop, inconspicuous behind the puffy, dog-eared *Collier's,* the boy had been witness to an exchange that fascinated him ever after. Standard Williams was waiting patiently for his turn in the chair when Mr. Billy Boy Carruthers walked in. Standard was a day laborer who had been too slow to go beyond the seventh grade, but he was well-regarded in the community because of his geniality.

"Standard! What in Sam Hill you doin in town today? I heard you just got married last weekend."

"Yessir, Mr. Billy Boy," responded the youth, "that's right. But my wife said I had to get a haircut today."

"Well, Standard, that's fine, that's fine. Always do what your wife says and you'll be a big success in life. Where did you go on your honeymoon?"

"We didn't go nowhere but home, Mr. Billy Boy. You know we po folks."

"Well, boy, that ain't what counts no how," the undertaker rumbled. He looked at Mr. Arthur Masters, winked, and belched.

"Tell me, Standard, how many times did you do it on the first night?" he asked, crossing his eyes and swallowing.

When Standard turned red and refused to answer, Mr. Billy Boy pursued.

"Aw, come on, Standard, everbody in here just about is married. We all know bout it. How many times did you get it that first night?"

The youth lowered his head and under the pressure of universal attention muttered, "Oncet."

"Oncet?" his tormentor yelled incredulously. "You eighteen years old and you only done it oncet? Why, good Godamighty, boy. Heapa these men here done it eight, ten times they first night. Hell, I was nearly twenty-five when I got married and I done it six or seven! I say 'oncet'!"

Standard raised his head and with all the courtesy in the world replied, "Yessir, Mr. Billy Boy, but you got to understand my wife wadn't use to it."

As Mr. Billy Boy Carruthers precipitously left, propelled by the explosion of delighted laughter, Mr. Arthur Masters picked up his cigarette holder and gave Mr. Boss Chapman an exaggerated wink.

When the laughter subsided Mr. Boss Chapman removed the stump of cigar from his mouth and growled in a comforting tone, "'Y golly, Standard, don't pay no attention to ole Billy Boy. 'Y golly, it ain't been two weeks since I heard him say he hadn't got none in six months. In fact, 'y golly, he said if it ever did git hard again he had a good notion to embalm the goddam thing."

Over the resurgence of laughter he looked at Mr. Arthur Masters and winked.

The boy confided to his magazine, "If I didn't know I was in Brewtonton, I'd think I was dreaming."

At Mrs. Fitzgerald's funeral, as Mrs. Carruthers squeezed the boy's shoulder and directed him with a whisper to the bench where the two girls were sitting, he thought what a nice lady she was.

When he sat down by Mattie Mae, he lowered his eyes reverently while everyone waited for the family and the body. He noted Mattie Mae's legs, fat and hairy, with marbled red lacework across the shins, denoting too much time spent standing close to an open fire. He thought them the ugliest legs he had ever seen and for once was glad that he was too little for anyone to think he was sitting by his girlfriend. About this time all the men shuffled into the church and climbed awkwardly over knees of neighbors to sit by their wives. He knew by this that the hearse was drawing slowly into the churchyard, followed by the crawling caravan of cars full of mourning family.

Mr. Billy Boy Carruthers walked slowly to the front of the church, his respirations wheezingly audible, but his face fresh-shaven. He swallowed, crossed his eyes, and said in an overly reverent tone, "Please rise." The boy looked studiously at Mr. Billy Boy's crotch. I don't believe he's had a chance to embalm it yet, he thought.

The undertaker's helpers rolled the heavy, swaying coffin down the aisle, the grieving family followed closely behind, and the friends filling the church clattered awkwardly to their feet. The boy noted that most of the men stared straight ahead, but the women followed the progress down the aisle. When everyone was seated again, he looked sidelong at the coffin. It stood open at the front of the church, nestled into the space Mrs. Carruthers had left for it. Mr. Lewis Fitzgerald and his seven children sat on the front bench almost able to touch the coffin. They all had swollen eyes, but no one was audibly weeping. The boy was relieved to see that they had not brought the new baby.

He looked at Sally. Sitting beside her older brother, she had an arm stretched protectingly over the shoulders of her two little sisters. Her face looked as though everything about it had melted and run forlornly downward. If it had started falling in blobs onto the floor, the illusion would have been complete. The boy thought that she looked as though she had never smiled before and certainly never would smile in the future. He felt a lump in his throat and tears freshen behind his eyelids. He tried desperately not to sniff.

The piano sounded a tin-pan chord, and there was a rustle behind the flowers on the left side of the church. His mother's sweet soprano, clear and unfaltering, floated across the church:

> There's a land beyond the river,
> That they call the sweet forever, . . .

The tears increased. He sniffled audibly. He looked at Mattie Mae's legs again. I'm glad they requested that song, he thought. Her voice is just right for it. That ought to impress Mattie Mae and Summerfield and Elsie. Bet their mothers can't sing in church. I'm sitting pretty close to Mattie Mae and I don't smell any fish. Excuse me, Lord, Satan got in my heart for a minute. It seemed he could never control his thoughts in church. He forced himself back to his surroundings.

> In that far-off sweet forever,
> Just beyond the shining river
> When they ring the golden bells for you and me.

There was another rustle among the banked flowers. As his mother sat down, the preacher arose.

"Dearly beloved," he intoned, "we are gathered here for a sad, yet a sweet, occasion. Look at this dear family in your midst. Behold the bereaved husband, look you at the sweet children weeping for their departed mother. It breaks your heart, doesn't it?"

Audience response was immediate. Everyone sniffled or blew a nose. There was an occasional audible sob across the house. One of Sally's little sisters and two of the smaller brothers began wailing. An older brother, whose voice had changed, was leaning against the father, and both were sobbing. The boy stole a glance at Sally. She was leaning over one of the sisters with comforting little pats. Her face was wounded, but her eyes were dry. The boy wondered about the look he thought she flashed at the preacher.

That master of manipulation, inspired by the reception of his beginning, continued, "Everything seems lost, doesn't it, beloved? All seems dark and drear. Well, let me tell you there is One who is King of Sadness. He is the Conqueror of Death. Listen you to the words of Jee-sus now. 'In my Father's house are many mansions.' " The boy lowered his eyes in reverence, careful to focus on the knees of his knickers rather than on Mattie Mae's legs. The smell of the hyacinths mixed with the heavy fragrance of tuberoses filled the church. The tuberoses were in a storebought wreath at the head of the casket. It had a tulle streamer across it with "The Children" in big silver letters. It looked expensive.

Sally's got some real stuff to her, he thought. She's not falling for any of that nonsense. If she wants to cry, she's not going to let any old preacher make her do it just to show off to folks how good a speaker he is. Look at her. She's got to be plumb grown-up from now on. She'll have to cook for that whole crowd, and wash, and sweep, and make beds, and help with the yard work, and raise those little girls. Oh, Lord, don't ever let my mother die, please, Sir. And forgive me, Lord, but that preacher of Yours is a real ninny. He needs some attention. I know he means well, but he oughta do better than he's doing.

"Beloved," the preacher was declaring in a fervent whisper, "this dear family, these precious children, these lovely daughters, these stalwart sons, this. . ." he paused, "this goodly husband and father can be comforted and sustained in the sure knowledge that their loved one, their beautiful wife and mother, is in a far better place. She is happier than we are. She's better off than she's ever been in her life."

Was there a note of reproach there as he looked at Lewis Fitzgerald? "She is in the arms of Jee-sus. She is today in the Bosom of the Lamb. She is on that happy, golden shore, smiling at us, reaching out her arms to us. She is saying to each one of you, beloved, 'Believe on the Lord Jesus Christ and serve Him with all your heart, and when death comes for you, then it is assured that you will join me here in this happy land.' Listen to her, beloved. Listen before it is too late. Let us pray."

As they bowed their heads, the sharp small drops of winter rain rattled against the window at the end of his bench. The boy sighed. At least he dried the tears with that one, he thought as he followed Mattie Mae down the aisle to pay their respects with a last look at the corpse. This was a ritual that still embarrassed him. As a small child, burning with curiosity, he had wanted to examine each corpse in great detail at funeral time and for this had been crossly reprimanded by his mother. Later he learned that some children were afraid to go down front because that was a dead person. Now he felt a surge of genuine reverence and respect, but he could force only a swift look at the face of Mrs. Fitzgerald. It was smooth and waxen beneath the protecting glass, the skin translucent and whiter than he had ever seen. The lips and cheeks were rouged and there was some penciling in the eyebrows. The hair was fluffier than Mrs. Fitzgerald wore it, and she was clothed in a ready-made, storebought robe. She looked altogether beautiful, distant, and dead, dead, dead.

Mattie Mae, move your fat ass out from in front of this coffin, he silently implored. You've looked enough for six people, and you'll have everybody looking at us.

Settled back into the anonymity of his bench, he refused to look when Mr. Fitzgerald and the boys walked by the coffin, crying aloud and blowing their noses. When Sally came up to her mother's casket, however, he stared and gaped as fixedly as anyone in the congregation. For a moment she leaned over the glass. The boy, from his seat, could see just the tip of her mother's waxen nose against the white satin lining. Sally made no sound. Her lips moved silently a few times. Then, sad-faced and resigned, with shoulders sagging, she turned back to her pew. As she slid past her father, she laid one hand on his shoulder for a moment. Lewis Fitzgerald, with bowed head, gave another sob.

The boy, electrified, thought, Oh, God, what if there's nothing to it? What if there isn't anything after this? What if that thing in the coffin is just as dead as it looks? Just as dead as my dog that got run over last summer? This is what Tabitha means when she says somebody's gone to Stony Lonesome. I don't think she believes in Jesus any more than she does in Santa Claus. What if this is all there is? What if Jesus didn't rise up really? Why do people hurt like this if God really cares about us? What's going to become of Sally and all those others?

As he realized with a start where his thoughts had wandered, he squirmed and sat bolt upright on the hard wooden bench.

Oh, Lord, he breathed in fear, You really will have to forgive Your humble servant this time. All those other times have been little nit-picking sins. I really let Satan get plumb inside this time. Help me get him out and I won't ever think like that again.

Going down the church steps, he heard Cuddin Sadie say to Miz Loggins, "Didn't she look beautiful? Just like she was sleeping. And did you see that robe? It must have cost a fortune. I offered Lewis my navy blue silk for her, but he said no, he wanted to get her something nice and new. She sure looked pretty."

"She looked so natural," agreed Mrs. Loggins. "Jes like she might open her eyes any minute and speak to you. Them Carrutherses sure know what they're doing."

Cuddin Edgar turned to Mr. Loggins. "That was a fine casket, too. Lewis is bliged to have borrowed on that last fifty acres for this. It's fine but he'll never pay it back with what cotton brings now. The land'll be gone in three years."

"You're probably right," answered Mr. Loggins. He paused, looked around, and leaned a little closer to Cuddin Edgar. "What in the hell do the Carrutherses want with any more land? They own half the county now."

The rain mercifully paused, and the boy walked out to the graveyard to watch the coffin creaked into the ground and covered with red clay.

The following week, working with Kathleen McEachern on their debate speeches, he was still thinking of the Fitzgeralds. Kathleen was a senior girl, rawboned, brash, and loudspoken. She was also highly intelligent. The boy felt secure in having her as his partner. They had drawn the negative side of the debate question this year, and he felt she would be particularly good on rebuttals, with her quick wit and her cutting tongue. Like most of the older girls in the school, she was tolerant and benevolent toward the boy. He decided to ask her the unanswered question.

"It sure was good to see Sally Fitzgerald come back to school today," he casually began.

"Yes," Kathleen replied. "I was right relieved to see her, too.

I was afraid she might have to stay out and look after all that family. I bet she's having to work her head off to do all that work and get to school too. At least she doesn't have to look after that new baby. Her paw gave it away to a cousin that doesn't have any babies, I heard. She's well-fixed. Her husband has a good job and they live up above Atlanta. The woman even has a car of her own. Everything will be easier now, I expect."

"Maybe so," agreed the boy. "Kathleen, do you know exactly what killed Mrs. Fitzgerald?"

"Sure," responded the girl, shuffling through some index cards. "She hemorrhaged when that baby was born. Everyone knows that."

"That's what I heard," said the boy, "and I know that means she bled to death. Kathleen, I don't want you to think I'm getting fresh, but what makes a woman do that? I mean, where does it come from? What causes it?" he stammered.

"Well, for Pete's sake," Kathleen exclaimed. She put down the index cards. "She bled to death from her womb. The baby is carried in the womb, and when it comes out of there there's an afterbirth stuck to the womb, and if things don't go right a woman can bleed to death. You know what a womb is, don't you?"

The boy was totally shocked and embarrassed. The previous summer he had found the word while virtuously following a resolve to read the Bible from cover to cover. "And when the Lord saw that Leah was hated, he opened her womb; but Rachel was barren." This was followed by an awful lot of going in unto and lying with and conceiving. The boy could figure most of this out in fairly explicit detail, but he wanted to know, clinically and precisely, what a womb was and just exactly where it was situated.

Sexually excited, guilty because of the excitement, confused beyond description, he went to the big, unabridged dictionary.

"Womb: any cavity like a womb in containing and enveloping; the place where anything is generated or produced; uterus."

He was triumphant over discovering a new noun which might clear up all mystery. Feverishly and exultantly, his penis jumping like a snap beetle, he flipped the pages backward. At last he was going to have this question answered. Maybe it would even have a picture! He searched it out.

"Uterus: in female mammals, an organ for containing, and usually for nourishing, the young during the development previous to birth; the womb."

Disappointed over the dead end, frustrated because of his lack of enlightenment, the boy had finally succumbed to guilt over being sexually aroused. He felt that he was somehow depraved to be running from the Bible to the dictionary with a stiff pecker and finally decided that the Lord had seen fit to punish him for some unrecognized evil deed by rendering him oversexed but under-equipped. He had hidden these thoughts as one of his darkest secrets. Now this older girl, this brazen hulk of an Amazon, was matter-of-factly and loudly asking, "You know what a womb is, don't you?"

Thankful that she could not possibly have any knowledge of his investigative and erotic forays into Webster, he stammered, "Sure—sure, I know. It's a uterus."

Kathleen's jaw dropped. "Huh?" she said. "It's a what? Oh! Well, I declare—I wouldn't have thought—but then, you always have been ahead of yourself, haven't you? In books, I mean. I wonder where you learned that."

Uncomfortable at the prospect of answering her question, desperate to keep his own personal life out of the conversation, he flipped through the index cards and pretended intense absorption in a rebuttal point. He knew her well.

"About Mrs. Fitzgerald," Kathleen resumed, "the night she was having that baby, Mr. Fitzgerald walked into town to get a doctor. Dr. Brisford is the one they use, because you know he'll go any time and he doesn't gouge for money. He's a good old man. But he was in the hospital getting his rupture fixed. Dr. Philpot had gone to Alabama to his brother's funeral. That didn't leave anybody in town but Dr. Hunnicut. By the time Mr. Fitzgerald found out about all this, it was getting on toward nine or nine-thirty. He rang Dr. Hunnicut's doorbell at that grand house

181

he lives in, and anyhow my mama says that when Dr. Hunnicut came here he had to borrow money to buy even a kitchen table. He's made everything he's got offa these folks right here in Brewton County, and he's got plenty. Anyway, Mr. Fitzgerald got him out on the front porch, because Mrs. Hunnicut won't invite anybody in the house. She thinks she's better than anybody here, and besides she has a new rug. He told him that his wife was down, and could he come in a hurry. Dr. Hunnicut told him sure he could come but it would be twenty-five dollars cash—in advance—for a maternity call.

"Mr. Fitzgerald said, 'Doc, I ain't got twenty-five on me, but I'm good for it. You can ask any of my neighbors or anybody in that end of the county, but we need to be moving. My wife's took bad.' And you know what happened then? Dr. Hunnicut started back in the house. Mr. Fitzgerald grabbed the door and hollered, 'Wait a minute, Doc, you can't do me this way! I got a milk cow that's half Jersey, gives three gallons of milk a day easy. You can have her. I don't know what the children will do for milk, but you can have her. Just, for God's sake, come help my wife.' And you know what Dr. Hunnicut said then? He said, 'Well, you'll have to take me and bring me back. I got a new car and I don't like to take it out in the mud.' Can you imagine that?"

"No, I can't," replied the boy. "What did Mr. Fitzgerald do? He doesn't have a car."

"That's what he told Dr. Hunnicut," Kathleen agreed. "And Dr. Hunnicut said, 'Well, I'll drive out there, but that'll be five dollars extra for using my car.' And he went and got newspapers to put on the floorboard so Mr. Fitzgerald's feet wouldn't get his car muddy. Well, they drove on out to the Fitzgerald homeplace, and Mr. Fitzgerald was about to have a fit because he hadn't heard from his wife in at least two hours. So he jumped outa the car and started running for the house, hollering, 'Come on, Doc!' But Dr. Hunnicut said, 'Wait a minute! Where's that cow?' So Mr. Fitzgerald took him down to the barn, and Dr. Hunnicut shone his flashlight on that cow and made her stand up in the stable and looked at her bag, and then he said, 'Hell, that cow ain't worth twenty-five dollars.'

"And you know what he did then? He got back in his car and went home. He oughta be horsewhipped and hung. And poor old Mr. Fitzgerald ran in the house, and the baby was coming, and he cut through the woods to get an old colored granny woman. And when he got back, the baby was just born. The granny woman saved the little baby, but when the afterbirth came out, Mrs. Fitzgerald bled to death from her womb. They say it soaked through two mattresses and there was a big puddle of clots on the floor under the bed when Mr. Billy Boy Carruthers finally got there. It was terrible.

"Now," finished Kathleen, "you know."

As he gathered up his debate material, the bell rang for the end of the period. Walking down the hall, he was oblivious to the noisy push of fellow students. He thought of the molten sadness of Sally's face. I think I really will be a doctor, he vowed to himself. No fooling around this time. I really will be a doctor, and I'll come right back here to practice. He took another step. I'm still not sure what a womb is. I wonder what one looks like.

When he left the building, the sun was shining. The little frogs were peeping in the creek below the school. There was a faint thrill of early spring in the air. He thought of Cuddin Edgar and Mr. Loggins. "I wonder what in the hell the Carrutherses do want with all that land," he said aloud.

the literary meet that year was a maturing experience. Having won first place in Declamation in the District Meet the year before, the boy approached the competition this time with a new speech, the same suit of clothes, and the confidence of a proven winner. In addition, he was on the debate team and was the sole entrant in the Ready Writer's Essay contest. He had entered the contest at the request of the senior English teacher, who had been instructed by Mr. Gill that she had better have a contestant in that event or else.

She had approached the boy with a flip remark. She said that she had heard he knew a sentence should have both a subject and a predicate and could tell them apart. She assured him that any theme he had already written would be an acceptable local entry. She did not even read it. He figured he had fifteen points sewed up for three first places just on the local level. He figured without Summerfield Hammond.

Summerfield, in the ninth grade, was as big as he would ever get. In addition, his voice was as deep and mellifluous as any voice in the whole world. The boy had an urge to sing him a ditty he had overheard a lady singing to his father one night in the back of the drugstore when the peach brandy was flowing and the presence of the boy was temporarily forgotten.

> Oh, do your balls hang low?
> Do they swing to and fro?
> Can you tie 'em in a knot?

Can you tie 'em in a bow?
Can you throw 'em over your shoulder
Like a continental soldier?
Oh, do your balls hang low?

His natural timidity forbade his acknowledging the presence of balls on any human, however, and it was particularly
unthinkable to associate them with Summerfield. Summerfield
was set apart. He had already decided to be a preacher. He had
"dedicated his life to full-time Christian service." The boy
sometimes wondered if his motive was partly to avoid the local
growth experiences of smoking, drinking, and girls, but he never
expressed this. He was more curious about Summerfield having
received "the call," and on two occasions had mustered the
temerity to ask what he felt like when the call came. Everyone
knew that in order to be a real preacher, this inspiring transformation, sudden, irresistible, and overwhelming, was an imperative
prerequisite.

All his life the boy had listened to preachers discuss being
"called." The implication was that this was the ultimate in ecstatic
and exotic experiences, a one-to-one communion with the Almighty comparable to Moses' experience with the burning bush.
The boy could not remember the call ever coming from Jesus;
such a nerve-shattering, life-changing event came from the Lord
God of Hosts, Jehovah Himself.

It could not be denied. It made uninhibited sinners drop
whatever they were doing, mend their sinful ways, and immediately begin doing the will of the Master, it being understood that
from that day hence the will was disclosed fully and freely to the
heretofore deaf and blind initiate. The boy had noticed that it made
people preach even when they murdered the English language
and could barely stumble through the reading of a text. Once the
Big Call had come, the recipient was ever thereafter subject to
lesser calls. A preacher never decided to move to another church;
he got called to go. This announcement was always associated
with the use of the royal "we." The boy observed that the Lord

always called preachers to churches that paid more money or else away from congregations that were on the verge of flaying them alive, but he was not critical about this. He just assumed it was the Lord's way of caring personally for His royal servants. He had always been intensely curious about the calling phenomenon but lived in terror of having it visited on him personally. He hoped fervently that he would never attract the attention of the Lord for such an unexpected and cataclysmic visitation, and he identified frequently with Adam hiding in the Garden. He really fancied himself as more skilled than Adam. At least he had not been caught and cast out of Paradise yet. It never occurred to him that perhaps he had not entered it yet, either.

The first time he asked how it felt to get The Call, Summerfield turned red and stammered. When the boy persisted and inquired if it felt like a coal of fire on his tongue or if he saw things like pigeons flying around, Summerfield had muttered evasively as he turned his head to cough that things weren't like that any more. By the time the boy had gathered his courage a couple of weeks later to repeat the question, Summerfield was prepared and with impressively distant demeanor replied in pious tones, "I don't want to discuss it. It's too sacred." The boy was sophisticated enough to recognize another closed door.

Summerfield's religious dedication made him immediately aloof from his peers, and he was not challenged to wrestling or other contests requiring physical superiority. It was automatically assumed that he would not be involved in sports, and his piety was the excuse for this rather than his natural lack of interest. He dressed more immaculately than any of the other boys and, in those predeodorant days, always smelled of talcum powder. Any older boy who was obtuse enough to imply to Summerfield's peers that he was a sissy was quickly corrected and told that he had been called. The ninth grade was proud of him.

Once in the eighth grade a crowd of burly upperclassmen, in ribald glee, had cornered Summerfield and the boy with the avowed intention of taking down their pants and checking them out. This was in retribution for the scornful distance the pair maintained from the cedar tree oracle at lunch time. Recognizing the futility of struggle, the boy had quickly succumbed to the onslaught with little more than token squirming, laughing all the while as though he thought the torture funny. They cornered Summerfield, however, with an entirely different result.

Summerfield looked soft, white, and puffy fat, but when he got through bucking, slinging, and kicking, six juniors and four seniors had been flung in crumpled defeat across the playground, and Summerfield's belt buckle had not even been undone. The boy, unbelieving witness to this foray, was ever thereafter slightly in awe of him. It was shortly after this that Summerfield got the call. Miss Beauty Graves did not wait for the UDC meeting but proclaimed from her millinery station in Pike's Mercantile that he would certainly Go Far. Rooster Holcomb said that them upper-classmen would have had an easier time trying to put a pair of pants on a bull than taking a pair off that dressed-up sissy. That Rooster was a sight.

Summerfield may have lacked athletic competitiveness, but he was fiercely determined to excel in oratory. The boy had no idea how badly disappointed and humiliated Summerfield had been by Patrick Henry and Mrs. Parker the year before. For their combined virtues to have propelled the pint-sized, shrill-voiced country boy into the District championship had almost devastated Summerfield. Isolated and aloof, he had mentioned his disappointment to no one outside his family, but the following fall he had begun "taking" from a music teacher in Brewtonton who also had a diploma in elocution and always wore a white hair net over her carefully waved silver coiffure.

By mid-November he had already memorized his speech. By the first of the year he was letter perfect, his gestures were an integral part of the message, and he could recite it backward in his sleep.

The night of the contest the boy spoke first. With the assurance of a proven champion, he addressed the audience with a shortened version of one of Cordell Hull's campaign speeches. Calmly, without the least sensation of stage fright or twinge of embarrassment, he began and ended a sweetly reasoned plea for consideration of the plight of people living in East Tennessee. Graciously he bowed to the applause which greeted his final sentence and walked nonchalantly back to his chair. He had not even bothered to pray about tonight's contest. He was bored himself.

Summerfield had chosen an address of Theodore Roosevelt to the American Congress. In addition, he was resplendent in a double-breasted new suit with padded shoulders. For six minutes he used his voice like a finely tuned musical instrument. He soared, boomed, and trumpeted. He even had deep bass trills and tremolos. He whispered and he thundered. The boy sat spell-bound. There was no shadow of doubt in his mind that Summerfield was winning the Declamation contest hands down.

Well, he thought, there I go. I mean he's really going to town on that speech tonight. He even looks pretty good. I can smell the Vitalis from here. His expression teacher has really helped him a lot. But listen to his voice—he can slide into a question with it as smooth as a buzzard on a downdraft. You might as well get yourself ready to look like a good loser tonight. Don't forget to shake his hand and be sure and look him in the eyes when you do it. And act like you don't give a damn. Just wait until next year. I'll start early and I'll win next year for sure.

At this moment, Summerfield demanded in a deep smooth baritone, "Is this, then, to be the end of Western Civilization?"

Reality confronted the boy. Aw, hell, he told himself, you're not ever going to whip that boy until you get a voice on you. Oh, Lord, aren't You ever going to let me grow? You could at least let me have some nuts. But then I guess You know best—a deep voice in this frame would rattle it to pieces. It looks like I can't do anything right. Just when I find something I think I'm really good at, somebody comes along and takes even that away from me. It really isn't fair.

He was saved from any further indulgence in self-pity by the end of Summerfield's speech and the applause that followed. As they lined up to march off the stage, he went over to Summerfield and held out his hand.

"Summerfield, that was great," he said, as he gripped the soft hand firmly and looked him in the eye. "I know you won tonight, and I want to congratulate you before the decision is announced. You spoke like a true continental soldier."

As he turned to step back into line, he thought smugly, That'll drive him crazy. If he ever asks me what I meant, I'll tell him I don't want to discuss it—it's too sacred. He marched out of the auditorium smiling with his head held high. I'll still get three points for second place, he comforted himself.

A little later he lost all thought of himself and his defeat in Declamation. He was seated in the auditorium in the very front row, right in the middle of the grammar school relatives of the contestants in the Reading Contest. He had applauded politely for Kathleen McEachern as she rather stiffly presented Robert Frost's "Mending Wall." He liked this girl in spite of her brassy approach to people and applauded loudly as she finished with ". . .Good fences make good neighbors."

And that's sure the God's truth, he thought. I'm not going to let the cows over into my pine trees to find out how I'm feeling tonight.

He listened patiently and pityingly to Geraldine Turnipseed as she almost mumbled a poem centering around somebody named Luke Havergill. He clapped louder than before when she concluded. He felt she needed it. He soon became bored as an eighth grade girl shrilled, "Bowed by the weight of centuries, he stands . . ." and a ninth grade girl jerked her way through "Richard Cory."

The last contestant on the program was Marietta Marsen-gill, the senior girl who depended on him to help her with general science. In his eyes she was the epitome of culture, the final distilled essence of feminine sophistication, as lovely as a movie star, twice as poised, and just as unapproachable. Although none of the students had cars of their own, Marietta's father had so much money that he bought an extra Ford for himself. Marietta drove it all the time, and school gossip asserted that it was really hers.

She had dominated the stage all through the Girls' Reading contest, sitting quiet and queenly as the other girls spoke, her feet crossed at the ankles and her knees pressed together and turned sideways. As she rose and walked slowly and undulatingly to the front of the stage, the boy thought he had never seen anything quite so beautiful. Her dark hair, fashionably waved and set, her dark flashing eyes, her deeply reddened lips, contrasting with her white skin and white teeth, all contributed to render him straight-necked in his seat, open-mouthed with wheezing admiration.

Tonight she was even more spectacularly beautiful than usual. She had on a new dress for the occasion. Her father had so much money that she always had a new dress—another small item that made all the other girls envious of her. This dress was light blue, and the boy had been around his mother and sisters enough to know it was a material called "crepe." It had short sleeves and a collar that followed the low cut neckline in a frilly vee.

The neck was so low that it showed the line made by her two breasts being squeezed together. The boy had recently learned that this was a phenomenon called "cleavage." He noted with worshipful admiration that Marietta had a long, deep cleavage and that a considerable amount of it was on view. He wiped his nose with the back of a forefinger to keep from calling attention to himself by digging out a white handkerchief in the darkened auditorium.

As Marietta came to a halt near the front of the stage, almost directly above him, he took in the rest of the gown and the vision it adorned. It clung snugly to the flare of her ribs and the flat stomach beneath. There was just the hint of a darkened spot in the middle, the slightest shadow of an indentation, and the boy was sure this must be her navel. Since he had never heard anybody say anything against navels showing through an evening dress, he assumed that this was permissible, but there was something a little scandalizing and very exciting about it to him.

Her stance and the angle of the footlights accentuated the tight fall of the dress over her hips and pelvis. From where he sat the boy could see, just below and to one side of the elusive, shadowy navel, a perfect outline of the flaring bone that delineated the brim of her beautiful pelvis. He began to hear the blood swish in his ears with each heartbeat and felt guilty about looking. Nothing, however, could have stopped him. The rest of the dress was an expanse of blue mystery, stretching from that tantalizing hip bone to the floor.

She began to speak. Her voice was a hushed, smooth contralto, so modulated that one strained to hear every word but so controlled that one did not really need to strain. She projected every syllable with ease all the way to the back of the auditorium but did not sound excessively loud to the enthralled audience on the front row. Her voice was not all she projected. With every rolling phrase, she lowered her lids and moved her eyes. For emphasis she shifted her feet occasionally, causing blue ripples to dance before the boy's eyes and moving the compelling line of her hip bone in tantalizing shadow.

He concentrated on what she was reciting. It was new to him.

> O what can ail thee, knight-at-arms,
> Alone and palely loitering!
> The sedge has wither'd from the lake,
> And no birds sing.

What's sedge? he wondered quickly to himself. This sounds eerie—especially the way she's saying it. I wish she'd hold still so I can concentrate. No, I don't, Lord. I take that back.

> I see a lily on thy brow
> With anguish moist and fever dew,
> And on thy cheeks a fading rose
> Fast withereth too.

Lord, she's talking about me. That girl is wise. She can look right inside you. Spellbound, he was carried helplessly through the poem, drinking in every word, catching every nuance, submerged completely in erotic identification.

> I made a garland for her head,
> And bracelets too, and fragrant zone;
> She look'd at me as she did love,
> And made sweet moan.

The boy shifted in his seat. Can that mean what I think it means? he wondered. I mean this poem is getting red hot!

> She found me roots of relish sweet,
> And honey wild, and manna dew,
> And sure in language strange she said—
> "I love thee true."

Openmouthed as an imbecile, oblivious of person and place, he fantasized until the denouement:

> I saw pale kings and princes too,
> Pale warriors, death-pale were they all;
> They cried—"La Belle Dame sans Merci
> Hath thee in thrall!"

Bewildered by the chilly aftermath of the fascinating lady's identification, unwilling to accept the concluding two stanzas, he sat stockstill, too absorbed in his own thoughts even to clap when Marietta finished. His attention was jerked quickly back to the present, however, as she acknowledged the applause that rewarded her. She bowed from the waist so deeply that both breasts were visible in shadowy pendulance, moving like things alive behind the lightly veiling blue ruffle that also fell forward as she bowed. The boy recovered his thoughts and applauded ecstatically.

As the girls came off the stage, they clustered right at the end of the row where he was sitting. Marietta was nodding and smiling and waving like an opera star who had just overwhelmed the audience at La Scala and is relieved to relax. The boy sidled up to her. "Marietta," he blurted in adoration, "that was wonderful."

She turned her beautiful eyes downward. "Why, thank you," she said graciously.

Encouraged by her response, he added, "I can tell you pretty quick what ailed ole knight-at-arms. You got ahold of him in that blue dress, and he couldn't take it. That's the prettiest dress I ever saw."

Marietta threw back her head and laughed in an almost hoydenish manner. He was enthralled anew. She stopped laughing and gave him a calculating look. Then she said, in a speculative tone, "You keep on thinking and talking that way, and you gonna be something if you ever get any size on you."

The line of girls started to move. She patted his cheek. "Marietta," he asked, "what does 'La Belle Dame sans Merci' mean? I haven't had French yet."

"Law, boy, I don't know," she said over her shoulder as she gracefully picked up her skirt and started down the aisle. "I was so busy memorizing that old poem, I didn't take time to look up any French. I just learned it this week." She smiled in a dazzle of rolling black eyes and flashing white teeth.

Kathleen McEachern was right back of her. She bent over the boy and said in carrying tones, "I have had French, and it means 'Good-looking dame without one speck of gratitude.'" She looked him straight in the eyes. "And don't you ever forget it," she said. Marietta was busy holding her skirt, smiling, bowing, and waving. She gave no indication that she heard Kathleen.

When the awards were announced, the boy was still so enchanted that his pain at losing the Declamation contest was deadened. Leaving the auditorium, inconspicuous as usual in the jostling crowd, he overheard the two ladies just in front of him. "And did you see her carrying on when they clapped? Putting on airs in that blue dress like she was the Queen of England."

He identified her as Kathleen McEachern's mother. "It's the truth," her companion responded, and added loyally, "A body'd do better just to be theyself."

There was a pause, and Mrs. McEachern replied in a judicious tone, "I wouldn't be atall surprised if she was, Miz Bottoms. I wouldn't be atall surprised."

That night he also dreamed.

A pack of boys was chasing him. They were yelling, Take his pants off and check him out. In the forefront were Rooster Holcomb and Summerfield Hammond. He was running as fast as he could, screaming with terror, and Summerfield was reaching out to grab him, his face contorted in an evil grin. Suddenly he ran by a tree and his father was standing there. He slowly handed the boy the long sword that his great-grandfather had carried in the War between the States and said, Try this, son. Flourishing the sword above his head, he turned on his pursuers, and they all disappeared immediately except Summerfield. Summerfield reached out both hands to him. The boy swung the sword and slowly, softly, without the shock of a blow being felt, sliced through both Summerfield's arms. As his hands flopped on the ground like chickens with their necks wrung, Summerfield begged in a high falsetto screech, Don't kill me, please don't kill me, just listen to what you've done already. The boy raised the sword with both hands and suddenly Summerfield faded away. In his place stood the boy's mother dressed like the lady on a silver dollar, one shoulder bare. Smiling, she reached out an arm and said softly, Why don't you give me that? He mutely shook his head and held the sword behind his back, whereupon his mother smiled, stretched her other arm out to the side in a welcoming gesture and said, Well, maybe you'll give it to her. The boy faced around to the new arrival who was a tall statuesque woman with red gold hair. She was dressed in a toga which left one breast bare. As she stretched out both arms toward him in an unsmiling but infinitely welcoming gesture, the breast rose on her chest in a slow gliding motion. Compelled to respond, the boy held the sword in front of him across outstretched hands as though presenting a gift. As he took one step forward he recognized her and said reverently, You're Ceres aren't you, ma'am, the head goddess of the earth? The lady responded, Since you've asked I'll have to go, and changed immediately into Marietta Marsengill. Marietta stood and smiled at him. There was a difference in her smile, however. It was tremulous and respectful and suddenly he was taller than she. As she stood in a warm swirling mist, she slowly raised both arms and the blue dress parted smoothly right down the middle and dropped out of sight into the mist around her feet. The sword in his hands moved and became hot and he realized that it was really his penis. Marietta looked at him demurely and said in reverent tones, Do you have something for me? As he stepped toward her, her manner changed. She flashed a flirtatious smile, rolled her eyes, and grabbed the proffered penis with both hands. This is more like it, boy, she said. Why don't we just drop on down to my elfin grot and make a little sweet moan?

Lightning flashed through his loins, and he awoke to feel one irresistible shudder after another passing with inundating ecstasy through his penis. The boy lay for a moment in bewilderment and then exclaimed with surprise, "Hey, I've had one! I've had a wet dream!"

He reached down and felt himself. Everything was dry. I know that was the feeling, he thought in cedar tree terms. That had to be the feeling. But I didn't shoot off. What's going on? The boys at school all say that you have wet dreams because all that stuff backs up in you and has to come out, and Burford Dettwiler says he's never had a wet dream because he fucks Minnie Fingers too much. He'd rather do that than mess up the sheets and have his ma fuss at him. Those boys must not know as much as they all act like they do. I ain't even manufacturing any of that stuff, and now this has happened to me.

He drifted back into a restless sleep.

His mother came downstairs the next morning right after he had built the fire in the cook stove. "Good morning, son. Are you feeling good? I thought you did real well with your speech last night, and I'm terribly proud of you. Did you sleep well? I thought I heard you moaning and bumping the wall."

"I feel fine, Mother," he answered, noting with relief that she was garbed in a familiar faded pink dress. "I ate a piece of sausage just before I went to bed, and I suspect that made me restless." He picked up his hot water and milk buckets and headed for the barn.

What in the world is wrong with you? he said to himself. How did your mother get mixed up in that dream anyway? You can't even tell anybody about it. And what kind of freak are you anyhow? Have you had a dry wet dream—or what? As he pushed the cow in the leg to make her expose her tits better, he sighed.

"Sah in there, back your leg now! Oh, Lord, how I wish I had somebody to talk to."

The District Meet convened in LaGrange that year. The boy dutifully put on his suit and attended as a contestant in Ready Writer's Essay. There was no audience participation, no keen and exciting feel of combat. The contest was no fun. The ten students who were competing merely sat in an empty classroom and were given a list of five subjects from which they could pick a title.

Then they were given two hours to write their essays, while the LaGrange teachers supervising them wandered around in boredom and visited with everyone who happened down the hall.

The boy selected "The effect of proposed rural electrification on Georgia," wrote for one hour, corrected his essay, and copied it over for the sake of neatness. He was neither stimulated nor enthusiastic but dutifully tried to make a creditable effort for his school.

He left early and managed to get himself included in an automobile full of older students who were going to a restaurant downtown for lunch. One of the girls was Marietta Marsengill. She had spoken to him in an offhanded, preoccupied acknowledgment of his greeting and then became her captivating, flirtatious best with a couple of senior boys. She was apparently no longer aware of his existence. The boy, neverthless, felt that she had to be carefully watching his every move. How could he be so intensely aware of someone else sitting at the same table without that person reciprocating?

He studied the menu carefully. He wanted to order the fried chicken, but, of a sudden, he was concerned about table etiquette. At home they ate fried chicken with their fingers, but maybe Marietta and these town boys used a knife and fork. Since he handled a knife so clumsily, he decided against ordering even the country-fried steak—it might wind up on the vest of his suit. Intimidated, he decided on the twenty-five cent vegetable plate. There was no way he could go wrong with just a plain old fork, and besides he really liked vegetables. Anyone who had gone for days when the larder was low eating nothing but turnip greens and cornbread had learned to like almost anything.

He remembered his manners and unfolded his napkin into his lap. Across the table the darkhaired, handsome senior on Marietta's left sipped his water and never took his eyes off her. The curlyhaired, athletic senior on her right was behaving identically. She sat between them with a hand on the shoulder of each, laughing and talking and rolling her eyes. She turned her head first to one and then the other, leaning a little closer to the favored one but never losing her tactile control of the other.

The two boys never took their eyes off her, even when her head was turned the other way. The three were oblivious of anyone else being in the world and never acknowledged the presence of the other three girls and the boy at the table. These four made labored conversation, always conscious of the peals of laughter and the animated discourse between *la belle dame sans merci* and her two knights-at-arms.

The boy, absorbed in the display, jealous of the two older boys, had his first glimmering of doubt about the lovely Marietta. He thought back to a stanza she would be reading this afternoon:

> I set her on my pacing steed,
> And nothing else saw all day long.
> For sidelong would she bend, and sing
> A faery's song.

More realistically he thought, What's she doing carrying on over those two ballplayers like that? She's supposed to be dating Manley Goodlow and nobody else. I'm glad she doesn't know I dream about her. Afraid to pursue that memory any further, he turned to the girl on his left.

"Are you nervous about your music piece tonight?" he inquired politely. "I know you're going to do a good job. We'll all be out there pulling for you."

About this time the waitress came to the table for their order. She was an older woman, at least twenty-five, and moved with the deliberation and patience of one who had worked long enough with the public to expect anything and to express surprise at nothing. Her uniform had been fresh three days before and had never been big enough for her. She was so fat that when she stopped walking it was several seconds before her buttocks settled down.

The boy tried not to look at them as he ordered the vegetable plate and iced tea. She took the orders of the other girls and moved on to stand behind Marietta and the two ballplayers. She shifted patiently from one foot to the other, pencil poised over her little green pad, while Marietta clutched a shoulder on each side of her and laughed charmingly into the ear of each boy. Finally the waitress interrupted.

"Honey, if you ain't afraid you'll fall off, how bout turning loose one them boys and yall gimme your order so's I can get some dinner in these other kids."

The two boys continued laughing like drunken sailors, but the transformation in Marietta was abrupt. Her back stiffened, her neck stretched, and in a regal and disdainful tone she answered, "I haven't even had a chance to look at the menu. Just bring me some fried chicken. I'm sure you have some. Places like this always do." She paused. "What do you fellows want? Fried chicken with me?" she cooed.

As the two boys hastily and enthusiastically agreed with this choice, Marietta turned back to the waitress. Aloof and haughty, she arched one eyebrow and looked pointedly at the massive bosom. "Don't put any potatoes on my plate. And you needn't bother to bring me any bread. I sure don't want to get fat."

The waitress did not blush nor change expression. Chewing her gum and gathering up menus, she replied without inflection, "Anything you say, honey. You sure you don't want some extra sugar in your tea, though?"

As she moved swiftly away, the boy stared raptly at her rolling, propelling buttocks. Harking back to the barbershop, he thought, They really do look like two coons fighting in a croker sack.

When the waitress returned with their food, Marietta sat icily erect, with her hands folded in her lap. The curlyheaded boy on her right unfolded his napkin and tucked it into his shirt collar. The blackhaired boy on her left picked up his chicken drumstick with one hand and took a huge bite; then he pushed some potatoes onto his fork with it. Although Marietta did indeed use a knife and fork very daintily on her fried chicken, she gave no sign of noting the eating habits of her companions. In fact, as soon as the waitress left, she was once again smiling and looking raptly into the eyes of first the boy on her right and then the boy on her left. They could say hardly anything that did not evoke from Marietta an impulsive squeeze of their biceps and a delighted and admiring peal of laughter. The boy noted that she was not getting much meat off her chicken bone and privately decided that was a silly way to eat.

He then addressed his own plate and wished he had displayed the gumption to order chicken. He had dried peas, dried butterbeans, cole slaw, and a scoop of mashed potatoes with gravy. Sitting in the middle was a pickled peach, its beautiful amber surface interrupted by the star of a fragrant clove. He loved pickled peaches and for a moment forgot his anxiety about table manners in appreciative anticipation.

The pickled peaches his mother made were cooked until they were soft and practically fell off the seed while being served. This peach on his plate was firm to the point of hardness. Relaxed and unsuspecting, he confidently speared it with his fork and gave a downward snap of his wrist to cut off a bite. To his horror the enticing fruit shot forth like a chinaberry from an elderberry gun.

It skidded across his plate, scattering peas and butterbeans on the tablecloth, and shot all the way across the table between Marietta and the curlyhaired boy to land with an audible thud on the linoleum floor. Marietta and the boys were so absorbed in each other that they did not even notice the intrusion. The waitress, on her way between tables, gave the boy a swift look and then kicked the peach with one deft motion into the corner.

The crimson-faced boy, his appetite completely destroyed, began picking butterbeans and peas off the tablecloth one by one, depositing them on his plate as inconspicuously as possible. The girl on his left leaned over and murmured, "Isn't that exasperating? I did that once with a baked apple. Tell me about that writing contest you were in this morning. I'm getting nervous about my music piece, and maybe that'll help get my mind off it."

Gratefully he began chattering away. Inside he seethed. She didn't even see it, let alone notice it, he thought. In a way I'm glad, but in another way, well, gee whiz, what does a guy have to do to get her attention? Cut his throat? I nearly knock her head off with a peach pickle and spray vegetables over the table like a Poland-china hog, and she doesn't even know I'm in the world.

He glanced across the table at the happy trio. Let's face it, boy, he admonished himself. She likes the continental soldier type.

Later that afternoon, he sat in the auditorium while she recited. The magic was gone. She sounded wooden and stilted and just a little rushed. He knew she had not even placed and felt disappointed. Disillusionment about himself had not extended to the object of his adoration, and he longed to comfort her.

When the awards were announced that night, not a single person from Brewtonton won first place. Summerfield was not mentioned in Declamation nor Marietta in Reading. His friend from lunch won third place in Music, and the boy clapped as loudly as he could. He had completely forgotten Ready Writer's Essay. He was, consequently, almost overcome with surprise when he heard his name called out as first-place winner in that event.

The memory of the peach pickle vanished. He almost floated down the aisle in amazed triumph, feeling more than a little guilty over this unexpected largesse. He could not for the life of him remember any details of what he had written and half suspected that he did not really deserve this award.

Maybe the judges got the papers mixed up. Everybody else must have been pretty bad if you were the best, he thought. He took the extended medal almost greedily. As he walked back to his seat with modest manner and lowered eyes, he thought in a rush of exultation, That's ten points you weren't expecting. You're way ahead of the game with this. You've landed on your feet again.

After sitting down, he belatedly and guiltily closed his eyes for a moment. "Thank you, Lord," he breathed in sacrificial propitiation. "Thy humble servant thanks Thee. To Thee be all the praise and honor for this. Amen."

A little later he asked his ride to wait for him while he went to the rest room. He wanted to find Marietta. He had the inspiration that he could comment obliquely about the intelligence of the Reading judges and then offer her his Ready Writer's medal. After all, it was the only first place medal in just the whole dang school. He fancied that this would make him look magnanimous, mature, and even a little sophisticated. He could imagine her looking into his eyes and laughing delightedly while he pinned the gift on her dress.

The boy spied her down the hall, swinging on the elbows of her two luncheon companions. He approached the group from behind on silent feet. Just as they rounded a corner he drew a breath to speak and extended a hand to offer his gift.

Marietta, unaware as usual of the rest of the world, pealed out to her mesmerized escorts, "Let's get out of here before that precocious child finds me and says something about me not winning that silly old Reading contest. I declare the way he looks at me sometimes gives me the creeps. When he went down to get that medal, I was surprised butterbeans didn't fall out of his britches. What is Ready Writer's Essay, anyhow?"

Stunned into immobility, smothered by his worst fears, he heard her add lightly, "Now let's settle something really important. Which one of you fellows is going to sit in the front seat with me and drive my car, and which one is going to ride in the back seat with good ole Tommie Lou?"

Bearing the terrible weight of reality and unwanted enlightenment, he crept disconsolately back the way he had come, walking as close to the wall as he could.

Thank you, Lord, he finally acknowledged. Thy humble servant thanks Thee from the bottom of his heart for letting him hear before he spoke.

He found his ride, climbed into the back seat, and pretended to sleep during the long ride home.

In the kitchen next morning his mother was ecstatic when he told her about winning first place. "That's wonderful, son! Why didn't you wake me up last night to tell me? What did you write about?"

"Aw, something about electricity, Prometheus, yankee entrepreneurs eating liver, and the sleeping South, Mother. To tell you the truth, I can't remember exactly what I did write. I don't really deserve the credit for it. The Lord must have been guiding my hand. Maybe He gave me first place to sort of make up for some other things. I sure want to be careful to give Him the honor and the praise."

"Son, that's wonderful," his mother beamed. "Sometimes I feel like Hannah. Have you ever thought about going into the ministry?"

He nearly dropped his milk bucket. "No, ma'am! I sure haven't!" He started out the door. "And so far," he added, "I've managed not to get the Call. I'm going to be a doctor."

A few nights later he was flipping through his sister's anthology of modern poetry. Under selections from *A Shropshire Lad* he stopped and read:

> When I was one-and-twenty
> I heard a wise man say,
> "Give crowns and pounds and guineas
> But not your heart away;
> Give pearls away and rubies
> But keep your fancy free."
> But I was one-and-twenty,
> No use to talk to me.

He sat straight up. Hey, this guy is talking to me, he thought. He's good. He sure knows what he's talking about. He read the second verse:

> When I was one-and-twenty
> I heard him say again,
> "The heart out of the bosom
> Was never given in vain;
> 'Tis paid with sighs a-plenty
> And sold for endless rue."
> And I am two-and-twenty,
> And oh, 'tis true, 'tis true.

He closed the book and thought. Then in a world-weary

tone he daringly spoke aloud. "You ain't just a-shitting, A. E. Housman; you ain't just a-shitting."

He felt boldly mature for having used such a manly and forbidden word. He opened the book and read the poem again.

How I wish I could talk to A. E. Housman, he mused. I bet he would understand. I wonder if he ever heard of a dry wet dream.

XIV

the boy stayed busy on the farm all that summer. Buddy came to him early in the season and persuaded him to talk to his father. As a result he and Buddy had five acres of watermelons that they were raising on halves. The father furnished the land, the mules, the fertilizer, and the seed. Buddy and the boy furnished the labor. It would be their responsibility to harvest and sell the melons. When the crop was finished, they would have a settling-up day. All the money would be turned in, the fertilizer and seed bills would be presented and halved, and then the profits would be split down the middle, one half to the father, the other half to Buddy and the boy.

This was standard procedure for all the tenants on the farm, except that the two boys would not have to pay a grocery bill in addition. They dreamed of making a fortune. Buddy still had to help his father work the family crops, and the watermelon venture was to be managed during his spare time.

They selected a five acre plot of land that had "laid out" the previous year and was head high in the dead stalks of weeds. They cleaned out the stables and the lot from the cowbarn and scattered the manure thickly over the favored spot. Buddy was enthusiastic.

"Everybody say gray land make de bes melons, Sambo, but dis here ole red land'll hold de moisture better. De almanac say it goan be a dry summer. Everybody else be plantin in gray land 'n hit won't hold de moisture. We plant de red. Hit rocky, but hit rich 'n hit won't dry out. We goan make some melons, boy. En we goan make some money."

The boy was impressed by Buddy's research into the mysteries of the almanac. The boy had finished the ninth grade and Buddy had stopped in the seventh; yet his partner could decipher the cryptic messages in *Grier's Almanac* in a flash. The boy floundered in cross references and always gave up. It did not occur to the boy that Buddy's sole reading material consisted of this very same almanac, with the addition of the Sears, Roebuck catalog.

"Are we going to plant by the sign, Buddy?" the boy asked respectfully, straining and puffing with a seed-fork half full of manure.

"You mighty right us is," his friend affirmed. "We goan do everthing jes essackly right bout dis ole melon patch. An we gwine make us some money, too. If I can clear fifty dollars on nese melons, I got me a project."

"What sort of project, Buddy? You know we ain't going to make fifty dollars apiece offa these melons. That's a heap of money."

"I know at's a heap o' money, Sambo. Nis a heap o' project, too. But nemumine what it is. Les see kin we make ne money first. C'mon, red land, I'm bettin on you!"

For weeks they labored. Buddy could work on the melons only when he was caught up with the cotton and corn crops that his father was sharecropping with the boy's father. While the boy was still in school, Buddy took the two-horse turner and turned the manure and dead vegetation under, his huge shoulders and steady hands guiding the mules into making furrows nearly knee deep. Then he harrowed it. No one knew for sure how long he spent with the harrow. When the boy went over to inspect it, the entire field was as smooth and puffy-looking as a quilt new-stretched over his grandmother's feather bed.

The field was a good three-quarters of a mile off the big road and down a wagon road which was the only remaining vestige of sawmilling some ten years earlier. The road wound along the edge of the bottom land, turned around the foot of the big red hill, and dipped up over a smaller hill through second-growth pines and sassafras trees. It went around another curve and of a sudden burst into the clearing that was the five-acre field.

It was nearly on the back side of the farm, a good two miles from home, and when the boy had questioned the wisdom of planting this far from the barn and pointed out the additional time in reaching it and the extra labor in transporting supplies this far, Buddy had looked at him and grinned.

" 'At's one ne reasons I like nis ole field in ne red lands. Hit ain't real handy to folks at wanna steal a wallermillion. Ain't nobody goan jus stumble up on it accidental-like. Ne only folks know it here goan be ne folks what live on nis farm, 'n when nese melons get ripe I be waitin right here in case we has visitors. Hit too far back in here for anybody to tote a melon out, 'n hit goan be too nerve-wrackin for anybody to eat one on ne ground."

"Gosh, Buddy, I hadn't even thought about anybody stealing from us. It wouldn't be enough to amount to anything, would it?"

"Boy, what chew tawkin about! Time you had twenty o nese hands live on yo paw's place help nayselves a coupla times, you be done lost any money you liable to make." He hooked his thumbs in his overall galluses and twisted a bare big toe in the dust.

"Besides," he continued, "way I look at it, if anybody want a wallermillion he kin grow his own. Nese melons gwine be for *sale*. Me 'n you ain't gwine wuk our heads off all summer jes to pleasure somebody else."

He looked at the boy again. "On toppa nat, you don't understand, boy. Nays sump'n about a nigger 'n a waller-million jus natchul draw each other. Ney don't think nat's real stealin. Hit's bout like a possum in a simmon tree. Ney jes go together."

Comfortable and relaxed with Buddy's use of the racial designation but well aware that it was a taboo word for him, the boy asked, "Well, how you gonna keep em outa here?"

"Nemumine," Buddy replied. "Nemumine bout nat right now. Les make ne melons first. I study on it, 'n we'll think o' somepen."

* * *

The day that Buddy finished harrowing the field, he was coming in at dusk with the mules as the boy was leaving the cowbarn with his two buckets of fresh-foaming milk.

"Sambo, I got done," he announced. "We can plant it Sarridy. I can lay off ne rows 'n list on em tomorer, 'n we can both git on it Sarridy 'n put ne seeds in ne hills."

"That's great, Buddy. I'm sorry you're having to do all the heavy work by yourself, but it's going to be another two weeks before I'm out of school. You must be tired enough to drop."

"I ain't all nat tired, an don you worry bout ne wuk. I young 'n stout 'n I can cold do it. You done yo part when you talked yo paw into lettin us have ne land."

The boy carried the milk up the lane to the house feeling uncomfortably inferior.

The next morning he waked unusually early, hurried through his milking chores, loaded the woodbox high with stovewood for the day, and figured that he had plenty of time to visit the field before breakfast and school.

It was good daylight but not sunup as he hurried along the field road through the woods. He loved being outdoors at this time of day. There was a silence that was almost heavy. All the night insect noises had stilled, and none of the day noises had begun except the very early, very secret call of the hermit thrush down near the creek. There was always a feel of expectant excitement this time of day at this time of year. He likened the ponderous turning of the sleeping earth toward the morning sun to a huge water wheel not quite ready to dump the wet load it had lifted to the top of its circle.

His fantasy was interrupted when a long black snake streaked across the path just in front of his bare feet. He leaped three feet in the air without breaking stride and felt the sudden lurch of his heart in his throat. "Good Godamighty!" he expostulated in a startled whisper, ashamed of being scared but unable to control it.

Excuse me, Lord, he apologized silently, for taking Thy

name in vain. Especially over a silly old black snake that isn't even poisonous anyhow.

I wonder if it's a coachwhip, he thought as he hurried on down the road. He had never been able to distinguish between a coachwhip, a black runner, and a chicken snake. He had about decided that adults couldn't either.

Tabitha had scared the wits out of him years earlier. She had asserted, in a tone so positive that no listener could possibly doubt her, that the wondrous coachwhip snake would chase a child until it caught him, wrap itself around the victim, and whip him to death. When this fell deed was done, the snake would unwind itself from the pitiful and crumpled body. Before it departed, however, it would run its keen tail up each little nostril to be sure there was no breath of life remaining. Bad children were especially attractive to coachwhips.

She had thereby done much to make berry-picking an exciting adventure for the boy but had seriously undermined her credibility as he grew older. Remembering this, he chuckled and forgave himself for being frightened.

As he rounded the last turn in the road, a large hoot owl sailed silently and mysteriously homeward just ahead of him, and he burst out of the leafy tunnel into the open infinity of the field.

It lay there, that field, in the early light of a pure spring morning, as red and round as a cabochon ruby. Rimmed about with the dew-softened green of very young grasses, its surface was smooth and unmarred, yet, by rows. A faint line of mist floated wispily some ten feet above its surface, and on the far side the tall trees caught the first light of the rising sun in their top branches. The field lay there, virginal and waiting.

The boy drew a deep breath of sweet and stinging air. This place is magic, he thought. I don't want anybody doing any stealing over here, either. Shoot, I don't even want anybody to see this except me and Buddy.

Conscious once again of time, he turned and hurried back. Just before he got to the big road, he met his partner driving the wagon full of plows and other tools.

"Good morning, Buddy. Isn't it a pretty day? You've really done a good job on that old field. I never saw one so pretty before."

"Yeah, you right. So far, hit look pretty good. We goan make some money offen it, too."

"It's so pretty I may not be a doctor. I may just raise watermelons the rest of my life," the boy said, and he laughed.

Buddy smiled in reply. "Don't change yo mind on nis kind of mornin, boy. Wait'll it be hot one day an yo back achin fo you decide for good. I gotta go. Giddap in nere, Pet." The wagon rattled and banged out of sight as the boy hurried home for breakfast.

The next Saturday the two friends planted their melon patch. Three seeds exactly went into each hill. The boy was dubious about planting them so far apart but was assured by Buddy that the vines would send out runners and overlap each other. The boy questioned the omniscient grandfather about this point, and he confirmed it. After that the boy did not doubt Buddy's judgment again.

He had a lot more spare time than Buddy, and he visited the field every day. He was thrilled the day he found the red surface dotted with little green specks down the wide rows, and he watched the hairy leaves develop almost overnight into good-sized clumps of vegetation that sprangled like green lace shawls over the red field.

When the runners were about four feet long, the boys dropped nitrate of soda round each plant. Then he went down the rows and tenderly moved each runner into line while Buddy followed behind with the mule and listed the crumbling red earth in snuggling richness around the plants.

The vines soon carpeted the field so thickly that only accenting patches of red showed through the green. The yellow blossoms appeared and were followed in short order by hard, tight little green balls which seemed to enlarge daily before the proprietary eyes of the boy. Too large and thick for any more plowing, the vines now had to be weeded by hand.

This became the boy's passion. Buddy was busy plowing

cotton for his daddy, and the boy soon discovered that five acres was a tremendous territory for one person to weed. He snatched cockleburs, wild coffee, ragweeds, and jimson weeds out by the thousands. As soon as he covered the field, it was all to do over. On Sunday afternoon inspection tours, Buddy assured him that he was overdoing it and that weeds out in the middles did not sap strength from the plants. The boy was not convinced.

"It *looks* so much better, Buddy, if you get the weeds out of the whole field instead of just around the hills," he remonstrated. "This is about the prettiest crop I ever saw."

"Yeah, hit pretty all right," his mentor replied, "but pretty different from money, 'n nat what we after. But you go right ahead 'n get nem ole weeds all out nere, Sambo. You right, hit sho is pretty."

When the melons were the size of a man's two fists, Buddy decided it was time to protect the crop from the arrogant and rapacious crows. They had fun fashioning two scarecrows from old clothing. One was a man and one was a woman, and they laughed a lot deciding whom they resembled. Buddy advised the boy to move them around to different positions in the field, since he was visiting it on a daily basis anyway.

Crows were hard to fool, he counseled, but were extremely suspicious of anything they didn't understand. The partners stuck poles in the ground around the periphery of the field and looped white string all around it and then in crisscrossing squares over the field. The crows were supposed to think this represented either a fence or a freedom-threatening net and be afraid to light within its boundaries. The boy marveled at Buddy's wisdom.

The day they put the string up, they had carried their lunch to the field: buttermilk, a ham biscuit, and a sweet potato apiece. After wolfing down the food, they had stretched on the ground in the heavy shade of a redoak tree. The boy leaned up on one elbow, pulled a piece of grass, and nibbled on the tender, juicy stem. "Buddy," he ventured, "what makes folks have wet dreams?"

Buddy raised his head briefly and looked at the boy. He

flopped his head back, looked up into the branches of the oak tree, and replied in an offhand tone, "Aw, you jes build up all nat stuff inside you en it got to come out nere. Is you had one?"

"Naw," quickly replied the boy. "You know I ain't big enough yet. What are they like?"

"I hates em, en nen ney sorta scary, too. Ne first one I ever had, my maw was chasin me wid a brush broom. En I run up unner ne table en turnt into Minnie Mouse, en Mickey Mouse come runnin up en jam his tail in my nabel en I woke up having ne feelin wid ne whole bed in a mess."

The boy held his breath and made no response.

"Ney say you won't have em at all if you do plenny of windin wid ne gals, en I know you don't have so many of em effen you wukkin hard. Les make 'as'e en finish nem strings.Nem ole crows smarter'n we is."

As they rose to their feet, Buddy looked over at the boy. "You know what ne project is I been talkin bout? I goan tell you why I want nese ole wallermillions to mount to somepin. Don't you tell nobody, neither. Effen I kin clear fifty dollars, I gwine get married nis fall. I been keepin company with Tutt for two years now. Her paw live on Mr. Carson Clifton's place, en he done tole Tutt's paw that he'll let me have a crop nex year. He got a two room house I kin have too. Hit little, but hit got a good well o' water. Tutt doan wanna hatta tote no water. Now you know why we gotta make some money, but doan you tell nobody. My maw 'n paw doan know bouten it yit."

"Gosh, Buddy, I won't tell a soul," the boy promised, wide-eyed at this confidence. They worked fast and walked home in subdued and companionable silence. When they parted at the driveway to the big house and the boy trudged on alone, he thought, Minnie Mouse's navel! Mickey Mouse's tail! Maybe you're not such a freak after all. He bowed his head. "Heavenly Father," he breathed, "send showers and sun and make those melons grow. Thy humble servant's friend needs to get married. Have mercy on all of us, Lord. Amen."

* * *

A few days later he made a new friend. The county was working the road in front of the house. The guards, with their rifles, shotguns, and pistols, brought the men on the chain gang from the convict camp above Brewtonton, riding on the back end of an old flatbed truck. They arrived every morning about an hour after sunup and departed an hour before sundown. They all wore identical suits with wide horizontal black and white stripes, and they all had their heads shaved. A motor patrol, or road-scrape, preceded them like the animated skeleton of a deliberate dinosaur, gouging out the contents of first one ditch and then the other, belching gasoline smoke and roaring when sudden extra effort was required.

The men on foot cut sprouts with bush-axes, moved dirt with shovels, or replaced culverts and put new oak timbers in worn-out bridges. They were supervised every minute by silent, stolid guards who never put their shotguns down for a minute. Two or three times a day the warden would ride out in a pickup truck to see that everything was proceeding correctly. There was little conversation on the chain gang and no singing at all.

The boy was appalled to see that four of the prisoners had heavy iron rings around their ankles with a cumbersome chain connecting them. Consequently, these men walked with a sidling, slinging gait for all the world, he thought, as if they had soiled their breeches. Three of them were white and one was black. Without anybody warning him, he was instinctively afraid and kept a cautious distance from them.

The man who ran the road-scrape was a Nigra, shiny black and keenly thin. He was a "trusty," which meant that he enjoyed certain liberties the others on the chain gang were denied. He could leave the road for a bowel movement in the bushes without a guard following him with a gun. He was sent on errands with complete confidence that he would return. In addition, he was afforded no small degree of respect because he knew more about the operation and upkeep of the motor grader than anyone except the warden himself.

The boy, inconspicuous but attentive, overheard one of the guards say that Garfield sure was a good nigger and it was a shame he was on the gang. His companion responded that he didn't have but two more years to serve and he ought not to have killed his old lady. They sure were going to miss him on the gang, though.

At lunch time, the boy inspected the tin plate each prisoner was given. It was served with a big piece of puffy-white biscuit bread, a piece of fried fatback with pure grease instead of gravy, and a good dollop of thick sorghum syrup. The men did not even need to use the spoons they had tied to their belt loops. They just sopped the grease and syrup with the bread.

The boy went to the house and procured from his indulgent mother a gallon of fresh-churned buttermilk which had been designated for the hogpen. The guards were eating fried egg sandwiches and vienna sausage. The boy approached one of them. "Please, sir, could I give this buttermilk to ole Garfield over there? He helped my father fix a flat tire one time, and my mother sent him this milk."

The guard looked up, one cheek distended with half a sandwich. "Yeah, it'll be all right," he replied. "Ole Garfield wouldn't hurt a flea. But you stay away from them boys down yonder by theyselves with the chains on em, you hear? Ain't you Mr. Porter Osborne's little boy?" Receiving an affirmative answer, he continued, "I thought so. You sho do favor him. You tell him Pete Goodwin said howdy. All my folks think a heap of yo paw. He paid my maw's poll tax, and we always vote for Mr. Porter."

"Thank you, sir. I'll sure tell him. After dinner, would it be all right if I rode on the road-scrape a while? I can hang on right behind Garfield and I'll be careful not to fall off."

"Sure, it's all right. He's gonna be so far out ahead of the other prisoners we don't have to worry about you being too close to them. That ole scrape goes so slow it's plumb safe, but you be careful and hold on tight anyhow. We don't want nothing to happen to Mr. Porter's boy."

The boy carried the buttermilk over to the black man seated

in the dirt, leaning against one of the wheels of his machine. "Garfield, my name is Sambo. I brought you some buttermilk. Do you want it?"

"I sho do want it," Garfield assured him. "Hit'll cut dis grease jes right, and I thank you." The boy hunkered down in the loose, moist earth from the ditch bank. The guard sauntered off.

"Mr. Pete Goodwin said I could ride some with you on the machine. I've never been on one, and I'll bet it's fun. You don't mind, do you?"

"Naw, boy, I don't mind. Hit's mo fun than swinging them axes and shovels, but hit's still work to me. I heard what de guard said. How come you tell him that lie? I ain't never hope yo paw fix no flat tire. I doan eben know yo paw. I come from Mr. Tip Swanson's place over close to Tyrone. You ought not to start lyin, young as you is. They'd a let you ride without you tellin no lie. Dis sho is good buttermilk, though, and I do appreciate it."

He stood up and stretched. "Lemme carry dis plate back to de truck, and we'll crank up dis ole baby."

"I'll do it, Garfield," the boy volunteered eagerly. "Hand it here. It won't take a minute." Scampering down the road toward the truck, he thought with discomfort, You ought to be ashamed of yourself, getting a lesson on lying from a black convict on the chain gang. He's right, you know.

He clung happily to the back of Garfield's seat for most of the afternoon, watching in bemusement the huge coils of fresh earth rolled up from the ditches by the slanting blade beneath him. Once, as they neared the north boundary to the big house, he ran through the pecan trees to the back porch. From the safe he got two graham biscuits, stuck a big piece of fried ham between them, and carried them to his new friend.

"Boy, that sho taste good," Garfield thanked him. "But doan you let nobody see you sneakin me vittles. Buttermilk all right, but dey might fuss about dis. Hit's better'n dey eatin."

The next day the boy checked the melon patch early, pulled up weeds for a couple of hours, but was back on the road-scrape well before dinnertime. A good distance ahead of the others, Garfield stopped his machine near the driveway and stepped across the road under the shade of one of the big pecan trees. The boy brought him a fruit jar half full of fresh string beans, some cornbread, and another container of buttermilk.

"Garfield," he ventured, "what did you do to get on the chain gang?"

"I kilt my wife, Sambo," the man answered. "Dat's de plain truth of it. I kilt my wife."

"How come you to do that?" the boy asked earnestly. "Didn't you love her?"

There was a long pause.

"Yeah, I loved her," Garfield said roughly. "How old you, boy?"

"I'm almost fifteen," the boy lied. "But I'm awful small for my age. It sure does bother me, too. I'm the littlest one in my whole school."

"Ain't no need to worry bout that. You goan grow. You got a heap a sense, too. You goan do all right."

"Thank you," said the boy. "How come you killed your wife?"

"I guess I kilt her cause I had to. I couldn't help it. My oldest boy told me I need to come home early from the field cause he think de letter carrier ain't got no business goin in de house where his maw cookin dinner and stayin for no haffa hour. I studied on it all night after he tole me, and nex mawnin when I caught my mule out, I tole him effen it happen again to come to de field and let me know. Didn't nothin happen dat day, en I thought mebbe he been wrong and de mail man mebbe jes step in for some water or somepin. De nex day, though, here come de boy down to de field, en he say, 'Paw, he done drove in our yard an turnt off his car an gone in ne house!'

"I tole de boy to stay wid my mule, an I cut through de woods an come up back ne house. Ain't nobody in de kitchen, where Maggie May spose to be. I got my razor off de shelf on de back poach where I keep my shavin stuff and step real quiet round

216

to de front room." He stopped for a minute, looking into the distance, and the spellbound boy felt that he had forgotten his presence.

"Well, I want you to know, dere dey wuz. Right in our bed. Both of em buck-nekkid. Her black and on de bottom and him white an on de top, and both of em just a goin at it, her a-moanin an him a-gruntin. I let out a yell and jump right in de middle of de room, an when I did dat man run to de winder and start out headfust. I run at him an slice one side his white ass plumb to de bone, but he keep a-gwine and get in dat old mail car widout his clothes an gone from there fo I kin ketch him again.

"I turned back to Maggie May, an she ain't tryin to run. She down on her knees by de side de bed, tryin to kiver her breastes wid her dress. I talk real soft, an I say, 'How come you do dis, Mag? How come you do dis to me—an to de chirren?' She ain't make a sound. Jes look at me real wall-eye and pitiful-lak. An I reach down real slow and easy-lak and pull her head back by de hair. An I cut her th'oat. She flopped over and jerked real hard bout fo times an bled dat man's shoes plumb fulla blood. An I walk down de road to Mr. Tip's house and tole him to tell de sheriff to come git me. An here I am."

He paused and looked down at the boy, whose eyes were swimming in tears. "I had to do it, Sambo. De chirren knew bout it. I had to do it."

The boy laid a hand on his shoulder. "Of course you did, Garfield. Let's crank up. It's time to go back to work."

The road work was progressing rapidly, and the following day the boy had to walk a half mile to carry Garfield his lunch. As they sat together in the shade, the boy timidly began, "Garfield, there's something that's been bothering me. Do you know anything about wet dreams?"

"My Lord, I reckon I do. I knows a heap about em since I been on dis ole chain gang. They bout the messiest thing in de world."

"Well, what I wanta know—well what I mean—well, tell me—can you have a dry one? I had this crazy dream last winter about this girl, and my mother and daddy and a boy at school were

217

all mixed up in it. I waked up having the feeling, but everything was dry. I can't shoot off yet, you know, not even when I beat my dog." He lowered his head in embarrassment but was relieved to have the question asked at last.

"Aw, don't you worry none bout dat. I spec dat's plumb natchel. You gwine grow up some day an be spillin seed all over dis county. Dem ole dreams always crazy, but ain't no need to fret yoself about em. You sho can't help what you dream about, and dat's a fact."

In green iridescence a July fly, mullion-winged and jewel-eyed, shrieked contentedly from a distant tree that midsummer was approaching. At ease and reassured for the first time in months, the boy stood up and stretched.

"You say you have em in the convict camp, Garfield. What do you dream about?"

The sleek black head jerked upright, and the tortured eyes of Garfield glared at the boy. He yelled, "I dreams about my wife, Sambo! God have mercy on me, I dreams about my wife!"

He clasped his hands behind his neck and bent his head between his knees. He made no sound, but long shudders racked his body and he rocked to and fro in a veritable spasm of grief.

Terrified by the release of such emotion, the boy turned to run. Something held him back. Slowly he turned and placed one hand on Garfield's quivering body. "Don't, Garfield," he begged. "Please don't do that. It's time to go to work." He patted him gently. " 'The sedge is withered from the lake,' " he whispered. " 'And no birds sing.' "

The man reached up without raising his head and covered the boy's hand with one of his own. "I be awright in a minute, Sambo. You run on an leave me by myself. . . . I don't want you to ride dis afternoon."

All of a sudden, it seemed, the weeks of work and waiting all came together in a rush at the field. It was accented all over its surface by the innumerable lumps of a bumper melon crop. The darker green mounds of the burgeoning fruit stuck up out of the blanket of green vines like the plump backs of submerged animals fattening and swelling on some hidden feast. Buddy was ecstatic.

"Sambo, we gwine be bout a week ahead'n anybody else, I b'lieve, 'n I know we got ne bes crop anywhere aroun. Nis ole red land sho come through for us in nat dry spell back in June. Us ain't had ne fust vine shrivel 'n turn yaller. Lookit nem ole melons out nere. Look lak hawgs rootin aroun wid ney heads down, don't it?"

He walked through the field with the boy, both of them being careful to take high, long steps and avoid stepping on any of the vines. Buddy thumped the larger melons at random, producing a slightly hollow and musical sound with strong quick strokes of his rapidly released forefinger.

"Uh-huh, nis whole patch be ready to move in a week. Some nese bigguns plum ripe right now. You tell yo paw de man he got comin wid de truck be here nex Friday, we be done pile em up at ne big road ready to go. Me'n you pick em, haul em to ne big road in ne wagon 'n help im load em."

"I'll tell him tomorrow, Buddy," the boy promised. "I can't believe it's really time."

"You believe it, all right, time we git done pickin em. Yo back ain't never ache lak it gwine ache next week." He added with a note of doubt, "I jes hope ne market hold en we make some money off nis crop."

"Oh, we will, Buddy, you know we will. Quit worrying and just relax; we've got it made now."

"Naw, we ain't, Sambo, 'n at reminds me. Moon full tonight en all nis nex week. I gwiner stay in nis patch twel midnight ever night. Tomorrow Sarridy, en all ne hands knock off at dinnertime. Here what we gwine do. I let everbody think I ain't goan play ball caze I'm gwine co'tin. I git my paw's fo'-ten, en you get yo paw's twenty gauge pump, en we slip in here ne back way en wait. Tomorrow or Sunday we sure to have company. I ain't save nis crop from crows to lose it to no two-legged ones what can't fly."

"Buddy, you mean you're going to shoot somebody if they steal a watermelon?" the boy asked incredulously. "I don't think we ought to do that. Why don't we just tell everybody this is our patch and give them orders to stay out of it?"

Buddy looked at him with a hint of pity. "Co'se we ain't goan shoot nobody, Sambo. You know I had better raisin en nat. Ney ain't goan know we won't shoot em, nough, en when you know you somers you ought notta be, you hear a gun go off, you might nere's well be shot. We jes shoot in ne air en I spec nat'll do ne trick."

He paused and then continued, "As for tellin em, you don't unnerstan yet. Nat jes fire em up mo. Ney be laughin behine yo back at yo preachments 'n plannin all ne time to do whut ney wanna do. Ney think you jes a chile, Sambo. You meet me soon as you kin after dinner tomorrow on ne back side nis field. Don't come in by ne wagon track. Sneak in th'u ne woods." As they parted, Buddy added, "En doan tell yo paw."

The boy was excited by the entire mission and kept the rendezvous next day with some sense of unreality, suppressing an urge to fantasize himself as the dashing Scarlet Pimpernel on one hand or a ridiculous Tom Sawyer on the other. He had his father's shotgun and a pocket full of shells loaded with bird shot. His friend was already there when he arrived, crouched behind a sassafras bush on the far side of the field.

"Gosh, Buddy, did you spend the night here? How long you been here? Did you see anybody?" the boy asked rapidly.

"Naw, I went home bout ten-thirty last night. I had to work all mawnin. I ain't been here but bout thirty minutes, 'n I ain't seen nobody yet, last night or today. May not see nobody nis evenin, but we gwine be waitin for em if ney come. Now, here's what we do."

He led the boy down the back side of the field to the other end, across the rich expanse of sprawling greenery from his own station. He found a concealing bush and showed him where to hide. It was at the narrow end of the oval field, directly across from the entrance of the wagon track and some two hundred feet from it.

"Now, Sambo, effen somebody come, you jes lay real low an real quiet. Let em git on out in ne field and think ney gittin away wid somepin. When I shoot, you shoot. Ney hear all nat racket comin from both ends ne field, en dat gonna scare ne daylights out'n em. En when ney run, don't show yoself en don't holler. Ain't no need lettin em know zactly who we is. En remember don't you shoot twel I shoot." He turned to leave and added, "Sambo, don't you worry. We gwine shoot straight up in ne air. You know I wouldn't really shoot nobody—not even over nese wallermillions."

The boy sat for at least two hours, his back propped against a stump, the shotgun lying across his lap, his bare heels gouging holes in the soft earth, peering occasionally through the concealing bush in front of him for sign of any intruder. He was obedient to his instructions about remaining quiet and hidden but felt that he was really only humoring his friend. He did not expect any thieves to appear. He was, however, not bored.

He watched butterflies float overhead, and he sat very still to see how close a wayward young rabbit would hop before realizing that it was in danger. He observed with delight two mockingbirds put an intruding crow to shame and rapid retreat when it came over the tree in which they were nesting. Always there was the field to watch, beautiful, rich, and rolling, dotted thickly with the huge and improbable looking fruits of a summer's labor. He hoped they really would make some money. He would like to have some himself, but he most fervently hoped that Buddy would make enough to get married. Maybe, he thought, if they didn't clear enough to reach his goal of fifty dollars he might add part of his own share. A little of it, he thought.

In his reverie, he became aware of voices. He peeked through the bushes and moved very quietly to a crouch. He saw no one. They were still on the wagon trail. As he watched, three teen-aged boys appeared, all wearing overalls and all barefooted. Two of them were Darnell's boys and lived on the farm. The third was a friend and baseball competitor from the Weaver farm down the road. Excited at the interruption of his vigil, he watched the trio with curiosity.

"Hoo-wee!" he heard one of them exclaim. "You ever in all yo life seen anything lak dis?"

"Gawdamighty, dat's de pretties patch a wallermillions I be ever seed!" responded the neighbor.

"I see de one I gwine git," announced the bigger brother. "I gwine git dat ole big un hidin under dem leaves where it be sorta cool. I gwine bus it open wid my fist an eat jes de heart out'n it. Les go!"

With this all three boys trooped out into the melon patch. The boy could not believe his eyes. They were making no effort at all to avoid stepping on the vines. They didn't even lift their feet up. They were trampling on the leaves with callous indifference, and he could tell by distant twitches of the vines that they were catching runners with their feet and jerking them carelessly with every step. Indignation filled him. The field was being profaned. The sanctity of a holy place was being violated.

He rose to his full height behind his bush, rage filling his heart so fully and so suddenly that he was indifferent to discovery. Just as two of the boys were bending over to tear choice melons from their vines, Buddy's gun boomed from the end of the field. It scared the boy so badly that he nearly dropped his own weapon. The effect on the three interlopers was immediate. With frightened bellows, they leaped in the air, turned, and began racing out of the field to the wagon road.

Raising his gun to fire in the air, the boy was enraged at the harm their fleeing feet were wreaking among the watermelon plants. It looked to him as though they were tearing up half the field. He lowered the pump gun and aimed it deliberately between the shoulders of the boy on the left.

"Bam!" the weapon echoed in his ears. The target gave a shriek and an extra leap. "Rattle, slide, click. Bam!" He breeched and fired at the second one, then quickly again at the third one.

Buddy had risen from his post and was frantically waving his arms and yelling, "Stop, stop, stop!"

If possible, this only made the marauding trio run faster. They vanished down the wagon road more quickly than rabbits and just as silently. The boy stood, the gun hanging loose in his hands, trembling with disbelief and subsiding anger, as Buddy ran up to him.

"Good Godamighty, boy! What come over you? You preachin to me bout not shootin anybody over a wallermillion, en you done shot three in a row!" He paused and added, "Dat was some good shootin, too. You got all three of em right in ne ass. Good thing you had bird shot en wuz as fur away as you wuz. Else I b'lieve to my soul you mighta kilt somebody."

"Buddy, you reckon they're all right? I don't know what came over me. The way they were messing up our field, all of a sudden I really wanted to kill them. I don't like the way I was feeling. Did I hurt them bad?"

"Naw. Don't fret. You ain't hurt em bad. Mighta raised a bunch o' whelps on em, but you didn even break de skin, fur off as you wuz. Effen ney doan die from heart failure, ney be all right."

"Buddy, please don't tell my daddy. And please don't ask me to do this anymore. I'm scared. I really wanted to kill those boys."

"I ain't gwine tell nobody, en I ain't gwine ask you to do dis no more. You sorta scairt me, too." He thought a minute and added, "I spec I ease on down here ne rest o' ne full moon, but I be awful s'prized do we have any mo company. I spec you done took keer o'nat. Word'll git aroun, en I jes b'lieve everbody steer clear o' nis place."

Weeks later he heard from a companion at the cowpen that Buddy was sure a bad one. He had actually shot three boys who weren't doing nothing but walking across his ole watermelon patch minding their own business. Two of them were even his cousins and it was a good thing for Buddy they hadn't told their maw. With a smug feeling of security, the boy assured his informant that Buddy wasn't anybody to mess around with and those boys were smart not to tattle.

The next week they harvested the crop. A large number of the choice melons weighed twenty pounds each. A few weighed even more. They hired one of the hands on the farm to help them for the unheard-of sum of a dollar and a half a day. The boy was named J.C. and was chocolate colored. He was dull as dishwater but had a back, arms and legs, and possessed the supreme virtue of doing what he was told. Buddy could whip him, and the boy could out-talk him, two points which made him an ideal employee.

For two days they hauled melons. They put sidebodies on the two-horse wagon, hitched up Pet and Clyde, and whipped them through the field—up one row and down the next. Buddy picked melons from one side, J.C. from the other. The boy stood in the wagon and placed them gently as they were handed to him. The iron-shod wagon wheels crushed and bruised the vines as they traversed them; the careless mules put their heavy feet wherever they pleased. The boy felt that he was the perpetrator of pillage and rape comparable to that of the Visigoths and the damnyankees. Buddy looked up and sensed that he was disturbed.

"Here, Sambo, let me drive awhile an you tote to ne wagon. Don't you fret bout tearin up ne vines. We done wid em now. Ney be gone des soon as ne melons ripe anyhow. Nis what we worked hard all summer for, en we done good. Specially you. I bet nis ne only melon patch in ne whole state of Georgia ain't got no hawg weeds or wild coffee in it."

Once reconciled to the necessity for bruising and tumbling the vines that he had cherished in their bucolic purity for so long, the boy thrilled to the harvest. He had not realized how many melons they had. By the end of the first day they had accumulated a pile that he fancied to be as high as Stone Mountain. They left J.C. on guard against thieves while they drove the mules in that evening.

Buddy took great pride in carrying a melon to every family on the farm and six to their own two mothers. He was as magnanimous as a black and glistening Santa Claus, and his reception was ecstatic. He had selected his gifts from the very largest melons in the pile, and they were so heavy the boy had trouble with their smooth, slick weight. Consequently he drove the wagon, and Buddy leaped off at each tenant house, hoisted a huge, green globe to his shoulders, and made his way through excited, chattering pickaninnies, his teeth and eyes flashing, healthy red gums shining, and his loud beautiful laugh booming through the sunset. The boy ached in every joint, but he was happy, too.

The next day Mr. Mark Hewell came with two hands and his huge truck, the side bodies on it towering high as a man's head above the cab. The father had contracted with him to haul the melons all the way into Atlanta and sell them to a wholesaler. They wound up with three big loads, and it was almost sundown when they loaded the last one.

Tired and hungry, the boy and J.C. picked out a melon. J.C. burst it open with one expert blow of his fist, and they each broke off a piece of the fragile, jagged red heart of the watermelon meat, free of seeds and looking frosted with sweetness. Buddy declined their invitation.

"Naw," he said, "I don't want none right now. In fact, I ain't sure I goan be want none ever again. I so tired of wallermillions right at nis minute I don't care if I never see another one."

He surveyed the loading area. "Sambo, we got about two hundred left here nat ole truck ain't gwine come back for. Les borrow yo paw's truck an peddle em ourselves tomorrow afternoon in Brewtonton. We kin ask fifty cent apiece for nem great ole big uns, right on down to a nickle for them little bitty knotty uns. We go in right after dinner tomorrow, we catch ever colored man in town what work by de day wid a little money in his pocket."

"That's a great idea, Buddy. I'll ask Daddy first thing in the morning."

"You know he gwine let you have it. I go on to de big house en git de key en bring ne truck back en we'll load it en leave it in yo yard tonight. You can ask him bout ne truck jes as good wid it full as you can wid it empty, and ain't nobody in nis whole county goan steal no wallermillions out'n Mr. Porter Osborne's back yard. I kin sleep easy tonight."

"I could sleep easy tonight if somebody stole the bed out from under me," laughed the boy. "You were right about waiting to decide what I want to do. There must be a better way to make a living than this. You go get the truck, and J.C. and I will wait here and help load it."

The truck was an ancient Dodge, its fenders and cab dented and crumpled by years of enthusiastic use, more rust showing now than black paint. It had a faithful, steady motor, however, which could be heard and identified a mile away. It had a flatbed on it with twelve-inch boards as side rails. Buddy had carpeted it with a thick layer of wheat straw to cushion the melons. The three boys worked rapidly and soon had the gleanings of their crop loaded in an evenly balanced mound of dark green ovals with yellow straw protruding between them. The boy thought the old truck had never looked so good.

They parked it in the back yard, right between the well and the washplace. Big Boy and Spot inspected it thoroughly and urinated on all four tires. The boy was sure that any intruder during the night would be announced by excited barking. He slept soundly and did not even hear his father come in.

When he went to milk next morning at sunup, one of the cows was missing. He knew she was in heat and found the hole in the lot fence she had squeezed through in her desperate and primordial search for a mate. There was no bull on the farm, and the boy figured she would be at the Whitaker place some three miles west. At any rate, he knew he would have to find her. He milked the other cow and hurried back to the house for breakfast.

The family was already at the table and the blessing had been said. No one was missing except the father, who had come home late, and was sleeping late. He slipped into his chair, served his plate with grits, a piece of ham, hot graham biscuits with melted butter oozing through the crust, and a slice of ripe tomato.

"Mother," he said, "old Stell got out during the night, and I've got to go find her. I spec she's over at Mr. Whitaker's. If Daddy leaves before I get back, tell him Buddy and I want to use the truck to peddle the last of our watermelons in town this afternoon and ask him if it's all right, please, ma'am."

"I'll ask him for you, son," his mother agreed. "He said last night when he came to bed that he bet that's what you were up to. He saw the truck when he came in. What in the world is wrong with that old cow, getting out of the pasture when there's all the feed in the world in it? And what makes you so sure she's over at the Whitaker farm?"

The silence following her question became uncomfortably prolonged. The boy glanced desperately around the table. All the adults were chewing like billy goats and staring into their plates as though they had discovered treasure maps beneath the food. The grandfather had poured his coffee into the saucer for cooling and was just raising it to his lips. The boy caught his eye with an imploring glance. The old man set his saucer down and wiped his mouth.

"Aaaaah, Lord," he said with relish. "Vera, don't fret about that cow, and don't ask any more questions." He turned to the boy. "Be sure and take a rope with you," he advised. He turned back to his daughter-in-law and added benevolently, "That's menfolks' business. You don't need to worry."

Later, walking alone and barefoot down the clay road through the still-cool summer morning, the boy was well-content. He was not at all annoyed by this unexpected interruption of his routine and the addition of an extra chore to his duties for the day. In fact, he anticipated this trip with pleasure. Of all the animals he had witnessed copulating so far, he liked cows best.

Dogs, he thought, were vulgar and plebian and were probably the inspiration for the word "frigging." He followed this thinking a little further. It was obvious from their anatomy that "screwing" best described pigs. Chickens were ridiculous and beneath one's notice, and there was something about the sexual activity of cats that made you want to kick them.

Whenever a bull serviced a cow, though, there was only one word that was adequate to describe the process. He decided that if you thought of a bull, it imparted a certain nobility to the word. He was loathe to use the word, however, even when he was alone, and he had noticed that most other males either said the word real fast or else lowered their voices when they said it. Women and girls, of course, had never heard it and would not know what it meant.

Earlier in the summer, he had sneaked off with one of the men on the farm who was carrying his milk cow over to Mr. Whitaker's bull to be bred. The heavily muscled man had a fight on his hands getting the animal to move down the big road for the first mile. He had a plowline over her horns, and she was either sulling, spraddle-legged with lowered head in the middle of the road while the man flogged her with the end of the rope, or tossing her head violently and trying to leap the ditches.

The man was sweating profusely and muttering fascinating curses. After having been dragged, jerked, and kicked for an hour, the recalcitrant cow raised her head, flopped her ears forward, let out a loud bellow, and started walking in a quick shuffle down the road to Mr. Whitaker's.

"Gosh, Wes," said the boy, "what came over her all of a sudden? She's good as gold now."

"Uh-huh," responded the perspiring man. "She done got a smell o' dat ole bull, an she know where she goin."

At that moment they heard a deep-throated, answering bellow in the distance. The cow broke into a loose-jointed run, throwing her head back in occasional communicating roars and slinging great ropes of slobber all around her.

"Dat ole bull smell her, too," Wes murmured. "Grab my hat, Sambo. I gotta hang on to dis critter now, sho-nuff."

The boy would never forget the last half mile to Mr. Whitaker's. Wes was holding a taut rope and being pulled at the full length of his running stride down the big road by the now-galloping, singleminded cow. The boy was running as fast as he could but was soon left behind. He figured Wes was setting some kind of speed record for a human until he stumbled and fell, the rope jerking out of his hands and singing into the air to fall in trailing contortions behind the runaway animal. Propelled by the momentum of sudden release, Wes tumbled over and over in the red dust of the road. The boy ran up to him as he rolled to a sitting position.

"Gosh, Wes," he asked as he handed him his hat, "are you all right?"

"Yeah, I'm aw right, but dat fool cow bout kilt me. Les git on down to Mr. Whitaker's barn fo she bus his lot fence down to git at dat bull."

"I didn't know there was so much to this," the boy said as they hastened down toward the barn. He added boldly, "Fucking can be plumb dangerous, can't it?"

Wes threw back his head and laughed in unbelieving delight. "Hit sho can dat, Sambo. An dis jes gittin sot for it, too." He looked at the boy with glee. "You keep dat in mind, an you be better off all yo life."

When they reached the barn, Mr. Whitaker and his son, John Wesley, were already there, attracted by the reverberating cacophony of the eager animals. The bull was part Jersey and a veteran at his job. He was bellowing and throwing huge clods of earth over his back with defiant thrusts of first one forefoot and then the other.

"Mawnin, Mr. Whitaker," Wes greeted. "Be aw right do I git my cow serviced? I can work a haffa day for you nex Sa'ydy."

"Howdy, Wes," Mr. Whitaker replied. "Be fine." He cut himself a chew of tobacco and jerked his head at his son. "Open the gate, John Wesley."

His son, who was twenty-five years old and had a wild look in his light blue eyes, was considered strange by everyone in the community. He had quit school in the fourth grade because he was twelve years old and still hadn't learned to read. He worked on the farm sporadically but spent most of his time arguing with his parents about politics or things he heard on the radio. He could figure as good as anybody, but he couldn't read a lick.

As he struggled with the big wooden gate, Wes leaped forward. "Lemme git de rope off dis ole cow fo she hang herself or break her neck," he said.

The actual encounter fascinated the boy. After all her frenetic scramble to get there, when she was finally admitted to the enclosure with the bull the cow became completely docile and apathetic. She simply stood there in the middle of the lot with head extended and legs spraddled. Occasionally she would urinate. The bull was active enough, however.

The boy watched every detail of the procedure with horrified curiosity. Wes and Mr. Whitaker leaned sideways against the fence, talking to each other desultorily about crops or the weather, acting as though they were unaware of the sexual activity just beyond their elbows. The boy thought their attitude the ultimate in nonchalance but had no desire to emulate them.

He climbed the fence and held on like a possum, his white head peering over the top in total concentration. When the bull interrupted his smelling and licking to arch his thick neck heavenward, wagging his great head slowly and ritualistically sideways with his thick upper lip rolled back in a taut grimace, the boy laughed aloud. He wondered if this meant it smelled so good the bull couldn't stand it or so bad he couldn't stand it. He did not laugh, however, when the huge creature suddenly vaulted on his hind legs and brought his great weight crashing down on the sagging back of the small, compliant cow.

He had never in his life seen such a pink, dripping extension of flesh as the bull now unsheathed into the cow. He hunched it deep within her with a few vigorous thrusts of his hips before falling awkwardly off to the side. The cow never moved except to stagger when the weight on her back was released. The boy recalled old man John Cox, and murmured in disbelief, "Just let it lay there, 'y God; I'll git it."

He watched with rapt attention as the mating was repeated over and over. John Wesley Whitaker joined him on the fence. Wes and Mr. Whitaker had walked on off and were sitting on the back of a wagon, still gossiping and whittling.

"You wanna go up in the hay loft and watch?" asked John Wesley. "You kin see real good from up there."

"Goodness, no," the boy responded, without diverting his glance from the barnyard. "I can see all I can stand from right here. Have you ever seen such big balls in all your life? I bet they weigh two pounds apiece."

"Git down off dat fence, Sambo," called Wes. "Hit's time f'us to go. He done used her five times, en if she ain't cotch by now, somepin wrong."

The boy was amazed at the transformation in the cow on the way home. She ambled along at the end of the rope as obedient as an old friendly dog—her attention was apparently elsewhere, but she was completely cooperative. He noted that her tail stuck straight out for the entire trip, and she dripped semen for a half mile.

"What John Wesley say to you?" asked Wes.

"Gosh, I don't remember. Something about seeing better from the loft. Wes, I thought your cow was gonna get her back broken. You reckon she's all right?"

"Law, yeah, Sambo, dey lak folks. A bull do all dat struttin 'n showin-off, en he look mighty big 'n dang'ous, but I ain't never yet see a cow so little she can't take all he's got. Don't you git in no barn loft wid John Wesley. Somepin bout him ain't jus esackly right. You keep yo feets on de groun."

The boy recalled that previous trip on this morning when he went alone in search of old Stell. His judgment had been correct. She was, indeed, at the Whitaker farm, and when he arrived she was already in the lot being mounted by the Whitaker bull. John Wesley was sitting on top of the fence, watching avidly. He swung down as the boy approached.

"I come down to feed this morning, and yo cow was waiting outside the gate; so I let her in. He done been to her six or seven times and she's about satisfied."

"I appreciate you looking after her," said the boy. "She got out some time in the night, and I figured she'd come straight here. If you don't mind helping me, I'll put a rope on her head and take her home."

"I don't mind helpin ya." He walked slowly towards the boy.

"But let's go up in the loft awhile first." He lowered his voice confidentially. "It's fun to watch the cows while you fuck ya fist."

He laid a hand on the boy's shoulder. The boy considered the suggestion with startled interest. He had never witnessed such activity in others, and the prospect of observing it in a grown man was tempting. Although he tried to imagine John Wesley so involved, he quickly decided it would be as ludicrous as dogs. Still, it might be fun to watch. He felt the man's hand kneading his shoulders and begin rubbing his back and realized that his penis was getting hard.

"We might even jack each other off," John Wesley confided as his caressing hand moved down to the boy's waist.

Fear and shame filled the boy with a sudden rush. He moved back and looked up into the big man's light blue eyes.

"We better not do that, John Wesley!" Suppressing any tremor of fear in his voice, he added earnestly, "I sure wouldn't want Jesus to come and find us doing that."

The man looked at him and turned his head. "Yeah," he muttered, "I guess you're right. Come on an let's getcha cow."

"Besides," the boy announced importantly, "I've got to get home in a hurry and help haul watermelons."

"I heard you had a good crop. Pa come down the road yesterday where they was loadin and said they was the prettiest he's ever seen." He handed the boy the rope to the now-haltered cow.

"Don't say nothin bout what I asked you," he directed. "I was jest foolin you."

"Gosh, I knew that all the time; you had to be fooling. I'd already forgotten about it."

Walking home with the rope over one shoulder and the docile cow trailing at his heels, he breathed piously, "Thank you, Lord, for the strength of Thy divine Presence in keeping Thy humble servant out of temptation in that barn loft. For Christ's sake. Amen." Deep in his mind in the secret place where he knew the Lord could not see him hiding, he thought, I'm really good not to have gone, but I'm really bad to keep wishing I had.

232

When he got home from his errand, his father had already gone to town. His mother told him that he and Buddy had permission to use the truck, but they were to stop at the drugstore before they sold any melons and see the father. He excitedly choked down his dinner and hollered across the field to Buddy's house.

The two of them stopped and picked up J.C., who was not getting paid to help them this afternoon but had made them promise to let him make the trip anyway. The boy made him sit in the middle while he hugged the right hand door with a clasping elbow. The wind blew deliciously through his hair as the old truck sputtered and roared up the dirt highway under Buddy's expert hand. They stopped in the shallow, sandy ditch at the courthouse, and the boy climbed out of the truck to go across the street to find his father. That gentleman, however, was already headed toward them, having both heard and seen their arrival. Reaching into his pocket, he extracted a quarter. Handing it to J.C., he said, "Run across yonder and get us some real cold Co-Colas, boy."

As J.C. scampered delightedly across the dusty street, the father turned to the two friends. "I wanted to see you two just a minute by yourselves. I've figured up the fertilizer costs and the seed, and I'm ready to settle with you boys for your half of the crop. Mr. Hewell paid me last night when he got in from the market."

He reached in the other pocket and pulled out a folded packet of green money. The bills were so new he had to lick his thumb occasionally as he separated them. They were all twenties. He counted off eight of them and held them out to the boy. "Here's one hundred and sixty dollars for yall's half of the crop. Don't forget to divide with Buddy. I want you boys to know I've never been so surprised. You made more than twice what I thought you would on that patch. I just wish I knew I was going to clear as much per acre on my cotton." He turned to the stunned Buddy. "I want to talk to you this fall. Big as you are and hard as you work, you might be ready to have a crop on your own. We'll talk about it."

"Yassuh, Mr. Porter, yassuh. I sho much obliged to you," said Buddy. "We bring you yo ha'f nese melons des soon es we sell em."

"No," the tall man in white linen said, "you boys keep the money you make this afternoon for yourselves." He placed a hand on the shoulder of each boy. "I want both of you to be through selling melons, though, and out of colored town well before dark. You won't forget that, will you? How much are you planning to ask for these melons?"

"Well, Buddy thought we might get fifty cents for these twelve big ones on down to a nickel for the smallest ones."

"You fellows do what you like, but if you were to ask my advice, I'd say charge a dime for the small ones. I haven't seen any other melons in town yet, and I think you can get what you ask. Then don't take less than a quarter for any of the middle-sized ones.

"Here comes J.C. with your Cokes. Don't forget to be back here or out of town before dark. Better still, come by the drugstore and let me know just before you go home."

"Yessir, we will," the boy promised as the three clambered back into the truck, J.C. in the back with the melons.

"I tell you what," the father added. "Here's a dollar. I'm buying your two biggest melons. Just leave them on the truck and bring them to me when you've sold all the others."

As the melon merchants swung around the corner of Church Street, leading into colored town, Buddy said, "Yo paw is one mo good man, Sambo. He done hand me eighty dollars nis afternoon, an he wadn't bliged to settle up fo fall. I can't b'lieve us done already made nis much. Nis goan be enough extra to let Tutt buy a bed 'n dresser. I be married by Christmas for sure."

He was so excited and so happy that his salesmanship was irresistible. They sold melons on Church Street, and they went on across the railroad tracks into Holly Hill and sold more. They did not have to hawk them from house to house. People clustered around the truck whenever it stopped. There were good natured banter and efforts at dickering, but Buddy clung to his predetermined price. There were even a couple of attempts at barter from girls who rolled their eyes and their hips in unmistakable suggestion.

When the boy primly confronted Buddy with this possibility, he laughed and said, "Ney jes wantin some anyhow an trying to see kin ney git a wallermillion thown in as a extra. I spec ney be back tereckly wid some feller what'll buy em one. If ney don't, we'll turn ole J.C. loose on em. I ain't got time for windin; I'm makin money. Hurray fo de red land!"

By sundown they had sold every melon they had except the two reserved for the father. Before delivering these two and going on home, they parked on the main street by the courthouse to count their money. They gave J.C. two dollars because they felt magnanimous, and he disappeared up the street in the direction of Pike's Mercantile and Putman's General Store. Buddy and the boy sat on the flatbed of the truck, raked a spot clear of hay, and emptied their pockets into one central pile. From this they extracted pennies, nickels, dimes, quarters, and half dollars into separate stacks. When they finished their final count, they had thirty-seven dollars and twenty-five cents. They were over-whelmed.

Riding a crest of euphoria over unexpected good fortune, the boy impulsively pushed the whole pile toward his friend.

"Here, Buddy, I want you to have my half of what we've earned today. You've done most of the work, and I haven't done anything today but have a good time. I'll give you this for a wedding present, and now you'll have about a hundred and twenty dollars."

"Sambo, you ain't bliged to do dat," his friend protested. "You got everthing set up fo nis crop, en you worked jes as hard fo yo size as I did, en besides I done tole you I don't b'lieve yo paw woulda let me hab de lan nout you bein in on it." He paused. "I ought notta take it, but de plain truf is I ain't man enough to turn it down. So maybe you bigger'n me. I thank you kindly. What's all nat comin up ne road?" he asked, suddenly and sharply.

The boy became conscious that, even in a town where the noise of traffic was at best sporadic, there was an unnatural quiet. No car was in sight or moving around the courthouse square. He was reminded of the unnatural hush just preceding a tornado, when even the birds quit cheeping. From south of town, just in front of the schoolhouse and extending on around the curve and over the hill, a long line of headlights shone, slowly and steadily approaching. Suddenly, even as he looked, a blaze of fire shot into the air above the car in the lead. The leaping flames were in the shape of a cross. He was roughly and precipitously hurled to the floor of the truck. Buddy's great heavy arm was over his shoulders, and his voice was desperate in his ear.

"Keep yo head down, Sambo! For God's sake, keep yo head down an be stiller'n you ever been in yo life befo! I oughta run, but I can't leave you, an besides ney might see me. Fo de love o' God, lay still!"

Frightened by the obvious panic in his friend's voice, the boy flattened himself against the bottom of the truck, his thin body clasped tightly against Buddy by the strong arm. He felt protected and cherished and strangely content. That must be the Ku Klux, he thought. I've heard about em, but I've never seen them. What in the world are they doing in Brewtonton?

Buddy pulled him even tighter against him. "Please, Sambo, keep yo head down! Don't go back on me now!" he begged again.

The boy became conscious of the acrid, smothering odor of Buddy's armpit. It was different from working sweat. This was the smell of fear. Of a sudden the realization overwhelmed him that his friend was not protecting him but was seeking protection. That great quivering, muscular hulk was in reality trying to hide behind his puny, scrawny frame. His friend was afraid because he was a Nigra! He was beseeching the boy's help because he was white!

All fear and consternation left him and were replaced by rage. In a fiercely protective tone, he said, "Buddy, you lie still! That's just the ole Ku Klux and they don't amount to anything any more. Don't be afraid. Trust me."

He could hear the motors of the approaching cars. They were less than a block away. Struggling loose from the clutching arm, he reached out and covered Buddy completely with the wheat straw. The great black head was pressed sideways against the wooden floor of the truck. He covered it, too. He stood straight up in the truck, his tow head shining in the lights of the oncoming cars, his glasses glinting in reflection of the flickering cross. Rolling the large watermelons forward into easy reach, he crouched behind them, his buttocks resting on Buddy's quivering behind.

The cross was held aloft from the rear seat of the open touring car which led the cavalcade. It smelled of kerosene and burning rags, but it was nevertheless an awe-inspiring sight. The humans in the caravan were even more awesome, and he almost panicked himself as he looked. Completely covered in white, they all wore high peaked white caps with strange insignia adorning some of them. Each one had a loose mask of cloth hanging completely over the face with holes for the eyes only. Some were dark and cavernous, but behind some of the holes could be seen the flash of an eyeball as it turned and caught reflected light. The most impressive thing was the silence.

The cars, loaded with stolid, immovable men, passed slowly up the dirt street, and not one man made a sound. The soft even chug of the smoothly functioning motors was the only noise to be heard. Although no head turned to acknowledge his presence, the boy was positive that every mask was staring straight at him. He could recognize no one, nor, indeed, in a hamlet where everyone's car and even mule was familiar by sight, could he recognize any of the automobiles.

Across the street some scattered men were pressed stiffly and motionlessly against the walls of the stores, but he felt all alone and conspicuous. Of a sudden he felt actively responsible for Buddy. In a high voice he called out, "Watermelons for sale! Nice, ripe, juicy watermelons for sale! Just got two left—seventy-five cents apiece."

The cars filed steadily by. No head turned. He felt Buddy's behind ball up in a hard knot. Again he violated the silence. He resented it. Nobody had any right to command that much respectful silence, not even a funeral procession or a word of prayer. Nobody had even coughed.

"Buy my last two watermelons, Mister," he yelled. "Soon as I sell these I can go home. Watermelons for sale!" No one noticed.

As the last car drew abreast, he hurled into the chugging, indifferent, infuriatingly reverent atmosphere of this deteriorated night a high falsetto taunt. In exaggerated dialect he yelled, "Don't yall *lak* wallermillions? Buy a wallermillion!" As the last car passed in deliberate procession, the intruders could be seen turning down Church Street, the cross still burning brightly. He heard Buddy say, "Sambo, you git in nat cab en crank nis ole truck, en les git outa town fo nem folks double back."

"Buddy, I can't drive this truck on the big road, and you know it. They're gone. You get in the cab and let's go."

"Yeah, you kin," Buddy retorted from under the hay. "You gotta. Jes remember to pull up nat little thing en slam ne gear stick way over to ne right to put it in reverse. Please, Sambo, git me outa nis town. I ain't movin from unner nis craw twel you do."

Too small to sit on the seat and reach the gas feed, the boy managed by dint of hanging to the steering wheel to crank and clutch and gas the old truck. He headed down the road. The air was cool and fresh. The blackness of the night rushed to attack the penetrating headlights of the truck, carrying insects squishing into the windshield. The faithful old motor roared around a forgotten muffler, and the boy felt a surge of accomplishment as he drove for the first time on the big road. When they turned off at Harp's Crossing, he swung from the top of the steering wheel and brought both feet down simultaneously on the clutch and the brake. The truck obediently lurched to a stop. He put it in neutral.

"Buddy, this is silly. Get up here in the cab with me. I'm driving pretty good, but we're off the main road now."

Buddy clambered over the side of the truck, picking wheat straw off his shirt. "You drivin plumb fine, boy, en I sho thank you. Nis ne second year in a row you done save my life. I doan know how I'd make it widout you."

"Aw, Buddy, don't be silly. I didn't save your life. Those men just scared you. They were just showing out. They wouldn't really hurt anybody nowadays, not even a Nigra."

"Nat's what you say, boy. You white. I know better. Nem folks come plumb up here from Griffin. I recognize nat ole car in front. I got a ontee stay in Griffin, en I seen nat car when I went to see her one Sunday. Hit belong to a man so mean he thow a nigger in ne river quick es look at him. Don't talk to me bout not hurt nobody."

"Gosh, Buddy, where in the world is J.C.? I forgot all about him. You reckon we ought to go back and get him?" the boy interrupted.

"Naw. J.C. awright. He may done beat us home. You sho needn't worry bout him. He slick. Ain't nobody hurt him caze they can't hem him up. Les go, Sambo. I feel better when I in my maw's house."

When they drove into the barnyard, the boy cut the motor and leaned against the steering wheel. "Buddy, it's not right, what happened tonight. I want you to know I hate the Ku Klux Klan. You're the best friend I've got. I want you to take some more of the watermelon money."

Buddy looked at him, one leg already out of the open door. "Naw, you don't. You don't give me no mo money. I done got what I earned, en I earned what I got, en nat's ne way it oughta be. Money ain't everthing, Sambo. I never forgit you." With a sudden release of tension, he threw back his head and laughed. "I ain't never forgit nis whole night, neither. Ain't many folks ever had a white chile settin on top ney ass sellin wallermillions to de Ku Klux Klan. You crazy, Sambo, an you got de devil in you, but you my bes friend, too."

Sleeping lightly that night, he overheard the father in the next bedroom. "I'm proud of that boy. I had made up my mind to see that they had some cash for that crop, but they really and truly earned almost a hundred dollars for their share. That Buddy is a good worker. I'm going to give him a crop of his own next year."

He chuckled, "I wish you could have seen the boy driving that truck. I think he had Buddy hidden under the straw. You see, Dr. Hunnicut raised hell because he said old George Glass grabbed his wife's titty when he was doing some painting for them. She wanted old George flogged, but Dr. Hunnicut talked her out of that. He got word to some of the boys from Griffin, and the Klan made a little parade through town and down to George's house.

"The boys had gotten out of colored town before dark and were on the courthouse square when they went through. One of the men who stayed on the street said he didn't see Buddy but that Sambo was trying to sell watermelons to the Klan. Then he drove the truck out of town later by himself, standing up to do it. That's what makes me think he had Buddy hidden. He never would have left without him.

"But don't you mention it to him. I don't want him to think I'm keeping too close an eye on him."

He heard his mother reply sleepily, "I wish you'd think how close an eye he might be keeping on you. Turn off the light and let's go to sleep."

The next morning the boy took a piece of his mother's stationery and wrote "Congratulations and best wishes" on it. He folded it over thirty dollars and tucked it into an envelope. On the outside he wrote "Tutt Bazemore, Peabody, Georgia, Rural Route, Box 95." He thought a minute, tore up the envelope, and addressed another one: "Miss Tutt Bazemore, Peabody, Georgia, Rural Route, Box 95."

The mucilage on the envelope tasted faintly of wintergreen as he licked and sealed it. He felt older.

XV

a week later, he went to church with Ole John Tom Westmoreland. He had already been to Sunday School that morning with his mother and sisters, but there was no preaching at his church because it was not first Sunday. The colored folk were beginning their revival service, which they called Big Meeting, and they did not have Sunday School at all. They were, however, having dinner on the grounds today, and the boy was eager to go.

He had extracted an invitation from Ole John Tom the evening before by directly and simply asking if it would be all right to go to church with him. Ole John Tom assured him that it would be fine for him to go but that he must first be sure he had permission from his parents. There were certain unwritten but nonetheless well-defined barriers of mutual respect between the races. Nowhere has the doctrine of religious freedom been more openly extended than in the rural post-Reconstruction South, except, of course, to Catholics and Jews. As long as a group designated itself Baptist, almost any code of behaviour was acceptable.

One did not, however, attend a strange church out of idle curiosity. Certainly one did not traverse racial lines as a titillated spectator. Although no one had ever bothered to tell the boy that he should not go to a colored church, he knew within his heart that such a venture was strictly taboo. He consequently went about obtaining permission to go with Ole John Tom in a very circuitous fashion.

"Mother," he said in his most soulful tones as they rode to Sunday School that morning, "I feel real good to be going to church this morning."

"That's fine, son," beamed his mother. "It makes me feel good to hear you say that."

"One of the boys in my grade at school says if you go to church too much, it might make you a religious fanatic. He says Summerfield Hammond is one. Do you think you can go to church too much?" he inquired earnestly as his saintly mother guided the square Chevrolet out of the path of an approaching car.

His older sister in the front seat was on a three-day program of ignoring him as punishment for some breach of conduct on his part. She sniffed. The two younger sisters, riding in the back seat with him, had never been able to find any modicum of safety in ignoring him and relied on a mutual assistance pact for survival. They rolled their eyes heavenward and elbowed each other.

"I certainly do not," replied his mother. "Summerfield Hammond is certainly no religious fanatic just because he has dedicated his life to full time Christian service. My greatest dream is to see our church go full time and be able to have a preacher every Sunday. No one in this community is going to church too much."

"No'm, that's what I think. I certainly agree with you," he lied. The prospect of sitting through a one hour sermon by Mr. Cloud every Sunday was not one of joy.

"Isn't there some place in the Bible that says, 'It is good to go into the house of the Lord'?" he continued, contemplating the while how he would enjoy putting his chewing gum in the older sister's hair and tying the shoe laces of the two younger ones together.

"There certainly is, son," responded the captivated mother. "It's in one of the Psalms."

"Well, then," said the boy with judicial demeanor, "that settles it. We all know we should do what the Bible says. I've been thinking about that talk we had on tithing, and I've decided you're right. I want to tithe my watermelons and give a tenth to the Lord.

242

Would you put this eight dollars in the Foreign Missions offering for me this morning?" He leaned over the front seat and slipped the money into her pocketbook.

"You make me so proud and happy, son," said his mother. She paused a moment. "But is this a tenth of all of it? Didn't you and Buddy get some money peddling in Brewtonton? The Lord is not mocked." She paused again. "Remember Ananias," she warned firmly.

"Yes'm," gulped the boy, "but I never did get any of that money. I gave it all to Buddy."

"Why in the world would you do that?"

"Well you see, it's kinda like this—well, what I mean is I figured he had done more of the work than I had and he deserved a little more of the profits than I did. Besides, they're a lot worse off than we are—they don't even have screens in their windows. I just felt called of the Lord to do it," he added valiantly.

"How sweet," murmured the mother, making mental notes about how she might recount this conversation at the next meeting of the Woman's Missionary Union. As they began piling out of the car in the churchyard, the mother looked across at him. "I certainly am a lucky woman to have a son like you." Then she added, "All my children are such a blessing to me."

"What are you up to now?" demanded the baby sister as they walked behind the car.

"I don't know what you mean, and you hush your mouth, you hear?"

In his Sunday School class after the group devotional, he leaned close to JoJo. "Whatcha doin this afternoon?" he whispered in preamble.

"Me'n Little Bob Stubbs goin to put crossed nails on the railroad tracks and let the train mash em together. You wanta come?" asked his baptismal buddy.

"Naw," said the boy. "I had thought we might get up a ball game in the Caldwell pasture, and you and Little Bob would come."

A few minutes later he recited his Bible verse for the

morning and, avoiding the attention of the teacher, whispered again, "The train sounds like more fun. Yall go ahead. I'll just read and fool around this afternoon."

The mention of reading always made JoJo uncomfortable, and the conversation died. On the way home the boy announced, "JoJo and Little Bob Stubbs are going to meet us at the Caldwell pasture right after dinner for a ball game. I'll have to eat in a hurry. He wanted me to go with them to the railroad tracks, but I told him you didn't like for me to play there—it's too dangerous. I thought I might go to the ball game, though, if I don't find something better to do. You don't mind if I eat and run, do you?" he asked his mother.

"No, son, it's all right," she answered, still entranced. "I've about given up on you being able to spend a Sunday afternoon with your sisters without fussing. I'm glad there are going to be some more white boys there. It worries me for you not to have any playmates but those colored boys."

He thought they would never get dinner served and the blessing said. He bolted his food and excused himself as unobtrusively as possible. The father was presiding at the Sunday table, but his eyes were red and the lids puffy, and his attention seemed to be elsewhere. The boy raced to the back yard, leaped on his old bicycle, and pedaled frantically up the road. Even allowing for the difference in the concept of time between the two races, he was afraid he would miss Ole John Tom.

I hope Mother stays too busy to notice I left in my Sunday clothes, he thought as he topped the hill and saw Ole John Tom standing in the middle of a crowd and presiding over the embarkation. He skidded the rear tire on his bicycle sideways to a sudden stop beneath the huge oak tree in the front yard and walked nonchalantly toward the black patriarch.

Ole John Tom Westmoreland was tall and thin and wrinkled. His hair was white as snow and his skin as black as soot. His eyes were yellow. At first meeting, after he moved onto their place some three years previously, the boy thought him the most fascinating person he had ever seen. He had three sets of children living with him, a grown son and two grown daughters from his first wife, five of his current wife's sons from her previous marriage, and three daughters of their own. In addition, one of his grown daughters had two yard babies and the other had one. He controlled a total of four plow hands and eight hoe hands and consequently could trade with almost any cotton farmer he chose.

The boy had assumed that any man who looked like Ole John Tom Westmoreland would rule his environment with dash and vigor and dignified fire. Punishment from him for disobedience would be quick and devastating. No man ever manifested a greater disparity between appearance and personality.

To be sure, he controlled his family well enough. He had the obedience of all his children and stepchildren when he lined out jobs and chores. He enjoyed the support and cooperation of a dutiful wife and the respect of everyone on the farm, for indeed he was a good and dignified man. He accomplished all this, however, through the use of tedium. He never whipped any of his boys. He gave them a talk. This torture might last for an hour, and he enjoyed it as much as they hated it.

His voice was a weapon, understated but indomitable. He never raised it. He simply launched it. It was a dry, rambling monotone, and it continued endlessly. In giving instructions he could nag and natter in such a reasonable fashion and for so long that his children were conditioned to move with alacrity in obedience. Their attitude was that it was better to work three hours than to listen to a thirty minute lecture on why and how they should. His children were all hard workers. A Sunday spent in the company of Ole John Tom made them desperate to leap into the physical release of the cotton field on Monday morning.

After the first year on the farm, the boy's father abandoned any effort to advise Ole John Tom about crops, fields, tools, or labor. After two years he avoided him altogether. The boy had overheard him tell the mother, "There's not enough time in my life for that old man. Having nothing to say, he says it all day long."

The grandfather, peppery with the impatience of dotage and one generation more paternalistic toward Negroes, had once roared at Ole John Tom, "Shut your infernal black mouth! I've heard enough. When I ask what time it is, I don't want somebody to tell me how to build a goddam watch!"

He had strutted off in a whitehaired rage, and Ole John Tom had shrugged his shoulders and mumbled to the boy in self-righteous equanimity, "Yo granpaw sho is fractious today which they ain't no tellin whut ail him which I stayed with a man in Senoia wunst name of Mr. Hutchinson McKnight what got so fractious you couldn't hardly never say nothin to him atall which it turnt out he wadn't gittin no sleep cause he had trouble passin his water an when he finely give in an go to a doctor it turnt out to be his prostrate glands an they tuk him plumb to Atlanta an bored a hole thu em an he come home passin water like a spiggot but his disposition never was the same no mo which it remind me of a ole coon dog I had wunst long time ago I guess it was befo I left Pike County whilest my first wife was yet alivin and seems like it was whilest I stayed wid Mr. Looney McElroy but I don't zactly rec'llect what year it wuz which it may been two maybe three years atter de bad drought in '25 an nat ole dawg got so snarly an snappified couldn't hardly nobody atall git anywheres aroun him. Anyways. . . ." He took a breath.

"Gosh, John Tom, I gotta go," interrupted the boy. "I forgot something I just have to do." As he walked off rapidly, he added over his shoulder, "I want to hear about that coon dog some time. I love to hear you tell about coon hunting."

Ole John Tom loved the boy.

This Sunday afternoon, when the boy approached him, he cocked an eye at him suspiciously,"Yo folks say it all right you go to church wi me, Sambo?"

"They sure did. At least Mother did. Daddy didn't seem to be feeling so good, and I didn't want to bother him, but Mother said she was real proud of me and that you just can't go to church too much."

"Dat Miss Vera sho a fine woman which you gwine hatta set in my lap an you hatta be a good boy an behave yoself in church now an make everbody proud of you an show you had some raisin

246

an Willie, you gwine drive of co'se which I can't let nobody but you tetch my car caze I don't drive myself an which I mainly keep one fo de fambly anyhow an to go to church in an, Pee-Ball, you an Shoatie gotta double up an set on each other's laps an, Sallie Mae, honey, you set on yo maw's lap an hold de bucket of vittles on top ne car an les see, Pint, you a big boy now an you kin hold two o' yo lil sisters an. . . ."

The monologue continued while children frantically piled into the car in a desperate effort to stop the sound at its source. They were all scrubbed shiny clean. The clothes of the boys smelled of lye soap and the girls' dresses of starch. The wooly hair of the girls was pulled so tightly in new braids that their eyes almost slanted, and it glistened with the sheen of Royal Crown Pomade. Packed into the car, they were all decorous and subdued on the way to church.

The boy, perched on Ole John Tom's bony knees, his head bent forward and neck arched against the roof, noted that there were thirteen people in the vehicle, five in the front and eight in the back. Nobody talked on the four mile trip to church except Ole John Tom. Once the boy tried to interrupt him to confide importantly that he had brought along a dollar for the collection. Ole John Tom's discourse about the virtues of going to church and serving the Lord continued as relentlessly as the turgid current of Flint River, and the boy's remark fell like a leaf on the surface and floated away unnoticed. He was glad when the ride was over.

The church was the usual white frame building, its outlines softened by feathers of peeling paint. Its steeple was oddly foreshortened and squat, proportions which the boy thought characterized colored churches so surely that one could separate them from white churches just by looking at the steeples. It was hugged into a curving arm of oak trees, and its bare yard was freshly swept. A scattering of automobiles was haphazardly parked near the scrawny little cemetery that had rocks and unpainted boards as grave markers. There was one wagon in the group of vehicles, its mules tied in head-drooping, tail-swishing patience to a cedar tree.

The yard seemed full of people. On the other side of the church from the parked cars was a long table improvised from planks and sawhorses. There was a profusion of food spread out, and women and children were slowly waving chinaberry branches above it to discourage the sticky and heavy-bodied flies. People were going in and out of the two front doors of the church in such steady streams that the boy was reminded of the mouth of an ant hill. He could hear singing from inside the church, and he assumed that services had already begun. At his own church, people would have gone inside as soon as they heard the hymns or at least have lowered their voices to hushed and reverent rumbles if they stayed outside.

He timidly confided this to Ole John Tom's wife, who quickly reassured him, "Law, Sambo, we ain't late. Dis de way we do. Sing a little, pray a little, take up a little money. Maybe three, four, five o'clock come out and eat. Jes whenever de Reverend git done preaching. He ain't even started yet. Lemme set my vittles down over here wid Mattie Kate and we go on in de church. Howdy, Brother Clemons, yall all doin all right?. . .Yeah, dat white chile Mr. Porter's boy. He come wid us."

Accustomed to his small size making him anonymous in a crowd, the boy suddenly felt that he stood out like a sore thumb. He was the only white person on the premises. Granted there were several mulattoes, even some with blue eyes—no one with any expertise could be deceived. He felt that his sunbleached white mop of hair was as conspicuous as a waving flag. Although he knew some of the Negroes present, the vast majority of them were total strangers. He was acutely conscious that there was a change in attitude whenever anyone saw him.

A man or woman could be greeting the Westmoreland family in a relaxed and jovial manner. When the boy was spied, there was an immediate change. The laughter would cease, the voices would drop, and the spines would invariably straighten a little. Although people resumed polite conversation at once, it was apparent that they were conscious of him. Even as they talked, they rolled their eyes and cast covert glances at him, their attention irresistibly drawn to the strange visitor.

The boy thought they behaved for all the world like a high strung horse approaching an unfamiliar object on a well-known road. If one of them had twitched his ears, snorted loudly, and then leaped sideways, he would not have found it incongruous. He felt different because they all behaved differently as soon as they saw him. Clothed in the armor of whiteness, with the protective mantle of being his father's son as additional security, he felt no fear. He did, however, feel distinctly uncomfortable. He realized this was because he was white, and he fancied himself a stranger in a foreign land.

With diffidence he sidled up to Ole John Tom. That individual had not ceased talking since he got out of the car. The rattle of his dry monotone cleared a space before him as well-defined as though he had personal bodyguards preceding him. People walked to the periphery of the charmed space and actually leaned over to shake hands. Their own respectful greeting dropped unnoticed on the ebb tide of his voice, and they retreated rapidly. In this fashion Ole John Tom was making steady progress through the crowd toward the steps of the church.

When they entered the building, the sound of singing, only dim background while they were outdoors, became the dominant stimulus. There was no piano or other accompaniment. None was needed. The loud clapping of hands in the beat of the hymn was as rhythmic and deliberate as a metronome. There were several soprano voices, keenly falsetto and penetrating, that skittered high over the congregation like violin notes or the trill of a flute. The tenors and the contraltos were saxophones and second violins, and some of the men were tubas or bass fiddles. The clapping, however, was what carried the music. Everybody in the building clapped.

Some stood up to clap. Some arched their bodies and swayed their hips in rhythm as they clapped. The clapping was so loud that the singing voices were heard only between the explosions of smacking palms, and the whole building shook in percussive rhythm. Mouths were stretched wide and some eyes squinted shut as the members sang their hearts out. The boy had never seen such total and enthusiastic group participation. He pressed his alien body to Ole John Tom's angular frame as that venerable patriarch ambled down to the Amen corner at the front of the church.

Seated on the distant side of his host and fused as closely and inconspicuously to him as possible, feet dangling in mid-air, the boy sought desperately to adjust to this new environment.

He had fancied himself no stranger to Negro music. For years, in the twilight evenings of deep summer, he had sat at the feet of his grandfather on the verandah and listened to Lisbon and his children across the fields at their house. At the end of a hard day in the cotton fields, their songs began after supper and always started with a low humming to establish both mood and harmony. Soon they swelled into crooning melodies that were softened by darkness and muted by distance into sounds as sweet and smooth as new-strained honey. Though the words through the dusk and across the darkened cotton fields were unintelligible, the message was clearly one of fulfillment and contentment. It served as reassurance that the universe was a place of order and happiness and that everything *must* be all right. He realized suddenly that his grandfather's rocker was not present and he was in a situation that he had never imagined. This was no evening lullaby of people compliant and satisfied. This was a new world for him, and he faced it on his own.

"He said, 'If I be lifted up,'" the congregation sang.

Ole John Tom began a belching bass right in his ear. The voices were ringing out, the feet of the men were tapping, the torsos of otherwise staid and dignified matrons were swaying from side to side, and rhythm filled the church from floor to ceiling. The boy fancied the hypnotic clapping was an escape valve for the unbearable pressure of the pure rhythm that was filling the building. The aisles were full of people constantly going in and out of the church. Most were young girls and women, who seemed to have no particular motive or purpose. They simply sauntered out and then presently sauntered back in. There was nothing shy or discreet about them, either—if they chose to laugh or talk in the aisle, they did so. Their elders gave no disapproving looks at them. In fact, there were no disapproving looks anywhere, and also no prim, pursed mouths, and no straight, stiff spines.

Of a sudden a middle-aged woman across the church rose to her feet, shoulders sagging, head rolling on limber neck, long arms waving in rhythm as if they had no bones in them. She clapped loudly to the beat and her voice rose out above all the rest, with passion and fervor greater than the words:

> I be yo father, I be yo mother,
> I be yo sister, or yo brother . . .

Behind him one of the old deacons yelled, "Sing it then," and clapped like a pistol shot. The other men chorused "Amen" or "Yes, Lord," and the woman's voice became higher and shriller. She wagged her head as though shaking a yoke loose.

> He said, "If I be lifted up
> I bring joy into yo soul. . . ."

She sat down as the singing and the clapping continued. The boy was mesmerized. This was like no church he had ever seen. This was joy and sorrow at the same time. This was pain and ecstasy combined. This was promise and denial.

This was total abandonment of self to something wild and unspeakably primitive. This was passion such as he had never imagined, and some small part of it had to be sexual. This, he decided, was no place for white folks. He wriggled a little closer to Ole John Tom. It took only the slightest imagination to transform the slow clapping to the more rapid rhythm of tom-toms, the swaying and foot tapping to frenzied dancing, and the shrill singing to wild supplications before mysterious gods. This was the jungle. He didn't understand it, and he was afraid all the way to his bones.

He became aware that Ole John Tom was talking to him, "Where yo dollar? They fixin to take up collection."

The preacher, as gaunt and double-jointed as a wooden puppet, was holding both arms outstretched for silence as the hymn ended. This did not slow the coming and going of the girls in the aisle. The boy noticed that the preacher's long extended fingers almost curled back on themselves. He thought they were proportioned like the toes on a tree frog and looked as though they might have suction cups on the tips. In a booming baritone that filled every corner, he announced that an offering was now going to be taken for the work of the Lord and that everyone was expected to contribute as much as he or she could afford. No matter what that amount might be, everyone was supposed to contribute.

The boy could identify with this exhortation. Give or take an inflection here, a cadence there, and two or three distinctively pronounced words, he could close his eyes and transpose the rigid-spined, dusty-gray preacher of his own church into this pulpit. The message was the same.

He reached in his pocket, dug out his dollar bill and showed it to Ole John Tom, who nodded approvingly. The preacher was leaning over the pulpit, swinging a simian arm over the table below it.

"While we sing the offatory hymn, let all dat love de Lawd come forth and lay de proof of it on dis here altar. Let the pee-pul come, saith de Lawd," he rumbled in irresistible rhythm. He moved to the side of the table, raised his long arm in the air, a green piece of money dangling from his fingers, and thundered, "Hit's my high privilege to be the fust to approach de tabernacle of de Most High wid my gift—uh. Follow de precepts of de high priest of de Most High—uh. See here, chirren of God, I'm givin mine, I'm givin mine—uh. Let de people come." He leaned over and planted his money firmly on the table top.

Then he straightened, clashed his two huge hands like startling cymbals, and led off.

Nobody knows the trouble I've seen;
Nobody knows but Jesus . . .

The whole church came alive in response. The swaying and clapping resumed. A keening soprano from the rear of the church soared out.

Sometimes I'm up, sometimes I'm down,
O, yes, Lord,
Sometimes I'm nearly to the ground,
Glory hallelujah. . . .

The boy was stunned with disbelief. He had assumed that the ritual of a collection plate being passed up one pew and down the other by solemn deacons was as universal as wearing clothes to church. These people were expected to march down the aisle individually and place their offering on that table beneath the waving, singing preacher and before the eyes of everyone assembled. As he watched, the congregation began responding.

There was no order or system to it. People rose from the front, the middle, or the back of the church, squeezed over the knees of their fellows, and came down the aisle to the front. They walked in rhythm to the clapping. The women untied corners of their handkerchiefs on the way down the aisle to release the coins they had knotted therein. The preacher was threatening, beseeching, and promising. The clapping pervaded everything. Some of the people were going to the table more than once. The preacher became frenzied. The boy was terrified. He felt Ole John Tom nudge him. He heard his growl, "Now a good time to go, Sambo."

Desperately he tried to hand him the dollar. Ole John Tom folded it back into his hand. "You gotta go yoself, Sambo. Don't be timmified about it." He pushed him again.

He felt that the deacons were all staring at him and willing him to rise. He knew the preacher was looking at him. He closed his eyes. Our merciful Heavenly Father, he implored, if You can

253

reach me through all this, help me now. Hold Thy humble servant in the palm of Thy hand. Remember Elisha and Naaman, Merciful Father, and help me down that aisle.

He rose on rubbery legs and stepped out into the aisle. As he did so, his roving, frightened eye spied Buddy across the church. Buddy was clapping and singing, but when he saw the boy, he grinned broadly and pointed a finger at him in derisive salutation. For a moment the boy was comforted by the sight of someone so familiar and so associated with security.

Looking again, he realized that Buddy was comfortable and at home and that he felt none of the terror and desperation that he was feeling. He thought back a week when Buddy was lying quivering and pleading under the straw on the floor of the truck. That's the fix you're in now, he thought. It's just your imagination. Nobody's going to hurt you. If the Ku Klux came through here now, everybody would run. I think.

He felt annoyed at Buddy for laughing. He drew himself erect and squared his thin shoulders. He imagined himself garbed in a long white robe with full sleeves and a tall pointed hood on his head. In his mind he pulled a mask down over his face. "Well, call Dr. Redwine," he murmured with bravado and marched down the aisle.

He made no effort to accommodate his step to the rhythm of the singing. As conspicuous and foreign as he was, he felt that any effort to blend with the crowd was completely futile. His palsied fingers made the dollar bill dance uncontrollably as he laid it on the pile of coins and scattered bills on the table. He had no feeling of worship or offering. This situation had nothing to do with the Georgia Baptist Orphans' Home or Lottie Moon or missionaries to China. He was dealing in ransom and hoped fervently that it was adequate.

Regardless of the words to the songs that were sung, Jesus and Jehovah, he thought, were nowhere near this building. They were off in the white man's world, listening patiently to the sermons of Dwight L. Moody or Sam Jones and making civilized contracts with the sweetly whining Louie D. Newton. Elijah at Carmel had to be the bravest man in history.

Thank you, Lord, he prayed, for bringing Thy humble servant this far in safety. Now let me see You get him back to Ole John Tom.

"Somethimes I'm nearly to the ground," a high falsetto voice screamed in dramatic insistent rhythm.

"Sing it, then."

"Praise the Lord."

"Hallelujah, Lord," interjected the deacons. Amid the clapping and swaying, the boy made his way back to his seat, eyes lowered in his old familiar pretense at modesty. He heard one sister yell to another between claps, "Ain't dat sweet?" As he wriggled into the haven of Ole John Tom's circling arm, he realized that the front of his pants was damp.

Intimidated and astounded by the offertory, the boy soon realized that his initiation had only begun. There was more fire and fervor in the very beginning of this preacher's sermon than in the evangelical climax of any sermon the boy had ever heard in the Peabody Baptist Church. Prancing like a drum major one moment, crouching like a cat, leaping in the air and gyrating like a dervish, that preacher was all over the front of the church. He jerked his body; he jerked his head. He screamed, he shouted, and he yelled. His great thick lips looked prehensile as they reached out to grab words, caress them, and then hurl them like lightning bolts across the church.

Soon he quit preaching and began chanting and crowing, his message broken into rhythms as definite as any iambic pentameter but much shorter and more basic. He opened his mouth so wide the boy thought his jaws would come unhinged, and the back of his throat seemed as visible as his huge flat nose. The boy could not tear his gaze away. He could not imagine anyone making himself look like that on purpose.

Within ten minutes there was not a dry thread on the preacher, and sweat was running down his face in streams. He mopped himself with a handkerchief as big as a quarter of a bed sheet, but he never stopped his dance and never broke the rhythm of his chant. The boy saw him as a savage jungle warrior or a rabble-rousing witch doctor and could not have been more apprehensive if a gorilla had been unleashed in the pulpit.

The response of the audience was total. In time with the rhythmic grunts and jerky pauses of the preacher, it moved as a single unit, swaying from one side to the other, its universal voice chorusing, "Yes, Lord," or "Amen," in perfect, punctuating cadence. As frenzy mounted and passion grew until it was almost unbearable, individuals began getting the spirit and falling out all across the church.

At last the boy learned the function of the ladies in the aisle. When a good sister screamed, rose to her feet, stiffened, raised rigid arms in convulsing motion overhead, and began "drawing," then a couple of the ladies would rush to her. With smooth competence they would lower her to the floor, stroke her face, and begin fanning her. Such an event caused no interruption in the sermon. It seemed to whip the preacher into greater frenzy, and this in turn produced more outpouring of the spirit as manifested by the screaming, falling women. The boy longed to run but was convinced that if he did he would be snatched up and thrown into a cooking pot. All he could do was sit very still and pray for this to be over soon. He longed for calm as a thirsting man craves water.

The preacher boomed,

> Daniel stood firm, uh,
> He did not move, uh,
> He looked at dat lion, uh,
> But he did not move, uh,
> De Lawd was with him, uh,
> De Lawd was on his right hand, uh,
> De Lawd give him stren'th, uh,
> Praise de Lawd, uh.

"The Lord is my shepherd. I shall not want," said the boy softly.

>   Daniel was not afeard, uh,
>   Daniel was not afeard of dat lion, uh,
>   De Lawd God of Hosts was with him, uh,
>   Dat lion growl, uh, he lash his tail, uh,
>   He open his big ol mouf, uh,
>   And he let out a roar, uh,
>   Daniel was not afeard, uh, I tell you
>   Daniel was not afeard of dat lion, uh,
>   Daniel was not afeard!

"He leadeth me beside the still waters," the boy continued determinedly.

"Lawd, I'm comin! I'm comin *home!*" screamed a thirty-year-old fat woman across the aisle. She arched her back and rolled her eyes. Two girls ran to her and started fanning her.

"Uh-huh," chanted the congregation, swaying to one side. "Yes, Lawd," it chanted, swaying to the other.

>   Daniel felt hot breath, uh,
>   He felt hot breath on his face, uh,
>   He didn't blink his eyes, uh,
>   He stood firm, uh.
>   He was not afeard of dat lion, uh,
>   Daniel was not afeard of dat lion!

"I shall fear no evil, for Thou art with me," murmured the boy.

Suddenly wild, erratic screams erupted from the back of the church, accompanied by stamping and bumping of pews. The preacher cried out, "Good Godamighty!" and stopped in mid-sentence. People began leaping out windows in shrieking pandemonium. The boy looked beyond the melee and saw two black men standing in the doors, covered with blood.

One of them was cut from the top of his head to the angle of his jaw. The severed meat hung in a flap over his eyes, and the gleaming white bone of his skull was exposed. Clotted blood slid like crimson snails down the front of his overalls. The other man was taller and a little bit blacker but just as bloody. His wounds, however, were not readily apparent.

Both men brandished knives. The boy recognized them as the brothers Clarence and Coot, who had worked on the farm forever. Coot was fairly stable and could stay married for two or three years at the time. Clarence usually boarded with him, since his efforts at matrimony never lasted more than two or three months. Both of them ritualistically got drunk every weekend but were always in the field on Monday with fetid breath and white scum in the corners of their eyes.

When the boy was very young, he had witnessed Clarence receive a whipping at the hands of the grandfather. He had been caught stealing from a neighboring tenant, and the punishment was preordained and swift. He was stripped to the waist and his hands tied overhead to the limb of an apple tree. The cool and impartial grandfather laid great welts across his back with a plowline in a series of almost interminable blows, the fleshy thudding sounds of which profaned the summer air.

The giant's piteous grunts and cries had sickened the boy, and he had vomited in the weeds behind the smokehouse, lying there in retching weakness long after Clarence was untied and quiet restored. He hated the memory of that morning so much that he had blocked it from his consciousness, but now he recalled it as Clarence flourished his knife overhead, spit blood out of his mouth, and roared, "Where Ole John Tom Westmoreland? I gwine cut his scrawny ole th'oat whilest I's at it! He think he so good; I gwine show him what a *bad* nigger can do!"

People thronged the aisles, screaming and clamoring for escape. The preacher had disappeared out the door behind the pulpit, and the faithful were stampeding to follow him. Many were still jumping out the windows. The church was clearing rapidly. Ole John Tom emitted an unintelligible groan and vanished into the crowd behind the pulpit. The boy climbed over pews until he reached a clear place in the aisle and advanced on the weaving black Goliath.

"Clarence," he ordered firmly, "give me that knife and behave yourself. If you don't I'm going to tell Mr. Porter."

After labored effort at comprehension, Clarence meekly handed over the knife and leaned against the wall. The odor of fresh human blood and cheap groundhog whiskey was nauseating.

"Coot," the boy began as he turned to the shorter, stockier brother with the gaping head wound. He never finished the sentence, for Coot crashed to the floor in such heavy unconsciousness that the entire church shook. The boy raced to the door.

"Help!" he shouted into the yard.

Total confusion greeted him. People were yelling and screaming and running in all directions at once. There were at least five men dripping blood. One was lying across the picnic table, another stretched on the roots of an oak tree, and three were staggering around the yard. The boy spied Willie Westmoreland.

"Come here quick, Willie," he commanded. "We got one bad hurt in here."

He flew back into the church and leaned over the unconscious Coot. Blood was still flowing in a steady stream over his face. He reached in his pocket with blood-sticky fingers for his handkerchief. It was too small to serve any function at all. He fumbled the buttons on his shirt loose, jerked it off, and crammed it into the head wound, securing it with the bloody handkerchief. Willie Westmoreland stuck his head cautiously around the door.

"He ain't daid, is he, Sambo?"

"Naw, he's living. But he's cut up something fierce. Pull your paw's car up to the foot of the steps and get somebody to help load him. We got to get him to a doctor."

As Willie hesitated, the dry voice of Ole John Tom directed, "Do whut he say, Willie, and make 'as'e!"

The boy looked up to see his friend, who had gathered enough courage to return. He still kept a wary eye on the disarmed Clarence, however, who by now was sitting on the floor in a drunken stupor, blubbering inanely and bleeding from a cut across his cheek.

"Hold this shirt tight on Coot's head, John Tom," he directed, "and give me your handkerchief so I can tie up Clarence's face. What in the world happened out there? It's as bloody as a hog-killing."

His fear of a few minutes earlier had vanished. The fantasies had stopped with the sermon. Although he was very excited now, his head was clear and his thinking had direction. These were his people who were hurt. They all belonged on the same land. Since he was the son of the owner of the land, these people, in the absence of his father, became his responsibility if they were in trouble. The rules were clear on this point, and he moved in obedience to them as he tried to think what his father would have him do.

Ole John Tom, delighted to be asked a direct question, was rattling in reply, "Law, Sambo, dese two boys come up out dere in de church yard which dey had been drinkin right sharply an dey tole Mattie Kate dey was hongry an to give em some vittles which she had a dish o' cabbage in her hand she was takin to de table an she tole em straight out dey ought not to be in de church yard adrinkin like dat which dey oughtn but dar dey wuz anyhow an everbody roun here know not to mess wit Clarence caze he so mean he kilt a nigger wunst 'n den went to de settin-up an Coot tole her to shut up effen he wanted to hear some preachin he'd go inside an he grab at dat dish of cabbage an spill it in de dirt an Mattie Kate lost her temper an slap him up side de head hard as she kin and Clarence yell out You can't do dat to my brother and slap Mattie Kate plumb to de groun an den her oldes boy say You can't do dat to my maw and he git his knife at Clarence but he duck an got cut on de face instid of in his th'oat which angerfied Coot an Clarence both an dey pulled dey knives an fust thing you know everbody in de yard was fightin an hit's a good thing dey was fightin over cabbage which effen it had been sweet potato pie wouldn't be a nigger lef standin an I believe Possum's oldes boy gwine die some 'un say he stab plumb to de hollow an Coot cut up de nex worse but here come Willie les git him in de car which he gwine mess it up but I guess hit'll wash. . . ."

As he and Ole John Tom and Willie roared up the road in a cloud of dust with Coot and Clarence as compliant passengers, the boy considered his own position. Ole John Tom was in the front seat giving Willie directions and innumerable reasons why they were going to the big house to get Mr. Porter instead of directly to Brewtonton to hunt a doctor. The boy realized that the real reason for his absence from home was about to be revealed in dramatic fashion.

The father, he had long since discovered, was not enthusiastic at all about being surprised, and was apt to react reflexly and violently, deferring questions until later. In the parlance of the boys who shot marbles for keeps, he decided that he did not have a good lay, and he was filled with foreboding.

"Set down on that horn, Willie," he commanded as they turned off the big road into the driveway of his home. That, he thought, should get his father so irritated with Willie that some of his anger would be diverted.

"Quit blowing that damn horn in my front yard!" roared his father moments later as the car jerked to a halt. He surveyed the bloody car with controlled calm, and the boy's admiration was boundless when he quietly said, "Tell me what happened and only one of you talk at a time."

Minutes later, that remarkable man had climbed behind the wheel of his own car and was saying, "You boys follow me into town and we'll get a doctor."

He turned to the boy. "No, you can't go. You'd better go find your mother. JoJo's mother brought him to play with you, and you're in trouble. They couldn't find anybody playing ball in Caldwell's pasture." He paused and added gravely, "That's a good job you did on Coot. I'm proud of you. Don't worry about him—he's going to be all right."

The boy walked around the corner of the house and mounted the back porch steps. His mother was waiting for him.

"Well, young man, you're pretty smart, aren't you? You really caught me off guard with your little act this morning. I want you to know that even the devil can quote scripture to his purpose, and you're not the only one who can do it. Listen to this," she said.

" 'Thou shalt not bear false witness.'

" 'Honor thy father and mother, that thy days may be long on the earth.'

" 'Bring up a child in the way he should go, and when he is old he will not depart from it.' "

She paused. Leaning over the table behind her, she picked up three freshly cut, keenly bending peachtree switches. The boy could smell their rank, unpleasant odor. As she opened her mouth to speak, the boy joined her and they spoke in unison. " 'Spare the rod and spoil the child.' "

"That's right," his mother said. "Also, 'God is not mocked,' and your mother is no longer deceived. Drop those pants!"

One month before his fourteenth birthday, the boy received his last switching. Of a sudden he resolved not to cry or dance. As the keen switches cut into his bare thighs and calves, he could not help flinching. He did not cry out or jump in the air, however. He stood straight and still and took the blows on his bare flesh, pretending that he was somewhere else and this was not really happening to him. The duration of the torture confirmed the premise of a lifetime that the louder one yelled and the more wildly one danced, the shorter the switching. He thought she would never quit.

When it was finally over and his red-faced and exhausted mother had left him to put on his pants, the boy examined the interlacing network of red welts that stung like so many bees and looked like a haphazard collection of earthworms. He felt peaceful and clean, absolved of guilt and free of sin.

"I wish I had my eight dollars back," he said aloud. Then he added silently, I didn't really mean that, most merciful Heavenly Father. Forgive Thy humble servant. He's had a hard day.

XVI

When school resumed that year, he was a junior, a position so much higher in the school hierarchy that it took several days for him to adapt to his new importance. The first day in English class, the teacher told them to write a theme on something they did that summer. The boy could not recall a single event enough out of the ordinary to be of interest to town sophisticates. He thought for five minutes and then wrote a completely fabricated account of a Sunday School picnic at Indian Springs.

He had no difficulty getting his subjects scheduled. Although he was still the smallest boy in the school, he noted with gratification that most of the freshmen and some of the sophomores treated him with respect. The freshmen boys threw up their hands and called his name when they met him in the hall, for all the world, he thought, like children who want to be noticed. He recalled the self-conscious discomfort he had experienced two years earlier and was cordial in his replies. He was unusually warm and solicitous to the ones who seemed most timid and country. It made him feel good.

It made him feel even better when one of the town girls in his class came to tell him that she needed his help. She and one other girl and the boy were the only students in the third year Latin class. Mr. Gill had confided to this particular girl, who just happened to be a child of the largest family in town and a member of his church, that he was going to drop third year Latin from the curriculum. He pointed out that only a small number of students would be benefitted and that the new Latin teacher was unwilling to expend her energies on a group so small.

This town girl, even in the relatively sophisticated and mature circles of the tenth grade, was still called Little Betty Lou. She was the same girl who had wet the floor in Mrs. Culpepper's fourth grade, and she had managed to turn that childhood trauma to advantage with consummate manipulative skill. All she needed to do when faced with a crisis at school was to breathe deeply, close her eyes, and begin trembling. This would bring an instant flurry of loyal girl friends around her, which in turn would attract an alarmed teacher, and in a matter of minutes she would be solicitously escorted from the classroom and sent home for the rest of the day.

The boy had noticed that these attacks in high school usually occurred during written examinations. Little Betty Lou never had a spell until the questions were all on the blackboard. She frequently was given the examination later, and some of the more deeply involved teachers would even drop it by her home so that she could suffer in the privacy of her boudoir.

Despite the delicacy of her nervous system and these periodic shocks to it, she managed to make consistently good grades. Her fellow students had been successfully conditioned over the years to regard her as a creature set apart who deserved unusual consideration. No one showed any of the jealousy that special privilege usually evoked, although the boy occasionally wondered if her life would have been different if her bladder had been more dependable in the fourth grade.

She was enrolled in the third year Latin class because she wanted to go to Sophie Newcomb College when she graduated, and she had been told that Latin was a prerequisite. The three students had already bought their grammar books and selections from Cicero and had been well into the third day of translations when Mr. Gill singled out Little Betty Lou to make his announcement. He prudently stopped her in the hall on her way to the rest room.

Although she breathed deeply, shut her eyes, and even trembled a little, her arts were futile. Mr. Gill just rocked from one foot to the other, jingled his keys, and plopped his lower plate about while looking fixedly at a point two feet over her head. As soon as he finished talking, he backed into his office, closed the door, and rang the bell for recess.

Little Betty Lou was so startled that she walked right up to the boy as he stood on tiptoe getting books out of his locker. He was also startled. He could not recall ever having seen her alone before, and he was quite certain that she had never before spoken to him without an audience. She was usually accompanied by at least two or three other girls, who surrounded her and did her talking for her. The implication was that she could not be bothered.

Now, as she spoke directly to the boy in a cracked tremolo of a voice, words coming out in breathless spurts, he decided that she was pretty cute.

"Little Betty Lou," he said, "don't you worry. Don't get excited and don't you worry." He resisted the impulse to pat her on the head.

"Today is Friday," he reflected. "That gives us plenty of time. I'll have to talk to my daddy and get him to put us on the agenda, and we'll go before the Board of Education next Tuesday."

"Go to the Board of Education?" Little Betty Lou repeated in panic. "I couldn't do that. I'd be scared to death."

"You won't have to say a word," promised the boy. "The rest of us will do the talking. We need as many as we can get, though. You reckon you can talk Annie Ruth and Wynette into taking Latin for another year? I know Virginia will go with us, and five will sure look better than three."

"Oh, I don't know," quavered Little Betty Lou. "Annie Ruth said before school started she wasn't even going to think about taking Latin again. She said she already can't forget 'amo, amas, amat' from the first year and 'Omnia Gallia in tres partes divisa est' from the second. She said she doesn't want any more stuff like that cluttering up her mind for the rest of her life and she doesn't even want to talk about a third year."

"She'll go with us if you ask her," said the boy. "She doesn't exactly have to say that she's going to take third year Latin herself. She can just say she would like to see it offered. And looking at it that way, I bet you could talk Leonard into going with us, too. He likes you."

"Ooh-wee," crackled the girl. "All this just plumb makes me dizzy."

"Don't get excited, Little Betty Lou," admonished the boy. "You just talk to your friends and I'll talk to my daddy. And tell them not to say anything about it. We don't want it to get back to Mr. Gill before we go."

"Law, me," whimpered the girl, "I hadn't thought about that. I sure wouldn't want to hurt Mr. Gill's feelings. He's so sweet. Do you think he'll get upset?"

"Now, Little Betty Lou, when did you ever see Mr. Gill upset? He's just enforcing some rule that's been handed down by the Board of Education. He probably wouldn't want us bothering the Board with our little problems, that's all. You want to go to Sophie Newcomb, don't you?"

"Oh, my, yes," breathed Little Betty Lou. "I don't believe I could face my parents if I didn't get in at Sophie. That's why I came to you in the first place. Mama met someone in Atlanta whose daughter went to that school, and she's determined for me to go."

When they parted and the boy was walking down the hall, he mused, Now, why didn't Mr. Gill say anything to me about that? Come to think of it, I don't believe he's even spoken to me since school started. I had made up my mind to steer clear of him, but do you suppose he's trying to ignore me? We'll soon find out, the old goat!

On Sunday when he explained the situation to his father, he was met at first with an explosion. "That dried-up old jackass! I should have pushed last spring to get rid of him! You don't need to come before the Board. I can handle this little matter with an executive order from the County School Superintendent."

He looked speculatively at the boy. "Wait a minute, though. You say there are six of you who want to come to the Board

266

meeting? And one of them is Bartow Braxton's daughter?" He narrowed his eyes. "This might be just the Trojan horse I need. Yall come on to the Board meeting. Come early, and we'll be waiting for you." He slapped the boy on the shoulder. "Don't you worry. Everything will turn out all right!"

As he left the room, the boy felt deliciously conspiratorial. For a moment he considered Mr. Gill and almost felt sorry for him. Then he shrugged and muttered, "Call Dr. Redwine. He sure done it hisself."

The following Tuesday, walking to town with his five classmates, he thought back to his trip the previous year and remembered his stop for a word of prayer. There's no need for that this year, he thought. I'm not even nervous. With my daddy on my side there's no need worrying the Lord with third year Latin. We can handle it.

He looked over at Little Betty Lou, flanked by two of her friends, all of them chattering animatedly in the excitement of doing something new and daring. Her daddy must be extra important, he thought. She's not much taller than I am. I bet she's not a bit over five feet. She sure has pretty titties, though. I wonder where Sophie Newcomb is.

When they entered the echoing old courthouse, the audacity of their errand became real, and they lowered their voices to whispers and walked on tiptoe. Their presence was obviously expected, and the boy shook hands only with the chairman this time. He lapsed once again into the security of formality as he introduced each of his fellow students. He saved Little Betty Lou for the last and carefully kept his voice expressionless as he said, "Last but not least, and certainly well-admired, Miss Elizabeth Louise Braxton."

Although all the Board members smiled, it was obvious that Mr. Gooch was overdoing it. The chairman almost simpered as he thrust his leonine head forward over his tieless shirt collar and fluttered his thick, plow-cracked fingers in a coyly welcoming wave. Little Betty Lou blushed but did not seem to think the homage inappropriate.

"Gentlemen, we thank you for this audience, and we want you to know that we students appreciate the wonderful job you do for us as members of the Board of Education. We know that each of you has to lay aside his personal business to come into town each month and be sure that our fine school is functioning properly and that we are getting the best education possible."

He paused. It was obvious that he had their attention. "We hate to take your time away from more valuable business, but this group of students needs your help. Mr. Gill has told one of our group that third year Latin is going to be discontinued because there are not enough students signed up to take it. We are here to protest that action and beg your intervention. All of us in this room want to go on to college when we finish high school next year. Another year of Latin will make it easier for all of us."

Deciding rapidly not to make any reference to the teacher, he continued, "I have to have a Latin background for the study of medicine, and one of our students will not even be able to enter the college she wants without a minimum of three years of Latin. Little Betty Lou, would you mind telling these gentlemen where you want to go to school?" he asked innocently, stepping back and turning his head.

The girl's face pinked up in the deepest blush he had ever seen. Bravely she raised her head, looked pleadingly at the chairman, and in her little crackling voice volunteered, "My mama wants me to go to a school over in New Orleans called Sophie Newcomb, and Porter's correct. They require three years of Latin to enter." She closed her eyes, drew a deep breath, and trembled slightly. Annie Ruth and Wynette moved protectively closer to her. The chairman rose to his feet.

"I don't know about the rest of you men, but I'm gittin plumb tired of hearing about this scheduling mess ever fall. I thought we settled that last year. I think we oughta tell ole Gill to teach that stuff just as long as there's one boy or gal down there what wants to take it. Kin I git a motion on that?"

In a short time the students were headed down the courthouse steps with a written document of permission in their possession. Annie Ruth turned to the boy in fierce indignation. "I thought you told her she wouldn't have to say a word!"

"I did, but it just seemed like the thing to do at the time. And didn't it work? Little Betty Lou was just great. She did a good job, and she was a lot better than I was. I'd have been begging for another half hour. Little Betty Lou, I think we all owe you a vote of thanks. I'm sorry if I embarrassed you."

"That's all right," the girl answered, leaning forward between the flanking Annie Ruth and Wynette to address him. "It wasn't so bad, and after all you were doing it because I asked you to. Thank you."

He hitched the left leg of his knickers up. He felt accepted at court. "Shoot, that wasn't anything. You wanta give this paper to Mr. Gill?"

"Heavens, no!" shrieked Little Betty Lou, grabbing a defending arm on each side of her. "I'd just die if I had to do that. I don't even want him to know I've been before the Board. Won't you give the paper to him? Please?"

He caught Mr. Gill leaning against his office door as classes changed. "Howdy, Mr. Gill. I don't believe I've spoken to you this year yet; I've been so busy. And I know you have, too."

Mr. Gill flicked one brief glance at him and did not speak. Slowly and surely, the lower plate appeared.

I believe he had fried eggs this morning, the boy thought. Aloud, he continued, "Here's a letter from the Board of Education I was asked to deliver to you, Mr. Gill."

The response was immediate and gratifying. With a snarl, the man snatched and rapidly read the proffered paper.

"Over my head and behind my back again, huh?" he yelled, insensitive to the students hurrying by. "One of these days you're going to stumble, and when you do I'll be there. Don't you forget it."

"Why, Mr. Gill, none of us thought about going behind your back. The word I got was that the teacher didn't want that small a class. We thought this would make it easier for you. Don't you see?" He began backing away. "Besides, I thought you knew that

Little Betty Lou Braxton wanted to go to Sophie Newcomb." He stepped in front of two senior boys hastening to class and was swept triumphantly down the hall.

Good morning, our Heavenly Father, he exulted. We just hit the Philistines a good lick. Thank You from the bottom of my heart, and keep on holding me in Thy hand, Lord.

Two weeks later, Little Betty Lou received a catalog from Sophie Newcomb and discovered that Latin was not a prerequisite for matriculation after all. The next morning, after five minutes of trembling, she was sent home for the day and allowed to drop her third year Latin class in an effort to relieve some of her work load. The boy and Virginia spent the rest of the year sharing the attention of a disgruntled teacher. As he labored through long evenings, virtuously translating the boring orations of a pompous and tedious Cicero, the boy had time to envy Little Betty Lou and to ponder one's involvement in Fate. He had enough insight not to call it God's will and enough manhood not to ask God's help.

XVII

heretofore, his mother had been able to help him when he had a difficult passage of Latin to translate, but now she informed him that he had passed beyond her limits. She had taken only two years of Latin when she was in school and did not feel qualified to deal with Cicero. She was a phenomenal person. After working hard all morning cooking and cleaning for her family and spending her afternoons in church and civic activities, she was always cheerfully available for help with homework in the evenings. She could help with almost anything. She was proficient in English, Latin, algebra, geometry, and spelling. She knew all the shortcuts that the teachers either did not know or would not bother to mention. The most valuable lesson she taught, however, was patience.

The boy had a tendency to rush through assignments, and a math or algebra problem that he could not solve with his first effort drove him into a frenzy of frustration. When this happened the mother would calmly leave the little sisters with their diagraming or spelling assignments and come to his rescue. Taking a difficult problem and finding the correct formula for its solution was an enjoyable challenge to her, and she managed over the long nights of tutelage to pass this attitude on to her son. It became more of a game than a chore, and all his life he could hear her delighted laugh and her excited exclamation, "That's it!" as she balanced in triumph an impossible equation.

In the winter, the children gathered in the big dining room, one of the two heated rooms in the house, to get their homework.

There was no choice. This was what one did, and it was considered to be one of the necessary routines of life. Each child had a segment of the round dining table as a work space, and they studied together while the mother darned or sewed until her help was needed.

She did not check individual assignments, nor did she inquire if all the work was done. So strong was the unspoken assumption that one worked until there was no more work that not one of her children ever thought of skipping any homework. She instilled in them such a sense of responsibility and conscientiousness that none of them ever went to school without an assignment prepared or turned in a late book report. The routine was so firmly entrenched in the boy's make-up that for years he considered families lacking if they had a square dining table.

Dimly, in the past, he could remember the father being at home in the evening. This was so long ago, however, that he had no clear picture of it. Over the years he had grown accustomed to his father's absence. Indeed, there were long periods of time when his children saw him only on weekends. They went to bed before he came home and went to school before he got out of bed. The boy knew from occasional encounters that his father usually had whiskey on his breath at night, and he gleaned from nocturnal eavesdropping and from innuendos at school that fist fights and women were part of his night time activities.

None of this was discussed at home, however, and the mother encouraged and exemplified absolute respect for the father. His authority was never questioned, and important decisions were deferred for his consideration and judgment. *Alcoholic* was a term that had never been heard in the county, and *drunk* was not an appellation that fit a charming war lord who sallied forth in immaculate white linen every morning to function with brilliant efficiency until sundown.

For years the boy had looked to the mother for guidance and support. There was the camaraderie of shared tasks and the companionship of special times when they were alone. The manifestation of her love for him was the sum total of his security.

He loved the early morning beginnings of life on the farm. He hastened to get fires built, cows milked, and wood toted, banging in and out of the cavernous kitchen while she moved smoothly and serenely through the preparations for breakfast. Their love for each other was an absolute of life, never questioned, needing no confirmation. He took her for granted as much as he did the sun in the sky. He instinctively knew the basic requirements for her approval and would have died in dishonor before violating them.

Consciousness of his father was ever in the background. He had always been at least half afraid of him. From his grandparents and the aunt, he had heard so many stories of the nobility of his father as a child, boy, and young adult that his image was heroic and kingly. It had gradually dawned on him that he was expected to mature into some facsimile of this grandest of all creatures. The enormity of the prospect filled him with awe, but it only rarely seemed unobtainable. He early decided that the transformation would be a religious miracle, wrought by a magnanimous Jehovah in benevolent reward for years of faithful service. When he sinned, he immediately and prophylactically implored divine forgiveness and comforted himself by recalling the unexpected and unmerited anointment of Saul as the King of the Jews.

By the end of the seventh grade, he was guiltily aware that he had become ashamed to be seen in public with his mother. When she was present, he felt vulnerable to the inquisitive eyes of his peers and fancied that his privacy was being violated. He never mentioned this shame to anyone and went to great lengths to deny its existence even to himself. By contrast, he liked to be seen with his father, walking timidly and respectfully in the shadow of masculine greatness. None of this had changed anything at home.

Now, in the tenth grade, he became aware of an extension of his feelings toward his mother. Goodnight kisses became a duty with which he secretly would like to dispense, and he grew resentful of instructions or directions from her. He had enough intelligence and a strong enough sense of survival to hide it, but he privately began thinking, I wish she'd leave me alone.

He yearned for his father. He had always coveted his approval, but now he consciously longed for his attention. He had occasionally been allowed to go to town on Saturday afternoons in his childhood. He remembered these excursions as fascinating experiences that involved sitting decorously on a high stool in the drugstore, eating ice cream and watching his jovial and gregarious father. The "nice lady" of the moment usually attempted to cuddle him and read him a story, an art at which he was, unbeknownst to her, more proficient than she.

He enjoyed even more the rare sorties to his father's office in the perpendicular, echoing old courthouse. Comp was the father's secretary, and he would invariably leave to go get a Coke or see about some mail whenever the father brought the child over. While the father talked on the telephone, an unusual event in itself, or discussed politics with some lieutenant in his satrapy, the boy was free to explore. He could peek, unintimidated, into all of Comp's filing cabinets, look through the magazines stacked in neat piles in a corner, or even approach that holy of holies, the rolltop desk. If he could get into the desk, he could pull out all its multiplicity of little drawers in search of hidden treasures. He was convinced there was some valuable secret in that desk, for if Comp by any chance was forewarned of his coming, he always locked it and pocketed the key.

On these occasions, however, he had not really had any companionship with his father. He had, indeed, been intent on the trophies he could obtain for being Mr. Porter Osborne's little boy and had actually tended to avoid the direct and discomforting attention of the awe-inspiring figure that had sired him. Now, as he impatiently strained at the bonds with his mother, he consciously desired to be included in his father's world. There had to be more exciting aspects to life than milking cows and going to Sunday School.

He knew he was unworthy, but he aspired to winning the notice of his father, for whom he felt more reverence and admiration and fear than for anyone else in the world. He gained the man's attention by writing notes. He began with a passage in Latin that he could not translate. He copied it on a sheet of note paper with a request that his father read it for him. He left this message tucked under the plate of food which his mother dutifully placed on top of the stove each night. Next morning a precise translation with an added sentence about the mysteries of the dative case was waiting for him. Two or three times a week he began leaving notes for his father. Encouraged by replies, he was emboldened to abandon fabricated problems and to ask simple, direct questions. Unless a larger than usual amount of alcohol had been consumed, he always had a written answer next morning, which he excitedly read before he milked and before his mother came downstairs.

Once he wrote, "Dear Dad, Can I go bird hunting with you Saturday?" and daringly he signed it, "Love, Sambo." Reading his answer next morning, he could almost hear the drunken dignity of measured sentences and realized that his father had come home just before he reached the wild and grandiose stage of his inebriety.

"Dear Son, You may go hunting with me Saturday. I shall be delighted to share your company. Have your mother awaken me early." Unbelievably, the signature was, "Love, your Dad." A little chastened by the grammar lesson, he was nonetheless elated by the acceptance implied in this note. He saved it for a long time. It evoked memories of the hunt on the following Saturday, when just the two of them set off across the frost-covered fields behind two bird dogs who soon curbed their frantic joy in the outing and began ranging competently in search of bobwhites.

There was no significant exchange of conversation that day. In fact, most of the communication between them was about the hunt. They noted aloud the discovery of a rosette of quail droppings left by a roosting covey. By the mere backward flick of a hand, the father admonished stealth of approach when the dogs pointed. The building tension was dissipated in the exploding flight of the flushed covey, the shocking blasts of the shotguns, and the snapping release of the point by the dogs. The man's cry of, "Watch those singles, Sambo," was followed by his calm, deep-throated cluck to the dogs. "Hunt dead. Hunt dead in there, I say," was a phrase replete with contented fulfillment.

The boy noted with wonder how gently the strong fingers removed the dead birds from the mouth of the retrieving dog, unconsciously smoothing the ruffled feathers into their proper direction before easing the crumpled little bodies into the back pocket of the hunting coat. The dogs then had to be applauded and petted and sent in tongue-lolling pursuit of the single birds.

Twice the booted, long-legged man had to carry the boy through thick tangles of briers, and once he lifted him across a creek too wide for him to jump. Most of the time, however, the boy managed to keep up on his own, plowing manfully through cocklebur patches as high as his head or half trotting to match the gait of his father. He hated the sardines and crackers they opened for lunch but pretended to enjoy them.

He missed every shot he had at a bird that day and realized that he was tense because he feared looking ridiculous to the mighty hunter accompanying him. Nevertheless he enjoyed the day. When they returned at three o'clock, he was so exhausted that he was delighted for his father to bathe and go to town, leaving him to settle into his own life once more.

A few nights later, he wrote a page and a half entitled "What I learned from you about quail hunting" and tucked it beneath his father's supper. Next morning, scrawled across the bottom in drunken penmanship, he read, "With a student like this, a teacher cannot fail. I would add to your list 'Never shoot a covey on the ground.' "

He thrilled like the lemon pointer being patted for a good retrieve and all the way to the cowlot felt like wagging his tail. He waited a day and then wrote, "May I stay after school Friday and ride home with you that night?" The reply was terse. "Sure," it said.

He could not hide his excitement when he told his mother that morning. He added importantly, "Better save me a plate, too, I reckon."

"I'll be glad to," answered his mother as he started outside. "Sambo," she called softly.

He stuck his head back in the door. "Ma'am?"

"I'm glad to see you and your daddy getting closer. I know you've been writing notes to him at night. Maybe this is an answer to prayer. You have a good time tonight, but remember who you are."

"Yes'm," he said, a little uncomfortable. As they both turned away, he paused a moment and heard his mother, unaware of an audience, say in a wondering tone, "And a little child shall lead them?"

He eased quietly across the porch. What in the world did she mean by that? he mused. Lord, You sure do have a lot of people talking to You, don't You?

That afternoon after school, he trudged to town with his armload of books and self-consciously pushed open the door to the drugstore. The soda jerk was behind the counter, an unshaven man who always wore a gray wool cap pulled down over his forehead, the bill of it greasy and warped from being tugged between thumb and forefinger. His cheeks were perpetually slack because he never wore his teeth, and his jaws were always in motion because he chewed tobacco. He was also a pretty good automobile mechanic, an accomplishment that his fingernails affirmed. It was an adventure to get him to fix an ice cream cone.

"Where's my dad?" the boy inquired politely of him. The gargoyle behind the soda fountain ruminated a moment, turned his head, spat an amber stream to the floor, tugged on his cap, and replied, "I reckon he's still over in his office. Old man Root Whitlock was in here a while ago looking for him, and I think he stepped over thataway. Yo paw don't hardly never get over here before four-four-thirty ever afternoon. When Mr. Comp leaves ever day he us'ly goes back to his office for at least a coupla hours. I'm forever sendin folks over there what come in here lookin for him. I spec that's where you'll find him at."

The boy crossed the wide dirt street to the courthouse. He had to push with his shoulder to open the tall outside door, which was closed against the winter cold. The hall was so long and so huge that he fancied it had its own weather. At least it was colder inside than outside, and a stronger wind was blowing. The nameless convict assigned as janitor for the building was hunched over a barrel of sweeping compound beneath the stairs.

"Howdy, Big'un," the boy greeted benevolently in conscious imitation of his father. He paused briefly for a reply but did not receive one. He walked importantly up to the office door and knocked. His father shook hands with him, introduced him to Mr. Root Whitlock, and said, "I'm just going to let you make yourself comfortable here at my desk. You can do your homework or whatever you like, but if you don't mind, you'll just have to excuse me for awhile. Mr. Root and I have some important school business to discuss. Here, I'll have to unlock that desk for you; I don't know why in the world Comp locked it before he left."

He clattered back the top of the desk for the boy before he joined Mr. Root in front of the coal fire sputtering in the grate. Both men leaned back in their straight canebottomed chairs. The father smoked one cigarette after another, and Mr. Root chewed tobacco, leaning forward occasionally to spit accurately and hissingly into the fire. The boy balanced on the father's swivel chair. With toes barely touching the floor and elbows resting on the desk, he tilted it forward against its strong spring. Opening his books, he began his homework.

"Root," he heard his father say, "like I was saying, I'm counting on you next summer when I run again. I may not have any opposition this time, but I always believe in running scared, and I sure want you and your folks to know I appreciate your standing by me before and I sure want you to vote for me again."

"Law, Porter, ain't no scuse for you to worry. I don't hear nothin bout nobody runnin but maybe Tommie Lou Creamer. Ain't heard a breath bout nobody else atall. Her folks has always been such strong Babcock men that ole man Henry Marsengill would even support you if she's the only one runnin against you. And if he comes out for you, you know Mr. Bob Newcomb will, cause he's Marsengill to the bone. Johnny Browning is always for you, and if the Marsengills, Newcombs, Whitlocks, and Johnny is all for you, then they can just forget about Winship district."

He paused and spit and then added, "Co'se hit might cost you a little, but not as much as usual. A few permanent waves fer some o' the women, a drink o' likker heren there, but no big money. You know where to put it out. Ain't no need for me to tell you bout that." He rose, divested himself of his cud of tobacco by extruding it from his mouth into his palm, and cast it on the fire.

"Reckon I better mosey on, Porter. I promised my ole lady I'd get her some things at the store. Effen you do git a chanst fer a new bus driver, I sure will thank you fer rememberin Junior. He needs it bad."

"Well, Root," the father replied, "it's like I told you. We don't have any money ourselves, but if the state ever gives us a new driver, your boy is as good as hired. I won't forget you, and I really appreciate yall remembering me at the polls."

They shook hands, and the visitor walked by the desk. "Goodbye, little fella," he said. "You study them books and git some smart. Yer paw says you gonna be a doctor when you grow up. Hurry back here and look after us country folks." He tousled the boy's head with a roughly affectionate hand and chuckled condescendingly.

"Yessir, Mr. Root, I sure will," replied the boy. "It was nice to meet you." He tried not to cringe as he realized that the hand on his head was the one that had recently cupped the spent wad of tobacco.

He sat through a few more business sessions, finished his homework, and began leafing through a *Liberty* magazine. His father turned from seeing a visitor out the door. "Well," he said as the clock in the tower above them struck a single reverberating note that traveled in booming vibration all the way through them and the wooden floor beneath them into the depths of the earth, "it's four-thirty. Let's step across the street and see what's going on."

He stuck his pistol into his overcoat pocket and leaned over with the huge folding key provided by the county to lock the office door. The convict shuffled up the hall on his way to the rendezvous that would carry him back to the chain gang to spend the night.

"Evening, Big'un," the father said.

"Good even to you, Mr. Porter," the man replied in grinning obsequiousness. "Nis here yo lil boy? I thought hit wuz when he come by me while ago. He sho favor you, Mr. Porter, he gwine be jus like you when he grow up. Yassuh, he a fine boy, sho nuff."

The father handed him a quarter. "Get you some tobacco for the weekend, Big'un. And be sure and get me a fresh scuttle of coal. I may not get here till late tomorrow, but I'll unlock the door soon as I come to town for you to build me a fire."

"Yassuh, Mr. Porter, Yas*suh*. I be waitin an I keepa eye out fer you. Thank you, *suh*."

"Gosh, Daddy, he wouldn't even talk to me when I came in," the boy confided as they went down the steps. "I guess he's just timid with strangers."

"Let's get on over to the drugstore," the father said. "I asked a boy to come by and teach you to play pool. I thought you might enjoy that."

"Yessir," replied the boy slowly. "That sounds like fun." He felt defensive.

The teacher was waiting, propped against the soda fountain with both elbows and one foot. A tailor-made cigarette dangled from his lips in an affectation that made his eyes squint. He was Denton Jones, one year older than the boy, two years behind him in school, and planets away in attitude. He was the youngest of six brothers, all of whom had been "raised on the streets."

Their father, a devotee of spree drinking, had worked sporadically and unenthusiastically as a brick mason until one spinning Monday morning he fell off a chimney and broke his neck. Their widowed mother was a vivacious, gregarious gadabout, who visited neighbors in the morning and came to town in the afternoon. She concealed a short attention span by moving from one audience to another in rapid succession. There was never a sick person in the town who did not receive a visit from her.

She was practiced at peering over the foot of a bed and shaking her head sagely at the incapacitated occupant, implying thereby that she knew something concealed from him. Her standard response to an invitation to sit down was, "No, I ain't got time to set. I'm like a pore horse's ass, in and out." She knew everything that happened in town and told most of it. She had once shocked the Baptist preacher by avowing, "I don't pay no attention to that Bible what was writ around a hundred years ago. I believe *The Atlanta Constitution*."

The children were provided clean clothes and bedding, and she cooked when she got around to it. Sometimes she prepared a bounteous meal which would glut a Nero, but she had to be in the notion. More often she fried something and boiled some grits, but no one knew what time she was going to do even this. Unlike most of the city residents, the family had no cow or vegetable garden, and the boys were free to roam the streets. The Jones brothers came and went as they pleased and observed no curfew whatever. Since they never went anywhere together, it seemed that there were more of them than there actually were.

They had the reputation of being the worst boys who had ever lived in Brewtonton, and the citizens anticipated their next misadventure with shocked enjoyment. At UDC meetings Miss Beauty Graves maintained such a detailed record of their activities that it was suspected she kept a Jones diary. Judging from Miss Beauty's report, Denton was by far the most active of the boys.

She even told that when he was thirteen he had already been drunk. It was a known fact that he had been in two knife fights and that even his older brothers did little to cross him. Although he was physically ahead of his age and performed well on the basketball team, it was a foregone conclusion that he would not finish high school. No Jones ever did. They all dropped out when they captured a steady girl friend.

John Seelbend could give an expert opinion on the physiological and psychological reasons for this change of motivation, but it was so crude and explicit that the boy wouldn't even think about it without looking over his shoulder first.

As he saw Denton leaning against the soda fountain and realized that this was the mentor his father had chosen for him, he had mixed emotions, none of which was pleasant. This vulgar youth with big pores and blackheads made the boy distinctly uncomfortable. Every word that Denton spoke was braggadocian and aggressive. Even standing still, he looked to be swaggering. The boy didn't feel awkward and inferior just because Denton was larger and physically stronger. It was also his cocksure demeanor and the arrogant assumption that in all the world only his opinions were fact.

The boy both loathed and admired him. Now, as he thought to himself that his father must be advancing Denton as a model, he felt ashamed and unworthy. He was suddenly overwhelmed by the feeling that his father did not really like him and that his puny appearance was an embarrassment to him. In miserable acquiescence to one more bitter fact of life, he decided that he would always be a disappointment to his manly idol. He knew there was no way he could ever emulate Denton Jones. Forcing his eyes to be guarded and dry, he wept in his heart.

Walking over to the pool table, he challenged without enthusiasm, "Come on, Denton. Let's see what you can teach me."

The father disappeared behind the green lattice partition into the dim and mysterious back room as Denton racked the balls and explained that they were positioned by the numbers painted on them. He nudged the boy in the ribs, winked, and said in a coarse voice, "You know what your old man's gone back there for, don't you? He wants a drink o' likker." His tone conveyed both acceptance and admiration.

"I bet you ain't never even tasted no whiskey. Livin way out, like you do—you don't know what you've missed. Ever now 'n then, when I do a favor for Buck or Bugger, one of em'll slip me a half pint of that corn they sell. I mean it'll grow hair on your chest. I bet you ain't even got none round your dick yet, but that stuff'll put it on your chest.

"If you can git hold of some of Houston Stargill's peach brandy, that's the best stuff in this town, but don't you never drink none o' that groundhog that comes outta Winship. They run it through old radiators out there and that stuff's ba-a-ad! Here, hold your cue further back and try to hit the ball solid. You can't hardly reach the table, but maybe you can learn something."

The boy rapidly learned the proper expletive to use when one missed a shot and that "goddam" was a masculine adjective implying admiration for a worthy challenge. "Oh, shit, don't drive your cue down the table like that. You'll tear the felt. Git outta the way and I'll show you how to make that goddam shot. . . . How'd you like that, hey? Now I bet you think I can't bank that goddam ten-ball in that side pocket. Watch this."

As Denton attacked the pool balls in rising self-adulation, he grew ever more loquacious. The boy, intimidated and repelled, grew quieter, answering direct questions in monosyllables and praying for the lesson to end.

"Rack em up again. We got just bout time for one more game. My ma's cookin tonight, and I gotta get home. Brother Bill helped ole man Thurston Adams kill hogs and he flat loaded us down with goddam fresh meat. We're gonna have backbone and turnip greens and sweet potatoes for supper, and Ma promised she'd make some cracklin bread. That's goddam good eatin and I can't miss that. You wanna bust, or you want me to?"

"Go ahead," murmured the boy. "I wish I was a little taller, and then I could hit em harder."

"You wish?" scoffed Denton. "You know what my ma says when we wish for something? She says, 'Wish in one hand and shit in the other, and see which one fills up first.' Here, stand on this stool and see what you can do."

Dutifully mounted, the boy leaned over the table, lined up the balls, drew back with all his might, and launched the cue stick. It caught the ball just a little below the top, and he watched helplessly as it rolled lazily down the green table and gently kissed its target with a barely audible click. The boy felt as if he were in a dream in which he had furiously struck out at an attacker, only to find his blow falling featherlight and unheeded.

He cringed as Denton reacted. "Oh, shit! Here, move over and let me show you how it's done. I'll bust them goddam balls wide open."

The boy looked around in time to see his father swiftly duck his head back out of sight around the doorjamb. He had been watching the debacle. The boy felt crushed and weary. He had no desire at all to beat Denton Jones or put him in his place. He felt a lump in his chest and realized that he really felt like crying over the futility of the situation. Resolutely, he slipped his cue stick back into the rack.

"Den," he said, "I've enjoyed it, but I've had enough. Besides, there are some grownups waiting to use the table. Why don't you go on home to that good supper?"

"Naw," said. Denton, "I don't wanta get there early. Maw would plumb hound the life outa me with things to do. Besides, I still got money your pa give me for the pool games. Come on, and we'll use it up in the goddam pinball machine."

Once Denton became absorbed in how many free games he could accumulate, it was easy enough for the boy to slip away. A group of men had taken over the pool table. They were busy in determined pursuit of entertainment, their faces starkly lit by the naked light bulb, their eyes squinted in aligning assessment of a difficult shot, their heads immersed in an ever-swelling blue haze of cigarette smoke. A changing, shuffling row of spectators made a loose ring around the pool table as newcomers drifted in to watch and exchange greetings.

There were not many places open after dark in Brewtonton. The boy was bored. He thought wistfully of his mother and sisters at home.

Looking at the Coca-Cola clock over the soda fountain, he knew they had finished supper by now. They were probably through washing the dishes and were having the evening devotional. He wondered if they missed him. He decided that his sisters were probably relieved at his absence, but he knew his mother would pray for him. He felt uncomfortable at the thought, but he felt more uncomfortable where he was.

Anxious not to find his father until Denton Jones had gone home, he procured a package of malted crackers from the glass jar with a mouth in its side and ordered a milk shake. He watched with interest as the soda jerk poured out the milk from a gallon jug, added a scoop of ice cream, a dash of vanilla, and then shook the mixture so vigorously that his whiskered cheeks quivered. As the foaming mixture was poured into a glass, the boy assured himself that at no time had even one of the black-rimmed fingernails slipped into it. He took his crackers and glass to an unoccupied corner and pretended not to see Denton as he waved a hand and left.

Not long afterwards, his father came out and joined the group at the soda fountain, chatting easily and smoothly with everyone who came in. Once he caught the boy's eye and winked quickly across the crowd. The boy immediately felt secure but was glad that he was small enough to be unnoticed by anyone else in the room.

Later, he could never remember exactly when Harcourt Matthews joined the group. To have missed the entrance of someone so massive would have required intense concentration on something else. Harcourt was six feet two inches tall, weighed over three hundred pounds, and appeared to be incredibly fat. His fingers stuck out like the teats on a cow's distended bag, and even his nose was puffed. Actually, his appearance camouflaged powerful muscles and great strength.

An only child, he had been named for his mother's grandfather, and all the ladies in town called him "Hahco't." Everybody else called him "Bull." Since he was only ten years younger than the father, the boy would have called him "Mr. Bull" had he ever had occasion to speak to him, but the giant had never bothered to notice the existence of any children in town except the Jones boys. He used them for various errands. Although an assignment from him usually had an interestingly nefarious quality to it, he paid poorly, and the Jones brothers did not give him an enthusiastic reference. In fact, the boy could not remember anything remotely complimentary of Bull Matthews ever having been said in Brewtonton by anyone.

The ladies thought him coarse and vulgar. The men tolerated his presence but referred to his various business enterprises with contempt. No one trusted him, and he, in turn, trusted no one. If he had any admiration for another man, he hid it very successfully behind an attitude of contemptuous cynicism.

Currently he was running a sawmill, an enterprise that depended on day laborers from the indigent group of alcoholic Negroes around town who were too unreliable for a farmer to consider trusting with a cotton crop. Each morning he collected the ones who were sober enough to work, loaded them on the back of his truck, and drove them wherever in the county his rig was located. The Joneses spoke in admiring awe of his highhanded attitude toward his employees.

He referred to them openly and loudly as "sorry niggers," both in their hearing and as direct salutation, and his physical treatment of them reflected the same callousness. He jerked, shoved, and kicked in impatient reprimand for delayed obedience, and any sign of objection on the part of the recipient brought stunning blows from the great fists or even skull-crushing attack with a length of two by four.

Bull had a legendary appetite for food as well as for violence. John Addison Bowen liked to have extra coffee at Buzz Pike's cafe every morning, and he said that Bull always came in and ordered a dozen fried eggs. He would then take a loaf of bread, cut the top off it, and hollow out a cavity in it with his switch blade. He would have Buzz put the hot eggs in it, stuff the torn bread back in, and head for the sawmill. This sandwich, washed down with a gallon of buttermilk, was his lunch. The boy would as easily have believed this was only a midmorning snack.

Bull was the biggest creature he had ever seen outside of a barnlot. His belly was so huge and so protruberant that no pants in the world could contain it; his buttocks actually looked skinny by comparison. The great belly could not be adequately covered by a shirt tail, either, and his navel was always on view, a cavernous, seemingly bottomless hole that hicupped obscenely when Bull laughed or coughed.

Tonight the boy noticed that the navel was hidden by the straining union suit Bull had donned for the winter, but there was still the triangle of gaping shirt to mark its location. He leaned against the soda fountain, sucking a tailor-made cigarette, grinning fatuously as though he thought himself the most popular member of the group.

"Porter," the boy heard him address the father, "I saw that new teacher you hired when I come by the school this morning. She was out there coaching the girls' basketball team. I mean you knew what you was doing when you hired her. She's a real looker."

"Thank you, Harcourt," the boy's father replied with a definite note of formality in his voice. "She is a very fine young lady."

"Uh-huh," Bull persisted. "I tell you I'd like to get them gym bloomers off her cute little ass and get with that good stuff she's got in em."

The father moved like a cat. He grabbed Harcourt by his shirt front, jerked the huge body forward, and slapped him so hard it sounded like a pistol shot. The boy, immovable, gasped in astonishment as the crowd around the pool table dissolved. His father roared, "God damn your sorry soul to eternal hell! You keep a civil tongue in your insolent head!"

He slapped Bull again just as hard as before. The giant staggered and let loose a bellow that was worthy of Mr. Whitaker's bull. He grabbed for the father. This time the father delivered a smashing blow of the fist squarely to Bull's bulbous nose and mouth. Blood gushed as the giant fell back. "I'll kill you!" he roared, pulling his switch blade from his pocket. He never got to open it.

The father, electric quick, snatched up a pool cue, swung it like a baseball bat, and with a solid and resounding crack laid open a gash above Bull's left ear. Slowly, Bull buckled to his knees, grabbed briefly at the pool table for support, and rolled lingeringly to the floor in reluctant surrender. The room was hushed. The father leaned over the fallen man, whose massive chest was rising and falling in stertorous rhythm. "Don't you ever say another word about one of my school teachers the longest day you live; you hear me?"

There was the flicker of a bloody eyelid which the father evidently accepted as an agreement to terms. He kicked the switch blade across the drugstore and turned to the bristle-faced soda jerk. "Get the doctor to fix him up. Tell him I'll pay. And now, if you gentlemen will excuse me, I think I'll go home. Come on, Sambo."

It took three miles of driving down the road for the father's breathing to return to normal. The boy sat in silence, staring through the windshield, his heart still racing. He was assailed by fear, embarrassment, humiliation, and even joy. He thought of all he had seen his father do this day.

I'll never make it, he thought with sad resignation. He saw Harcourt Matthews' bloody head lying on the floor. I don't want to, he added.

He would have liked to pray, but the strong smell of tobacco mingled with whiskey emanating from his father precluded inviting the Almighty into the automobile. He felt it would be almost like telling on his father, for the Lord would be sure to notice the whiskey.

"Sambo," the father interrupted his thoughts, "there are some things that a man always has to fight for if he's really a man, and the good name of a woman entrusted to his care is one of them."

"Yessir," the boy answered.

"That teacher is young enough to be my daughter, and I couldn't let a slur like that, occurring in a public place and delivered by a lout like that repulsive Harcourt Matthews, go unpunished. You understand that, don't you?"

"Yessir," the boy replied, looking through the windshield and wishing the car was not weaving quite so erratically between the ditches.

"Now, I think we ought to protect our womenfolks at home from undue distress and worry, don't you?"

"Oh, yes, sir," the boy dutifully replied.

"Well, let's don't mention this little episode about Harcourt Matthews to them. It would only upset them, and we can keep that as a little secret between us boys, don't you think?"

"Oh, yes, sir. I think I see Paul Arnold's cow up ahead in the ditch, Daddy. Maybe we better slow down just a little bit."

He thought longingly of his bed waiting at home. No matter how cold the sheets were, he wanted to crawl into it and pull the covers over his head. He never wanted to see that drugstore again, he decided. His father's world was distinctly frightening. He certainly could not return to his mother. He looked upward through the windshield into the darkened sky.

Oh, where do I belong? he implored.

His note writing ceased. Although his father never implied it and the boy never heard the subject mentioned in his nocturnal eavesdropping, he felt very strongly that his father disapproved of him and was disappointed in him as a son. He bitterly resented being compared, in his father's eyes, with the likes of Denton Jones. Denton was the antithesis of everything he had been reared to regard as admirable. Just the way he used the Lord's name in vain was enough to make the boy spurn him. If his father wanted him to be like Denton, then he would just have to fail his father.

He nursed the hurt inside of him until it became an embedded sadness. He grew stubborn. Refusing to compete for his father's respect, he withdrew from the field.

Frequently he thought of his evening in town. He over-looked the manipulative interplay with Mr. Root Whitlock. After all, men conducted all kinds of business by the code of mutual advantage, and a politician did have to get elected. He soon forgot the embarrassing encounter with Harcourt Matthews and came to regard his father as a gallant knight defending a fair maiden by delivering well-earned punishment to a miscreant knave. He could not, however, get far enough away from his own emotions to forgive his father Denton Jones.

Once his mother commented very innocently to him, "I don't believe I've seen any notes lately that you've left for your father."

"No'm," he responded evasively, "I haven't had any trouble with Cicero in the last few weeks."

He felt unspoken pressure in the simple statement of his mother, and he began to feel increasingly guilty about not writing to his father. A couple of nights later he contrived a rather stilted message, thought for several minutes, and finally signed it, "with love."

The next morning he found the note intact under the plate of food, which had not been touched. With a shrug, he assumed that the father had been so drunk the previous evening he had neglected to eat. When he stepped outdoors in the cold dawn, however, he saw that the car was not in the yard and realized that his father had not yet come home. When he returned from milking, it was good daylight, and there was still the shrieking vacancy where the car should have been.

He carried the buckets of milk into the kitchen and prised his cold and reddened hands from the handles. His mother was standing at the kitchen cabinet, her sleeves rolled to her elbows, her firm white hands kneading biscuit dough in the old bread tray. It had been hollowed from a single poplar log and generations of use had crusted it to almost feather lightness.

In the corner next to the woodbox, hands extended for the warmth around the stove pipe, stood " 'at Damn Charlie Porter." The boy did not like him. No one, in fact, liked him. 'At Damn Charlie Porter was one of those people doomed to go through life being barely tolerated. The boy had been unobtrusively present at a conversation between his father and grandfather.

"Pa," the father had announced, "I guess we have 'at Damn Charlie Porter on our hands again. This new wife has just kicked him out, and old man Bob Mask has run him off, and he doesn't have any place to go."

"Well, son," the whitehaired grandfather answered, "that's the same old story. 'At Damn Charlie Porter can't stay anywhere long. The last time you brought him here, he sneaked off just before I could get around to killing him."

"I know it, Pa," the father continued. "That's why I wanted to be sure it was all right with you before I gave him a job. I don't like him any better than you—in fact, I've had to whip him twice in the last five years—but his old daddy was one of our slaves. I've heard you and Mammy talk about how faithful old Andrew was in the bad times, and I remember him, too. I hate to turn my back on his baby boy, even if it is 'at Damn Charlie Porter."

"Well," sighed the grandfather, "there ain't anything else you can do, son, and we both know it. Some of the other hands'll run him off in less than three weeks. I'll try to leave him alone. I don't know exactly what it is, but there's something about that darkie that makes it hard to keep your hands off him."

The boy had curiously and judiciously observed 'at Damn Charlie Porter since his arrival some six weeks earlier. Everything about him was annoying. He walked back on his heels so that he seemed to be strutting, and he swung his arms with bent elbows as though he heard music. He carried his head tilted inquisitively to one side, but his shoulders and neck were always squared off and stiffly erect. He had a perpetual little half smile that could only be described as condescending, and he spoke to the other Negroes in patronizing tones that imputed abysmal ignorance to them and lofty wisdom to himself. Even when, goaded beyond endurance, some of the other hands threatened him or threw rocks at him, 'at Damn Charlie Porter would bestow on them a tolerant little smirk that left no doubt that he felt above such raffish and infantile behaviour.

He emanated such a strong and unmistakable aura of self-esteem that there was neither room nor need for regard from anyone else. He performed his farm chores with an air of noblesse oblige as though he were stooping to mollify an unreasonable child. If he had ever learned to read or write, he would probably have been a power in some northern city. In his present environment, his mere survival was a tribute to his nimble footwork and an instinct for the limits of human endurance. The boy had heard Darnell, Central, and Freeman on separate occasions all avow, "Some day somebody gwine kill 'at Damn Charlie Porter."

As the boy set down his milk buckets that morning, he realized that something was wrong. When he spoke his usual hearty greeting to his mother, he was answered only by a bowed head and a mumbled monosyllable. As he looked more attentively, he saw a tear slide off her nose into the biscuit dough she was working. His mother was crying.

In consternation he started to go to her and then remembered 'at Damn Charlie Porter, who was ensconced behind the kitchen stove with his eyes averted, refusing to meet the boy's glance. An unwritten but rigid law decreed that one did not show emotion before the servants. It was not proper for them to know intimate details of family crises in the first place, and, secondly, they might gossip among themselves. He knew in a flash that it would be much better for 'at Damn Charlie Porter not even to know that his mother was crying. Not only would the dignity of his mother be violated, but the entire family would appear in an unfavorable light.

He knew that if he approached his mother she would probably cry aloud, and he was certain that in the event she did he also would relax into tears. As he stood in his quandary, undecided and miserable, the whitehaired grandfather erupted into the kitchen.

"Hello, Vera," he said in a farmer's morning voice. "I mean it's cold out there. My thermometer says thirty-two. Do you have some coffee made yet?"

His voice stopped as he reached the middle of the kitchen and realized that his daughter-in-law had not answered him. He peered at her long enough to see another falling tear disappear into the dry flour of the biscuit tray. Swiftly he turned toward the corner behind the stove. "What are you doing hunkered over that warm stove when there's work to be done?" he roared.

'At Damn Charlie Porter rolled his eyes toward the ceiling, head cocked jauntily to one side, erect as a turkey gobbler, only the faintest hint of a smirk on his face.

"Confound it, answer me when I speak to you, you black limb of Satan!" challenged the grandfather.

With an alacrity belying his age, he leaped forward, grabbed a stick of stove wood from the box, and caught the man a solid blow on the top of the head. In a flash 'at Damn Charlie Porter was on his all-fours, crawling rapidly around the stove to avoid the irate grandfather. The boy opened the kitchen door for him and followed him onto the back porch. As the Negro rose to his feet to launch a proper flight, the boy blocked him and grabbed an arm.

"Hold still, Charlie, and let me see how bad hurt you are," he directed. The hair was clipped so short it was easy to inspect the wound. "It's all right, Charlie," he asserted. "You're bleeding, but it's not a deep cut. You're not going to need any stitches. Hold this cloth on it tight, and hush that crying."

"How come Mr. Jim jump on me like dat, Sambo?" wailed the bloody man. "He fractious over nothin. Now I gotta find another place to stay. I be skeered to stay here no longer. He act like it my fault yo maw cryin. I can't hep it Mr. Porter been layin out all night in town an ain't come home yet. Ain't no need to whup a nigger jes cause de boss man layin out."

"You hush your mouth!" the boy shrilled. "You don't know what you're talking about!"

He turned and reentered the kitchen, empty now except for the mother, who was determinedly rolling out biscuits and arranging them in the greased pan. He slipped both arms around her waist and leaned his head against her upper arm.

"I'm sorry, Mother," he whispered as he hugged her.

"Oh, my son," she said with tremulous voice and brimming eyes. "What would I do without you? You mean so much to me." She kissed him on the top of the head and kept her floured hands aloof for the bread.

"I feel so sorry for you, Mother. He ought not to do you this way," the boy said fiercely as he stepped back from the embrace.

The mother straightened her shoulders and raised her head. "Don't feel sorry for me, son. I'm the luckiest woman in the world. 'Of him to whom much is given, much shall be demanded'; and the Lord has given me a lot."

Her voice became stronger and she added, "Don't ever let anything make you criticize your father. There's a verse in

Jeremiah: 'If you run with the footmen and they weary thee, how will you contend with the horses? If they weary thee in the land where thou dwellest secure, how will you fare in the swelling of the Jordan?' We are not a family of footmen to start with, and you have to run with the horsemen whether you always feel like it or not, but this is still the land where we dwell secure.

"I'm sorry I let you catch me crying. Fill up the woodbox, and check on Charlie. It's getting late."

As he left the kitchen, beset by divided loyalties and with a lump in his chest, the boy thought wistfully that he would not mind right now becoming the third generation to whip 'at Damn Charlie Porter.

At school that day, Denton Jones came up behind him at recess and nudged him with an elbow. "You know whatcha daddy done last night? He tell you anything about it?"

The boy moved away behind a mask of preoccupation and indifference. "I went to bed before he came home last night, and I didn't get a chance to talk to him this morning."

"Well, let me tell you about it," volunteered Denton in his coarse voice. "Yo paw was standin at the front counter with his overcoat on all ready to go cause he'd promised Miss Evelyn he'd give her a ride home cause it was gitten late and had started drizzlin rain a little. Anyway she was gitten her packages together from behind the pinball machine and Tollison Inman come in the drugstore with another nigger man and a nigger woman.

"He walked up to ya daddy and said, 'Mr. Porter, this is Mr. so-and-so'—I didn't hear the name too good—'from Atlanta. He done brought one o' yo teacher supervisors down here to meet you.' And that Atlanta nigger stuck out his hand and said, 'Mr. Osborne, I'm glad to meet you. This is Miss Marguerite Rainbow from the State Department of Education.'

"Yo paw is quick as a cat. He snatched off his gloves and slapped the shit outa that goddam nigger fo he knew what hit him.

He hit him about three times and kicked him out the front door and then turned around an said, 'Where's the black son-bitch that's introducing me to such exalted society tonight?' "

Denton paused for breath and then continued importantly, while the shamed boy listened with pounding heart and flaming cheeks.

"I hollered out, 'If you talkin bout Tollison Inman, Mr. Porter, he's runnin up the street.' Yo paw grabbed that Luger outa his pocket and hollered, 'Stop or I'll shoot,' but that just made Tollison run faster. He hit that rough spot in the sidewalk just in front of Pike's and stumbled. He was carryin a package of plates he'd bought for his wife, and when he stumbled they slipped and he grabbed down between his legs and caught em and goddam if I'm standin here if yo paw didn't shoot the shit outa them goddam plates right from between Tollison's legs as far away as it was and as dark as it had got.

"Them goddamn plates just exploded, and Tollison never missed another step. I mean he went around that corner doin ninety to nothin. Me'n yo paw walked up the street and kicked the glass out into the ditch, an he give me some money an said, 'Run over to Putman's store and get him another set of dishes. Take em down to his house and tell him I didn't mean to break his plates,' and he give me a whole goddam dollar for doing it."

The boy was filled with resentment that this other boy knew more about his father than he did, and he was humiliated that his father had again done something that would have the whole town buzzing behind the family's back. Denton was looking in momentary reverie at some distant horizon. With a long sigh, he turned to the boy and said, "I wish I had a daddy like that."

Startled at the implications of this revelation, the boy carefully steadied his voice into just the right mixture of innocence and smugness and replied, "What is it your mother says, Denton? See which hand fills up first. I gotta get to class."

He hurried away before his street-wise acquaintance could begin speculating on the fate of Miss Evelyn. He felt that his heart was filling up with things that he could never tell anybody.

XVIII

In February, when the days grew longer and warmer and the little peepers could be heard along the creeks in the afternoon, he occasionally went home with Sally Fitzgerald so that they could study together. The bus route went by Sally's house, and it was fun to travel the county roads almost smothered by children of every age from grades one through eleven. When the bus stopped at the Fitzgerald's house, so many children popped out the door one at the time that the boy fantasized a great orange sow farrowing a litter of enthusiastic pigs.

The Fitzgerald house was a mean, four room wooden box set head-high on pillars made of native rock. It had a front porch with a tin roof and steep wooden steps leading up to it. It had been painted white so long ago that it was now softened and muted into a silver gray. There was a sandy front walk outlined with the sharp points of diagonally submerged bricks, and a huge old magnolia tree overhung the walk and almost shaded the porch. The yard was swept so clean and bare that not even a fallen magnolia leaf interrupted its austere surface. The inside of the house was even cleaner and almost as bare.

The boy and Sally sat at the kitchen table, elbows propped on the cracking oil cloth, and did their homework. The planks of the bare floor were always a marvel to the boy. They smelled strongly of homemade lye soap and were bleached by such frequent scrubbings that they were almost white and the splinters in them were pliant and soft. Sally's face was not as mournful here as it was at school, but it was still slightly sad, and she gave instructions to her siblings in a low, crooning voice that reminded the boy of a nesting dove. He liked to make her laugh, and it was fun during study breaks to regale her with some outlandish tale that would make her throw back her head and gurgle softly in controlled delight.

They both enjoyed studying together on those afternoons before the boy's mother would come by to drive him home in time to milk. Sally had a good mind but had been remiss about learning her axioms and theorems in plane geometry. The boy felt important as he coached her into not only understanding but enjoying this discipline of mathematics. As her confidence grew, her eyes would sparkle when she successfully solved a problem, and her pleasure in accomplishment was contagious. He suggested that she come to his house to study for the monthly examination, pointing out that his mother could as easily carry her home as come to fetch him.

When they arrived at the boy's house that afternoon, they launched themselves into a scholastic orgy. They had the round dining table to themselves, and Sally, before the afternoon was over, had worked every single geometry problem they had covered for the last six weeks. She was a perfectionist about her penmanship and the neatness of her paper. The boy teased her.

"Sally, for Pete's sake, you act like you were going to take those problems in for a grade. And you've only written on one side of the paper. The way things cost, that's plumb scandalous of you."

"I know, Little Porter. I feel really wasteful, but you've no idea how much fun it is to do these problems when a month ago I hated them like the bad man. It makes me feel good to have them look sort of like a drawing or something on one sheet of paper."

After she had left in the car with his mother, the boy noted that she had forgotten to carry with her the problems on which she had spent the whole afternoon. He realized that she knew the subject so perfectly there was no need for her to review these work sheets, but with the idle thought that she might need the unused backs of them for scratch paper later he stuffed them in his notebook.

The following day, when the examination was written on the board, the boy worked quickly and quietly. There were ten problems, and by writing on both sides of the paper, he wound up with a three page examination paper, which he folded, labeled, and set aside on the edge of his desk. Taking out a history book to appear busy, he spent the rest of the hour looking at his fellow students. The examination had been the type of exercise that a well-prepared student finds too easy to be either challenging or fulfilling, and the boy was just a little bored.

He looked across the room at Sally Fitzgerald. She had her head down, hair hanging loosely around her face and almost touching the desk, and she was so absorbed in her work she seemed oblivious to her surroundings. Little Betty Lou was chewing first on her pencil and then on her fingernails but seemed to be fairly calm today. Further back in the classroom Jacob Turnipseed and Seaborn Huddleston were trying to look at each other's papers, an exercise in futility, since one knew almost exactly as little about the subject as the other. Mattie Mae Simpson was playing with her hair, Winona McElwaney was playing with her chewing gum, and Oliver Betsill was picking his nose.

All in all, it was an ordinary, usual classroom scene at test time, everything under control and everyone quietly busy. He studied the teacher. Mr. Herschell Hubbard was just one year out of the University of Georgia. He was six feet two and had buttocks which the boy thought looked like a barrel sitting crosswise on stilts. His hair was so black that his closely shaven beard contrasted sharply with his unusually white skin. He used lots of Vitalis and carried in his shirt pocket a comb which he plied frequently and publicly to his sculptured pompadour. His lips were unusually thick for a white man and unusually red for any man. He had little short peg teeth with gaps between them, and when he breathed the air made a whistling noise through the thick hairs in his nose.

He doubled as basketball coach and math teacher. He was paid no supplement for extra effort but received the same eighty dollars per month as all the other teachers, and he was very glad to have a job. He was not as intelligent as about a third of the class, but he excelled in both dignity and self-esteem. The girls thought he was handsome, and he deigned to agree with a condescending air.

The boys on the basketball team thought he was a mama's boy and ran circles around him at practice. They were careful to conceal their opinions, however, and to obey promptly, for he had a hair-trigger temper and was more inclined to punish than to persuade. The boy, a little scared of him, was careful to be on his best behaviour in geometry class and to pretend respect which he did not fully feel.

He noted now, with casual interest, that it must be almost time for the bell, for the parade of the dollies had begun. This was a private amusement that he shared with no one. He had noted that just before the exam had to be turned in, a hesitant girl would slide sideways out of her seat, mince up to old Liver-lips Hubbard, and murmur a question in his ear. Mr. Hubbard would answer in just as low a voice. This stimulated others so that there was a steady stream of supplicants. The boy wondered if Mr. Hubbard was dumb enough to think that these girls had not already finished their geometry problems or conceited enough to notice that no boy had ever approached his desk with a question.

The bell shattered the silence and the room erupted into disorganized activity—students turning in papers, grabbing up books, struggling into coats or sweaters, and chattering their way into the hall for their next class. Sally Fitzgerald reached down and squeezed the boy's arm as he walked up.

"I knew every one of those problems—I made a hundred on that test!" she chortled softly. "Thanks for studying with me. That's the first math exam I ever took that was actually fun. I mean it was fun just to write it all out. I knew when I saw the questions on the board that I knew every bit of it. It was *fun*!"

Her eyes were shining. The boy thought, Gee whiz, Sally's really pretty when she's happy! "I know what you mean, Sally. You'll feel that way from now on. You're a good math student. All you needed was a little faith in yourself."

"I still want to thank you, Little Porter. This will give me the first A I've had on my report card in math since I came to Brewtonton. See you later."

As she walked down the hall, the boy thought he had never before seen her shoulders back and her head held high.

On Friday when report cards were distributed at the end of the day, the boy looked first at his deportment grade. He had been making a conscious effort this year to improve his conduct, having just decided that being a holy terror was juvenile. He remarked with satisfaction that he had a good solid C this month. There was no need to overplay virtue. From force of habit he counted the pluses behind his string of A's, lost interest in the report card, and slipped it into a book. It had to be signed by a parent before Monday. Heading for his locker in the crowded hallway, he passed Sally, huddled over her armload of books, shoulders bowed and head drooping.

"Hi, Sally. You liking that A?" Three steps later he noted her lack of response. He looked back. Sally was leaning against the wall with her face turned aside. She was crying, and she was doing it as silently and unobtrusively as she did everything else.

"What in the world is wrong, Sally? I can't stand to see you cry."

Silently, she handed him her report card. His eye leaped to the math column. Out from it was a solid string of B's until the end. This month's entry was a screaming F, blacker and bolder than the other entries. After the initial shock, he quickly assured her, "Quit crying, Sally. This is some mistake. He just got your card mixed up with Seaborn Huddleston's or somebody else's. Take it to Mr. Hubbard and he'll straighten it out."

Sally began sobbing. "I already did that. You know what he said? He said—oh, I can't tell you—he said. . . ." She stuffed a balled-up handkerchief against her mouth and slumped even more limply against the wall.

"Get control of yourself, Sally. What in the world did he say?" demanded the boy.

"He said I'd been *cheating*! That's what he said," moaned Sally. "He said I cheated on the final exam. He said he knew I had because I had each problem on a separate sheet of paper. He said I had worked all those problems ahead of time and had just slipped them in on the exam. He said he didn't see me do it but he knew I had."

"Why, that's ridiculous! We worked three times that many problems the afternoon before. Did you tell him that? Did you tell him I had teased you about wasting paper? Did you tell him you knew that exam cold?"

"I didn't tell him anything," whimpered Sally. "I was afraid I'd start crying, and I didn't want him to see me. Oh, Little Porter, what am I going to do? I can't show this to Daddy. Oh, I just want to curl up and die. It looks like everything's no use."

"You hush your mouth, Sally Fitzgerald. Don't talk like that, you hear me? You're just upset! Give me that report card. You blow your nose and wait right here. I'll be back in a minute. I'm going to see Mr. Hubbard."

As he plucked the report card from her unresisting fingers, she added, "He gave me an F in conduct, too, Little Porter. I didn't even say anything about that to him. That hurt worst of all."

"Don't worry! No problem! I'll be right back."

He was so excited and indignant, so filled with purpose that he completely forgot himself. It never occurred to him to be afraid or even self-conscious. As he hurried into Mr. Hubbard's room, Little Betty Lou was just leaving it, accompanied by a couple of the ladies of her court. He brushed by them without speaking and approached the red-lipped teacher, who was rocked back on the two back legs of a straight chair behind his desk, his arms outstretched in a self-satisfied yawn.

"Mr. Hubbard, I'm so glad I found you before the buses run," the boy began excitedly. "A terrible thing has happened! Sally Fitzgerald is out in the hall crying her eyes out because you thought she was cheating on our geometry test, and. . . ."

"I don't think it; I *know* it," interrupted the teacher. "She had copied every problem ahead of time and just turned them in as her test. Why else would she have each one on a separate piece of paper with times as hard as they are? She turned in ten pages for ten examples! How many did you turn in for yours? She can cry from now on, if she thinks I'm that big a fool! On top of that, she's been making all B's before, and she comes up with a perfect final examination? Don't tell me she wasn't cheating."

"But that's just exactly what I am telling you, Mr. Hubbard! You see, we've been studying together—I guess I've been coaching her a little—anyhow, all of a sudden she caught on to geometry and just loved it. You know how that can happen to you, don't you? Why, she knew every problem in the book with her eyes closed. She was so proud of it, she was a different person.

"Why, the night before the exam, when we were studying together, she did just what you're saying about the separate sheets of paper, and I teased her about it, just like you say, you know, how can you be so extravagant with paper, and she said it was so good to finally know geometry that it was fun to do it that way. I even saved the work papers for her to use the backs of later. . . ."

Inspiration seized him. "Wait a minute. Why hadn't I thought of that before? I've *got* those papers right here somewhere. I'll show you."

He scrambled through his notebook and produced the thirty work sheets he had been saving for Sally. They were slightly crinkled around the edges but nevertheless sparkled with authenticity. He thrust them into the hands of the teacher.

"Besides, Mr. Hubbard, you just don't know Sally like all of us do. She wouldn't do anything dishonest. She'd die before she'd cheat."

The teacher was leafing through the sheaf of papers, carefully perusing every page. He raised his head. "Well, it looks like I may have made a little mistake here," he finally acknowledged. "I never ran into anything like this before. Tell Sally I'll raise her grade, and we'll just forget about the whole thing."

"Yes, *sir*. I knew you would. I already told Sally soon as you understood, you'd do just exactly that. You're wonderful, Mr.

Hubbard! Here's her report card." He proffered the offending document.

"Well, now," hedged the teacher, "I'll have to change the grade on my record book first. Tell her to take this on home and see me Monday."

"Oh, she can't do that, Mr. Hubbard," remonstrated the boy. "She'd die if any of her folks saw it. Go ahead and change the grade now on the card and get the record book later. I think that'd be much better." He was so obsessed with the pursuit of justice he assumed Mr. Hubbard was also concerned.

"Well, hand it here," said the man. "I'll change it to a B, and it won't even show on the card. That's what she usually makes."

"Aw, Mr. Hubbard, you can't *do* that. She made a hundred on that test and that'll give her an A on that report card. You can change an F to a flat-topped A just as easy without it looking tampered with."

"All right, we'll do that," the teacher said shortly as he altered the letter. "I guess you're right. Here." He offered the card back to the boy.

"But, Mr. Hubbard, you've got to change that F in deportment, too. If she wasn't cheating, she doesn't deserve a bad conduct grade."

This time Mr. Hubbard snatched the card. The boy realized that he had been overlooking danger signals and that he stood perilously close to an explosion of temper.

"You really are a kind and considerate man, Mr. Hubbard," he said placatingly. "Not many people could be as good a teacher as you are and also as understanding of the student."

"Well, I try," Mr. Hubbard replied, partially mollified. "Here—I've raised that to a C. Does that satisfy you?"

"Oh, yes, *sir,* Mr. Hubbard, yes, sir. I think C is a good grade in deportment! Thank you *so* much. You've been great." He hurried off to Sally, who had dried her swollen eyes but was now hiccuping.

"Here you are, Sally," he announced triumphantly. "You'll feel better now. I told you not to worry. All I had to do was explain

303

it to Mr. Hubbard. I told you it was bad to waste paper on those art masterpieces."

Sally rubbed the sodden ball of her handkerchief upward beneath her nose, opened the report card, and said softly, "Look at that A in geometry! I don't blame him for wondering about it. I can't get over it myself."

Suddenly she let out a fresh wail.

"What's the matter now?" the boy asked.

"Oh, look at that C in deportment!" she cried. "I can't go home with that!"

"For Pete's sake, Sally! What are you talking about? I've carried home F in deportment many a time. That grade doesn't count on your permanent record or anything like that. Forget about it."

"I can't! I've never made anything less than A on deportment in my life! Besides, Little Porter, don't you see? The only reason he gave me an F in deportment was because he thought I'd been cheating. Well, if I wasn't, I sure deserve an A because for sure and certain I haven't done anything else. I'll just go see him about this myself."

"Wait a minute, Sally," interrupted the boy. He remembered the set of Mr. Hubbard's jaw and the look in his eye just minutes earlier. "You better let me go back and see him. I may have gotten him a little bit riled, and I'd hate for him to take it out on you."

He took the card back into Mr. Hubbard's room. That gentleman was obviously packing up for the day. "Whatta you want now?" he asked abruptly.

"Well, Mr. Hubbard, we have a little problem here that neither one of us thought about," the boy said deferentially. "Sally's never made anything but A on deportment before, and she said the only reason she made an F was because she made you think she was cheating, and since that's not so then she ought to have an A in deportment now. I hadn't even thought about it that way," he laughed nervously, "and I told her I was sure you hadn't." Before the steady black stare of the teacher, he fidgeted a little but added determinedly, "I told her I was sure you'd understand. It won't take a second for you to change it. She's right, you know." He slid the card over the desk top.

The teacher did not even look at the card. "What's this girl to you?" he demanded. "You're sure sticking your nose in her business! She your kin or girl friend or something?"

"Oh, no, sir, she's just a friend, a classmate, a girl that's sort of, you know, had a hard time. I mean she's shy and can't talk up for herself, if you know what I mean."

"I know I'm getting damn tired of you trying to tell me how to run my business," the teacher said with reddening face. His voice trembled a little. "That C stands, just like it is, and there's nothing you or she either one can do to change it. She deserves a C for making a monkey out of me, if nothing else, let alone all this confusion with you about it. Here, give this card back to her, and don't you mention it to me again."

The boy cast all caution aside. "Mr. Hubbard, you can't do that," he said defiantly. "It's not logical and it's not fair, and it won't stand up."

"We'll see about that," rasped the shaking, red-faced teacher. He grabbed the boy by the ear, lifting him half off his feet and began pulling him across the room. "We'll just let Mr. Gill settle this," he pronounced. "He's told me about you, and I think you'll find out you've gone too far this time."

The boy could not decide whether he minded the pain or the indignity most as Mr. Hubbard rushed down the hall with his ear twisted firmly in an unrelenting grasp. Sally was the only student left in the hall, and the boy managed to fling the report card at her feet as they swept by.

If Mr. Hubbard even saw her, he gave no indication of it. The two of them exploded into Mr. Gill's office with a shuffle and bang that brought the principal to his feet, teeth clenched firmly in emergency reaction.

"Well, well, well," he intoned with a rising note of satisfaction.

"Tell me what's going on, Mr. Hubbard." He rubbed his hands together with a dry and leathery sound.

"Well, Mr. Gill," the teacher began, breathing heavily, "this little smart-aleck is trying to tell me how to teach school, grade papers, and discipline a student, none of which is the least bit of his business. I thought I caught this girl cheating, and I flunked her. I changed her failing grade after this boy interceded for her, but then he had the nerve to rebuke me for cutting her deportment grade and actually defied me to tell me what I could and could not do. I can't let him get away with dictating to me."

"Well, well, *well*," the principal repeated. "I've finally got him. Open insubordination. This calls for a paddling. I'll be glad to administer it for you, Mr. Hubbard, since you may still be a little excited. Close the door."

He began removing his coat. "Bend over that chair," he directed firmly as he took the paddle off the wall.

The boy looked desperately around. There was no way to dart around Mr. Hubbard and run down the hall to freedom. The humiliating horror that he had avoided for ten years was on him so suddenly that he had no time to dwell on it. He was about to get a whipping at school. He made a resolution that come what may, live or die, he would not cry aloud. He faced Mr. Gill and, with one final effort at last-minute salvation, said, "You're making a serious mistake."

He was grabbed by a shoulder, twisted around, and shoved roughly into position. "You're the one who's made the mistake—a lot of them!" growled Mr. Gill. "Grab the arms of that chair and don't you move, or I'll have Mr. Hubbard hold you."

He drew back the paddle and let go. The boy thought dynamite had gone off in his pants. The shock of the blow was so great he could hardly maintain his footing and the pain so intense that he thought he would scream aloud despite his resolve.

He thought of Jehovah, Lord God of Hosts and King of Battles. Help me, Lord, in my great hour of need! Even if his enemies kill him, help Thou Thy humble servant not to cry. Help me, Lord, he prayed.

As the blows rained, he repeated the prayer over and over. He had never felt such pain. Every nerve in him urged him to scream and kick, to turn and try to run. From somewhere, cold anger settled like a pilot light in his chest and he concentrated on its flickering tongue. He tasted a raw sweetness in his mouth and realized that he had bitten the blood out of his own cheeks. Still, he made no sound. Finally he heard Mr. Hubbard say, "Mr. Gill, I think you'd better stop. I believe that's all he can stand. Who would have thought he was that tough?"

Mr. Gill's upraised arm fell slowly to his side. "Turn around and sit down," he told the boy between deep, heaving breaths, "but don't you move. I'm not sure yet you've had enough."

As the boy sat down, he was surprised to find that he could not feel the chair with his numb buttocks, although that entire area seemed to be on fire. He kept his chin on his chest. He heard Mr. Gill say, as though he were not in the room, "Now, Hubbard, tell me everything from the beginning so I'll have it all straight. We may hear from this later, you know. We need to be together. I'm like you. Who would have thought the little scoundrel could take it?"

The boy listened passively to the account and thought it essentially accurate, although it was overlong in explaining why Mr. Hubbard had thought Sally was cheating in the first place and overly petulant in recounting Mr. Hubbard's indignation at the confrontation over the grade in conduct. As the teacher neared the end, the voice became less sure and positive and finally ended on an almost questioning note.

Mr. Gill had begun rocking on his feet and jingling his keys. Although the boy did not raise his head, he was sure that he was by now looking out the windows and sliding his lower plate on his tongue. After a long moment of silence, the principal spoke, his tone weary and final. "My God, Hubbard, he's right. If he has those work sheets as proof, there's no doubt the girl wasn't cheating. And if she wasn't, you'll have to change that deportment grade.

"She's a little nobody, but this loud mouth here could spread it all over town. Change the grade to A." He turned to the boy and spoke in as conciliatory a tone as he could muster. "Well,

well, well. It looks like we've made a little mistake here. Maybe we acted a little hastily. I guess maybe I owe you an apology. You can go now if you want to."

The boy could not believe he was hearing correctly. He rose to his feet and raised his eyes. Mr. Gill was looking at some distant spot two feet above his head and a little to the right. He continued, "I guess you'll be telling your father about this. I can't stop you from it. But be sure to tell him I apologized."

"Mr. Gill," the boy began, and discovered to his embarrassment that his voice was quavering. He cleared his throat, gulped, and began again in a steadier tone, "Mr. Gill, I'm not going to tell my father. I'm going to let you do that before you go to bed tonight. If he doesn't know about it when I wake up tomorrow, I'm going to tell the Board of Education."

In the silence that followed, he walked to the door. He felt six feet tall and mean as a hungry snake. He looked upward at the principal and waited for his eyes to shift into focus. Triumphantly, he hissed, "You old fart-buster!" and turned away without fear. In the empty hallway he bowed his head. "Thank You, our Great Heavenly Father. That was a real unexpected bonus, but Thy humble servant thanks Thee most of all for not letting him cry. To Thee be all honor and glory and praise. Amen."

He knew full well that the impatient Comp had left him when he was not on the steps immediately after school. Shrugging resignedly, he began walking home, hoping to get there in time to milk before dark. Mr. Walter Buford picked him up and gave him a ride as far as Harp's Crossing, and the boy was painfully aware when he tried to sit down that he had been brutally punished. Walking felt better than sitting.

He managed to get the cows milked but could hardly bear to squat for the procedure. He evaded questions from his mother and sisters about the reason he was late, muttering vaguely about a debate meeting. He suffered through family prayers and then announced that he was going to read in bed. The truth of the matter was that he was having misgivings about his parents' finding out about the whipping.

He knew he had been right in defending Sally, but his anger and sense of martyrdom were giving way to fear that the family threat that a whipping at school would be followed by a whipping at home might be fulfilled. He was not at all sure now how his parents would react. He knew he was in no condition to risk another whipping.

Gently he lowered his pants, stood in front of the mirror, and pulled the union suit apart in the back. Looking over his shoulder he was aghast at the swollen, black buttocks that greeted him. No wonder he could feel the throb of every heart beat in his seat. Alarmed at the sight, he also felt self-righteous and nobly abused. He tried to think of some comparable martyr with whom to identify, but the location of his wounds thwarted him. Despairingly, he murmured aloud, "You don't reckon anybody ever died just from getting his ass beat and nothing else, do you?" He knelt and reverted to childhood in prayer as he fervently offered up, "Now I lay me down to sleep. . . ."

He was still awake later when the light was turned on. Lying on his stomach, he turned his head to see a tall figure standing over him. "Sambo, are you all right?" his father asked in a low voice.

"Yes, sir, Daddy. I'm fine."

"Old Gill came by the drugstore to see me tonight," his father informed him. "We had a long talk. He told me everything that happened this afternoon. He said he had apologized to you for the entire incident and that he was afraid he may have hit you too hard.

"Knowing him, I knew that if he had apologized to anybody for anything we had something serious on our hands, but I was very calm. When he got through, I told him he had three possible plans of action we could discuss: He could resign tonight in writing; I could carry this matter before the State Board of Education; or I could cut his goddamn throat. He chose the first plan, and he won't be at school Monday. Let me have a look at you."

He pulled the covers back and gently parted the underwear. The boy heard the hiss of sucked-in breath and smelled the sour-sweet odor of metabolizing whiskey. As his father laid a finger almost caressingly on one throbbing, swollen buttock, the boy tried hard not to flinch. There was a long silence. Finally with a tone of wonder, almost of reverence, the father asked, "Why did you do it, son?"

The boy thought a long moment, and replied, "There are some things a man always has to fight for, Daddy. The good name of a woman was involved."

The father reached down and grasped one frail shoulder in a strong hand. He held it a long time without slackening the grip. No word was spoken. Finally the man switched off the light and left. The boy lay very still and pondered for a long while. Heavy tears came streaming in cleansing freshet from his eyes, and he wept himself to sleep.

that spring he went to the Junior-Senior Prom. Theoretically, this was a farewell party for the senior class hosted as a gala by the junior class. In reality, it was the only social function which occurred at night during the entire school year, and nearly everybody got excited about it. First of all, it was formal.

The boys in the class got many mysterious connotations from the word because the girls intoned it with special emphasis and reverence and seemed to use it during class meetings more often than was necessary. Each year some boy would raise his hand and ask just what was meant by formal. This always produced a twittering among the girls and a spate of irrelevant conversation that completely confused every male in the room.

By the time the boys were assured that it meant evening dresses for the girls and Sunday suits for the boys, not a one of them was convinced that that was all there was to it. Nothing that simple could provoke so much female conversation. Rooster Holcomb, en route to the cedar tree with a bunch of companions, was heard to growl that he believed it meant you had to paint your balls blue and wear a red ribbon on your peter. This comment so delighted the boys in the class that when the word was used in the later planning meetings it always caused snickers and knowing winks.

The next issue to be decided was where the prom would be held. There was no public meeting place in Brewtonton suitable for a party; so it was traditionally held in the home of some junior class member, with the understanding that the class would do the decorating and furnish the refreshments. It was also understood that it would be a house belonging to a town student, the reason given being that a central location was desirable and it was easier for everyone to get into town. The real reason, however, was plumbing. Nearly all of the town students had bathrooms, generally as appendages to the back porch at the end of an antebellum hallway. To have relegated the girls in formal finery to using an outhouse was as unthinkable as it was unmentionable.

This class was fortunate in that it did not have to worry about finding a home or making a diplomatic choice. Jane Reynolds offered the large house which belonged to her father, Mr. Charley Reynolds, state senator and cigar-chewing political boss of the county. This house was two doors off the courthouse square on the road that went to Holley's peach orchard.

It was white, two-storied, and had a verandah that wrapped around two sides of it, an adornment that doubled the living area in warm weather. It was perfect for the Junior-Senior Reception, and all the girls on the various committees were voluble in their praise of Jane for her graciousness and magnanimity. She was immediately appointed chairman of the committees on decoration and refreshments.

The girls were getting so excited about the prospect of the reception that they could talk of nothing else. They babbled breathlessly every day over new details and discussed at great length the latest news about who would be whose date. They also discussed those who had announced that they were definitely not going. Most of these were girls. There were just as many boys planning not to go, but they were reticent about it and felt no compunction at all about being socially correct. They just kept their mouths shut and did not show up.

It was a foregone conclusion that Rooster Holcomb was not going. He was dating a girl who was in the senior class, and rumor was strong that they were going to be married when Rooster finished high school. At any rate, she held a tight rein on the irrepressible Rooster, and for all his worldly posturings he was not allowed even to look at another girl. There were other couples in similar situations.

Indeed, there was small point in attending a prom if one was already committed to a romantic liaison. The best entertainment one could expect at the prom was an occasional furtive kiss, and even this was not guaranteed. It was assumed that real smooching was occurring between regular sweethearts every date they had.

This, of course, was assumption only, because the credo that a gentleman kisses but never tells was still one of the inviolates of county conduct. It was also assumed that smooching was the total extent of amorous exercise between real sweethearts, since another credo held that nice girls did not copulate, and no boy would think of getting serious about anyone but a nice girl. At any rate, couples who were really going together rarely attended the prom.

The boy learned from listening at the cedar tree that the big boys who were planning to attend were really on the prowl. The battle plan was simple enough. If one really wanted to experiment with sex, the clever approach was to sign up the same girl for three or four proms in a row. Each prom lasted ten minutes, and one did not really have to appear until intermission at the end of the fifth prom. This was the signal for a head count by the two faculty members chosen as chaperons, who were surprised at little and impressed by nothing. It had been years since anyone had been able to spike the punch.

The chaperons rang a big dinner bell at the end of each prom to notify the young celebrants that the prom was over. The bell could be heard for a good half mile, and the boys who were walking girls around the courthouse square in their evening finery had no excuse for not returning on time. It thus became fun to borrow the family automobile and disappear in it for each prom, teasing one's partner by threatening not to get her back on time.

The boy resolved to attend this fascinating social function, and he resolved to attend it in style. Skilled in family protocol, he approached his mother with request for permission to go.

313

"Ask your daddy," she replied.

"May I go to the Junior-Senior Reception?" his note read that night.

"Certainly you may go," was the parental rejoinder he found next morning.

He followed immediately with, "May I get a date?"

The response to this note was a little florid and obviously written after a larger ration of alcohol. "I find your desire for companionship of the fairer sex both appropriate and timely. You not only have my permission; you have my blessing."

The boy boldly pressed his case. His note that night was an exercise in guile. "Thanks, Dad," it read. "You are a great guy and the most understanding father in the world. I have a date with Gladys Walker. She has funny teeth, blonde hair, and blue eyes. She is really pretty from the side. Her mother is making her a pink dress. I've ordered her a corsage of pink carnations. It cost fifty cents for three, but I decided to splurge. May I borrow your car?"

He knew perfectly well the request would be denied. It was merely the opening move. The answer he received held no surprises.

"Dear Son, Of course I know Gladys Walker. Her father is the section foreman. She is a lovely young lady and I extend you my congratulations. Your selection of flowers is in good taste. If you need any more money, just let me know. I cannot lend you my car, for I will be using it that evening. Your mother can take you in her car. I do not think your skills commensurate yet with the demands of nocturnal driving. I trust you to understand."

Carefully, he perused his reply. "Dear Dad, I've already driven one time at night, and everything went OK. No other boys will have their mothers bringing them to the Prom. I will see Gladys tomorrow and break the date. Maybe she won't think too badly of me, and maybe the other kids won't laugh too long. I know that being a father is a hard job, and I am not questioning your judgment. Maybe the reason I have trouble understanding is that I have not been a father yet. At this rate, I may not ever be one. Love, Sambo."

314

Hoping he had not gone too far, he tucked the note under the plate of food. He awoke unusually early the next morning. Breathlessly he approached the cold cook stove. The plate of food had been only half eaten. No piece of paper showed beneath it. The boy's heart sank, and he thought that he had angered the father by being too impudent. As he turned away with a shrug of resignation, he looked through the open door. He spied a full sheet of paper on the dining table, held in place by great-grandma's salt cellar.

Eagerly he snatched it and read, "Sambo, dammit! You may borrow your mother's car. I am very well aware that you have driven one time at night, under more extenuating circumstances than these. You cannot drive by yourself to this party, but I will get Wes to drive you. That's the best I can do. Love, Your struggling Dad. P.S. If incipient fatherhood is a problem for you, I will be happy to instruct you in averting it. P.P.S. If you ever decide not to be a doctor, it is my opinion that you would make a damn good lawyer."

Recalling his grandfather's admonition that half a loaf was better than none, the boy turned with elation to the big dictionary in the corner. He looked up *extenuating* and *incipient*, nodding with approval and understanding as he added two new words to his vocabulary. Speeding barefoot through the early spring morning to the cowlot, he said aloud, "Let's face it, boy. You have one really smart man for a father."

That very morning he sought out Wes as that muscular man was harnessing his mule and announced importantly to him, "Wes, Mr. Porter says tell you that you are to drive me to the Junior-Senior Reception the end of this month."

Wes expertly tied his hame string and adjusted the mule's collar. "Say which?"

"This is the biggest party of the school year, and you can't even go till you get to the tenth grade," the boy explained. "It's at night and it'll last over two hours and we may be eleven o'clock getting home. It's at Mr. Charlie Reynold's house in town, and Mr. Porter won't let me drive the car by myself and that's why he said you could take me. You don't mind, do you?"

"Naw, I don't mind. What night is it?"

"It's the twenty-fifth of April. On Friday."

"Lessee," said Wes, raising his straw hat and scratching under it with an inquisitive finger. "Dat'll be two days befo de foth Sunday in dis month. Yeah, I can remember dat, an I be glad to do it. I gotta git to de field befo Mr. Jim start yellin. Git up, Worry."

When he left, the boy thought, Yeah, and it'll be the first Friday after the third Sunday following the fourth full moon, too, but it's still April twenty-fifth. He had never figured out the rationale for the elaborate manner in which rural blacks calculated dates and kept their appointment calendars, but he was too polite to be derisive of it in their presence.

At school he was careful to be nonchalant when he announced that he was going to the prom in a car. Sure that the news had spread, at dinnertime he actually approached the cedar tree with anticipation and a feeling of belonging. This sensation was rapidly dissipated. Rooster Holcomb made the first comment.

"I hear you got a car for the reception."

"Yeah," the boy responded in an offhand tone. "I'm borrowing my mother's."

"Well, whatta you know!" exclaimed Will Kelly, dragging deep on a palm-cupped cigarette and looking over his shoulder to be sure a teacher didn't catch him. "Whatcher goan do? Line up three, four proms in a row, park in the graveyard, and try to git a little? I hear Mattie Mae's sister has started."

Discomforted by the very idea, appalled at the public utterance of such a thought, the red-faced boy drew himself erect and with what dignity he could muster piped back, "Certainly not. I have a date with a nice girl!"

He turned and walked around the corner of the building, hoping he looked mature. The laughter following him destroyed that hope and exaggerated his loneliness. Fuming and indignant, he muttered, "If you weren't such a coward, you'd have knocked his teeth out, even if he would half kill you later."

Presently, he was joined by Moo-cow Mullins.

Oh, Lord, that's all I need right now, he thought.

Moo-cow was the son of an affable, ne'er-do-well father who stayed drunk even while he worked as a jack-of-all-trades. The mother, an even more affable woman, was reputed to accept financial remuneration for participation in adultery, an activity which she was said to conduct with great gusto. Moo-cow was an only child. He was so pampered and indulged that it never entered his head someone might not like him and yet so neglected that he had an inordinate craving for attention and inclusion.

He belonged to Epworth League and the Boy Scouts, but the boy had surmised from listening to the town boys that Moo-cow was tolerated more than liked and was included in special activities only from a sense of condescending compassion. Although he was a senior, shaved every day, and made straight C's on his report card, the boy privately thought him retarded.

Listening on the periphery of a discussion about dog-beating, the boy had personally heard Moo-cow boast of attaining three feelings on one hard. The summer after Moo-cow's sophomore year, he had joined the Boy Scouts, which indirectly accounted for his nickname. The scoutmaster was a married-in native of north Georgia who had confided to his charges one evening that when he was a boy, the little girls wouldn't let them have any and so they had to screw cows.

This fired the imagination of the Boy Scouts, condoning by confession an activity so scandalizing it had heretofore been regarded as mythological and sanctioning its indulgence because of the unchanged attitude of the little girls of this generation. Discussing this new horizon shortly after it had been opened to them, four of the scouts joked, supposed, and finally dared each other one summer afternoon to the point they actually went to Nelson Mullins's house with the fell purpose of bovine fornication.

Catching the old milk cow, tame and trusting creature that she was, posed no problem, and they soon led her to the concealing shadows of a black locust thicket, well-hidden from the eyes of any neighbors. Nelson Mullins insisted that he would be the first participant, since after all it was his father's cow. While two confederates held the cow by her lowered head, the third stood at the rear and watched with horrified prurience. Nelson inverted and mounted a five-gallon paint bucket, lowered his overalls, and actually accomplished his purpose, leaning forward over the back of the cow and grasping her hip bones.

As it began dawning on the other three boys that they would shortly be expected to duplicate this barbarism or be branded forever as chicken, the activity was precipitously ended. The venerable and docile old cow, completely unimpressed by the human indignity being visited upon her, of a sudden deposited a steaming, six-pound bowel movement into the lowered bib of Nelson's overalls.

Leaning backward to escape this unanticipated horror, Nelson lost his balance on the paint bucket and fell flat on his back, his head coming solidly to rest in another generous deposit, this one some thirty minutes older. As the released cow hunkered to urinate and then began nonchalantly eating grass, the other three boys exploded into the uncontrollable laughter of escape from doom.

In the midst of their hilarity, they earnestly assured the weeping Nelson that they would never tell anyone, a promise they scrupulously kept until the following evening at Epworth League. There all the males were informed, and the new title of Moo-cow was bestowed upon the hapless Nelson. Nelson buddied around for awhile with Denton Jones and dropped out of the Boy Scouts, but his mother forced him to continue Epworth League. Everyone tried to remember not to call him Moo-cow in front of the girls.

"Little Porter," Moo-cow said, as he leaned an arm across the boy's shoulders, "I got an idea."

"You have?" said the boy, twisting away and facing him. To himself he added, Yeah, and I bet I know what it's about and where it's coming from and it ain't your head.

"Yeah," responded Moo-cow eagerly. "You got a date with a nice girl. I know who she is. I heard this morning. She's Gladys Walker, and you're right! She won't do nothing. Besides, she's twicet as big as you."

Failing to see the boy wince, he continued, "But I got an idea. You only have to have the first and last proms with your date, and then you're sposed to have the others with a whole lot of girls. Well, line you up one o' those ole dumb country girls for three or four proms in a row, and you don't have to let having a date with a nice girl spoil your evening.

"Everybody knows these country girls are hotter than the ones in town. Comes from spending they lives watchin cows and hogs and chickens fuck. They're ready and they know what to do. You know what I mean, dontcha?"

Averting his eyes to avoid acknowledgment of a conspiratorial wink and leer, the boy replied, "I know what you mean, Moo-cow, but that's not for me. I don't believe in it."

"Yeah, I heard you were a real big Baptist. I spect you'll come around to it. Yo nuts just ain't come down yet. Well, anyway, lemme tell you what let's do. Let's me'n you double-date."

"Wha-a-a-at?"

"Yeah. Why not? My folks ain't got no car, an I sho ain't never goan get no pussy without one. I know a good place to park, and you'n yo gal can set in the front seat and not look in the back—that is, if it bothers you. I don't care myself. Whatcha say?"

"Moo-cow," the scandalized boy answered in as kind a tone as he could manage, "we can't do that."

"Why can't we? You can pick me up on the way into town and drop me off on your way back to the country. Why cantchew?"

"Well, it's this way—I'm not—this is a formal event, you know."

Inspiration seized him, and he decided to put as much caste distance between them as possible. "My folks are very proper, and they're insisting on a chauffeur attending me that evening; so there just won't be room in our car for but one couple. I'm sorry, but that's final." He thought he sounded adequately priggish and condescending.

"They doin what?" demanded the incredulous Moo-cow. "You ain't got no chauffeur. What's his name?"

"His name, I'll have you know, is Bradley, but he's been with us so long we call him Wes, which is his first name. One of his duties is chauffeuring my grandparents, but they don't ever use him at night. Just wait; you'll see."

"You lyin and you know it. Yo folks jes makin some field nigger wet-nurse you cause you so little. You jes don't want me along cause you afraid you'll lose yo cherry if you go out with a big boy to show you how."

"I am not lying," the boy replied, hiding his anger beneath a coolness he did not feel. "And you were just complaining that you haven't lost your own cherry yet. I'd like to point out to you that people were doing it long before there were automobiles, and there are some people with automobiles who still aren't doing it. Maybe it's your attitude you need to work on."

"Don't get highfalutin on me," shot back the Mullins boy. "I ain't never seen yo pa walkin to my house, and I ain't never seen his car there when my pa was at home."

Head spinning, almost reeling from shock, the boy managed to answer in a steady tone, "If you can even mention that, you've got less sense than I was giving you credit for. Think about it."

His voice quavering, but still with bravado, Moo-cow blustered, "Well, if everbody knows somepin, how come they can't talk about it? I git tired actin like I'm the only one in town what's blind."

His anger replaced by a sudden rush of sadness, the boy reached up and touched the older boy on the shoulder. "Nelson, the only thing I can tell you is that there're some things you just don't ever mention, not even to the Lord."

As he turned and walked away, he comforted himself by thinking there was someone in worse shape than himself.

After school that afternoon, he hurried to the field where Wes was laying off cotton rows. The mule was glad to stop and breathe for awhile. "Wes, since you're gonna drive the car the night of the reception, I decided we'd just make a real genuine chauffeur outa you. If that's okay?"

"Well, at depends. Whatcha talkin bout?"

"Oh, just the way it looks, really. Course you're already planning to shave 'n take a bath 'n put on clean clothes. This just means wearing a white shirt 'n black tie with that black suit you had on last year at Jesse Porter's funeral."

" 'At's my brother suit an he staying over to Hampton now on Mr. Israel Lindler's place," responded Wes. "I guess I could get it Sunday, though, since yo party ain't twel nex week."

"Good. I'll find you a cap to wear with it. I wish we had some of those shiny black boots I've seen in pictures or some of those pants that stick out at the sides, but this'll do fine. You're gonna look great. Be sure and wash Miss Vera's car real good for me."

Wes leaned on his plowstock and nodded assent but said nothing.

The boy decided to ensure his cooperation. "Wes, I've got a little of my watermelon money left, and I'm going to give you three dollars that night just because you're so nice to help me out."

"You is? Dat's de bes news I heard out'n nis yet. You ain't gotta do dat, cause Mr. Porter done tole me I gwine drive you, but I sho be much obliged. I kin use de money."

"I want to do it, Wes. Now, the other thing I want you to do is *act* like a chauffeur."

"Okay, Sambo. How do dey do?" he asked agreeably.

"Oh, you know, every time you stop the car, get out and open the door for me and stand there and hold it 'til I get out and get my girl out, and then you close the door while you sorta tip the bill of your cap with a finger. And when you see me coming back to the car, open the door and hold it for me to get in. Stuff like that. You know. You can do it."

"I kin? I jubious bout dat. I mought git mixed up. Hit sho sound lak a heap o' jumpin in an out to me."

"Naw, you'll do fine," promised the boy. "You'll see. We'll practice that night on the way to town. And every time I get in the car, I'll give you directions about where to go. That's the way they do it in books I've read and in those stories by P.G. Wodehouse in *Saturday Evening Post*."

"Say which?" asked the perplexed man. "I thought dis thing was on Friday."

"It is," the boy said hastily. "Don't pay any attention to me. I was thinking out loud. I guess I'm a little nervous about it. You know, one more thing, though. I may decide to call you Bradley that night instead of Wes. It has a grander ring to it, and this is a formal event. You don't care, do you? I don't want you to misunderstand."

"Naw, I don't keer. You can call me heap wuss'n nat for three dollars. You better go 'n lemme git nis mule to turnin." He turned to grasp the plowhandles, looped the lines over his wrists, and remarked, "Dis must sho gwine be some mo sight of a party. Giddup, Worry."

The boy spent the rest of the time before the reception falling completely in love. Having expended considerable courage by even daring to ask a girl for a date, he had to keep himself constantly braced to avoid panic at the prospect of filling it. He so endowed Gladys with all the noble traits of the heroines peopling the books he had read that she would have been the one to panic could she have seen inside his head.

He fabricated a girl blessed with all the virtues and none of the faults of Juliet, Portia, Rowena, and Queen Guinevere. He convinced himself that this girl of his fantasy, this mythological female, was embodied in Gladys Walker. After all, she did have blue eyes and blonde hair. The mystery and beauty of this romance were too delicate to voice. Instead, he sighed a lot.

He sought her out at school for occasional pointless conversations and even sporadically carried her as trophy a twig of wild azalea or sweet shrub. She dimpled and smiled and thanked him in a sweet, melodious voice, sending him into wilder flights of fancy than ever before. By the twenty-fifth of April he had convinced himself that this was the romance of his life, that he was overwhelmingly infatuated by this gorgeous creature, that she was his girl and consequently belonged, body and soul, to him. He was scared to death.

On the afternoon of the reception, he flung his books in the back porch and hastened out to inspect his mother's black Chevrolet. It glistened from radiator to trunk, fresh-washed and impressively clean. As he opened the rear door to check the upholstery of the back seat for any speck of dust, he conjured up a vision of himself and Gladys, riding happily along in a chauffeur-driven limousine. He was urbane and smooth, leaning over occasionally to share some sophisticated witticism with her and being rewarded with silvery peals of laughter and the delicate flush along her throat.

As she became more comfortable with him, he reached over and took her hand, tenderly stroking it as they arrived at the Junior-Senior Reception. He smiled tolerantly as she blushed, lowered her eyes, and slowly but firmly withdrew her hand. After all, she was a very nice girl, and he was probably being a little too worldly for her.

He brought himself back to reality. The car looked good, but it was not a limousine. He thought a minute and hurried into the house. Returning with a handful of big safety pins and a brightly striped beach towel, he set to work. Within a surprisingly short time he had pinned the towel across the roof of the car midway down the length of the interior. Pulling it tight, he fastened the other side securely to the top of the upholstered front seat and stepped back triumphantly to view his handiwork.

The back seat of the car was now a cloistered nook, private and sequestered. He broke some roses off the vine at the side of the garage, made a bouquet of them with English dogwood, and pinned it to the back of the front seat. He thought the car was now the grandest and most romantic thing he had ever seen. Nothing was too much trouble for Gladys, he vowed silently. He could not see through the towel, of course, but then neither could Wes see into the back seat. Who knows, he thought, I may hold both her hands.

When he bathed and dressed, he put on extra Vitalis and slicked his hair down. Scrub as he might he could not, however, get the odor of milk and cows' udder off his hands. Experimenting, he decided that his hands were odorless at a distance of eighteen inches from his nose and assured himself that should not constitute a social handicap.

When I get to be a doctor, he promised himself, I'll never milk another cow. I'm tired of smelling like this. He hurried downstairs to see if Wes had arrived.

Wes was lounged against the front fender of the car, resplendent in his brother's funeralizing suit, white shirt, and black tie. It was obvious that he had scrubbed himself squeaky clean. He was puffing on a hand-rolled Bull Durham cigarette and had a soft, checkered wool cap on the back of his head.

"Hidy, Sambo. You bout ready to go? Whoo, you look nice. Yo hair look nice, too. I kin smell it fum here. What chew got in at box?"

"This is a corsage for my date—you know, some store-bought flowers for her to pin on her dress. You look good, too, Wes. Stand up straight and hold your shoulders back, and let me get a good look. George's suit fits you good, and you look mighty fine, but that cap won't do. It's too informal. Wait a minute. Hold the corsage for me, and I'll be right back."

He hastened into the living room, which was closed off and separated from the rest of the house. Refusing to think beyond his immediate need, he approached the rack that his father had designed and mounted on the wall to hold the military relics of the family. Great-grandpa's Civil War sword hung there, a Very pistol from the American Expeditionary Forces, a Prussian officer's dress helmet, and several other souvenirs from 1918. He reached up and took the dress cap his father had worn as a captain of infantry in the World War. With its flared out crown, flattened top, and its shiny leather visor, he thought it might be just the item to round out Wes's livery. He slipped it out to the back yard. "Here, try this on," he directed.

The cap rested squarely on the top of Wes's ears, covering his eyes. The top of his head made a definite bulge in the flat crown. "That won't do at all," the boy said in dismay.

Taking some strips of newspaper, the two padded the inside of the cap until it rested at the proper level on the new chauffeur's head. "That's fine," the boy said, admiring the finished product. "Of course it looks like if you turned your head the cap would stay still, so be careful. And of course it's khaki, and your suit is black, but we can't have everything. It'll still be daylight when we get there but it'll be dark before we leave, and the color won't matter all that much.

"I think you look great, Wes. Now don't forget, I'm going to call you Bradley. And be sure to open the door for me. And try to remember to touch two fingers to the bill of your cap when I get out. Not a real salute, but just sort of a casual gesture of respect. Like this. But be careful you don't knock that cap off. And, Wes, don't smoke in the car or in front of any of my proms. You'll just have to wait and smoke at intermission. I'll try to bring you some refreshments. I reckon we're ready to go, but we're going to be early."

"Whoa up a minute, Sambo," said Wes. "You bout to git me mixed up. I never knowed ney's so much to drivin befo. Hit goan be bad enough wid nis here towel hangin up here 'n me can't see out'n ne window, 'n what chew plannin on doin back nere anyhow? Nen you say I can't smoke cept at ne intermission 'n I don't eben know where dat is, but I do know nis here is Mr. Porter's hat, 'n I skeered he skin my head do he catch me wid it. I b'lieve you done overreached yoself."

"Listen, Wes," soothed the boy, "my daddy told me he'd do anything to help me with this date. He'll know you didn't go in the living room and get that hat. He'll know I did it. And he'll know I told you to wear it. He was a captain, and he's not going to punish a private for doing what a lieutenant ordered him to do. So you quit fretting.

"Here, take this. This is the three dollars I promised you. Now you've been paid in advance. That makes a contract and you can't renege because if you do the law might get you. Now, let's go."

"Uh-huh," responded Wes as he carefully folded the three bills and put them in his pocket. "All nat probly so, but I take my chances wid de law any day fo I cross yo paw. Git in and les go."

"Git in, nothing. Open the door for me, touch your cap, and then let's go."

As he settled into the corner of the back seat and Wes cranked the car, he directed through the partitioning towel, "To the village, Bradley."

Arriving at the section house, the boy almost forgot and jumped out of the car by himself. Recovering, he loftily reminded Wes, "Bradley, the door."

"Say which?" responded the driver through the terry cloth partition.

With aplomb and dignity, the boy patiently cajoled, "Aw, Wes, you remember. You're supposed to get out and open the door for me. Stand straight and tall when you do it, cause you really do look good tonight. And do the same thing when you see me coming toward the car with the girl. This is the real thing, now, Wes. Please don't forget again."

"Uh, huh. I won't. I just disremembered. I won't forgit no mo. Sambo, yo paw say for us to come by ne drugsto on our way to nis party. I might nigh forgot nat, too. I ain't never been in nothin like nis befo. You reckon we better get on down an see him now?"

"No," answered the boy. "It's too late now. I'm sure the Walkers know we're out here. I thought I saw somebody peeking through the dining room window, and it'd look funny if we backed out of the driveway now. Besides," he added as he looked at his father's hat on the chauffeur's head, "I spect it'd be better to have Gladys with us anyhow. I'm sure Daddy wants to meet her. Get ready now and open the door."

As he stepped out of the car and nodded condescendingly at his chauffeur, he was sure he saw a curtain flicker in the parlor window. Even so, after he knocked he had time to pull his coat down, feel his tie, run a hand over his head, and polish the toe of each shoe against the back of his other leg. Just as the door swung open, he was in the process of checking to be sure his fly was

326

securely buttoned, and he jerked himself so abruptly to attention that the corsage box leaped from under his arm like something alive and popped into the grasp of Gladys's mother. "My goodness," murmured that lady. "Won't you come in and have a seat?"

The boy's embarrassment was tempered by relief that Mrs. Walker had answered the door rather than her husband. Mr. Walker had a booming, harsh voice and an overly hearty manner that intimidated everyone, but his wife had never been heard to raise her voice. In fact, she spoke only in the softest of murmurs and sometimes did not even finish sentences.

She was tall and thin but was not the least bit angular. To the contrary, she looked as though she had not a bone in her body. When she walked she always slid along, and when she sat she melted into a chair, her long legs pressed flat against each other and folded at the knees, collapsing sideways like two adherent strips of pastry. The long neck always wilted to the opposite side from her knees, giving the impression that her head was an over-large blossom balanced precariously on a very fragile stem.

Her teeth were wide and large, and her lips were hardly ever closed completely over them so that she made frequent little silent tasting motions with her lips and tongue. Her eyes were the same pale blue as her daughter's but bulged more prominently and tilted downward at the outer corners. Her eyelids were so heavy that they were always half lowered, and this, combined with the downward slant of the eyes themselves, gave her a constantly bored and disenchanted air that the boy thought was elegant. Indeed she reminded him of impoverished English aristocracy, and he imagined that she might be the American descendant of some long-forgotten British earl.

As she limply waved the corsage box toward a chair, she murmured, "Gladys hasn't quite finished dressing. She'll be out in just a few. . . . Just have a seat and chat with me until she's. . . . It won't take long. . . . How are your payrents?"

"They're just fine, thank you, ma'am." He discovered that if he sat on the edge of the upholstered chair, his feet would touch the floor and decided this looked better than snuggling against the back with his legs stuck straight out. He sat in silence a moment and covertly watched her tasting some unknown substance. From her expression, he decided it was not pleasant. She must be anxious, he thought.

"Mrs. Walker," he ventured, "what time do you and Mr. Walker want me to have Gladys home?"

She slanted her lowered eyes at him, looking detached and only faintly interested. "Why, I don't know . . . I guess . . . whenever . . . what time is the prom over?"

"Well, the prom is over at eleven, and I'll try my dead level best to get Gladys home by five after eleven. Is that all right?"

She looked at him a little straighter. "Why, yes, I think that's fine. What time are the other girls expected home?"

"I don't know, Mrs. Walker, but I don't want you worrying about Gladys. I'll take good care of her."

"I'm sure you will," Mrs. Walker murmured.

"I mean, I know yall are probably extra particular about her, with her being an only child and all," the boy earnestly pursued, "and I want you to know that she is safe with me."

"I'm sure she is," Mrs. Walker almost whispered and looked around for a place to deposit the corsage.

"I mean, this is my very first date and all, and I want you to know that I respect your daughter and for that matter all womanhood, if you know what I mean."

"I'm sure you . . . I'm not at all worried about Gladys," Mrs. Walker said, continuing her tasting exercises.

The boy thought of Gene Stratton Porter's Freckles and Laddie, and decided that this was good sound material to allay the anxiety of a worried mother. "Well, what I really mean, Mrs. Walker, is that I want to assure you and Mr. Walker that I'm as pure as the day I was born, and I'm sure Gladys is, too, and I'll get us both back that way, so don't worry. You know what I mean?"

Mrs. Walker rose. "My goodness . . . where is . . . let me check on. . . . Gladys!" she called in the loudest voice the boy had ever heard her use. "You come on out here, you hear? You've kept this boy waiting too. . . . Mercy, what can be slowing you?"

Gladys swept into the room as though she had been waiting for a cue. The boy slid out of his chair and looked at her, openmouthed with wonder and admiration. Her head was bouncing with coils of freshly curled hair, and her radiant smile was delineated by the reddest lipstick he had ever seen. Her eyelashes looked longer and darker than he remembered. It was the dress her mother had made, however, that really transported her into a creature of mystery and beauty.

He had never seen so much pink net in all his life. It stood up in a cloud around her shoulders almost as high as the top of her head and fell in fluffy layers all the way to the floor. Somewhere near the top of the cloud was an artfully designed peephole that unmistakably showed her milk-white breasts, looking, he thought, like two white leghorn hens snuggled into the same nest. Underneath all the net she wore something that whispered and rustled every time she moved. He was so beguiled at the noise that his nervousness vanished.

"Gladys, you're just beautiful! That dress really does a lot for you."

"Thank you," she twinkled. She spread her arms and whirled around to the noisy accompaniment of her petticoat. "You really like it?"

"I mean I do! You look like a Campbell Soup kid in a ball of cotton candy.

"Here, I brought you some flowers." He proffered the white cardboard box.

"Ooh-wee. Aren't they pretty! Here, pin them on me."

The boy took the corsage and the long pin with the pearl head and moved toward the slightly stooping girl. He found himself looking straight into the cleavage showing through the nest of pink net and could not imagine pinning the corsage to any surface that did not involve his hand coming perilously close to those fascinating breasts. With a faint tremor he held the corsage out to Mrs. Walker. "You better do it," he gulped.

As the lady languidly pressed the bouquet down into the pink froth of one shoulder and secured it with the pin, the boy chattered nervously.

"See what I mean, Mrs. Walker? You can trust me. As my mother says, 'Avoid the very appearance of evil' or like my Latin teacher says, 'Caesar's wife must be above suspicion.' Those flowers look real pretty where you put them."

"Mercy," murmured Mrs. Walker into the pause that followed, "you children had better run along. Have a good time. . . . I mean behave yourselves, now. . . . I mean. . . . Well, mercy me, what are you waiting for?"

XX

Wes, eager to demonstrate mastery of his intensive training, hopped out of the car as they approached, opened the back door, and stood straight as a stick while the boy helped Gladys and her bundlesome swathings into the back seat.

"Well done, Bradley," the boy said loftily. He settled back against the cushions. "To the drugstore now, if you will," he directed through the tautly stretched towel.

As the car turned the corner around the church, Gladys was tilted against him in a melange of pink net and bouncing curls. His own gyroscope stable, the boy, before he thought, cast a steadying and protecting arm around the shoulders of the girl. Unbelievably, she did not move as the car straightened into the dirt street and chugged toward town. The blonde head rested on his shoulder, and she was actually snuggling into a natural embrace. The boy was momentarily breathless and ecstatic.

"Oo-wee," Gladys breathed, totally ignoring her position. "I just love this car and you having your own driver."

"You do?" said the boy, thinking of nothing in the world except his position. He had never in his plans for the evening afforded himself such a beautiful fantasy. He gently and stealthily slid his arm more snugly around the vision's shoulders. She pressed more comfortably against him. He furtively moved his hand under the angle of the soft jaw and stroked the velvety chin. As he did, he smelled the unmistakable milking aroma coming from his hand. Horrified, he realized that Gladys must be smelling it even more strongly than he, since her dainty little nose was

331

certainly closer to the offending member than his. Panicked, he jerked his arm away from Gladys and pushed her abruptly upright with the other hand.

"Excuse me," he blurted. "I don't know why in the world I did that. I certainly didn't mean to."

"Did what?" Gladys queried innocently. The boy barely heard her. He was slouched into his corner of the seat, mortified and humiliated, resisting the impulse to sit on both his hands. He was saved by their arrival at the drugstore.

In the early twilight, he could plainly see the white clothes of his father as he leaned against one of the supporting posts of the tin shed over the sidewalk just below the drugstore. He was in conversation with two overall-clad cronies. As the car slid slowly to the edge of the dirt street, his father straightened up, threw his cigarette aside, and stared incredulously.

As he slowly approached the car, the boy ordered masterfully, "The door, Bradley."

With Wes at attention, he descended grandly from the back seat and proffered his father a handshake in greeting. That gentleman did not seem to be bestowing his undivided attention on his only son. His glance kept straying from the hat on Wes's head to the brightly colored bath towel and back to the hat. Just as he drew a deep breath to speak, the boy impellingly announced, "Daddy, I'd like for you to meet Gladys Walker. She's my date for the evening."

While Wes still held the car door and the boy hopped from one foot to the other, the father, magnanimous master of all situations, postponed nonessentials and rose to the occasion. Leaning through the open door, he said with exquisite courtesy and just a flattering hint of formality, "Young lady, I'm delighted to make your acquaintance again. If you would not consider me forward, I'd like you to know that you are a veritable vision of loveliness in that dress."

He straightened, and his eyes went back to the top of Wes's head. "I won't detain you any longer. Have a good time. Here's the little retainer I promised you," he said and slipped a five dollar bill into the chauffeur's palm.

"Now," he added briskly, "there are certain incongruities here, some ludicrous and some invidious, to which the three of us will address ourselves later—in the morning, shall we say? Good night."

As they backed into the road, Gladys waved to the tall figure in white. "Ooh-wee," she exclaimed, "your daddy sure is nice. He's so educated."

"Yeah," the boy muttered absent-mindedly. He needed to get to the dictionary to find out if he or Wes was in the most trouble.

The prom was already very active. The front porch was full of girls in evening dresses with skirts so full their occupants had to bend awkwardly forward at the waist to bestow kisses on new arrivals. Feminine shrieks and nervous laughter filled the air, and each girl there assured at least six others, individually, that her dress was just beautiful and she was the prettiest thing ever seen in Brewtonton. No male voice could be heard anywhere.

Gladys, in her cloud of pink net, moving like a marionette, was pulled into the vortex of this female frenzy, and the boy was left at the top of the steps, alone and awkward.

Looking around, he noticed that Mrs. Jarvis across the street and Mrs. McLean next door were not letting the Junior-Senior Prom interrupt their daily routine. Having washed her supper dishes, each lady was ensconced in her usual chair on her front porch, slowly and rhythmically rocking the busy spring day to rest in contented ritual. If a little snuff was being dipped in twilight satisfaction, it was accomplished genteelly and unobtrusively, and no one need be concerned.

Comforted by the familiarity of the sight, the boy worked his way around the periphery of the chattering girls to the corner of the porch where he had spied a group of other boys. Some were stiffly standing around trying to remember not to put their hands in wrinkling forgetfulness into their pockets, and others were lounging against the columns or sitting on the bannisters of the wide porch. As alien as he usually felt with these older and bigger boys, he sensed tonight that they were all bound together in the common fear of being pulled into the tittering, shrieking mass of femininity that swirled all around them. With a comforting sensation of belonging, he edged into the masculine group, feeling instantly camouflaged and inconspicuous.

His arrival, however, had been remarked and nearly every boy there made some comment about his car. Since these comments, however phrased, expressed underlying admiration for either his basic ingenuity or the finished product, the boy began feeling accepted and at ease. Indeed, as the group of boys grew, all of them became more relaxed, and it was not long before they were exchanging not only jokes but detailed observations about the girls in their formal finery.

"Line up, fellas," he heard Dennis Rockmore say, "here come the Bishop twins." Within moments every boy in the group was hanging over the bannister to watch the procession of these two girls down the sidewalk and up the path to the porch. The other girls always tried to ignore them. Renda Belle and Linda Nell Bishop were lushly proportioned sisters who lived three miles south of town on a small cotton farm. Family economics forced them into the field with their four brothers. Their mother fancied herself well-connected and always acted as though she had married beneath herself. She insisted that the girls hoe and pick cotton in long-sleeved dresses and sunbonnets to protect their milkwhite skin from any exposure to the coarsening sun. She taught them early to fetch and carry for her and to regard every whim of their mother as a sacred obligation. She also taught them that the ability to please a man was the true measure of a woman's success and to walk up on their toes like ladies.

This produced in the twins gaits that were marvelous to behold, especially when they affected spike heels and chiffon finery as they had this evening. Linda Nell prissed and Renda Belle pranced. Both of them held their elbows stiff with hands sticking out to the side and swung their arms from the shoulders as they made their ebullient and vivacious entrance to the Junior-Senior Reception.

The boy had privately labeled them the "still-and-yet" girls. Linda Nell had the conversational habit of following a conjunction with the phrase "still and yet," and Renda Belle did the same with "yet and still." The twins did not disappoint him tonight.

As they mounted the steps and leaned forward to bestow and receive the insincere kisses of greeting, he overheard one sister squeal, "I declare this place looks like a fairyland, but yet and still it ought to with all the work the decorating committee has done. I jes love the way they've twined roses and honeysuckles round all the white colyums."

"I know," her twin gushed in counterpoint. "Jes look at that servin table. It's the prettiest thing I ever saw. Still and yet I believe that punch bowl's real cryshtal."

"God!" the boy heard Will Kelly breathe behind him. "I sure would like to cut that!"

"Which one?" the boy inquired.

"Don't make no difference. They're just alike. But ain't nobody got a chance les you could separate em. God, look at them titties!" He eyed the boy speculatively. "I tell you what," he said, "ain't no gal here gonna be able to turn down a chance to ride around town in that car you've fixed up. You ask one of em for a prom and I'll be right there and ask the other one. Me'n James Herman Malone are double-dating in his granddaddy's car, and he's already got ole Winona McGraw lined up for three proms in a row. He thinks she's bout ready to put out. You get two of em together sorta inclined that way and it's easier than with just one."

"You're crazy," scoffed the boy. "We've known Winona since the third grade and she's not about to do anything like that. She's got her tenth year Sunday School pin from the Baptist church for perfect attendance. And those Bishop twins, you might as well forget it. Their mama has raised them so strict they don't even chop cotton without gloves. They're scatterbrained, but I'm sure they're pure. You're crazy."

"You let me worry about that. They can wear gloves all night for all I want em to do. We sure ain't gonna chop no cotton. An we ain't plannin a thing that'll make Winona miss Sunday School day after tomorrow. You jest help me get those twins separated."

"Okay," the boy shrugged, "but I betcha it won't do you any good."

"Little Porter," Willie Mae Perdue interrupted, "would you please help me pass out these prom cards? You give one to everybody on the porch and I'll pass em out inside the house. Pink ones to the girls and blue ones to the boys. We're bout ready to begin."

"I'll be glad to if you'll save the second prom for me," the boy replied gallantly.

The cards had a bouquet of flowers on the front with "Junior-Senior" printed in gold at the top. Inside, beneath the large word Prom, were ten numbered lines, and attached to the card by a silken tasseled cord was the tiniest pencil the boy had ever seen. When the cards were all distributed, the boy wrote Gladys's name in the spaces for proms numbered one and ten and Willie Mae's for number two, discovering that for all its attractive appearance that pencil was the most difficult writing tool he had ever used. As he approached the bubbling Bishop twins, he felt Will Kelly nudge him in the ribs.

"Linda Nell," he blurted, "how bout signing me up for prom number three?"

"Well, Law, I declare, that'll jes be heavenly," she gushed. "Who you double-datin with? We need to get Sister signed up with him, you know."

"Well," he demurred, "I'm not double-dating tonight. I have my mother's car and my grandmother's chauffeur, and there's just not room for more than one couple."

"Ooh, I don't know," said Linda Nell. "Me'n Sister like to stick together. Why, just before we left home Mama said, 'Remember, girls, united you stand.' Maybe I better wait. I sure would like to ride in your car though. Me'n Sister seen it when we come up the sidewalk a while ago, but still and yet maybe we better wait."

As the boy began to shrug his shoulders in relief, Will Kelly interrupted, "I am double-dating, girls. James Herman Malone's got his granddaddy's Buick. I tell you what let's do. I'll take Renda Belle with us for the third prom, and then me'n James Herman will have the fourth prom with both of you. Sambo can prom with Winona McGraw that time. How bout that? James Herman can ride us around the courthouse and yall can wave at everybody that's walkin. Whatcha say, Renda Belle?" He held a firm grip on the boy's arm.

"Mama did say for Sister and I to stick together," said the second twin, "but yet and still it won't be but one lil bitty ole prom. They can't be no harm in that, Sister. Besides, Mama knows James Herman's mama, and everybody in the family always votes for his granddaddy."

Linda Nell was easily persuaded, and the boy moved on to finish filling the spaces on his prom card. He did not envy Will. By the time the fourth prom rolled around, it would be pitch dark and you couldn't see the Bishop twins. You could still hear both of them, however, and that, he thought, would be a lot to tolerate in the confines of one automobile. "Oh, well," he muttered, "call Dr. Redwine," and dismissed Will Kelly from his mind.

He claimed Gladys for the first prom, and they set off excitedly down the walk amidst a crowd of chattering, animated couples. The boys without cars steered their partners toward town, since the only paved sidewalks were those around the courthouse and fronting the businesses around the square. The Braswell brothers, best-raised boys in town, were careful to walk on the outside of the sidewalk with their dates on the inside. They waved to Mrs. McLean and Mrs. Jarvis, but everyone else went by the rocking figures as if they didn't exist.

As Wes snapped the door open and the boy helped Gladys into the car, he noted that her thin, fine hair was beginning to relax itself in the back from the tight curls of early evening and was straggling in disarray over the ruff of pink net.

"To the drugstore, Bradley," he directed and turned to Gladys. "Well," he said inconsequentially, "did you enjoy filling out your prom card? I guess yours was all filled in five minutes. I saw a lot of boys over there close to you."

"That line was around Myrtle Parker, not me. I did pretty good, though. I have all my proms filled except number eight and number nine. You have number ten. Do you want those other two? If you do, we could go for a long ride."

"Gosh," blurted the boy, "I wish I'd thought of it. I have all of mine filled up and I can't change them now. I thought you'd have all yours filled in no time. I guess the fellows thought that, too, and just didn't ask."

"Maybe so. You know there's a lot more girls here tonight than boys, and we can't go ask—we have to wait for some boy to come ask us. I think there's three girls that stood around through all that scramble and didn't get asked for a single prom."

The boy felt uncomfortable. He squirmed a little. "Gosh. I'd love to have all ten proms with you, Gladys. You're the prettiest girl here. But if a girl has more than one prom in a row with the same boy, everybody talks about her. They think she's smooching. Or," he added darkly, "worse. Wave to the Braswell boys. They're waving at you."

He thought of trying to hug her again but smelled his hands surreptitiously and quickly thrust them beneath his thighs.

Wes drove up to the drugstore and stopped.

"You may sound the horn, Bradley," the boy directed. "Once."

When the soda jerk appeared, rubbing the dappled gray stubble on his toothless jaw and tugging his greasy cap, he looked disbelievingly at the car and then peered into the back seat. "What kin I do for you?" he inquired softly.

"Two cherry smashes, please. If that's all right with you," he deferred to the girl. "Mr. Bama here makes the best ones you ever tasted."

"Comin right up," the gargoyle assured and turned to spit a copious stream of tobacco juice.

The boy added, "With straws, if you don't mind." He tried to ignore the slow shaking of the head as the man walked back into the drugstore.

When he returned with the sparkling red drinks, the boy served the girl, took his own glass, and deposited three nickels on the tray.

"Hit's just a dime," Mr. Bama told him. "You done put fiteen cent up there."

"I thought I'd leave a tip," the boy told him.

"Hit's just a dime—no tippin allowed. Take yo nickel." He shook the tray with a greasy hand until the coin threatened to dance into the boy's lap.

"Yes, sir." The boy cooperated. "Thank you, sir." He felt very young as the man turned away, shaking his head again.

"This sure is good," Gladys said. "What's the matter with that man? He acts like he has water in his ears."

"I'd be very surprised if he's ever had that problem," the boy declared. "We'd better finish our drinks; it's bout time for them to ring the bell at the party, and we don't want to be late."

By the time he had carried Willie Mae and then Linda Nell to the drugstore for cherry smashes, both Wes and Mr. Bama had grown familiar with the routine, and the boy thought the two of them were functioning smoothly and efficiently. When he carried Linda Nell Bishop back to the reception after his prom with her, they looked around for Renda Belle and Will Kelly. It soon became apparent that they were missing.

"Oh, well, Linda Nell," the boy said, "come on and we'll just prom together again. Don't worry, she'll show up. Let's go get another cherry smash."

"Ooh, no," responded the anxious twin. "I better stay here in case she comes back. I'm s'posed to have this prom with that Will Kelly. I know they're all right, but still and yet I can't help worrying. Besides, the last thing Mama told her and I was not to prom twicet in a row with the same fellow in case we was to get separated. You run on, and I'll stay here and worry."

As the boy started down the steps, bemused by the relief that the absence of Linda Nell produced, he spied three girls coming down the sidewalk, arm in arm and singing. These, he decided, were the three who Gladys said had not been asked for a single prom. One was fat, one was painfully thin, and one had blue-nosed acne. All three were well-behaved and quiet at school, made good grades, and were liked and respected. That was at school.

Obviously no boy liked or respected them well enough to ask them to the Junior-Senior Reception.

It dawned on the boy that they were making the best of a bad situation. Instead of skulking around the house and verandah, forcing polite conversation with the chaperons, they were out on the courthouse downtown circuit promming with each other. They seemed to be having fun, although he had heard "Row, row, row your boat" sung more harmoniously.

He thought how he would feel if every girl had refused his invitation to prom, and he was filled with a great sense of injustice and futility. Geraldine could lose weight, Mavis could gain weight, and Fannie Clyde, in time, would get rid of those bumps, but this was poor solace for having bought evening dresses and being ignored right now. He stepped purposefully in front of the trio, bent deep in as courtly a bow as he could manage, and said, "Would you three fair damsels do me the honor of sharing your company with me for this prom?"

"What ho!" said Mavis, immediately matching his spirit. "This can't be knave or varlet but must be goodly knight come to release us from durance vile. Let's go, girls!"

With all four of them laughing, they piled into the back seat, Fannie Clyde admonishing coyly, "Don't try to kiss us, now, for we'll all three turn into toads."

Geraldine drily rejoined, "That's your particular spell, honey. If it ever happens to me, I ain't going to be hopping and croaking or giving folks warts."

The boy was laughing so unself-consciously that he forgot to give Wes directions, and that bewildered man stuck his head out the front window and called into the back seat, "We gwine carry dis whole load to de drugsto, Sambo?"

"You can carry us to the cowlot if you'll drive around the courthouse first," laughed Mavis. "We wanta wave to all the folks we've been walking with."

When they finally pulled up to the drugstore and the boy had ordered four cherry smashes with straws, he was more relaxed than he had been all evening. When Mr. Bama returned with the order, he shifted his tobacco cud, tugged at his cap, and spoke to Wes, "Here, boy, I done brought you a Co-Cola. It's on the house. Enjoy yoself. An let me tell you somep'n. I been in the Merchant Marine and the CCC and I ain't never seen anything to top what you're right in the middle of tonight. First time I ever worried about gettin low on cherry syrup."

He pulled his cap lower and wagged his head all the way back into the drugstore.

The group got back just a few minutes late for the boy to claim his fifth prom. The voluble anguish pouring from Linda Nell Bishop, peering over her breasts as she descended the steps, clutching her skirt with one hand and a Braswell brother with the other, assured him that Renda Belle was still missing.

"But still and yet they ought to be back by now," he heard as he mounted the steps.

"Oh, I'm sure they're all right," Archibald Braswell told her. He caught the boy's eye and winked in the fraternal complicity of unspoken knowledge.

He brought his fifth prom back a few minutes early. All the cherry syrup and carbonated water he had imbibed required that he urinate immediately. This urgency produced problems he had not anticipated. If he excused himself while parked at the drugstore to utilize the loathsome toilet in the courthouse, not only would his date be left unattended, but she and every couple on the square would be notified of his need.

Directing Wes back to the house, he entered the front hall walking stiff-legged and breathing lightly, only to be appalled at the prospect of using the Reynolds's bathroom. It seemed there were girls clustered all over the place. Even if he managed to close the door and urinate silently down the side of the bowl, he would be forced to flush the toilet before he left. This distinctive noise would announce his presence and mission to everyone in the house.

He bolted in near-panic to the verandah, walking red-faced on tiptoe and resisting the urge to grab himself in clamping security against the irresistible pressure in his bladder. Averting his gaze from the liquid in the punch bowl, he scampered around the side yard and dived beneath the low-sweeping branches of a magnolia tree into dense and concealing shadow.

He fumbled his fly open, managed to flip his penis out with only one agonizing spurt into his pants, and relieved himself with such force that his head felt light and the dead magnolia leaves rattled as though a hail storm had hit.

Sauntering nonchalantly back across the lawn and onto the porch, he found himself in the confusion and babble of intermission. Assuring himself that in this dim light a small wet spot on dark pants was invisible, he sought out Gladys. "May I bring you a cup of punch?" he asked with loose-bellied comfort. As they held their paper plates with paper lace doilies for individual little cakes with "Jr.-Sr." in pink icing on the top, he heard a shriek behind him.

"Sister! You all right? I been jes frantic!"

"Oh, Sister! C'ose I'm all right. That old Buick just wouldn't crank, but yet and still I done stood up two boys for proms. Help me find em and pologize," the prodigal Renda Belle announced.

As soon as he could politely leave Gladys, the boy approached the cluster of males on the end of the porch. Seeking out Will Kelly, he punched him with an elbow. "Well?"

"It like to worked," Will told him. "It wadn't any trouble atall to get Renda Belle to smooch, and I'm here to tell you she's sump'n else, but James Herman was drivin an he finally parked way down in the cemetery close to the colored graves. He commenced tryin to smooch Winona up a little, an she didn't want to play, but he told her if she didn't he wadn't goin to ask her out any more and so they got to neckin pretty heavy in the front seat.

"An then he asked her how bout it, an she said no, she hadn't never done nothin like that, an James Herman says, 'What's wrong? Ain't you havin a good time? An here I was plannin to get my granddaddy's Buick and ask you to a movie all the way over in Jonesboro nex week, but now you go actin like a ignorant lil ole country girl, an I can't date you no more if this is all you kin do.' An I ain't standin here if that didn't break ole Winona down an she said, 'Well, I will if Renda Belle will.'"

He laughed and slapped his thigh.

"Well," persisted the boy, "what happened?"

"Aw, that sweet lil ole Renda Belle snuggled up in my arms an run her hand across the back of my neck an told her, 'Well, Winona, I'd really like to do it, only I got the lady sickness,' an me'n her gotta date nex weekend if I kin find somebody to date Sister. I know I ain't gonna get none with Linda Nell around, but that Renda Belle's so sweet I don't care. But James Herman missed his chance. If Winona was that close to givin in, he oughta cracked that tonight."

"Yeah?" interrupted James Herman. "If you uz doin all that much, you oughta known about the rag without havin to be told. I come a heap closer'n you did. Wanna smell my finger?" he offered.

As the boy recoiled, both physically and mentally, Warren Littlejohn spoke up, "Well, I tell you, both you fellows come a heap closer'n Moo-cow here. We all need to talk to him bout technique. I'm a son of a gun if he didn't run his last prom plumb off. We were walkin roun the courthouse square, and he was prommin Myrtice Whitmire, an you all know there ain't a sweeter, nicer girl in the whole class than Myrtice, an she an my prom was talkin about clothes an things girls always talk about an ole Moo-cow wadn't even holdin hands with her or nothin an all of a sudden outa the blue he said loud enough for everbody to hear, 'Myrtice, you wanta fuck?' and po ole Myrtice never said a word. She just acted like she ain't heard him, an when we turned the corner, she kept walking straight an come on back to the reception by herself an she was cryin. An Moo-cow ain't got no more sense than to stan there'n holler, 'What's the matter, Myrtice? How come you cryin?'"

"Moo-cow," Will Kelly admonished, "that's the worst thing I ever heard of." He paused. "Well, next to the worst," he amended. "That would stop any girl cold in her tracks. What you need to do is just keep your mouth shut. Start gradual. Hold hands, an then hug, an then kiss a little, and then try'n see how much feelin around she'll let you do, but don't ever, ever, ever mention it to a girl. Talk about somep'n else an act like you don't even know what your hands are doin. You ain't ever goan git nowhere talkin like that."

"Aw, yall make me sick," said Moo-cow. "I'm gettin as much as any o' yall, an I still got my cherry."

Moo-cow wandered off in one direction, and the boy disappeared in another. He found Gladys and spent the rest of intermission in stilted small-talk with her. Although he was sure he still loved her, he tried not to look at her hair, which had now lost nearly all its curl and was dragging in loose hanks across the pink net flounces of her collar. He also tried not to think about the shocking conversation he had just heard. He hoped the Lord would forgive him for being interested enough to have listened but avoided confronting Him directly with a plea. He carried Wes some cake and punch and was very careful to return his cup to the kitchen, since everyone knew that Nigras, no matter how clean they were, carried terrible diseases and no one should ever drink after them. He felt exceptionally virtuous.

Promming after intermission was almost an anticlimax. He dutifully escorted the girls to the car, directed Bradley to the drugstore as grandly as possible, and ordered cherry smashes from the now-jaded soda jerk. The freshness of new adventure was gone, however, and by ten o'clock he was anticipating with pleasure the end of the festivities.

Embarking on his eighth prom, he saw his beloved Gladys standing lonely by the punch bowl, chatting listlessly with one of the chaperones, and waved to her with a mixture of guilt and embarrassment. When he departed for the ninth prom she was nowhere in sight, and he surmised approvingly that she had probably joined the promless trio for a walk. When he returned for the tenth and final prom of the evening, however, she was nowhere to be found. Discreet inquiries proved fruitless, and finally he was impelled once again to seek the shelter of the magnolia tree in the back yard. Cutting loose with all the force he could muster, he did not hear the spattering rattle of dry magnolia leaves. Instead a male voice yelled out, "What the hell!"

This so startled him that he swung wide and almost wet himself again as he frantically hunched his buttocks backward, trying desperately to clamp the flow. A close look into the shadows showed unmistakably a male hand being withdrawn from beneath a pink net dress. Incredulous and furious, the boy retorted, "What the hell yourself!"

Moo-cow Mullins rose to his feet and in injured tones said accusingly, "You pissed right on me, goddammit!"

"I'm glad I did, and I'm sorry that's all I had to do. You better go on home," the scandalized boy replied.

As Moo-cow, aware of his indefensible position, vanished around the corner, the boy extended his hand to the now-sitting Gladys, "Come on. I'll take you home now before the party's over so you won't have to see anybody."

"The front of my dress is all wet," the girl wailed in a stricken voice as he led her across the side yard to his car.

"Tell your mama you spilled punch down it," the boy said shortly as the now-perfected chauffeur held the door open.

"To the section house, Bradley," the boy said with dignity. After a moment he added, "Don't spare the horses." Then he settled in silence into his corner.

When he escorted the crestfallen Gladys up the walkway, she turned at her doorstep. "I'm sorry for what happened. I hope you're not too mad at me."

He grasped the word with relief, clutching it like a familiar friend, and immediately used it to his advantage.

"Mad?" he said. "Mad?" He modulated his tone to one of injured hauteur. "I'm not mad! I'm just hurt!"

He turned on his heel and made a perfect exit into the waiting maw of the back seat.

Before they reached the city limits, he had unfastened all the safety pins, folded the bath towel, and crawled into the front seat. "You did a great job, Wes," he bragged. "But stop the car in the flat down there before I pee all over myself."

"I know whatcha mean. I bout to bus open, an I ain't had nowhere near's much to drink as you."

As they stood back to back on the side of the ditch, Wes spoke over his shoulder. "What is a cherry smash anyhow, Sambo?"

The boy, of a sudden, began laughing. They climbed back in the car and proceeded down the dirt road.

"It'll cost you five cents to find out, durn your time. And if I didn't know you well enough to know you'd throw 'contract' up to me, I'd make you give me back my three dollars. You knew all the time Mr. Porter had that five bucks for you. You've made more money tonight than you'd have made in a whole week plowing for Mr. Whitaker. You're a crafty, high-yellow rascal, that's what you are."

He looked at Wes and yelled with laughter.

Wes began grinning. "Yeah," he said, "I sho did, an I done had cake an punch an a Co-Cola. Sides which I smoked twicet en I wadn't eben at intermission. I done learnt a heap tonight, Sambo."

He threw back his head and joined in the mirth. After a mile they settled into a companionable silence. Just as they topped the tickle-stomach hill by the Holiness church, the boy drew a long, shuddering breath.

"Wes," he said in a bemused tone, "I done learnt a heap tonight, too. I guess I know a lot for a fourteen-year-old boy. Sometimes I think I know more than I want to. Someday I may tell you about it."

XXI

that summer the boy immersed himself in farm life and made no effort at all to see any of his former friends from town. Feeling separated by differences in values and interests, he discovered anew that six miles of dirt road made a very effective barrier to social contact. He hugged loneliness to himself and felt comfortable and secure in his isolation.

He wondered occasionally if Gladys had ever had a date with Moo-cow or if Will and Renda Belle were sweethearts, but these thoughts produced such painful memories that he avoided them. In fact, the only part of the Junior-Senior Reception that he recalled with pleasure was the prom he had with Fannie Clyde, Mavis, and Geraldine, after being stood up by Winona. He thought about those three girls often and decided that in a number of respects they were kindred souls. He remembered them with sadness, indignation, and affection, often projecting himself into imaginary solutions of their problems.

The Atlanta Constitution was filled with stories about Roosevelt and about some German named Hitler. The grandfather kept muttering darkly about each of these men, prophesying that the blue-bellied yankee with infantile paralysis would ruin the country and that the little pissant with a moustache was heading out for another war. The boy impatiently turned past these stories to find the funnies.

His older sister, home from college, let him read *Anthony Adverse,* a book which he found scandalously erotic. He had difficulty understanding how a nice girl like his sister could admit in public she had even read such a book, let alone brag on it as entertaining literature. He finally assured himself that she probably didn't understand all of it and that certainly the masturbation scene had gone completely over her head. It never occurred to him to discuss it with her.

The two younger sisters were growing up some. It took a little more effort on his part to precipitate a satisfactory fuss between them, but it could still be done when a rainy afternoon became too boring to bear. He voluntarily weeded the grandmother's flower border on Saturday afternoons, motivated by love rather than being forced into it as punishment. He still enjoyed the early morning times with his mother, finding it easier to relax with her spoken declarations of affection and her thinly disguised efforts at guidance when he was absolutely sure there were no witnesses. Another cow had freshened, a heifer which had been given to him when she was a calf. This brought the total of cows he was milking to three and produced a surplus of milk and butter in the family larder. The hogs got a lot of buttermilk that summer, but his mother sold the extra butter and gave the money to the boy.

He saw his father for the most part only on Sundays but still maintained a sporadic correspondence with him about the crops and his changing assignments on the farm. He slipped a streaky-field lizard into Freeman's Prince Albert tobacco, and when that man thrust a loosening forefinger deep in the can to prepare a cigarette, the lizard obligingly ran up his wrist and arm to disappear in the hollow between the black shoulders. Freeman, bellowing in uncontrollable terror, sought frantically to disrobe even as he wheeled round and round slapping at his back, and the boy and Darnell's sons laughed uproariously.

The boy delighted in the fear everyone on the farm had of snakes and suppressed his own revulsion for them enough to capture one occasionally with a head-flattening stick. Grasping the writhing reptile behind its jaws with a viselike grip, he found it gratifying to stride through the yards of the tenant houses and send everyone, regardless of age or gender, scampering to the safety of the raised porches. This compensated, somewhat, for his

348

lack of expertise in the cowpasture baseball games and increased his stature among his black friends. The comments he overheard ranged from "He crazy," to "De debbil in him," to "He ain't skeerda nuthin," and he relished all of them.

One afternoon during laying-by season, stretched out reading beneath the window to the front porch, he eavesdropped on a conversation among his visiting aunts. The three of them were sisters of his mother and had come from various towns in north Georgia to spend a week in the country with Vera. Wedged in powdered corpulence into chairs on the porch, they rocked and fanned. With indulgent affection, the boy half listened as they ruminated over family gossip and news they had already digested earlier in the week. Suddenly he heard the oldest one, whose husband had left her ten years earlier for another woman, "Poor Vera! I heard his car come in a little before three this morning." Creak-crack, poppity-pop went the rocking chairs.

"I know," replied the youngest one, currently living with her third husband in a one room apartment, "an I thought he'd never make it upstairs. He musta bounced off that bannister three times. Poor Vera."

Ship-whoosh, ship-whoosh went the funeral-home fans between the creak-crack, poppity-pop.

"Ain't it awful?" added the other sister, who would still weep at a moment's notice because the father of her seven children had walked out some three years before. "When I came in on the bus the other day, one of those women had the nerve to walk up to me on the sidewalk and actually speak to me. Poor Vera."

Conflicting loyalties boiling up in partisan indignation, the boy rose and thrust his skinny torso through the open window. With his little gold-rimmed glasses sitting crookedly on his face, he piped authoritatively, "She's the only one of you sisters still living with the same man she started with. Maybe she knows something yall don't. It looks to me like yall'd do better to break up this 'Poor Vera' club and spend a little time feeling sorry for each other."

As he retreated to the solitude of the barn loft, he wondered at his audacity and his disrespect and pondered on the pleasure of assuaging pain in himself by inflicting pain on others.

All in all, it was an uneventful summer, and when it was over he strode eagerly into the schoolhouse to begin his senior year. Gone was all trace of the diffidence of previous years. The thirty-nine students in the eleventh grade were as well known to him as siblings, and they comprised the senior class. That group obviously was running the school. One could tell by the way they walked down the hall, laughing and self-confident. Happy to have achieved this peak in the progress of life, they were benignly oblivious of the underclassmen who stepped respectfully out of their path. The seniors were the elite, the aristocracy, the cream of school society. This was their year.

The boy was right in the middle of them. Waiting for his fifteenth birthday the last of the month, weighing ninety pounds and measuring fifty-eight inches by the last notch he had cut on the kitchen door, he managed to persuade himself that he was a very mature young man. Physical development and good looks were certainly not as important as mental ability and social sophistication. From this pinnacle, he even joined the cedar tree luncheon club with a certain measure of confidence.

He listened in tolerant amusement as the juniors regaled the sophomores and freshmen with graphic sexual descriptions, promulgating forevermore the same myths they had inherited. He feigned indifference to the repetitive barrages of four letter words affected by some of the tougher boys.

He had easily arranged five subjects this year by signing up to take vocational agriculture. This was a brand new course taught by the brand new principal. The new man was as different from Mr. Gill as it was possible to be. Blond, with a jutting jaw and sun-bleached eyebrows, he was as vibrant as spring steel. From the very first day of school, there was an excitement in the student body and the faculty that had not been there before, a feeling of purpose and commitment, an almost electric sense of direction. This man could make the lowest student feel important and excite the most indifferent teacher to an interest in excellence. Before his

350

driving determination that each student be educated to the extent of his capability, sloth gave way to industry and apathy to joy and hope.

From the first, the boy impressed the principal with his academic ability. That man, in turn, had let the boy know that none of his wiles or maneuverings went unnoticed and that he did not attribute innocence automatically to a boy just because he was undersized, had little round glasses, a forlorn countenance, and big pleading eyes. The boy thought him one of the wisest and kindest persons he had ever known and would have worked until he dropped for him.

The advent of the principal was enough to make the boy's last year his finest, but there were two teachers who also influenced his life during that fabulous senior year. Both met the principal's challenge of excellence with an ease that manifested grace. One was Miss Berry, a recent graduate of Bessie Tift, the very Baptist college where the older sister was enrolled. From the sister's annual the boy had learned the motto of the college: "That our daughters may be as cornerstones, polished after the similitude of a palace." This awareness imparted an exotic and lady-like aura to Miss Berry the moment he met her.

She had a nose so intricate it looked laminated and sculpted. Wafer-thin, the long bridge was as delicate as the breastbone of a sparrow. The septum at the end was highly arched and pulled her upper lip just a little short. The nostrils were vaulted high and deep, giving the whole organ a pinched, aristocratic appearance—the boy thought she made Basil Rathbone in *A Tale of Two Cities* look like a plowhand.

The brow was wide, bulging forward beneath her fine, fair hair just enough to imply delightful intellect. The eyes were blue, and her gaze was tranquil, suggesting that her self-awareness and self-assurance were in serene harmony. Those eyes could twinkle in acknowledgment of a student and then warm into laughter before ever the lips or voice moved.

She was never depressed, never angry, and her classes were oases of joy. Discipline was subtle, since she could accomplish more by lifting one eyebrow than most women could by screaming and scolding. Misbehaviour in Miss Berry's room seemed so uncouth that even the crudest student avoided it. She joyously taught English, and this was her milieu. Here she sparkled and shone. She made even grammar and composition exciting, and she approached literature with such verve and vivacity that the most indifferent of students was pulled into the vortex of her enthusiasm. Miss Berry only dutifully taught French, and since no one could graduate without passing it, the students dutifully studied French but regarded it as an onerous duty—an attitude they transferred later to an entire country.

The boy soon realized that he was once again falling uncontrollably in love. He thought back to Marietta Marsengill and Gladys Walker and Miss Duncan and assured himself that this time he was succumbing to an emotion that was far nobler and more mature than any he had previously experienced. He accepted with cheerful resignation and a sense of security the knowledge that it was completely hopeless. He vowed to present to her perfect themes, memorized poems, and even the mastery of irregular French verbs as undeclared testimonials of his devotion.

Her approval of him in any fashion was sublime reward. He smiled benignly when one of the more loutish members of the Whitmore clan avowed, "I tole my ma that Miss Berry is the best English teacher I ever seed. If you don't do nuthin but just set in her class, she'll learn you sump'n."

Mr. Dorsey was the other teacher whose brilliance and ability had a lasting impact on the boy. He was all of nineteen years old when he signed and mailed a contract to teach school in Brewtonton, but he had the self-confidence of a man twice that age. It was from him that the boy first began getting the idea that his hometown might be extra-special and not just a duplicate of all other towns across America.

Mr. Dorsey recounted with merriment his arrival in Brewtonton on the evening train for his very first job. He had assumed that the crowd of local citizens gathered along the tracks was a welcoming committee for the new teachers in town. Later, amused at himself, he learned that this daily hegira to the depot was a community ritual second in social importance only to Sunday morning church attendance. From that day there was a mutual love affair between Mr. Dorsey and the community. Both delighted in discovering the character traits of the other, all the while developing an unshakable loyalty and admiration that brooked no mean nor petty assessment of either. The man could do anything. Everything about him was quick—his movements, his speech, his perception, and above all his intellect. He had an impudent irreverence about what people assumed to be their fate. His slanted green eyes would twinkle puckishly as he exclaimed in mock dismay, "You really think you can't do that? Well, with that attitude, I daresay you won't. It's a pity, too—you'd have been good at it."

He inspired more farm boys to achievement than anyone before or since. He stimulated a pride in self that squared drooping shoulders and raised hanging heads. His boundless energy and enjoyment of everything he did were as infectious as his quick laugh. His American History was the most popular class in school. He presented the Founding Fathers as personal acquaintances and the Constitution as a living document, the revered depository of everything fine and noble in Western civilization.

"What we need is a real class election," Mr. Dorsey announced one day. "You young people are treating these Whigs and Tories like something dead and dry. They weren't. They affected the lives of the people who voted. You seniors need to form a couple of political parties and nominate candidates with real platforms to support. I'm going to see the principal and Miss Berry about it. Most class elections are nothing but a popularity contest, but they should be based on what a candidate can contribute rather than on how well you like him."

Concealing his immediate excitement, the boy raised his hand. "You mean we should have a political campaign?"

"Certainly I do." Dorsey's ideas tumbled out. "Set the date of the election, nominate slates of officers, have speeches and debates over issues, and stir up some real interest in politics and the democratic process."

The boy lowered his eyes to hide the excitement in them. "That sounds like a lot of work," he ventured, "if it's done right, that is. Seems like extracurricular points ought to be offered for each office."

"Oh! I agree with you! I'll speak to the principal about that, too. Stay after class a few minutes and let's talk about it.

"Now, then," he began a little later, "just what is your interest here? I value your opinion and I want to learn what you're thinking."

"I think it's a great idea," said the boy. "I think you're right about stimulating interest in the mechanics of democracy, and I think there's a ready-made issue someone could run on and get elected." He looked into the piercing green eyes and for the first time in years abandoned himself to complete honesty. "Besides," he blurted, "I'd like to be president of the class. I've never been elected to anything. The main thing, though, Mr. Dorsey, is I want to be first honor graduate, and I need all the extra points I can get. Do you think that's too selfish or stuck-up?" He shivered a little as though naked. He felt that way.

The green eyes twinkled but did not mock. "Oh, no. I think what you're afflicted with is ambition, and I think it's wonderful. This country would never have survived without it. What issue were you talking about running on?"

Bolstered by this approbation, the boy drew himself up straight and tremulously began, "Well, you see, there are just a handful of town students compared to the number of kids from the country, and yet the town children have always run everything just the way they want it. What's so bad about it is that they act like they're better than anybody else and that it's their divine right to boss everything in the class. They give the impression that if somebody is from the country, he is just ignorant and beneath notice. Some of the town boys are pretty arrogant, especially to the country girls."

Incautiously, he even told Mr. Dorsey about Winona McGraw's debasement at the hands of James Herman the year before. "So, don't you see," he said finally, "at the most there're not more than fourteen votes a town ticket could get, and if somebody united all the country kids together there's a solid block of twenty-five votes right there. And I believe I could do it."

"Oh, I do, too. But I can see where it may be a disruptive campaign. I'll talk to the principal about it. You've been honest with me, and, in confidence, I'm going to be the same with you."

He paused. "Although I certainly won't be in any position to take sides, I think this needs doing. Lots of luck."

He reached out and shook hands. The boy was so elated that he walked home without the slightest sense of injustice at having missed his ride. He had told Mr. Dorsey exactly how he felt and exactly what his motives were, without trying to make himself look noble, and that man had not only seemed to like him but had actually approved of his activities. He puzzled for awhile over the difference between greed and ambition, finally shrugged his shoulders, and spoke out loud to himself on the deserted country road. "Who do you think you are? If you look okay to Mr. Dorsey, you're pretty silly to be worrying about what Jesus would say."

He had developed a most formidable case of hero worship. The next morning his new-found idol sought him out.

"I talked to the principal yesterday afternoon," he informed the boy. "He approved the election project, and your home room teacher will announce it this morning. I also looked at the records. I didn't have time to add everything up accurately, but I believe you're ahead for valedictorian. Of course, I know you want to get as many points as possible, but I believe it's within your grasp." He squeezed the boy's shoulder and walked quickly down the hall.

In home room the lovely Miss Berry informed the senior class that she had met with the principal and the history teacher. She outlined the nominating process, announced a one week campaign culminating in a secret ballot, and then concluded, "The principal has decided that, in view of the new importance and the concurrent responsibilities of these senior class offices, extracurricular points will be awarded—ten for president, five for vice-president, three for secretary, and two for treasurer."

The boy could not believe his ears. President of the class would be worth as many points as winning a district literary event! This filled him with such a resolve to win that his campaign was irresistible. Capitalizing on three years of snobbish rule and wounded feelings, he pointed out the power of political unity and made succinct promises about committee appointments and presidential policies.

The ticket was swept into office by a margin of three to one, with one hundred percent voter participation. He immediately made a modest acceptance speech and read off his committees, each of which consisted of one town student and four carefully chosen country students. Most of them had been advised privately that a committee chairman could not vote except in the event of a tie. As a result each committee wound up with a town student as chairman and a year-long record of unanimous accord. Never had a class had a greater spirit of cohesiveness and never had the lessons of democracy and practical politics been more poignantly demonstrated. The boy believed in the righteousness of his cause, but he also gloated over the ten points he had accrued.

A few days after the election, Miss Berry called him aside. "Porter, we need a good speller to represent our school at the state fair. We're going to have a local contest in two weeks, and I want you to enter it."

"Oh, gosh, Miss Berry," he demurred, "you know I've about got my hands full. This president's job is more than I thought it was going to be, and I'm taking five subjects. I don't know whether I ought to add anything else or not."

"Well, all right." She shrugged. "I just thought I'd mention it. You're making A's in all those subjects, but you know what you want to do. The principal talked to me about it and said he was giving five extracurricular points for it this year."

"Well, now, Miss Berry, I'd do anything in the world for you. I'll be glad to try out for spelling champ from our school."

He worked diligently for two weeks and walked off easily as the winner in that contest.

The principal stopped him one day after an agriculture class which had been devoted to the startlingly new idea of planting crimson clover and lespedeza as cover crops to restore fertility in farm land that had been row-cropped to yellow-leafed thinness.

"Porter," he said, "I want to see you for a minute. We need to organize a Future Farmers of America Club, and I want you to study this material and present it to the agriculture class. This is going to be a real service club with work projects all year, and I thought whoever wound up being president ought to get five extracurricular points. Would you do that for me?"

"Oh, yes, *sir*! I'd be glad to do anything I can to help you out. The agriculture class has been a great addition to our school—outside the new farming techniques we're learning, it's really got all the country boys together. I'll be glad to talk to them about the club."

After a couple of days of energetic discussion under the cedar tree and one formal presentation to the class, the first local chapter of the Future Farmers of America was formed. The boy was elected president of it by unanimous acclamation and accepted the new honor with a self-deprecating grace that was becoming perfect through repetition.

Mr. Dorsey accosted him the following day. "Congratulations on the FFA Club. The principal is real excited about it. He talked to me awhile yesterday, and he was impressed with the way you presented and organized it. He says you have real ability. I told him I knew that all along. I'm sure proud of you."

Ecstatic at this open accolade from such an exceptional person, the boy actually squirmed and blushed.

"You know what I wish you'd do?" Mr. Dorsey said. "I wish you'd go out for basketball. They're signing up for it today and start practice next week."

"Huh?" yelped the boy in surprise. "Basketball? I can't play basketball!"

"Nobody can until they learn how. That's why they have practice. The ancient Greeks had an ideal of the combination of scholar-athlete being the perfect man. You have a fine mind, but I feel like all your endeavors are slanted toward the academic side, and you'd really enjoy participating in a sport. Besides, you get five points just for going out for basketball, as long as you don't miss practice enough to get kicked out. What have you got against trying?"

"Gosh, Mr. Dorsey," the boy said defensively, "I'm already busier than I've ever been. Besides, I have three cows to milk and I have to ride home with my uncle and they practice after school. I wouldn't have time."

"No," the hero demurred, "the principal is changing that this year. They're going to begin practice the last period and get through in time for the last bus at least. If you miss your uncle occasionally, you can ride the bus to within two miles of your house and walk the rest of the way. I've milked many a cow after dark. That's no real hindrance."

Abandoning excuses, the boy faced Mr. Dorsey with honesty. "The real reason is I'm too dam' little," he blurted. "All those boys are twice as big as I am." He averted his eyes and tried to keep the quiver out of his voice as he confided, "I'm afraid they'll laugh at me."

Mr. Dorsey threw back his head and burst into unself-conscious laughter as he slapped the boy between the shoulders. "Of course they'll laugh at you," he said. "They'll also tease you when you make dumb mistakes on the court, but that doesn't mean they don't like you. If you'll just think a minute, every boy on the first string is already a friend of yours.

"I know how you feel about your size. I was a real runt when I was in high school, and it used to bother me. But, believe me, you're going to grow, and some day you'll laugh at having worried about it." He paused, looking like Puck, and then added merrily, "It's important to learn coordination in a sport early, and then you're better when you get the size for it. My grandfather used to say, 'It ain't the dawg in the fight, it's the fight in the dawg.' "

"Gosh, Mr. Dorsey. I can't believe you're telling me that. I've heard my own grandfather say exactly the same thing, I bet a hundred times, but I thought he was the only one who ever said it. Shoot, yeah, I'll go out for basketball!" He hesitated a moment. "How much did you weigh when you were a senior in high school?" he asked.

"Oh, I forget," Mr. Dorsey became a little vague. "I probably grew off a little earlier than that, but I sure remember feeling exactly as you do. I certainly understand, and I'm telling you not to worry."

Uncomfortable at having asked such a personal question, the boy left quickly so he could volunteer for basketball. Recalling the conversation later, he thought, I wish I'd had the nerve to ask him how long it took his pecker to grow. Then he blushed at his temerity.

Settling into the routine of practicing basketball was no easy matter, but he worked at it doggedly. Dressing out was humiliating. His hairless legs stuck out of his shorts like broomsticks, and one of the big junior boys remarked that his knees looked like onions in white stockings. Mustering all his strength, he could lob the basketball only half the distance of the court, while the bigger boys could hurl it like a cannon ball from one end to the other. He bravely stepped in to catch one of those hurtling passes and was carried twenty feet backwards, while the gym erupted in laughter. After this, he sidestepped the long fast ones and concentrated on learning to dribble and get rebounds.

Having determined to play basketball, he endured the torment of his inadequacy and the condescending gibes of the other boys. In the process he finally earned not only their tolerance but their compassion. They kindly looked the other way when he undressed, and no one ever commented on the humiliating fact that he didn't even stink when he sweat. Committed and resolved, he would not admit that he hated it. If Mr. Dorsey wanted him to do something, he was glad it was no more demanding than this.

When Miss Berry handed out the report cards, she held his until last. "Porter, I want to congratulate you. This is the second month in a row you have had all A's." She paused. "Including deportment. I've looked at your record, and this is the only time in your high school career you've accomplished that. I'm proud of you."

"Yes'm," the boy responded, "thank you. I've even been working hard."

He was ashamed that she knew about the F's he had made when he was young and immature. He noted that by tilting his head he could see the light shining through her nose. Surely no person in history had ever been more fascinating.

"I wanted to tell you about a change in the rules for the District Meet this year," she continued. "Instead of having the contestants do their writing on the spot, the officials are going to send a list of topics to each school. These will be distributed two weeks in advance to the students who are interested, and then they will be required to write an essay in the presence of the local sponsor. Whichever essay wins on the local level will be sent on to the District Meet and judged there, rather than having the students come and write an entirely different essay. I thought I'd tell you this because I know you've earned fifteen points each year by winning the District Meet for the last two years. You just don't know how proud of you I am!"

"Yes'm," he replied, "thank you. I'll do my best." He looked at her tenderly and vowed never to do anything to disappoint her.

A few days later the principal called him aside and informed him that the FFA was sponsoring an oratorical contest based on original speeches about some aspect of farming. He volunteered the information that he had decided to award extracurricular points for this event on the same basis as the literary meet.

He assured the boy that he was proud of him and that he was sure he would do a good job. The boy promised to try and vowed silently to deserve this man's admiration. That night in the barn, his head pressed into the flank of a cooperative cow as he milked by lantern light, he considered his lot.

"Well," he said to the cow, "I thought this senior year was sure to be a breeze and I'd just loaf my way through it, and I'm blessed if I'm not working harder than I ever have in my life. I sure do have three good teachers, though, and you can't let a good teacher down. They're too hard to find."

He moved on to the third cow and began washing her bag. "You know," he told her, "I've gone all through high school and nobody has ever mentioned extracurricular points to me before, and now, all of a sudden, every time I turn around some teacher is telling me how many points you can get for this and how many points you can get for that. The way I figure it I'm having my nose rubbed into forty-five extra points, and it's not even Christmas yet. That's more than I ever heard of anybody winning in one year, and I'm sure to make the debating team again, too. Sah in there now, you're having your tits pulled by a sure-fire valedictorian. Back your leg."

XXII

On the farm the cotton had been picked over twice, and there were only scattered flecks of white dotting the dead stalks. This was called scrap cotton and would be picked at leisure by the women and children sometime before Christmas. Most of the good cotton had already been hauled to the gin on wagons with high bodies, homemade extensions that raised one to a dizzying height if one rode on top of the load. These vehicles, properly packed by the stomping feet of young men and boys, would hold between thirteen and fifteen hundred pounds of seed cotton, which in turn would be ginned and compacted into a five- or six-hundred-pound bale of lint cotton. If a finished bale of cotton weighed only four hundred pounds, there was the unspoken feeling that someone had been lazy about packing.

During dry, pretty weather in August, September, and early October, everyone on the farm subordinated every other activity to cotton-picking. It was important to gather the crop before rain lowered the value of the lint. Early in the season all the sheds and barns were filled with the loose cotton. As soon as the outbuildings were filled, the dwellings themselves were pressed into service. Slats were nailed around the porches of the unpainted tenant houses, and cotton was packed to the roof, leaving only a small passage to the front door.

Darnell and Ole John Tom had so many children that they made more cotton than anyone else on the place. Storage until ginning time became a problem for them. They expediently solved this by knocking down the bedsteads and moving all the furniture out of the two front rooms in their houses. Then they packed these rooms almost to the ceiling with the precious white fleece for which they had labored all summer. If the womenfolk grumbled about this inconvenience, the boy never overheard them. They were just extra careful about their cooking fires and scolded the men about smoking.

The children in the family had an attitude almost carnival about the arrangement because, for the few weeks involved, everyone simply climbed into the packed rooms at bedtime and slept on top of the cotton. This was attested by the fuzzy white shreds clinging to hair and clothes for the better part of the following day. Harvested cotton had a distinctive odor, reminiscent simultaneously of both the vital sap of growth and the sun-drenched languor of ripeness. The smell was very comforting and fulfilling. It made the boy wistful about sharing the communal sleeping accommodations at Ole John Tom's, but he knew better than to mention it either to the Westmorelands, the family, or himself.

The wagon was loaded with the cotton at twilight in preparation for a daylight departure. If an industrious farmer was early enough to be near the head of the line when the gin began operating, he could get two loads of cotton ginned in the same day. The family got its mail from Brewtonton, but it hauled its cotton to Peabody. This was only two and a half miles from the farm, but with a loaded wagon it was still a long trip, since a team of mules encumbered by a generously packed, unginned bale of cotton could not walk as fast as an energetic man. Long since, the boy had discovered that going to gin was like many experiences in life—getting there was more fun than being there.

When the boy was very small, the grandfather was still energetic and vigorous. With an eye to efficiency, he would volunteer to go to gin himself, thus allowing at least one adult Negro to continue picking while the weather lasted. Frequently the boy was taken on these missions. The grandfather also carried the sisters to gin, but he never carried more than one child at the time. He was not a baby sitter. He was a grandfather.

The boy could remember going along when he was so small that the old man would not let him sit beside him on the front of the wagon with legs dangling high above the traces. He had to sit further back in the middle of the load lest a sudden jolt fling him into the big road. The wagon was loaded so heavily that the rattling noise of the wheels was obscured and the jarring, bone-jolting bumps were softened. Consequently, for an hour he was free to lie on his back in the softly supporting cotton and look his fill into the sky. When viewed from this position the sky was deep and benevolent and seemed to caress with blue and silver light the cruising buzzard that tensed its airborne slide through silent heights.

A few feet above the sunbaked red clay of the road, an occasional grasshopper hung suspended in warm, spiced air and chirred its Indian Summer song. When the wagon approached Peabody Creek, the tantalizing drifts from the ripe muscadines and the dank river smell of marsh vegetation mingled in the boy's nostrils with the fecund odor of the cotton. Even his fantasies were softened by the overwhelming assurance that once again nature was fulfilled in harvest, and he was well content.

The weightless reverie of the trip was violently interrupted by arrival at the gin. Mounted on timbers, the two-storied gin was completely covered with corrugated sheets of galvanized metal. It was filled with horribly complicated machinery that spun and rattled behind glass-covered lids in a dizzying whirl, separating seeds from the cotton. The noise level was soul-shattering, and conversation had to be conducted by yelling at maximum volume over a distance of no more than four inches. If the line of wagons dwindled, the operator blew a steam whistle to announce to all farmers within five miles that the gin was eager for business. Muted by distance, the whistle was a not unpleasant part of the rural scene, but added to the cacophony of the vibrating machinery, it was a totally unexpected screech that hurt the ears and made a small boy grab for his grandfather.

Abandoned to jimson weed and morning glory for nine months each year, the gin rose abruptly in an exaggerated perpendicular over the village. It looked to the boy like a gunmetal

363

and rust-colored idol, malevolent and mighty, requiring no telling what in the way of horrible sacrifice. He thought there was no building in all the world uglier than a cotton gin.

The most fascinating part of the conglomerate was the loading tube. This was a long metal cylinder with telescoping sections that hung suspended from the roof of the high shed on the east side of the gin. By some alchemy the squat gasoline generator that ran all the frenetic machinery in the building produced in this flexible tube the strongest vacuum the boy had ever encountered. When the tube was not in use, one could hear only the gentle sound of wind blowing through its tubular confines. When pulled down and swung back and forth over a loaded wagon, however, it became a violent force, sucking the cotton in great wads into its tremendous maw with ravenous insatiability.

Occasionally some careless client would get his head too near the tube, and his hat would be sucked off and would vanish into the complicated doomsday above. While the victim whirled around and tried not to look chagrined and foolish, everyone else shouted, the whistle screamed, and the operator slipped the main belt and stopped the gin.

At first the boy thought this was for the courteous retrieval of the hat, but he soon learned that it was to keep from damaging the delicate mechanism of the gin. The grandfather explained that if the hat got carried into the knives, pieces of the machinery had to be removed and carried all the way to Macon for repair, which meant that the gin would be "broke down" for at least two or three days. Fortunately, a hat could be retrieved by opening the bin upstairs and hooking it out with a long stick.

When old man Pascall Perdue's hat got sucked up the chute, there was a chocolate-colored adolescent named Tom Junior Attaway working for wages at the gin. After he opened the heavy door to the bin and retrieved the hat, they started the machinery back too soon and Tom Junior fell in. They stopped it again right away, but not before he had been pulled into the knives and mangled so badly he had to be carried all the way into Atlanta to the Gradys.

They kept him two months and managed to save his penis and one testicle, but something called the cord was damaged, even on the good side, and he came home patchworked with skin grafts and stiff in the knees. The boy had overheard the grandfather discussing the case with a neighbor, and the pronouncement was made that, "He'll be able to do some good, but he'll always be sterile." The boy did not inquire about particulars, but he was puzzled.

Later, Tom Junior Attaway married a real fat black girl with simian features and they had seven children, including two sets of twins. The day the second set was born, Tom Junior Attaway left his wife and moved to Cincinnati to stay with his ontee until he found a job. The boy had overheard Central tell Freeman that he saw him just before he got on the train and Tom Junior cried like a baby. Freeman had responded, "Ain't nobody blame him. At's mo barrassment nan any man kin be called on to stand."

Over the next several years his wife had three more children, but Tom Junior never returned from Cincinnati.

It was about this time that the family acquired a truck that could carry four or five bales of cotton at the time and make the trip to Peabody in ten minutes. The boy lost all interest in ginning and could not look at the building without thinking how Tom Junior Attaway had almost been sacrificed to the idol. He was glad when it burned down.

As soon as ginning was far enough along so that two or three grown men could be freed for awhile from their bondage to King Cotton, the grandfather began making syrup. Of all the activities on the farm, this was the one that was exclusively under his supervision. Each fall he personally selected the stalks that he buried in the field deep enough under the soil so that they would not freeze and would be available for seed cane in the spring. He pointed out to the boy the little triangular blebs at each joint, called "eyes," which by the next year would grow into full-sized stalks of ribbon cane.

365

He was the one who selected the spot to plant the cane. This had to be low-lying land with more moisture than other areas in order to support the rank growth. Ribbon cane required less plowing than cotton or corn or pimentos. It grew so fast and its foliage was so lush that the ground was soon shielded from all sunlight, and the middles were as free from weeds as a well-traveled path.

When it grew tall enough for its fronds to overlap, a boy could lose himself in a patch of sugar cane for the whole of a hot afternoon, stalking bears, wolves, or yankees up and down the dappled aisles or squeezing between the closely growing stalks into the next row to avoid pursuit by cannibals or Killer Kane.

At harvest time every single stalk was cut by men using heavy knives. The tall, feathery forest was transformed in less than a day into a shambles of fallen trunks. There is nothing that looks more immediately naked and devastated than a newly cut patch of sugar cane.

As with most other things in farming, time was an urgent factor. If the cane lay too long on the ground after harvest or if it were rained on or if it got too hot, it would sour, and then it would be good for nothing and would be wasted. Waste on a Piedmont farm between Reconstruction and World War II was as unthinkable as murder or theft. As a disciple of the grandfather the boy knew with certainty that this was a condition that led only downhill to poverty, pain, and possible loss of the status of God's chosen landowner.

The grandfather could get more work out of hired hands than anyone else in the world. His language was the most expressive in the county, and he could show his mood by the way he cut a chew of tobacco from his plug and returned the knife to his pocket. The boy's neck thrilled with prickling hairs to hear him yell, "You, Pomp, there! Look alive! You act like the dead lice are dropping off you! You're so slow I have to take a sight on you to be sure you're moving. You can do better than that!"

The boy held his breath and shrank small when a misdeed was bad enough to merit, "You infernal black limb of Satan, you! I've a good notion to thrash you to within an inch of your life."

366

He did not have a bullwhip nor did he ever mention selling anyone down the river, but the implication of each was there. When the boy grew old enough to watch the hands instead of the explosive grandfather, he discovered that amused glances were secretively exchanged that clearly attested both tolerance and affection. The boy relaxed and tried his best to understand.

The grandfather worked harder than anyone else. After the cane was cut, it had to be stripped and then hauled on the wagons to the syrup mill. The yield was prodigious. A two acre patch of cane could produce a mountain of stalks.

The syrup mill was a magic place. It was situated on a promontory in the swamp just below the main tenant house on the Red Land. The cane press which provided the raw juice for the mill consisted of two huge cast-iron rollers, weighing so much that it took two grown men to mount them on a post. A long sweetgum tree was cut and trimmed and then mounted over the top of these rollers and bolted to them. It was balanced with a short, heavy butt end and a longer, tapered end which served as the guide pole. A mule was then hitched to the thinner end of the log and walked round and round in a circle all day long, turning the rollers in apposition to each other.

Sugar cane was inserted by the armload between the rollers, and the juice came gushing out in a cloudy, spurting stream. It was directed by a hand-hammered tin spout into a large wooden barrel with a burlap bag over the top. The grandfather would dip a cup of the sweet juice up for one to drink, but it never tasted quite so sparklingly good that way as when he peeled and quartered a section of the cane with his tobacco-tainted pocket knife and gave it to one to chew and suck.

The burlap strained the juice of fibers and was also supposed to exclude yellow jackets. These visitors came by the thousands to the impelling sweetness of the ribbon cane juice and were a constantly annoying part of the syrup-making scene. Any child or adolescent who went to the syrup mill barefoot had fat feet all day long from stepping on the stinging insects and always remembered to wear his shoes the next day. When grown men were stung by yellow jackets, they only slapped and muttered without interrupting their work, but it was a serious enough wound in a child to justify screams and to merit the administration of freshly chewed tobacco to the site with a soothing cluck from the grandfather.

Grinding the cane was a highly organized process. A man with lots of stamina was chosen to feed the ribbon cane into the press. Another hand had to tote stalks from the mother pile to another smaller pile at the feeder's feet. Then the complicated action pattern began. The feeder bent, gathered an armload of stalks, stood erect and pushed them into the rollers, which grasped them and pulled them through to let them fall in feathery lightness as "pummy." The feeder had to hold the stalks until they were halfway through the rollers, and this meant that the sweetgum bar would make a minimum of one or two swings at the level of his shoulders during the process, requiring that he duck to avoid decapitation. What with bending, standing, raising his hands, and bobbing his head, the grinder man was the most constantly active figure on the scene except the ever-encircling mule. It was fun to grab the butt of the revolving pole and hang on for a round or two, but one had to be careful not to provoke the forbidding roar of the grandfather. He had an aversion to anyone playing when it was time to work.

The cane press with its ever-growing pummy pile and its puffing, lunging mule was just a few yards from the clump of blackgum trees with thinning crimson leaves that surrounded the syrup mill. The mill itself was a furnace fashioned of local rock and red clay with its stacked-stone chimney to the south, near the creek, and its hip-high bed running due north and slightly downhill for a length of some twelve feet. On top of the furnace bed was the syrup pan. This was an object of family pride and was carefully stored in the top of the corn crib when not in use. The grandfather had personally supervised the crafting of it, and it functioned perfectly.

It was fashioned of sheet copper fastened securely over a framework of partitioning timbers with artfully arranged holes that could be opened or closed at will for the progression of the juice. Each year it was fitted over the furnace and carefully caulked with clay so that smoke would not curve around the edges into the workers' eyes.

Cords of pine wood were cut into fence-post lengths and stacked to the side. Feeding the fire was an art in itself, since the fire had to be hot enough to boil the juice but not so hot as to burn the pan. A half-barrel was mounted over the pan near the chimney with a section of peeled cane serving as bung in the hole near the bottom. Juice was carried from the press to this tank and poured through its covering burlap, which strained it even further, still excluding the yellow jackets. Juice was then let into the first compartment of the pan, the fire was stoked, and syrup-making was begun.

As the fresh cane juice boiled, a thick green froth foamed up from the opaque liquid and was removed by the skimmers. These men were equipped with square tin strainers on the ends of poles as long as a hoe handle. As the juice boiled, they skimmed the froth from the surface and deposited it in another barrel just to the side of the furnace, the sticks of the strainers making a whacking noise against the lip of the barrel.

As the boiling juice was released in thickening and clearing progression from one compartment to another, the character of the skimmings changed from lime green foam to thickened white ropes. The skimming continued until the boiling liquid finally flowed into the last compartment like a creek reaching a lake. By now it was glisteningly transparent and the color of a good violin, and it was strained off through fine white cloth into tin buckets and tightly sealed. One always carried cold buttered biscuits to the mill and ate them with hot new syrup for lunch.

The barrel of skimmings fascinated the boy. It was as evil-looking as boiling mud flats and rimed around with scabrous green drippings, which trickled down the outside and crusted before they could reach the ground. The liquid inside the barrel was covered completely with a four inch layer of foam that attracted swarms of yellow jackets, a good proportion of which became fatally trapped and eventually sank to the liquid beneath. The boy had heard that an occasional foraging possum would lose its balance and perish in the skimming barrel. He had never witnessed this, but he never doubted it. If an evil, fetid-breathed, red-eyed dragon had erupted from that barrel, he would have been terrified but not surprised.

This reservoir of slops from syrup-making was not emptied. When the pan had been removed, cleaned, and stored and the other barrels carried on the wagon to the protection of a shed, the syrup mill looked abandoned and lonely. The barrel of skimmings, however, remained. As the boy grew older, he learned the reason.

The skimmings would ferment without another thing being added. The warm October days would produce a seething and rumbling deep within the liquid left in that barrel, and big thick bubbles would come plopping through the covering foam. When the bubbling had ceased and the barrel was quiet once more, it was full of beer, or "cane buck." This was left by the grandfather for the Negroes on the place, with the tacit understanding that no one spoke of it. Once the boy had heard the grandfather tell Freeman, "Don't get in that stuff before it quits working, else it'll make you sick as a dawg. Wait a coupla weeks."

The boy had never heard of a white person drinking cane buck, and actually not many of the Negroes indulged. Coming back from the cowlot with two brimming buckets of milk on the Saturday after his class election, the boy saw Freeman coming down the lane. Unfailingly courteous and soft-spoken, Freeman had an inherent sweetness of nature that made everyone like him. He would have been a favorite of the boy's even had he not been Buddy's father.

Many years before some mules had run away with him and hurt his shoulder, and it had not healed properly. As a consequence his right arm hung like a limp flail. He could grip and pull with it, but any motion of the shoulder was impossible, and the arm had to be lifted into place with the left hand. When Freeman walked, he had a loose, shambling gait anyhow, and the effect of the dangling arm was to make him look like a rag doll flapping down the road.

Now as he approached, about an hour past a chilly November sunup, the boy did not at first note anything unusual and hailed him with a cheerful, early-morning, outdoor greeting. "*Good* morning, Free," he called.

Freeman did not reply but shuffled along with no indication of awareness. His eyes were swollen and red-rimmed and had gummy deposits of glue in the corners. His mouth was agape, with the lower lip pendulous in slobbering relaxation. He was breathing with great blubbering sighs and muttering incoherently to himself in a crooning, whimpering monotone. The boy had to step aside to let him pass, and still Freeman did not see him. The boy got a good whiff of his breath and gagged. He did not try to speak again but watched the man career his way between the crib and hullhouse and start up the path leading to his home.

As he resumed his trek to the big house with the milk, the boy shook his head. Poor Buddy, he thought. I know how he feels. At least mine never stank that bad.

Later that morning the boy wandered up the road to the house that Wes had moved into when Jesse Arnold had died. Wes was now Freeman's closest neighbor, since the driveway to Freeman's house ran directly through his side yard. He found Wes splitting and stacking a winter supply of stove wood for Mae, and the man was glad to stop, roll a cigarette, and visit. After an exchange of pleasantries, the boy asked, "Wes, what's the matter with Freeman?"

"Whatcha mean, 'Whassa matter wit Freeman?' " responded Wes. "When you see Freeman?"

"I saw him this morning early. I don't know where he'd been, but I guess he was headed home after laying out. He came within three feet of me and didn't know I was there, even when I spoke to him. He looked awful." He paused and added, "He smelled awful, too."

Wes cast a look toward Freeman's house and then confided, "He be nat away over two weeks now. Mos ne time he slip an stumble his way home thu my yard, cause he don want nobody at ne house to see him, specially Mr. Porter." Wes developed a slightly crafty look and added in a superior way, "Free goan be powerful put out when he fine out you cotch him lak dat. He never woulda come thu de big house yard wuz he sober nuff to think anybody roun to see him."

"He looks bad, Wes. I'm worried about him. His skin looked right ashy, and I've always heard that a colored person wasn't healthy unless his skin was shiny."

"I spec you right, Sambo. If them skimmins don't play out pretty soon, Free liable to kill hisself. Everbody else done got a bait of em and let em alone, but Free layin wid dat ole cane buck ever mornin, afternoon, and evenin. He done let it git im by de shawt hairs, 'n hit gwine kill im sho ef he don lay offin it."

"Well," said the boy tartly, with a slight tinge of imperiousness, "I think I can take care of that problem."

He said nothing to anyone in the family, but after dinner he set out across the fields. His destination was the syrup mill. The sun was shining brightly, and he was warm enough to walk at a normal pace. The woods were already gleaned for winter, and all the trees were bare except for an occasional postoak that stubbornly held its brown leaves each year until the cleansing winds of March screamed them all the way to the river. A poplar tree with limbs sticking straight up, a seed pod on the end of each branch, shone like an immense candelabrum in the November sun. The boy strode with pleasure through his world. He was on crusade.

"You really are growing up," he congratulated himself. "You see a problem, find the cause, and correct it. That's real responsibility, and you haven't had to ask advice from anybody else. You're even going to be a good class president." He felt very virtuous.

When I grow up and take over the place, he thought, I'm going to run it differently. First thing I'm going to do is buy every farm that joins us and wind up with the biggest plantation in the whole state of Georgia. I'm going to tear down all these tenant houses and build solid brick ones with electric lights and running water. It'll be so nice around here that everybody will be begging to live on Mr. Sambo's place. And I'll look after them and be real good to them, but they're going to have to behave.

There's not going to be any drinking at all on my place, and everybody's going to bathe every day and put on clean clothes. And I'll inspect the houses every week, and nobody can burn any part of the house just cause they're too lazy to get firewood. And the babies and kids will have to wear diapers and quit running around naked so the houses won't smell like pee. And I won't whip anybody or cuss em. If they don't live right I'll just make em move, and everybody will love Mr. Sambo.

He stayed bemused until he reached the syrup mill. Without functional bustle and activity, the place looked insignificant. The cane press with its dangling guide pole stood deserted in the circle of the pummy pile, which had already rotted to half its original height. The furnace without a fire and minus the gleaming copper pan looked like the chimney of a long-abandoned cabin.

The barrel of skimmings stood in lonely solitude. The boy approached it with purpose. He stood on tiptoe to look inside. It was still over half full. As he leaned over the barrel he jostled it, and the liquid moved, sending forth a stench that so nauseated the boy that he moved back six feet. He was reminded of the hogpen when the sated animals had reached a level of obesity that made them content to lie placidly in the foul mixture of soured corn and excreta which coated the pen. "How in the world can anybody stand to drink that stuff?" he muttered aloud. Then silently he added, No wonder Freeman's skin looks like ashes.

He went back to the barrel and grasped the rim with both hands, trying his best not to inhale deeply. He pushed, but the barrel, mired by its own weight into the soft red earth beneath, moved only inches and did not overturn. The liquid within sloshed more vigorously, however, and the boy had to move back again. He heaved until his eyes watered. At this moment he heard a cry.

"Hey, Sambo!"

Looking up, he saw Freeman coming down the hill from the Dolliver house toward the promontory in the swamp. He never knew whether the man's appearance at this particular time was a coincidence or whether he had been warned by Wes that the boy was messing around the syrup mill. He never bothered to find out. The shambling figure was lurching rapidly down the hill. The boy approached the barrel again.

"Lawd God," yelled Freeman, "don't stir it up! *Please* don't stir it, honey chile! Hit h͘ ruint if you do."

The boy grabbed the barrel firmly and leaned his shoulder into the side. It tilted.

"Lil Cap!" came the frenzied bellow. The boy looked up again when he heard the affectionate courtesy title. The figure had broken into a shuffling run. The left arm was raised and extended and waving frantically from the shoulder. The right arm was jerking and flopping disjointedly from the elbow. It was at once a pathetic and ludicrous sight. The boy laughed. Free looks like Step'n-Fetchit in the movies, he thought.

He pulled the barrel toward him in a rocking motion and then pushed again. It leaned even further but did not overturn. One more time oughta do it, thought the boy.

"Listen to me, Lil Boss," came the frantic plea of the fast-approaching man. "You my good frien an I love you lak my own. Please don't po it out! Effen you don't I'll do anything in de world you ax me to, but in the name of sweet Jesus, please don't po it out!"

He might as well have saved his breath. In the rock and pull of the barrel the boy determinedly mustered his very maximum strength, and the heavy vessel overturned, cascading the contained swill in a malodorous torrent over the feet of the disbelieving Freeman. Snatching the hat from his head, Freeman dropped to his knees and tried to capture the last of the feculent liquid coming from the overturned barrel. The boy noted the grotesquely angled wing of what he assumed had once been an English sparrow. "You can't drink that, Freeman!" he proclaimed.

The man looked up at him, his reddened eyes weeping and tragic. "How come you done nat?" he demanded. "I ruther you strike me dead. How come you done it? Nere wuz plenty in here do me almos to Chrismas. I give anything you hadn'ta done it."

"I did it for your own good, Freeman. You're about to kill yourself drinking that old stuff, and I came over here because I don't want anything bad to happen to you. I did it for your own good and I did it on purpose."

"My own good?" muttered Freeman incredulously. "My own good?" His voice rose. "You think I drink dis slop could I afford good likker like yo paw? How you know what make a man lak me need a drink in de fust place? How you know what go on inside me I don never talk about? Who put you up where you know what good for me and what ain't? What you know bout sleepin deep an forgetful? You done gone an messed in nigger business, boy, when you oughta stayed in yo place." He peered in puzzled concentration at the wet feathers in his leaking hat. Slowly he emptied it and dropped it between his knees.

"I'm sorry if I upset you, Freeman," said the stricken boy. "I was trying to help you."

The man looked up at the boy and stared him straight in the eyes. Then, with an anguished howl, he screamed, "God damn yo soul, Sambo!"

Generations of instinct caused the boy to draw his arm back reflexly. Protocol was clear, and this was an unforgivable offense that demanded instant retribution. Freeman lowered his eyes and waited for the blow. Slowly the boy dropped his arm and turned away.

Gray clouds had covered the sun, and the little sconces of the poplar tree were after all only dull, dried seed pods. The November wind was thin and mean. The thick dark twigs of the redoak tree in Henry Dolliver's yard were sprangled against the somber sky like ancient Druid runes.

As the boy turned thoughtfully homeward, he did not feel virtuous. He felt uncomfortably young and very small.

He felt faintly sick that night and was unable to eat any supper. He finished his chores with a gnawing pain in the middle of his belly which he attributed to hunger, but the idea of food repelled him. He kissed his mother goodnight immediately after evening prayers and climbed the stairs to his bedroom. The pain grew worse, and he was unable to sleep. He heard everyone in the house go to bed, and still the pain became more severe. He got up and vomited and thought he would feel better. Instead the pain came in waves of greater intensity. By midnight he was moaning and crying. The pain was so bad he felt he could not stand it. He heard his father's car in the back yard and in desperation climbed out of bed and met him in the dining room with tears streaming down his cheeks.

"What in the world is wrong with you, son?" his father asked. "You get in a fight today?"

Bending to his right side and limping, the boy cried, "Oh, Daddy, my stomach hurts so bad I can't stand it. I've been vomiting, and I know it's not anything I ate because I haven't had anything since dinnertime."

"Let me see," said the father. "It's not like you to cry. Is this where it hurts?"

After a little probing and a few more questions, the father waked the mother. "Vera, get the boy out some clothes. I'm going to carry him into town and find a doctor. He's got bad pain down in his right side. —Hell, no, I don't think he needs a laxative! I think he needs a doctor. Don't try to fasten that top button. Can't you see it hurts him? —No, I don't need anybody to drive, dammit! I'll let you hear something as soon as I can."

He scooped the boy up in his arms and carried him out to the car, depositing him gently as a baby on the back seat. The ride over the rutted roads into town was an endurance contest. The boy tried to suppress his moans when the car hit a bump because every time he moaned his father drove faster and hit the bumps harder. Despite the pain the boy exulted over the concern and anxiety evinced by his father. He really does love me, he thought as he vomited silently into the towel his mother had given him. Nothing was coming up any more, but he kept gagging and heaving.

His father drove to the doctor's house and roused him, then went to the drugstore to await his arrival. He kept assuring his son that everything was all right and lit one cigarette off the other in the process. When the doctor made his examination, he straightened up and pronounced, "His belly's hard as a board and he's got the rebound all right. There ain't no doubt atall this is appendicitis, and you got to get him to Atlanta to a surgeon, quick. I'll get you the best one I know of, right now."

He cranked the phone, spoke to the operator, and after a seemingly endless conversation instructed the father, "Carry him to Crawford Long Hospital on Linden Avenue right off Peachtree Street, what used to be old Davis-Fisher Sanitarium. I got a good surgeon going to meet him."

To the father's gruff request he answered, "Well, there ain't a bit o' use me ridin up there with you— there ain't a thing else I can do for the boy, but," in a relenting, kindly tone, "if it'll make you feel better, I'll go with you. Let's move."

The trip into Atlanta was a blur of pain and confused impressions. The father leaned over the steering wheel, his head in a cloud of cigarette smoke, and drove as if he were possessed of a demon. The doctor hung tightly to the arm rest, smoked about as much as the father, and talked as though he were trying to placate a demon. The boy lay on the back seat and wondered if he were going to die. He tried to imagine being dead, but the pain kept him from concentrating on it.

There was a huge expanse of echoing hallway and bright lights at the hospital with a crowd of people in white rushing around even at that early hour of the morning. It seemed like no time before the boy found himself in a half-gown, lying on a rubber-wheeled cart, with the doctor bending over him in a reassuring fashion.

"Your daddy can't go no further than this, and I'm going to stay with him. Don't you worry, cause old Doc Stancil is the best in town, and he's gonna slice your belly open and get that ole rotten appendix out, an when you wake up we'll be there and you won't be hurtin and everything's gonna be all right."

The boy lay in terror. His belly hurt worse than anything he had ever imagined. He thought of John Mark Cowan. He thought of all his extracurricular points and Mr. Dorsey, the principal, and Miss Berry. He thought, of a sudden, of the UDC and American Legion Auxiliary and WMS Combined and Holy Cut-short Award. He knew then that he was going to die. He knew that he deserved to die. He tried to pray to Jesus but kept thinking how upset his mother was going to be.

As they wheeled him into the operating room with its stainless steel glittering like ice in the sun of the bright light suspended in mid-air, he abandoned his efforts at prayer and resolved to die like a man. He bit his lips and suppressed the grunt of pain when he was transferred to the operating table. A nurse cradled his head in her arms and showed him something that looked like a tea strainer with cheesecloth wrapped around it. "I'm going to put this over your nose and I want you to breathe deep. It'll smell funny, but don't be afraid."

He looked up into her face and with dry eyes and steady lips proclaimed the biggest lie of his life. "I'm not afraid. Do whatever you want to me. I'm ready to go."

When the sweet thick odor of ether began choking his very breath away, he still had enough conscious resolve to resist fighting and screaming. He breathed deeply. He was on a revolving phonograph record, turning faster and faster, and lights were flashing brighter and brighter. He heard the nurse, "He's the best boy I ever saw. He's just too sweet to live." He spun faster and faster. The phonograph record melted in the middle and became a whirlpool. The words came faster and faster, "too sweet to live, too sweet to live, too sweet to live too sweet live live live live live," and everything was black and still and he was falling. Endlessly and forever—Down.

He awoke, vomiting and groaning, to the awareness that he still lived. As he became a little more oriented, he realized that he was in a regular room and that a nurse was holding a little pan under his cheek as he retched. He opened his eyes. His father and the doctor were at the window, smoking cigarettes and watching the sun come up. His pain was gone. He ran a hand over his belly. The right side was covered with a firm bandage as tight as a corset. There was a little soreness underneath it. His hand slipped away and struck his penis, and he winced with pain. Looking under the cover, he saw that his penis was shrouded in a bandage that was sticky with bright red blood. The only thing he could think of was that the best-in-town good ole Doc Stancil had let his knife slip.

"Daddy!" he screamed.

Propelled instantly to the bedside, his father responded, "Good Godalmighty, son, what's the matter?"

"Oh, Daddy," the boy quavered, "they've ruined me. It's been cut off and I'll never be able to carry on the name."

"What's been cut off?" his father demanded. "Nothing happened except you've been circumcised. After you were asleep, Doc Stancil sent word out to me that you needed another little operation and he'd do it for an extra ten dollars, and I told him to go ahead. You're all right. Doc got that appendix just before it busted, and you're going to be fine."

The family doctor leaned over the bed. "You're fine," he placated. "We got to go home. But you let me tell you something about that circumcision. You're sewed up around the head of that thing just like a baseball. You better not get up a hard or you'll bust ever stitch in it wide open."

With that comforting phrase, the two men were gone. As the boy became drowsy and relaxed, he mused a moment over a new implication to the Combined and Holy Cut-short Award. He was glad he had never told anyone about it.

"Thank you, God, that I'm still a Go-Far boy," he breathed.

XXIII

When the boy returned to school, he felt that he was something of a hero to his classmates. Basketball practice had been forbidden for three weeks, and his father had assured him that he would continue to have the milking done for that long. The teachers were solicitous of his welfare, and he smugly enjoyed all the extra attention. He adopted a prim look with lowered lids when people inquired if he felt all right, and he was beginning to consider the advantages of chronic invalidism.

Late in the afternoon, his only study hall was supervised by Miss Hancock and was held in the auditorium. She was a conscientious disciplinarian and allowed no whispering or visiting between the students. She insisted that there be at least two seats between each person, and she patrolled the room as though a final exam were in progress. Full-bodied and loud-voiced, she wore tighter sweaters than most of the teachers and came perilously close to earning the appellation of "common."

She was eighth grade home room teacher and taught no senior subjects. This was her second year on the faculty, and she had been a loyal admirer of Mr. Gill the year before. She hated the boy. He had tried all his wiles and charms on her to no avail. She rejected any advance from him with open hostility, and when he had campaigned for class president, she had openly advocated the town ticket. When he had won she had volunteered to him that she was sorry, and he sensed such venom in her that he scrupulously tried to avoid her.

He was very, very good in her study hall. He used the time

to do his homework, but even his industry seemed to annoy her. She was incapable of ignoring him. At irregular intervals she would ease up behind him on gum-soled shoes and make a sarcastic comment or ask a vicious question. He had walled himself off from her barbs with such a thick shell that he had not even winced when she had remarked in a voice loud enough for his neighbors to hear, "All the girls tell me that you are a sight to behold in your basketball suit. I'm sorry for you," or, "Someone told me your father owns half interest in the drugstore. Is that true?"

He pretended not to recognize any sarcasm in her comments and feigned a meekness which she misunderstood. She could not leave him alone. Three days after his return to school, she padded silently up behind him. When he became aware of her presence and looked up, she said, "I see you're back."

"Yes'm," he replied. "Thank you, Miss Hancock."

"I wasn't real sure you'd been operated on," she continued, "until I heard Mr. Dorsey ask the principal if we could give extracurricular points for an appendectomy."

Lethal as Medusa she moved away. The boy, with cold detachment, noted the insolent roll of her buttocks and vowed silently, Just as soon as I decide that I don't want another A in deportment, I'm going to make you wish you'd never even heard of me. I don't know yet how I'm going to do it, but I'll get even with you for this if it's the last thing I do. He buried his head in his book and decided he wouldn't tell Mr. Dorsey about this encounter. Yet. . . .

A few days later they had important company at the big house. The grandfather had a younger half-brother who had moved to Mississippi as a young man when one of the Giddens girls at Peabody turned up pregnant. There he had studied law, married a local belle, and prospered mightily. He had sired four sons and a daughter, and all of them had college educations. Two of the boys had gone to West Point, and the daughter had met and married a friend of one of them when she was invited to a West Point dance.

The Mississippi branch of the family visited the home place only on rare occasions, and such visits were always exciting events. The daughter, Sara Margaret, dropped in for the weekend with her husband, William Elliott, who was a first lieutenant in the U.S. Army Air Corps, a former West Point football player, and a handsome blond giant of a man. The family had never met him before, but he impressed everyone very favorably. He won the boy immediately when, at introduction, he squeezed his hand in a huge grip, looked him squarely in the eye, and said, "Call me Will." To be on a first-name basis with such a lordly individual made the boy feel very grown-up, and he quickly abandoned the preconceived reserve he had nurtured because Will was a yankee.

In addition to the Elliotts, another visitor had arrived some few days earlier. When the father had held his first teaching job at a small private college, Buckalew Tarpley had been one of his students. A friendship had developed between the two that had survived the World War and a generation of disparate lives. Buck Tarpley had spent twenty years in the Merchant Marine working his way around the world as first mate on cargo vessels. Now he was ready to retire and was, unlikely as it seemed, considering buying a farm.

Of all people the boy had ever met, Buck Tarpley was the most fascinating. With spring steel control and graceful balance he walked on Brewton County soil as though it rolled beneath his feet in a high wind. He was lizard-lean and debonair, and his blue eyes gleamed like neon from the depths of a perpetually sunburned, wind-wrinkled squint. He was softspoken and unassuming, but there was an exciting aura about him as though he was constantly tensed to grapple with the unexpected.

If no one was around, he would quote Kipling and Service to the boy or explain the locks in the Panama Canal or describe the streets of Cairo or the waters of the Ganges. He had ridden dugouts on the Amazon and rickshaws in Shanghai and in ten minutes could give the boy enough dreams to last six months. Everyone in the family enjoyed Buck Tarpley's rare and unexpected visits, but the children actually fought for his company.

This weekend, the father had instructed Buck Tarpley to bring Will Elliott into town for a visit before supper. The boy had coaxed to be included, and the father had magnanimously responded, "Well, it's only ten days since you were operated on, but you were a real man through all that—so come on. You deserve a little celebration with the menfolks."

When the trio converged on the drugstore, they had time only to speak to the proprietress before the father came out of the back and invited them in. It was cold enough to have a fire in the cavernous space behind the brightly lit pool table, but even the glow from the potbellied stove did nothing to add light to the corners of this gaping, unfinished room. Illumination in the back of the drugstore was supplied by a single bulb on a drop cord over the doctor's dusty desk, and the smell was one of medicine, dank earth, and stale urine. The father reached into one of the darker shadows and produced a brown paper sack, which he placed on the desk. From his measured sentences, the boy could tell that he had already had at least two drinks.

"This is a very special occasion," the father began. "We have a representative of our nation's Air Corps present, a member of the Merchant Marine, and I, in my own humble and limited capacity, was privileged to serve in the American Expeditionary Forces in France, where I led my men through the Argonne forest and Verdun and was twice wounded in the process."

Embarrassed, the boy tried to slip more inconspicuously into the background. He succeeded in overturning the coal scuttle. With a flicker of annoyance, the father continued, "But enough of that. We are three comrades-in-arms here tonight, and such a convocation calls for the absolute best in refreshment that can be provided. Now," with a deep bow to Will Elliott, "I realize that you customarily move in more sophisticated company and that the speak-easies of New York may provide anything for which a man can pay.

"And I know that you," with an equally deep bow to Buck Tarpley, "are accustomed to wine flowing like water in the foreign ports you visit, but," he paused for emphasis, "I submit to you gentlemen that, to the best of my abilities, I have here tonight procured for your consumption and enjoyment the very finest nectar available in this entire region.

"It is made from the best peaches that ripened in the orchards of this county last summer. Those beautiful orbs took the red earth, the gentle rain, and the warm sun and distilled those natural elements into a fruit that would melt in your mouth. Then the local artisan, master of his craft, refined and distilled that fruit into the essence I present you—an ambrosia worthy of the occupants of Mount Olympus. Gentlemen, your glasses!"

He stripped the paper sack away with a flourish. The boy, craning his neck around the stove, was disappointed to see a half-gallon fruit jar of seemingly ordinary water. He decided his father had already had three drinks.

"Hold it to the light, boys. Observe that bead. It's one hundred proof at least. —What? You want Co-Cola in your peach brandy?" the host inquired of Will Elliott. "Certainly, suh, just a moment." The incredulity in his tone was just changing to condescension when the boy took a step backward and bumped the coal scuttle over again. As he knelt to retrieve it, he saw Buck Tarpley throw his head back, drain his glass, and shudder like a mule in fly-time.

"By God, Porter, that stuff's all right. I've never tasted better. Pour me about a half one if you don't mind," he said calmly.

As the boy watched the level of liquid in the fruit jar fall and the geniality of the men increase in inverse proportion, he wondered anew why he ever forgot and begged to come to town with his father. He always wound up being bored, uncomfortable, and embarrassed. The third time he stumbled into the coal scuttle, he found that the lumps he recovered from the floor were wet. Shortly afterwards he observed Will Elliott quietly and dexterously pouring the majority of his drink into the scuttle. This took a little skill, since by this time the three men were standing with locked arms singing "Mademoiselle from Armentieres."

"I've got another drink I want you boys to try," the father announced. He produced a flat pint bottle from beneath a pile of magazines. "Now, this," he informed Will Elliott, "is a more traditional Southern drink, and we'll be interested in receiving your unbiased evaluation of it. This is corn liquor from Shakerag district."

In the clamor arising from Buck and the father, Will Elliott was able to insert a polite but almost unheeded approval of this regional delicacy before dashing the entire contents of his glass into the now-sloshing coal scuttle.

The boy moved carefully to the other side of the stove. I don't know what this yankee's trying to prove, he thought, but one thing's sure and certain — it'll be an unholy mess if you turn over that scuttle of coal again.

The evening moved right along. Buck and the father began to interrupt each other as they more and more eagerly recounted anecdotes and adventures of earlier years. Familiar with all of them, the boy amused himself by watching the three men. He noted that all the tales began with, "Will, have you heard . . .?" or, "Will, let me tell you about . . ." and were ostensibly recited for the information or entertainment of the guest from the Air Corps.

This succeeded in demanding Will Elliott's constant attention but in reality drew him into the group no more than it did the boy. Their ebullient but nostalgic recital served to increase the camaraderie between Buck and the father but in the process only accentuated the exclusion of others. The boy wished he were home with his mother and then immediately resented such an unmanly desire.

Finally, as Buck Tarpley's head began wobbling on a more and more elongated neck between rounded shoulders and he began repeating once-told tales with a definite slur in his speech, the father called an end to the evening. "We'd better go, fellows, so these folks can close this drugstore. Let me pour the rest of this peach brandy into a bottle, and we'll carry it and the corn with us."

He produced an empty pint bottle and carefully decanted the contents of the fruit jar into it, not quite filling the bottle halfway. As he considered units of volume, time, and consumption, the boy was thankful that they were all headed for home and bed. As they were leaving the drugstore, the boy heard his father begin singing under his breath, "Who's your little Whoozis? Where's your little Whatzis?"

Oh, Lord, he thought, it's later than I thought.

Approaching the car, the father handed Will Elliott the two pint bottles. "Here, Will, we'll make you the official custodian of our resources. Buck, I tell you this ole boy my cousin married is a real prince of a fellow. He really sticks in there with the menfolks. Anything I like to see is a guy who can hold his liquor, an I tell you, this un can hold it with the best of em."

"Lemme tell you bout this ole boy," Buck responded, feet firmly planted while his body rotated in a full, swaying circle. "He's aw right. You hear me? He's aw right. I worried a lil bit at first bout him bein a yankee and gonna turn out to be a stuff shirt, but he's aw right. You find some yankees now'n then can hol their liquor and act like real folks, 'n you know somepin else? That kind always got enough sense to marry a Southern girl." He paused and swayed counterclockwise. "That is," he added profoundly, "when they got little enough sense to get married at all."

"Don't you want me to drive, Porter?" Will replied in response to this compliment.

"Hell, no," he was answered. "You're my guest. I wouldn't think of making a chauffeur outa you. Besides, I just remembered we haven't eaten. Miss Vera will have saved us some supper, but it'll be cold, and I'm gonna carry yall somewhere for a hot meal."

He turned to his son. "Get in the car, boy. As much coal as you've picked up tonight, you mus be half starved to death. Will, you know this boy here had his pen'ix out not much more'n week ago? He's tough, isn't he? A lil small yet, but he's plenty tough. Got what it takes. Chip off the ole block, or's my mammy says, 'Blood will tell.' Get in, boy, get in. We goin to Griffin."

With that praise the boy would have mounted a tumbril and followed him to the guillotine. Sinking into the back cushions of the Buick, he thought tolerantly of his earlier wish to be home with his mother.

Despite Will Elliott's protestations that he really wasn't

hungry and would just as soon go home to bed, the father jerked the car over the dirt highway in bucking pursuit of the erratic beams of the headlights, careening from the brink of one ditch to the other in breath-stopping abandon.

In the back seat Buck Tarpley tumbled about in rag-doll slumber. Three miles from Griffin they turned onto a paved highway, and even the boy relaxed a little.

"Will," the father ordered, "pass me over one those bottles an we'll have another lil drink before we get to town."

"I really think we've both had plenty, Porter," Will Elliott demurred.

"Hell you say," came the peremptory response. "Don't you know nobody goes home til the liquor's finished? Pass me the corn an you take a drink of the peach. Maybe we oughta wake Buck Tarpley up an give him another one."

"Oh, let him sleep," advised the lieutenant. "Here's your corn."

The boy heard the gurgle as the father upended the pint bottle, but his eyes never left Will Elliott. Although that man turned the bottle up to his lips, the boy heard no sound and could see no bubbles climbing through the liquid. That's a pretty smart yankee, he thought. That's just what I'd do in the same fix.

With the two bottles safely returned to Will Elliott's coat pockets, the quartet arrived at the only place in Griffin that appeared to be open. A wooden sign, suspended at right angles over the front door and lit on each side by a shaded light bulb, proclaimed in faded blue letters "Pelly's All-Nite Cafe. Steaks, Chicken, Seafood." The Buick made a U-turn in the street and came to a fast-dipping stop at the curb directly in front of the cafe.

"All out!" the father intoned. "At last we eat. Shake ole Buck awake and let's all go get a steak."

"Porter, don't you think you're parked a little too far from the curb?" Will Elliott asked.

"Hell, no, I'm not a little too far from the damn curb. Not much traffic anyway this time o' night an they'n get by. You bout to make me decide you worry too much, Will. You jus relax an have a good time an enjoy our Southern hospitality. You our guest an we want you to have fun. Don't worry bout a thing." He leaned into the back seat. "Hey, Buck Tarpley, boy, wake up an let's get a steak. Come on, boy! We're there."

Buck roused with some difficulty but was still in a jovial mood. "Who's got a drink?" he inquired.

Will Elliott, still serving as reluctant Ganymede, produced the two bottles silently and handed one to each of his companions. There was absolutely no expression of any kind on his face. Following a gurgling onslaught on each bottle by his two companions, he just as silently returned the bottles to his coat.

The liquor's almost gone; we can soon go home, the boy thought, but forced his eyes to be noncommunicative as they momentarily met Will Elliott's glance. Don't worry about him, he advised himself. He's in the Army and is a lieutenant and graduated from West Point and is from up north. You'd better worry about getting some food into Buck and your daddy. It's after one o'clock.

When they entered Pelly's All-Nite Cafe, the room seemed unduly large because it was almost empty. There were two women at the end of the room talking to each other—one behind the counter and one leaning over the counter. The one on the near side was pressing her shoulder against the only man in the room, who was leaning backward against the counter, resting on his elbows and chewing a toothpick.

As the quartet moved between the empty tables, Buck Tarpley's foot caught a chair, and in his efforts to prevent its falling he knocked over two others. When the boy straightened from retrieving them, the trio at the end of the room was watching the group of strangers in town with a wariness familiar to the boy. No one moved to meet them and no one spoke in greeting.

"Well," said the father, "well, well well." His voice echoed in the silent room, and he lowered it a bit. "We are four ravenous wayfarers who are delighted to find you fine people still open for business. It is permissible, I presume, to seat ourselves anywhere."

He had quit slurring syllables but now had a tinge of

aristocratic impatience in his tone that was unmistakably challenging. The boy tensed.

The man at the counter straightened, took his hands from his jacket pockets, rolled the toothpick to the other side of his mouth, and seated himself on a stool, leaning forward on his elbows this time with his back to the group. The message was clear. He was outnumbered and disinterested and did not work here. The boy relaxed.

The woman who had been leaning against him straightened the apron of her uniform and approached their table. The woman behind the counter never moved, but the boy was aware that she was watching every move of theirs.

"Kin I he'p you?" the waitress asked in a slightly hostile tone.

"Ah," boomed the father, "you certainly may. We are absolutely famished. We feel very fortunate to have found such a fine hostelry at such a late hour presided over by such a fine young lady as yourself."

"Yeah," interrupted the woman. "Whatcha want?"

"Well," replied the father with determined geniality, "we'd like the best steaks you have in the house. I have two out-of-town guests and I want your best fare for them, and," he squeezed his son's arm, "would you believe this boy here had a very serious operation just a few days ago? He's been very brave, but I'm afraid his stamina may be flagging. So I'd like to get something for him just as quickly as possible if you don't mind, please, ma'am."

Cooperating with this ploy, the boy raised his gaze and smiled tremulously at the waitress. Her eyes were unblinking and coldly impersonal.

"I'll see what we kin do," she said and walked back to confer with the woman behind the counter. Neither of them moved toward the kitchen. Silence fell. Buck Tarpley folded both arms on the table and rested his chin on his crossed wrists. "You know what, Porter?" he said. "Don't believe these folks want to feed us. Whatcha think?"

"Miss!" the father called. "Could I trouble you for some water while we're waiting for our order?"

There was a whispered conference at the counter. The waitress brought four glasses to the table and placed one with a bang before each of them. The man at the counter rose and walked down the side of the room to disappear out the front door. More time elapsed.

"Miss!" the father called again, no hint of placating friendliness in his voice now. "You haven't even given us napkins and silver yet."

She approached the table again, empty-handed. Her tone of voice, the boy noted, had become friendly. "I'll bring em in just a little bit. Don't you fret or worry."

"Where'd your boy friend go?" Buck Tarpley interposed. "That's what I wanna know. Always wonder when a card player leaves the game. Where'd your boy friend go?"

"He's not really my boy friend," the waitress replied. "I just know him real well. But he's gone to a restaurant down the street to borrow some steaks for us. We're fresh out, but don't worry. It won't be much longer." She joined the woman behind the counter.

Will Elliott leaned over and spoke in a low voice to the father, "It certainly looked as though this was the only restaurant open in this little town."

The boy was impressed at Griffin's being called a "little town." To him it seemed like a large city, second in size only to Atlanta, and reputed to have almost twenty thousand people in it. That Will Elliott had sure been around!

He looked at his father and tensed again. Oh, Lord, he thought. He's getting that look. In just a minute I know he's going to say it. Things could really get bad around here. I had hoped with all this company to entertain we were going to escape the Pusillanimous look tonight.

The boy had recognized a certain tightening of the lower lip and puckering of the upper lip accompanied by a wrinkling of the nose and an expression of hauteur that his father affected just before he pronounced something "pusillanimous." This was one word that the boy had never bothered to look up in Webster. He was sure that it meant "to smell bad and incite to rage." He hated the word, for it always presaged the unleashing of wild, unfounded accusations, generally followed by berserk behavior. His father used the word only when he was very drunk.

Now the noble features assumed the unwelcome but familiar cast. "You're right, Will," the big man said and added in a louder voice with arrogant disdain. "This is certainly intolerable treatment we're receiving. The service is the most inept I've ever encountered, and the entire establishment is pusillanimous. I think we'll leave here, boys. Right now."

As the four filed out of the restaurant, the two women behind the counter never moved.

"Wait a minute, Porter," Buck Tarpley remonstrated when they reached the sidewalk. "I never did eat my steak. Did you eat yours?"

"Hell, Buck, we never were served," the father answered. "There's something fishy going on in Pelly's All-Nite Cafe. We decided to leave."

He buttoned his overcoat and took his rabbit-lined gloves from one pocket. "Here, Sambo," he said. "Hold the car keys while I get my gloves on. We'll go somewhere else to eat."

"Why don't we just go home?" Will Elliott ventured. "I can scramble eggs as good as anyone you ever saw."

"Nothing doing," the father vetoed firmly. "You're our guest and we're going to entertain you."

He was interrupted by the arrival of another car which moved to the curb on the wrong side of the street, right in front of their Buick. Total silence fell as two policemen got out and approached the quartet.

"Be real quiet, Buck," the father admonished softly. "Let me do the talking." He stepped forward to meet the uniformed pair. "Well, well," he spoke in his rich baritone and with his best campaign manner. "Good evening, officers. I'm Porter Osborne, County School Superintendent over in Brewton County. These are my friends and this my son. We had driven over to get a midnight meal here in your city, but it's grown so late we decided to go home. We were just leaving when you drove up. You boys are patrolling in mighty cold weather. Is everything quiet around town?"

His air of camaraderie and his tone of friendliness were so genuine that the boy was amazed.

"Pretty quiet, Mr. Osborne. We're just checking. Saw a strange car and thought we'd better be sure Miss Pelly's all right. You any kin to the sheriff over in Brewton County? He's an Osborne, I think."

"Sure am," the father smoothly replied. "He's just my brother, that's all. Grif's doing a good job over there, too, and making a mighty fine law man."

Buck Tarpley gave an audible yawn and lurched against Will Elliott.

"Ya friend here's had a little too much to drink, hasn't he, Mr. Osborne?" the second policeman asked. "I could smell it pretty strong on you, too."

"Well, we had a few before supper, fellows. You know how that is," the father answered easily. "But certainly no one is *drunk*." He pronounced the word as though it was a condition so far beneath the code of a gentleman as to be unimaginable.

"Just the same, who's driving this car?" the policeman continued.

"My son right over there," the father triumphantly answered. "Certainly you don't think he's had anything to drink."

The boy cooperatively held up the switch keys which he had not returned. He tried to look relaxed and assured.

"Naw, I'm sure he ain't. How old is he, though?" the policeman asked.

"Why, he turned sixteen the last of September," the father answered, so promptly and so authoritatively that even the boy almost believed him.

"He's small for his age, but he's a real sweet little driver. And now if you gentlemen will excuse us, I really do think we'd best be getting on toward home. It's been a pleasure meeting you. Come on, fellows."

When Buck Tarpley tried to move, his equilibrium was so

impaired that he looked as though he were trying to play hopscotch on the cement octagons of the sidewalk.

"Wait a minute, there," admonished the second policeman. "I don't care what you say. That man's drunk, and we better check him out."

"Who's drunk?" demanded Buck Tarpley. "I ain't drunk. One thing we can do is hol our liquor. I ain't drunk!"

"Well, I think you're holdin too much and been holdin it too long," responded the officer.

" 'Zat so?" queried Buck, argumentative but still affable. "Well, lemme tell you what you do. You jus draw a line on this lil ol sidewalk and see, by God, if I don't walk it straight as you can."

"Officer," the father interrupted, "my friend is a veteran of twenty years in the Navy, and naturally you men know that all those years on the high seas have given him sea legs that cause him to walk differently from us old farm boys."

" 'S right," agreed Buck. "You won't draw me a line I walk one anyhow. How's thish?"

He stepped away from the group and nearly fell sprawling. The first policeman grabbed him by the arm.

"Thanksh," said the affable Buck. "Musta slipped or stumbled. I'll try again."

"Mr. Osborne," the second officer announced, "this man is definitely drunk. Now, we'll let you and this other man and your little boy go on home, but we'll have to hold this fellow for a public drunk."

"Well," the father responded, "that puts an entirely different complexion on things. We're all for one and one for all in this outfit, and we're not about to leave our companion alone in a strange city."

With a delighted shrug of his shoulders, Buck Tarpley looked squarely at the father. "Aw, hell, Porter," he said, and with no warning whatsoever unhooked a fist that caught the second policeman on the jaw with such force that he fell on his back, slid across the curb, and came to rest under the mud-spattered Buick, toes of his shiny shoes pointing upward.

As the first policeman moved toward Buck, the father spun him around by one shoulder and hit him so hard that he fell over the hood of his own car. The father and Buck looked at each other a moment and then threw back their heads and erupted into bellowing laughter. Still laughing, they pulled the policeman from under the car, propped him on his feet, and began brushing him off. "Man, you sho can slide," Buck Tarpley told him with a grin.

The father was helping his victim off the hood of the car. He proffered a hand and with a grin assured him, "Nothing personal to all this, officer. I'm sure you understand and will be a good sport about it." He and Buck looked at each other and exploded once again into laughter.

"Jus like ol times, Porter, jus like ol times," gurgled Buck Tarpley. "Can't that p'liceman slide pretty?"

"I mean he can, Buck!" the father agreed. "He slid like he was greased! An did you see mine roll over the hood o' that car? They must be the ol Slide an Somersault brothers. Never extended us the courtesy of introducin themselves, but I believe to my soul that's who they are." The two friends clapped each other on the back in chortling congratulation.

It seemed to the boy that within minutes the street was full of policemen. In a calm moment later, he made a retrospective count of only six, but at the time he felt that there were hordes of them. He heard his father say, "Uh-oh, we're outnumbered now, Buck. They'll sure take us down and book us. Just take it easy, boy, and cooperate with them. Easy, boy, easy. We'll be all right. Just take it easy, now."

Talking to Buck Tarpley as if he were soothing a bird dog, he got him through a body search that yielded a pocket knife and a buckeye. With hands in the air, he told a policeman approaching him, "There's a knife in my pants pocket, son. Be careful about my overcoat, though. My Luger's in the right-hand pocket, and I don't want you to hurt yourself."

"Hey, Cap, he's got a gun," the policeman announced incredulously. "Yall lucky he didn't use it. Now we got him for carrying a concealed weapon, ain't we? Gee, that must be bout twenty charges by now."

He was interrupted by the arrival of the police wagon. The boy had seen pictures of them in the Sunday comics, but this was the first time he had ever seen one in reality. It really did have barred doors in the back of it and a little step under them.

His father and Buck Tarpley were escorted into this conveyance with dispatch and no ceremony at all. The boy rushed up as a policeman was closing the doors and got one foot on the step. "Hey, wait for me!" he yelled.

"What the hell's wrong with you, kid? We don't want you. You can't git in here," the policeman rebuked him.

"That's my daddy, please, sir. The big one. I'm with him. Why can't I ride in there?"

"Because you can't," the policeman answered. "You just can't." Apparently he had never been faced with this request before. He added with inspiration, "You ain't done nothin wrong, and only folks what been arrested can ride in here. Now get back."

The doors slammed shut with a metallic clang, and the Black Maria began chugging away. Left alone in the middle of the suddenly quiet and empty street, the boy realized with panic that he did not know where the jail was or even if that was where they were going. He began running behind the vehicle as fast as he could in pursuit of the red tail light.

"Hey, Sambo," he heard someone call cautiously, "get out of that street and come back here."

He had absolutely forgotten Will Elliott. He could not recall even having seen him after the policemen had arrived. Here he was, however, walking rapidly down the sidewalk and calling to the boy.

"Will, they've got Buck and Daddy and I don't know where they're going with them and I've got to at least keep sight of that wagon. I've got to help em somehow. Did you see all that fracas back up there?"

"I saw it," said Will. "Get out of the middle of that street and come back here on the sidewalk. I can see the paddy wagon turning two blocks down to the left. The jail must be just around the corner. Come on over here. We'll find them."

Comforted by the companionship, the boy joined Will, who was walking so fast it required a half-trot to keep up with him. As they passed a vacant lot, the boy saw Will's arm arc in the shadows and heard the crash of shattering glass. The action was repeated. No word was spoken, but the boy realized what had happened.

"Well, the liquor's all gone at last. I guess we can go home now," the boy said to Will.

"Sambo, I want you to do me one favor. Don't say anything to any of those people about me being in the armed forces. Will you do that? Just don't mention it. Okay? There's the jail right up there on the left. See it?"

"I won't mention it, Will, but why shouldn't I? Looks like that might help. It would show em what a responsible and important person you are."

"After your father's credentials, mine don't look too impressive, and his didn't seem to make any difference to this bunch of cops. Besides, I'm supposed to make captain next month, a little earlier than most guys in my class, and anything that happened to get on my record might delay it."

As they mounted the steps, Will looked across at the boy. "Why don't you just let me do all the talking, huh?"

The jail was brightly lighted and seemed bigger to the boy than the entire courthouse in Brewtonton. They opened a door where an older man in uniform was putting objects into a brown manila envelope. The boy recognized his father's white gold Hamilton watch and his pearl-handled pocket knife. He darted from behind Will Elliott and shrilled, "Where's my daddy?" He forced his voice lower and added, "Please, sir?"

The man looked at him without speaking and jerked his head to the left. Turning, the boy saw a wall of iron bars going all the way across the room and a corridor beyond that ran between more iron bars. At the end he could definitely see his father's head above the heads of several policemen. Pressing his face between the bars, he shouted, "Daddy! Are you all right?"

"Sure, boy, I'm fine. Don't worry about anything. Just go get your Uncle Grif and tell him where I am." The boy heard the creaking of a heavy iron door and a policeman's voice.

"Now just get in there with your friend, and yall get a nice nap," the voice said.

He heard another voice. "Wait a minute. Give me that ring before you go in there."

"Oh, no," the father responded. "That ring doesn't leave my finger."

The boy knew well the item under discussion. Years before the father had bought himself a diamond ring with the biggest stone in it the boy had ever seen. It was bigger than anything Mrs. Holt or Miss Nevayda Dettmering ever wore and, in addition, was set in heavy white gold with yellow gold laurel garlands on the sides, which made it appear even larger. The boy had privately thrilled to the idea that it perhaps had been plucked from the eye of a heathen idol and probably had a curse upon it. It lent distinction to the entire family.

Now, to some unintelligible reply from the policeman, he heard his father's voice. "I don't care what you say. You're not taking this ring off my finger. At least not back here. You take me back up front and I'll put it with my other valuables, but I'm not giving it up back here. What's that you say? I'm not worried about anybody in that cell stealing it—I'm worried about your interest in it. . . . Here, suh! Take your hands off me!—All right then—Goddam your immortal soul to hell, you uniformed son of a bitch!"

The boy heard the solid smack of a fist, and a policeman came reeling backwards toward him. Then he heard his father's voice in rallying battle cry, "Up from there, Buck! Back to back now, boy! We got business!"

The policeman yelled. Reinforcements poured in, but the barred corridor was so narrow no more than two could function at a time. Everyone was yelling and cursing. The boy clung to the bars, weak with terror. He saw clubs raised by blue-sleeved arms, and the curses increased in volume. Finally, above it all, he heard, "Sambo! Sambo! Can you hear me? Are you still there?"

"Daddy!" he screamed. "Here I am, Daddy!"

"They're trying to get my ring, Sambo. Just remember that! They're trying to get my ring! Take that, you sniveling bastard!" The night sticks rose and fell. The boy felt two hands under his arms as he was lifted up and plucked away from the bars.

"Look, boy," the older man in uniform said to him as he set him down by the side of the desk. His voice was gruff, but the tone was kind. "Why don't you go on home? This gentleman here says he'll be glad to drive you if you know the way an can show him."

"That's my daddy! They might kill him. I can't leave here!"

"They ain't gonna kill him," the man assured him. "An I don't really think them two gonna kill any our boys. But you can't do no good here. Now I heered him tell you go get somebody. Why don't you do that?"

"Yeah," the boy replied. "That's my uncle. He's the sheriff at home. I'll do that." He turned and added over the din still erupting from the cell block. "My mother's president of the Woman's Missionary Union. Should I bring her, too?"

The policeman stared a moment, swallowed hard, and said, "Son, 'les yo mama's different from any other woman I ever seen, hit'd be better she don't even know bout it. All you need is somebody can put up a cash bond." He paused, turned his head toward the melée, and added, "A *heap* o' cash bond."

There was little conversation between the boy and Will Elliott on the way back to Peabody. The boy perched on the edge of the seat, peering through the windshield, and automatically gave directions to which Will gave perfunctory responses. His brain whirled, and he kept trying to organize his thoughts and plan what he should do. He realized that it was well after three in the morning and that he was tired and sleepy. This was not adequate explanation, however, for the feeling he had that he was still gripping iron bars with both hands and that those bars extended all the way up to Heaven itself, forever dividing, forever separating.

"Help, us, God," he implored, "for Thy Sweet Son, our Lord and Saviour Jesus Christ's sake, help this entire family." Vainly trying to recall all the formula, he belatedly remembered another ecclesiastical admonition and several miles down the road, added, "And bless our enemies, those policemen, who have despitefully used us this night." He was so oblivious of Will Elliott that he did not realize he had spoken aloud.

It took both of them calling and pounding on the back door to awaken his uncle, but the stimulation afforded by physical effort was welcome. The solid presence of the uncle in the doorway was reassuring and calming to a degree the boy could hardly believe.

"Both of em locked up?" the stalwart man queried in a level tone. "Must have been some more fight from what yall are telling me. Were they both . . . had they had a little too much to drink, do you think? Well, I'll get my clothes on and mosey on down there. No, son, you positively cannot go with me. You go home and get in that bed. And don't worry. I'll have your daddy and Buck Tarpley home by sunup. I got good connections with the boys in Griffin, and I'll tend to it. Sure, I'll check and be sure your daddy has his ring, but I'm not worried about it. You get on home."

As the boy and Will Elliott mounted the stairs in the big house, they were careful not to wake the grandparents, who occupied the only bedroom on the first floor. At the top of the stairs, Will Elliott turned to the right and tipped down the cold hallway to the guest bedroom.

Alone and reeling with fatigue, the boy was strangely reluctant to approach his own bed. He stopped a moment and leaned on the newel post at the head of the stairwell. He heard a murmur of voices from Will Elliott's room, and then he heard Sara Margaret's genteel voice, clear and musical, interspersed with Will's unintelligible rumble.

"Buck and Porter are in *jail*? You don't mean it! . . . Well, what in the hell are *you* doing *here*? . . . Well, let me educate you, darling. There are some things more important in life than a promotion in the Air Corps. . . . Oh, that's nonsense, that boy was *not* terrified. He's weasley, but he was just playing his cards. . . . But, baby, I *do* know what I'm talking about. Being tough when it looks like we're being stomped is what has kept Southerners alive for the last seventy-five years. . . . Look, he's probably even going to *look* handsome in ten years or so. Quit worrying about that boy and come on to bed. I'm freezing." Her laugh pealed beautifully down the darkened hall.

The boy felt both caressed and stimulated. He thought awhile and squared his shoulders. If he could fool Sara Margaret, he could fool anybody. There was one thing he felt compelled to do before he went to bed.

Stepping to the door of the sleeping porch containing his parents' bed, he stumbled against the doorjamb with a solid thud. Hearing only the regular, uninterrupted breathing of his mother, he rattled some papers on the bedside table. Still receiving no response, he coughed, loudly.

The breathing stopped.

He coughed again.

His mother's voice called sleepily, "Is that you, son?"

"Yes'm, Mother," he answered softly. "I just wanted to tell you goodnight."

"That's sweet. What time is it?"

"It's about four o'clock, Mother."

"My goodness, that's awfully late, son," came the sleepy response. "Where's your daddy?"

"He's in jail," the boy answered in his gentlest voice.

"*What!*" came the explosion. His mother hit the floor without, he thought, bending a single joint in her body, her long braid of hair popping like a lariat.

After fifteen minutes of the most gratifying pandemonium of which he had ever been the center, the boy crawled between the cold sheets of his bed and listened to his mother's car leaving the driveway for Griffin.

I'm glad this is Saturday and I can sleep late, he thought while his teeth chattered.

I hope Mr. Dorsey and the basketball team don't ever find out about this, he added as he shuddered with a chill. He tried to pray but was so exhausted he could think of nothing but "Now I lay me," and abandoned the effort. His body warmed a spot in the bed, and his muscles relaxed. He thought of his father. He could not truly imagine anything bad having happened to him. It was like trying to imagine there was no God. One couldn't get past His living presence to do any serious doubting. Drowsily he considered Will Elliott. Gosh, he told himself, I wonder if that yankee knows how lucky he is to have married a Southern girl!

He slept.

Despite the best efforts of his uncle, the sheriff, the authorities in Griffin would not release their prisoners until noon. The insult of having six of their finest policemen battered and bruised had to be atoned, and none of the formalities was shortened. The father had a cut, a swollen lip, scratches on both hands, and an assortment of lumps on his head. Buck Tarpley, however, looked as though he had stuck his head into a sausage grinder. Both eyes were swollen shut, and there were only small patches on his face which contained whole skin.

The boy was in disfavor with the father for having told the mother. Her presence at the sergeant's desk when he was released had been an embarrassment to the father. To her single spoken greeting of "Hello, Porter," he had made no response but had stalked past her to his brother's car and left her to drive home from Griffin alone. He gave the boy a stern lecture about the manly necessity of concealing things from womenfolk when knowledge would only inflict pain. His rebuke was peppered with numerous references to the axiom that woman's place is in the home. The boy accepted the lecture with genuine contrition, leavened with gratitude that his father did not realize how deliberate his sin had been.

Buck Tarpley had very little to say for the several days before he caught a bus and went home. The Elliotts left early Sunday morning, with Sara Margaret calling everyone "darling" and inviting a reciprocal visit from all and sundry. She released the grandmother from a final hug. "Bye, Aunt Sis," she trilled. "Take care of yourself. We all love you and Uncle Jim *so* much. It's wonderful to get back to the place we all came from and see that nothing's changed. Goodbye, darlings. All of yall come to see us, heah? We'll be back whenever we can."

The boy was holding her door open for her.

"Thank you," she said. She leaned forward and gave him a peck on the cheek. "You know you have to carry on the name, don't you? You're the only son your father has."

The boy waved to the disappearing car and considered that he and that name just might be reciprocal burdens to each other. He shrugged and spent the rest of the day being very lofty about doling out scraps of information to his two little sisters as they clamored for details of the adventure in Griffin.

He was a little jumpy in school for a week or two, but no one ever found out about the disgrace of his father's having been locked up in jail. He knew this for a fact because Miss Hancock never made any allusion to it.

XXIV

he continued to do well in his studies. He wrote a speech for the FFA entitled "The Effect of the Proposed Wage and Hour Bill on Agriculture in America." He won the subregional oratorical contest with it and so delighted the principal that he bestowed another five points to the boy's credit. The principal invited the father to accompany them to the regional contest, but the invitation was politely declined. When the boy won that contest also, the principal awarded him five more points and in his excitement called the father long distance to relay the wonderful news. Hanging up the phone, he looked thoughtful and detached for a moment and then said to the boy, "Your father sure thinks the world of you. You know what he told me? He said, 'I'm not at all surprised. He told me he was going to win, and he's never lied to me yet.' Not many boys have that sort of relationship with their fathers. You're lucky."

The boy made some deprecatingly correct murmur but rode home with a surging heart. Not only had he pleased his father, but he had parlayed his agriculture class into twenty points that no one else could approach.

The following week Miss Berry gave out the list of broad topics for Ready Writer's Essay. The boy was able to narrow one of them down to "The Southern Farmer and Pending National Legislation." Changing his agriculture speech only minimally, he won first place locally with the essay and then won at the district level. Captain of the debate team this final year in high school, he and his partner from the junior class won first place in that event at the District meet. That made a grand total of fifteen points for debate this year and fifteen for Ready Writer's Essay. When spring came into full bloom, it was a foregone conclusion that he would be the class valedictorian.

He happened to overhear Miss Hancock one afternoon authoritatively instructing a girl in the study hall concerning the bumblebees that hung in stationary buzzing beneath the eaves outside the auditorium. They would occasionally zoom after another intruding bee, only to return to hover with hypnotic hum in precisely the same spot.

"Demaris, that's the silliest thing I ever heard of. All bees will sting. You're not going to sit there and convince me that there's one that doesn't sting just because its head is white. Besides, who would ever examine their heads? It's their tails that give you trouble. At any rate, I'm scared to death of all bees, and I don't care how hot yall get, we're not going to open any of these windows. You won't smother, and I can't stand the idea of one of those creatures getting in here."

Pretending to be absorbed in his homework, the boy twitched as an idea was born. He knew there were city-bred folk who lived unaware of the white-headed bumblebee. It was identical to its feared counterpart except that it had a white spot between its multifaceted, prismatic green eyes and it had no stinger in its tail. He had heard one learned man say that this was the female of the species, and on another occasion he had heard an equally learned man vow that the white-headed bee was the male.

The white-headed bumblebee was a fascinating addition to the sole-tickling barefoot days of early spring. It was absorbing sport to swing at them with a broom handle as they hovered around the eaves of the smokehouse or other outbuildings of the farm. When one connected with a solid whack after many fruitless swings, it was easy to fantasize one was Babe Ruth while inspecting the quivering, silent object on the ground.

It had been more fun, however, before he grew up, to catch one in glistening, buzzing vigor and put it down the back of a visiting city child. The memory of prissy visitors screaming in anticipation of a searing sting could still evoke snickers from the boy. He had one bit of secret information about white-headed bumblebees—he had access to an unlimited supply of them. His mother in years past had transplanted two redbud trees from the woods on Jones Hill, one in the front yard and one in the back. Sprangling lacily in pink counterpoint to dogwood while in their native state, these redbuds, taking advantage of full sun and noncompetitive solitude, had grown into small trees with crowns thirty feet across and limbs that swept the ground.

Each April they were dense mounds of pale magenta which worked alive with thousands of hungry insects. The white-headed bumblebees, in particular, loved the redbud trees.

That afternoon after school it took a little time but no great amount of work to procure a quart fruit jar, poke holes in the lid, and fill it with the busy, noisy bees. He was enthusiastically assisted by his two little sisters, who would do anything to keep from having to practice piano lessons on a singing spring day. Even the boy was impressed when the jar was completely full, its occupants crowded into wriggling but nonbuzzing silence. "There must be at least six hundred bees in there," he marveled as he screwed the lid on tightly.

He swiped a new spool of thread from his mother's sewing machine drawer and spent several minutes soaking it in very muddy water to change its color. Next morning it was a simple matter to smuggle the jar of bees in his lunch sack into the schoolhouse and store it in his locker. During history class that morning, he excused himself and visited the empty auditorium. About midway down the aisle, behind a row of seats, he tied one end of the spool of thread to the leg of a chair. Then he unrolled it along the floor back to the end of the room and secreted the spool behind the corner seat on the raised platform at the back. At noon while everyone, including the faculty, was basking like lizards in the warm sun outside, he slipped back into the auditorium, this time carrying the jar of insects. He carried them down the empty aisle to the chair where he had anchored his string. Tying the thread to the neck of the fruit jar, he unscrewed the lid until it balanced loosely on top of the angry, crowded bees. Carefully he placed it upright. A number of things would have to go exactly right to make the plan work, but at least there should be nothing to implicate him.

Immediately after lunch, Miss Hancock held eighth and ninth grade study hall in the auditorium. Five minutes into his math class, the boy begged permission to visit his locker and get his homework assignment. He eased to the edge of the dividing wall between the auditorium and the hallway, reached over the top, and found the spool. Miss Hancock was at the other end of the auditorium, arms folded across her bosom, prowling the aisles in gum-soled stealth. The students were quiet as mice.

Miss Hancock turned and in slow rhythm strolled back down the aisle. As she approached the spot where the bees were hidden, the boy held his breath and pulled on the thread. He heard a resounding clatter and jerked the string. Feeling it snap somewhere in the distance, he hastily pulled in the loose end and stuffed it in his pocket while he heard Miss Hancock say, "Sallie Kate, what in the world did you drop?"

She moved between the rows of seats and bent over just as the released bees buzzed to freedom all around her. She screamed. A bee got tangled in her hair. She screamed again, made her way to the center aisle, and screamed again. As she leaned over and fought her own hair, the multitude of bees zoomed through the auditorium to the windows. All the girls in study hall screamed. A bee flew up Miss Hancock's skirt. She turned loose her hair and screamed more frantically. The bees buzzed loudly, bumped the windowpanes, and zoomed across to the opposite windows. The boys yelled. Miss Hancock screamed over and over and over. The principal came running into the auditorium.

"What in the *world* is the *matter*?" he demanded.

Miss Hancock lurched toward him, grabbed him around the neck and in gibbering hysteria, pointed wildly at the bee-covered windowpanes. The boy looked at her contorted face with satisfaction, noting that her eyes were rolling white like a heifer's in heat.

She's even slobbering, he thought as he walked back into his classroom.

"What in the world is all that racket out there?" his teacher inquired.

"I don't know for sure," the boy replied as he closed the door. "I think Miss Hancock's having a problem with something."

As he walked by the office after school, he overheard Mr. Dorsey addressing the principal. "It couldn't have been. He had math that period."

"Well, it couldn't have been little Sallie Kate Jackson," the principal replied. He chuckled. "I wish you could have seen it, Dorsey. Fifteen years in the school business, and that's the funniest sight I've ever seen."

The incident seemed to have a beneficial effect on Miss Hancock. For one thing she tended to spend more of her study hall time in the back of the auditorium and stopped making regular trips up and down the aisle. For another, she made fewer sarcastic remarks to the boy, and there were whole periods when she completely ignored him.

One Friday afternoon she walked up to his seat and spoke in such a soft, sweet tone that the boy twitched in alarm.

"Would you do me a big favor?" she asked.

"Yes'm, if I can."

"We got paid this afternoon, and I'm going home to North Carolina for the weekend. My problem is that the bank is going to close in twenty minutes. My bus leaves right after school—I've even got my suitcase ready in my homeroom—and I won't have time to get my check cashed before I get on the bus. It's the only money I have to pay my bus fare with, and I'm afraid the driver won't have the change."

She paused and even worked up a smile although she did not quite have the sang-froid to meet the boy's level gaze. "What I'm wondering is would you mind going to the bank before it closes and getting my check cashed for me? You make such good grades you can sure afford to miss study hall, and it really would be a big favor to me."

"Miss Hancock, you know the principal is real rough about students being on the streets. He's got a rule that if you're caught in town without a written excuse, you automatically get a whipping. You gonna write me an excuse?"

"Oh, sure." The teacher began scribbling on a piece of paper. She took the blue check and endorsed it. Thrusting both of them into the boy's hand, she looked at her wristwatch, "But you'd better hurry. It's only fifteen minutes until the bank closes."

Glad of an excuse to be outdoors in the beautiful weather, the boy accepted the mission from this archenemy and even pretended to be friendly. "I'll be happy to run this little errand, Miss Hancock. How do you want your money?"

"Oh, it doesn't matter," the teacher replied. "I don't care. I don't want any big bills and I'll need some change on account of the bus driver, but I really don't care. You're mighty sweet to do this for me, but you'd better hurry!"

By the time he passed under the water oaks in front of the Culpepper house, bright and airy with the new green of unfurling spring leaves, he was indignant. "Old sow!" he muttered. "Spend all year treating me like a dog and then when she wants something buttering me up like I was a fool. She thinks I've forgotten all those things she said? I've a good mind to tell her the bank closed before I got there and just give her back her old check."

He progressed to Miss Roxie's picket fence that enclosed the trimmed maze of boxwoods in the prim and tight front yard. There was still enough yellow jasmine blooming over the front porch to perfume the sidewalk. An idea flickered in his mind, dimmed, and then blazed into inspired clarity. "Oh, boy," he said aloud, "that's wonderful. I'll show her once and for all who she's been messing with."

Entering the bank, he saw Mr. Bannister, long and lean in white linen, sitting at the corner desk with Mr. Charley Reynolds, who had a cigar in his mouth and his hat pushed to the back of his head. Both men were leaning back in their chairs with their feet propped on the desk. Mr. Charley had his thumbs tucked in his suspenders.

"Howdy, Mr. Reynolds. Howdy, Mr. Bannister," the boy said, remembering the social rule that a younger gentleman always spoke first to an older gentleman and also remembering to speak loudly enough for the deaf Mr. Bannister to hear him. As he moved on to the teller's cage, he heard Mr. Reynolds: "Who's that nice boy, Wes? He's a fine young fellow."

"Why, Charley, that's Porter Osborne's son. You know him."

After a pause, he heard Mr. Reynolds's response. "Of course I do. He takes after his mother, doesn't he?"

As Mr. Cranford Sims, the cashier, leaned over the marble slab that penetrated the bars of the cashier's window, both he and the boy pretended not to hear.

"What can I do for you, Little Porter?" he asked with a nasal twang, holding an amber cigarette holder with a furiously burning Camel in it to one side. Everybody in town liked Mr. Sims, and the boy was no exception.

"Miss Hancock wants her paycheck cashed, Mr. Cranford," the boy explained, pushing it across the marble. "She's catching the bus out of here for North Carolina and didn't have time to come herself before school let out."

"Okay. It's all endorsed and everything." He turned to the cash drawer. "Do you know how she wants it?"

"Oh, yessir. I'm glad you asked me. She was most emphatic about that. She wants it all in pennies."

Mr. Sims choked on his cigarette and looked at the boy. "She couldn't possibly want all this in pennies. This check is for ninety-seven dollars."

The boy met his questioning look with blue-eyed candor and never a wavering of his glance. "That's sure crazy, isn't it, Mr. Cranford? She's going home for the weekend, and maybe there are a lot of children there or something. I don't know why she wants it like that, but that's sure what she told me. She's a real strict teacher, and I didn't ask her why. You know what I mean. She's from North Carolina. Would that have something to do with it? Or maybe it's just that she's a woman. I'm not sure why she wants it like that. Here's the note she gave me to come to town, though, if you want to see it."

It was Mr. Sims's gaze that broke away first. "All right. I believe you." He reached into the drawer and pulled out rolls of coins all wrapped in heavy brown paper and stacked them on the counter before the boy. "I can't do it. I don't have but forty dollars' worth of pennies."

The boy blithely reassured him. "That's all right. Give me the rest in nickels. She told me to make it up in the smallest change I could."

As Mr. Sims began stacking rolls of nickels, the boy shook his head solemnly. "I don't mean any disrespect, Mr. Cranford, but that lady must be crazy. Do you realize that's four thousand pennies there? That's more'n anybody could need!"

"It sure is, son," Mr. Sims replied, a note of enthusiasm creeping into his voice as he became involved in the project. "And you know something else? I don't have but forty dollars in nickels. That means she doesn't get but eight hundred of them." He looked over his rimless glasses. "I guess you want the rest in dimes, don't you?"

"Yes, sir," the boy said firmly. "Exactly one hundred and seventy of them, I believe. I sure hope she's not going to be disappointed."

"Well, you tell her we done the best we could on such short notice. You're gonna need a sack to tote all that back to the schoolhouse." He procured a small, heavy sack that looked like a canvas shopping bag, securely stitched and equipped with canvas handles. Together, he and the boy stacked the rolls of coins in it.

"Thanks a lot, Mr. Cranford, sir. I hope I haven't made you late about closing your bank. I see Mr. Charley and Mr. Bannister are already headed for the Ford place."

"Oh, no, Little Porter. Don't worry about that. I'm all locked up in the back. All I've got to do is close the vault and lock the front door. I'm just a few minutes late, but that doesn't matter."

When the boy lifted his sack of coins and left the bank, he realized that his trip to school was going to be work. These damn things must weigh thirty pounds, he thought. I didn't know coins came rolled up in wrappers like that. He peered into the sack. "They sure look formal and regimented like that," he murmured. "Nothing like a rich treasure heap that a lady could run her hands through in joyous abandon."

He stopped under the trees in front of Miss Pearl Woolsey's house and squatted down. Emptying the sack, he carefully unwrapped every roll and refilled the canvas sack with loose coins, dimes on the bottom, nickels in the middle, and pennies on the top. The bulging load of naked coins was much more satisfying to him.

He heard the courthouse clock groan and then bong the half hour. Gosh, I'd better hurry, he thought. He tossed the empty wrappers under Miss Pearl's elaeagnus bush and began walking as fast as he could, changing hands frequently with his load. You really are mean as hell, he gloated admiringly to himself. You may get the beating of your life for this, but it's worth it.

When he entered the school, Miss Hancock was waiting with her suitcase at her feet. She had put on a hat and short white gloves. She was obviously dressed for traveling. Mr. Dorsey, new owner of a thirdhand car, had been euchred into driving her to the bus and was standing at her side, chatting with two lady teachers.

Miss Hancock exclaimed, "Thank God, you're back. My bus leaves in fifteen minutes! Where in the world have you been? We were just fixing to come looking for you. I thought maybe you'd gotten lost or robbed or something."

She accepted the proffered sack of coins without looking at it, sagging to the right under its weight. "Why are you giving me this sack to hold?" she demanded. "It sure is heavy. My bus is going to leave me if I don't hurry. Where's my money? . . . What do you mean, it's in the bag? . . . Oh, oh, oh. . . . I don't believe. . . . You did. . . . Oh, I'll kill you, you little. . . ." Hampered by the coins, she raised her left hand threateningly.

"But, Miss Hancock," the boy replied. "I asked you how you wanted that money, and you distinctly said you didn't care. It came to me on the way to town that this would be romantic, like having

411

your own treasure chest or something. I went to a lot of trouble. It sure hurts for you to be disappointed."

As she quivered and drew a deep breath, he added in a soothing tone, "It looks like a lot more than it really is."

Mr. Dorsey interrupted, "Miss Hancock, we'd better be leaving if I'm going to get you to that bus on time. Here, let me take that. It's heavier than the suitcase." He turned to the boy. "You'd better go to your homeroom and check out."

As he moved away, the boy carried the image of Mr. Dorsey's green eyes shining out of a reddened face and from under slanting brows. How can he laugh without moving his mouth? he wondered.

A few days later, the principal sent for him to come to the office and the boy felt that denouement was imminent. Reflecting on the marvelous relationship he had enjoyed all year with this superior being, he resolved to take his punishment like a man. After all, he asserted, you deserve it. He entered the office with a lump in his throat and a quiver to his lower lip that could be controlled only by biting the lip firmly.

"Yes, sir?" he announced his presence to the tall blond figure standing by the window.

"Ah, yes, Porter, or Sambo, as your dad calls you. I want to talk to you about something. You're president of the senior class, and, I might add, you've done a darn good job with it all year. Well, I've got something I want you to present to the class. A man with a firm that rents caps and gowns to graduating classes came through here, and I've decided it would be a good thing for this class to do."

"What do you mean?" the boy asked, trying to rearrange his expectations. "He'd rent us the caps and gowns to graduate in and then we'd turn 'em back to him? I thought you had to be in college to do that. Besides, wouldn't that cost a lot of money?"

"It would certainly be establishing a precedent, all right. That's why I wanted to explain it to you and let you present it to the seniors. It would cost three dollars and a half to rent the outfit, but you would wear it three times—on class day, at the baccalaureate sermon, and on graduation night. Most of the girls try to get three different dresses for these occasions, and it sure would save them some money.

"In case you don't know it, it's still pretty hard times around here, and there are some students in your class who couldn't afford three different outfits. The other thing about these caps and gowns is that they are all exactly alike."

"Gosh, I don't know," the boy interrupted. "I've already heard some of the girls talking about wearing long white dresses and carrying red roses. They act pretty excited about the prospect."

"That's exactly the point. It's *some* of the girls. How many of them have you noticed who haven't said *anything* about it? How many of them have you noticed get real quiet or pretend to be interested in something else when the subject's brought up? I tell you one thing. I hope I never see another graduation where some of the girls are embarrassed because their dresses aren't fine or because they can't afford any flowers except what their mamas may have in the yard.

"Graduation is the biggest event that ever happens for some of these kids, and it's just as important or more so to a tenant farmer's child as it is to the mayor's daughter. The girls would wear white caps and gowns and the boys would wear black, and nobody could look at what they're wearing and use that as an estimate of how much money somebody's old man has in the bank." He checked the passion in his speech and asked, "What do you think of it?"

Remembering Mavis and her friends at the junior-senior reception the previous year and recalling his visits to Sally Fitzgerald's house, the boy replied slowly, "It's so wonderful, I'm ashamed I didn't think of it myself."

"Well, why don't you pretend you did?" chuckled the principal. "That detail is unimportant."

"You know this is going to raise one big ruckus in the class, don't you?" asked the boy.

"Some of those town girls will nail my hide to the barn door. There's no way I can handle this through committee and keep things pleasant on the surface like we've been doing all year. This is going to be one big fuss and there'll be some evermore mad womenfolks, and they'll be out for blood."

"I didn't know you backed off from that," the principal replied. "See what you can do with it, and if you need me to talk to the class, I'll be glad to do it."

As the boy turned to leave, he was stopped dead in his tracks. "Miss Hancock came to see me," the principal said in an almost casual voice.

"Yessir?"

"Dorsey had already told me what had happened, and I'd had the weekend to think it out."

"Yessir?" the boy said again, thinking briefly, with a tingle in his buttocks, of Mr. Gill.

"Miss Hancock was still spitting mad," the principal said, "but I told her that it was just as reprehensible for a student to be sent to town as an expedient instrument for a teacher who had the power to write a note as it would be for a student to be there on his own personal business without a note. I also told her that I was aware she had been badgering you all year, and that this was a personal matter between the two of you and that I expected it to cease right now with a truce for the rest of the year. Do you think you can live up to it?"

"Oh, yes, *sir*," the boy promised with relief. "Yes, *sir*. That'll be no problem at all."

"Wait just a minute. We both know that was a fiendish thing to do, and I ought to wear you out." He paused, chuckled, and added, "How did you talk *anybody* into giving you that many pennies, you rascal, you?"

The boy did not trust the situation enough to acknowledge any relaxing humor in it, but he answered, "It wasn't easy."

He almost ran up the hall.

It was also not easy to get the seniors to accept the caps and gowns. The actual process was simple enough and the vote was

414

overwhelmingly affirmative, but the buildup and aftermath were emotionally devastating. It became almost a caste war, and the boy was caught squarely in the middle. He discovered that as long as he felt he was in the right, he could face antagonism and anger with equanimity.

It was strictly a female war. The boys could care less what they wore and cast their votes purely to please the girls toward whom they felt loyalty. Despite conflicting feelings and in the face of pressure from girls he truly admired, the boy argued vigorously for the new precedent. He wished he could forget some of the vehement accusations and protestations. When it was all over, despite being solidly aligned with the majority of his peers, he felt honest remorse at the disappointment of the frustrated town girls. He knew they hated him. He had not been lonely for almost a year, and now he welcomed the prospect of loneliness as a returning friend.

When he finished writing his valedictory, he sought out Mr. Dorsey and asked him to read it. Right in the middle of it, Mr. Dorsey stopped, rolled up his shirt sleeve, and said, "Look at this— I'm breaking out in goose bumps! That means this has to be good."

The boy immediately forgot that he had ever been lonely in his life.

"There's something I have got to tell you," Mr. Dorsey said later as the boy was returning the speech to his notebook. "You remember last fall when you told me about the first-honor ambition you had? And I told you I checked your record and it looked as though you were leading a little? Well, you had it won hands down even then. There was absolutely no doubt who would get it."

In response to the dawning question in the boy's eyes, he added, "I just wanted to see what you could do if you really tried and if you had a little direction."

"Yeah, and you had me so busy you kept me out of trouble all year."

With an eye-squinting laugh, Mr. Dorsey amended, "Almost all year!" He hit the boy between the shoulders so hard that he nearly fell. "Congratulations!" he said.

* * *

On graduation night, the seniors filed into the auditorium looking impressively scholastic and serious in their caps and gowns. Every student there had someone in the audience proud enough to burst. No one commented that most of the graduates balanced their mortarboards as if they had cricks in their necks. Two of the girls were still so angry at being cheated out of white dresses and red roses that they hissed at the boy, "I hope you're satisfied." Nothing else, however, marred the processional. The boy was so full of memories that he was almost tearful. The affection he felt for his classmates was diluted by his awareness of his father's presence on the stage. He was there as School Superintendent to deliver the diplomas. He had a brand new pair of white buckskin shoes for the occasion and looked better than anyone's father had ever looked before.

Throughout the invocation and the visiting speaker's address the boy kept remembering the now-blended events of the last four years. He marveled at how many of the memories centered around his father and how many more included him. He noted that this was the first time since the eighth grade and Patrick Henry that his father would have heard him speak in public. He vowed to do the best that he possibly could with his speech tonight, not for his classmates, not for Mr. Dorsey, not for himself, but for his father. I owe him so much, he thought.

When his turn came on the program, he was calm, controlled, and eloquent. He used every trick he had ever learned from Mrs. Parker and delivered his valedictory with great confidence. As he came to the end, remembering never to be sing-song or yield to meter in reciting poetry, he began Rudyard Kipling's advice to young men:

> If you can keep your head when all about you
> Are losing theirs and blaming it on you

and a few minutes later concluded with,

> If you can fill the unforgiving minute
> With sixty seconds' worth of distance run,
> Yours is the Earth and everything that's in it,
> And—which is more—you'll be a Man, my son!

As he turned to the accompaniment of applause to resume his seat among his fellows, he faced his father. Their eyes locked for a moment. No wink was exchanged. No expression moved that could have been detected by another, but the boy felt accepted and approved in a manner and to a depth he had never experienced before.

As the principal introduced his father, the boy recalled previous graduations and the short, moving speeches his father always made. Frequently he became so emotional that his children were uncomfortable or occasionally even embarrassed. The boy wondered what he would say to his class tonight. He hoped there would be no personal references to him or his part on the program. He tensed. The father rose, walked to the table where the rolled certificates were stacked, and with squared shoulders stood at attention.

Oh, Lord, the boy thought, he looks like a general reviewing his troops. We're going to hear about the World War. He always cries and gets everybody else to crying when he uses the World War in a speech.

The audience stilled. The tall, straight figure stood in commanding immobility. A long moment passed. The silence was total. Reaching out a hand, the father picked up the first diploma and intoned the name inscribed thereon. Graduation was ending.

As the boy marched across the stage to receive his diploma, he could detect no special look in his father's eyes. Nor did he feel that the strong handshake was any different from that bestowed on any other student. Back in his seat he told himself, I hope you've got sense enough to know that's the greatest compliment you've ever been paid. As he bowed his head for the benediction, tears filled his eyes and he added, I hope you'll be strong enough to live up to it.

three nights later he was awakened from a
sound sleep. His father was shaking him.

"Wake up, Sambo. I want to talk to you."

The boy blinked himself to the present, recognized the sour-
sweet smell of metabolizing whiskey being blown off by active
lungs, and became thoroughly awake.

"Yessir," he answered. "What's the matter?"

"I hate to do this, but I want you to know about something
firsthand. I want you to hear it from me before you hear it
anywhere else." His tone was so portentous of calamity that the
boy sat up in alarm.

"You haven't been in jail again, have you?"

"No, no," his father replied. "Nothing like that." He paused,
and then continued, "I've just beat the living hell out of a good
friend of yours, and I realize now I shouldn't have done it."

"Oh, Daddy," gasped the boy. "Was it Mr. Dorsey? What did
he do? Or say?"

"Hush just a minute, son, and let me tell you about it,"
interrupted the father. "Hell, no, it wasn't Dorsey. Wes came to
town this afternoon and called me out. You know he hasn't got a
crop of his own right now with your grandmother but decided that
he wanted to do this whole year as a wages hand. I'd told him that
was all right and he could still have his house and wood free, and
everything's been going along fine."

He paused, adjusted his shoulders in his coat, and stretched
his neck. The boy realized that, although the smell of whiskey was

very strong, his father was speaking simply and succinctly with no slur of words and no grandiose metaphor.

Gosh, he thought, he's already sobered up.

"Anyway," his father continued, "Wes told me this afternoon that Buddy had come by his house at dinnertime and got to talking to him. You know he's been living with Carson Clifton ever since he got married. Well, he told Wes that one of Carson's hands had moved off to Detroit in the middle of the night. He left an empty house and ten acres of cotton that's already been chopped, and it seems Carson is looking for somebody to take over the crop. Buddy put in to tell Wes how much better Carson's house is than ours and then told him that, if he didn't want to sharecrop the cotton, Mr. Clifton would give him fifty cents a day more than I'm paying for him just to come work it. Seems Buddy was awfully friendly and pretty persuasive about the delights of living on Carson Clifton's farm. Enough so at least that Wes came to town to see if I wanted to raise his wages."

"And you beat Wes up," the boy inserted.

"Hell, no," the father said with a note of impatience, "I didn't lay a finger on Wes. He's been with us for over twenty years. I didn't even say anything to him. I just looked him dead in the eye real straight for a minute. He got to squirming and shifting and then assured me that he didn't want a raise, that he just wanted me to know that a meddling nigger was messing with my hands, and that I was the best boss-man in the world.

"I told him he'd done the right thing and gave him two dollars to buy himself some new overalls. I never raised my voice to Wes—I didn't have to."

The boy stared in owlish silence, and his father continued, "I went back to the drugstore and took a drink or two and got to thinking about the situation. You know the one thing you have to do is look after your hands. You have to let them know they can depend on you to help them if they're in trouble or let them have extra money for an emergency or keep anybody from off the farm from pestering them. There come times when you have to do something you really don't want to because if you don't everything is going to get worse."

He paused, and the boy asked incredulously, "And you whipped Mr. Carson Clifton?"

"No, I didn't whip that son of a bitch, at least not yet. He may have been the one I should have gotten, and I still may need to do it. No, I decided that a real lesson had to be taught to everybody concerned, and much as I hated to, I went after Buddy."

"No," whispered the boy, "you didn't! Not Buddy!"

"Yes, I did. Don't you see? It's like even Wes was saying it— 'You can't have niggers messing in white folks' business.' I went down to Buddy's house to teach him a lesson and to let everybody know that I'm in control of what happens to my people. All I intended to do was slap him around a little and scare him good."

"Oh, no! You didn't hurt him, did you?"

"That's what I'm coming to," his father replied, "and that's the part I really hate and that's why I'm waking you up to tell you about it. He wouldn't answer me, and I had to kick his front door in. He was in bed with his wife, and I'm sorry she had to see the whole thing.

"I told him to come out of that bed, that he had a whipping coming to him for upsetting my hands and trying to tend to my business, and he commenced begging. He said, 'Mr. Porter, you don't wanta do this. You been jus like another daddy to me. Now please, sir, you look at this whole thing real hard and you think again real close an go on home.' And you know what? I very nearly did it.

"I thought about his mother and daddy and how faithful they've been down through the years and how much we all think of them, and I very nearly walked out. Then I got mad at Buddy all over again for messing it up and I grabbed him by his shirt and slapped him real hard, and you know he put in to fight me? He pushed me back in the other room and I knew I had some action on my hands. I finally had to club him down with my pistol—he's strong as a bull—and by then I was so mad at him I started choking him with both hands, and when I came to my senses I had damn near gouged one of his eyes out."

420

The boy lay in horrified rigidity, staring at his father with dilated pupils, sickened to his soul, not daring to breathe.

"Well," his father said brusquely, "what's done is done, and water over the dam, and spilt milk and all that. I got him in my car and went by Carson's house and told him what I'd done. Then I carried Buddy on to the doctor and told him I wanted the best medical treatment money could buy and I'd pay for it.

"He sewed up a few cuts in his head, but he says the eye can't be saved. I had him call the best eye doctor in Atlanta and tell him I'd stand for the bill. Carson Clifton and his boys have carried him on to the hospital. I thought I'd come on home and tell you how sorry I am it all happened."

For the first time in his life, the boy heard an indecisive note in his father's voice but was too distraught to pick up on it.

"Why don't you tell Buddy that?" he asked in a tight whisper, trying to control a scream.

"I did," the father answered. "And you know what he said? He said—and this in the gentlest, quietest voice you ever heard—'At's awright, Mr. Porter. Everthing goan be awright. I know you been drinkin.' "

He stopped talking and looked at the boy. The silence was expectant. Eyes blazing with hatred, his body yearning for the release of a violent blow, voice still rigidly held to a whisper, the boy leveled his look squarely into the eyes of his father.

"I'll die and rot in hell before I ever say that to you!" he said.

There was an even longer pause. Never breaking the stare that formed a bridge between their eyes but a barrier between their souls, the man finally said, without inflection, "I wanted you to know."

He turned and left the room.

Pulling his knees under his chin and stuffing the sheet in his mouth, the boy wept until his eyes were swollen and hiccups jerked him in painful spasm. He thought of the watermelon patch, the Ku Klux Klan, the brown swirl of Whitewater Creek, the Patrick Henry speech, the smell of the office in the courthouse, Freeman at the syrup mill, the brightly lit stage at graduation.

Falling on the floor, he knelt shivering and bare kneed against the bed. Shuddering with a deep sigh, he forced his body to be still. With deep and simple passion, he prayed, "Our merciful Heavenly Father, what in the world am I going to do? I love him so!"

FOR THE BEST IN PAPERBACKS, LOOK FOR THE

In every corner of the world, on every subject under the sun, Penguin represents quality and variety—the very best in publishing today.

For complete information about books available from Penguin—including Puffins, Penguin Classics, and Arkana—and how to order them, write to us at the appropriate address below. Please note that for copyright reasons the selection of books varies from country to country.

In the United Kingdom: Please write to *Dept. JC, Penguin Books Ltd, FREEPOST, West Drayton, Middlesex UB7 0BR.*

If you have any difficulty in obtaining a title, please send your order with the correct money, plus ten percent for postage and packaging, to *P.O. Box No. 11, West Drayton, Middlesex UB7 0BR*

In the United States: Please write to *Consumer Sales, Penguin USA, P.O. Box 999, Dept. 17109, Bergenfield, New Jersey 07621-0120.* VISA and MasterCard holders call 1-800-253-6476 to order all Penguin titles

In Canada: Please write to *Penguin Books Canada Ltd, 10 Alcorn Avenue, Suite 300, Toronto, Ontario M4V 3B2*

In Australia: Please write to *Penguin Books Australia Ltd, P.O. Box 257, Ringwood, Victoria 3134*

In New Zealand: Please write to *Penguin Books (NZ) Ltd, Private Bag 102902, North Shore Mail Centre, Auckland 10*

In India: Please write to *Penguin Books India Pvt Ltd, 706 Eros Apartments, 56 Nehru Place, New Delhi 110 019*

In the Netherlands: Please write to *Penguin Books Netherlands bv, Postbus 3507, NL-1001 AH Amsterdam*

In Germany: Please write to *Penguin Books Deutschland GmbH, Metzlerstrasse 26, 60594 Frankfurt am Main*

In Spain: Please write to *Penguin Books S. A., Bravo Murillo 19, 1° B, 28015 Madrid*

In Italy: Please write to *Penguin Italia s.r.l., Via Felice Casati 20, I-20124 Milano*

In France: Please write to *Penguin France S. A., 17 rue Lejeune, F-31000 Toulouse*

In Japan: Please write to *Penguin Books Japan, Ishikiribashi Building, 2-5-4, Suido, Bunkyo-ku, Tokyo 112*

In Greece: Please write to *Penguin Hellas Ltd, Dimocritou 3, GR-106 71 Athens*

In South Africa: Please write to *Longman Penguin Southern Africa (Pty) Ltd, Private Bag X08, Bertsham 2013*